FEVER

A Novel

by

David Kettlehake

Cover design by Alex Saskalidis

187designz.deviantart.com

For my wonderful wife Lisa,
who puts up with so much.

Chapter 1

The last thing Ari Van Owen expected to see that Saturday morning was his ex-girlfriend's furious husband on his front step.

"Where is she?" Butch Brubaker demanded. "Where's Frankie?"

Butch was livid, his fists clenching and unclenching at his sides, nostrils flaring, leaning forward as if ready to attack. Ari showed no immediate reaction, since for very personal reasons he didn't think very highly of Butch. He had to be careful to temper both his tongue and his body language.

"I mean it, you son of a bitch. Where's my wife?"

"What do you mean, where's Frankie? How the hell should I know?" That much was true. He had no idea where she was, and it was news to him that she was missing.

Butch clearly didn't believe him. He took a menacing step closer and stuck a finger two inches from Van Owen's nose. The end of the finger was stained a dull orange, that particular burnt umber of a nicotine stain, and there was some dark grit under his fingernail. "I know you two still talk behind my back. Don't deny it!"

Ari crossed his arms and stood his ground, refusing to give a physical or psychological inch. "I don't know what you're talking about, Butch. Your wife and I haven't talked in years." That wasn't true in the least. They had spoken on the phone just days earlier, and did so a few times each month.

"Don't lie to me! Frankie told me you two talk all the time."

That last accusation lacked conviction. Ari was certain Butch knew nothing about their conversations. For Frankie's sake he'd vowed that her husband never find out about their talks. He could imagine nothing that would make him break that promise. He refused to take the bait.

"Hold on a second," he ordered, steering the heated conversation in a different direction. "Start over. Why do you think she's missing?"

Butch took a few deep breaths before he took half a step back. When he finally spoke his voice was measured and low, a strained, throaty whisper that hissed through his teeth. "She's gone. I came home from the airport Thursday night, and she wasn't there. I figured hey, no biggie, she's late a few times a week, nothing to worry about. But she never came home from the hospital that night, and she didn't answer her phone either. Then nothing all day Friday or Friday night, and now it's Saturday and still nothing. All her clothes are still there. So's her suitcase."

"Did you call the police? Or talk to her mom?"

"Of course I did," Butch snapped. His brown eyes, set so far apart as they were in his wide face, flashed in anger. "You think I'm a fucking idiot? Work said they haven't heard from her, but her car's still there in the parking lot. The cops checked the other hospitals and the morgue but didn't find anything. All they said is for now they'll keep their eyes open for her."

Ari quickly recounted the last conversation he and Frankie had had. He couldn't recall anything in it to explain her sudden disappearance. Their talk had revolved mainly around the two of them and work, normal topics. She hadn't mentioned a trip or plans to go away. She absolutely would have told him if she'd had anything planned.

"I don't know what to tell you. Wish I could help."

Butch looked like he couldn't decide whether to start swinging or storm off. Fortunately for both of them, he chose the latter. He stalked back to his green pickup truck and got in, slamming the door

2

so hard the driver's mirror vibrated like a struck tuning fork. He stuck his head out the window and pointed at Van Owen.

"You're somehow involved in all this, *Arjen*," he yelled, using Ari's proper name like a slur. He almost pronounced the Dutch name properly: *Iron*. "And if I find out you are, I'll kill you this time, I swear I will!" He jammed the truck into reverse and dug up a matching set of trenches in the gravel as he roared back out of the driveway. He tore off down the country road and was gone in seconds. The angry growl of his engine could be heard for a little while longer; then that was gone too.

Ari stood framed in the doorway of his small brick house. "Don't call me Arjen," he said to no one in particular. "I hate that name." Then he went back inside for the keys to his own truck. He needed to get to a computer.

Twenty minutes later he parked outside the Newburg branch of the Louisville Free Public Library. The gray brick building was low and squat with an oddly designed V-shaped roof. Ari had been there before and knew there were several dozen computers in cubbies scattered around. At that hour of the day, less than half of them were in use. He found an open machine near three older patrons, two of whom were intently playing solitaire, while the third was reading the local paper online. Ari slid into the seat and logged onto the Internet, then brought up Facebook and signed in. It didn't surprise him that he didn't have any notifications, and honestly he would have been shocked if he'd had any. He typed Frankie's full name in the search bar and went to her profile page, then clicked on her wall. Her profile picture was from a benefit golf outing the hospital had staged a few months before. Her long blondish-brown hair was pulled back in a tight ponytail. She looked happy with a big smile on her face, holding a small trophy aloft in triumph. Her soft green eyes gazed at him as if Ari were the only person who could see her. He smiled warmly back at the familiar photo and stared at it a few moments before making himself leave the picture to check out her latest notifications. Her most recent update had been on Thursday with a time stamp of 1:15 in the afternoon.

Off work right on time for once! Yay! Going to hit the driving range before dinner. Wish me luck!

He perused the earlier entries, but nothing caught his eye. He pondered her page for another few moments, then went back to his own. He thought for just a second before he updated his status:

Great catching up with old friends on FB. Who needs a cell phone nowadays??

That should do it, he thought. The "FB" was directed at Frankie Brubaker, and the reference to a cell phone and "nowadays" was simply telling her to call him right away. It was no Enigma cipher, but was one of many variations of a loose code they'd figured out over time, one that had flown under the radar and worked well. He checked to make sure his pay-as-you-go phone was on and charged.

He sat back in the hard library chair with his hand still resting on the mouse, tapping his finger. Vanishing like this was very un-Frankie and totally out of character. Her responsibilities in the Rehabilitation Wing at the hospital were something she took very seriously, and she wouldn't miss her shift without letting someone know. Even as little as they spoke "real-time," he was sure she would have told him if she'd had plans to go away.

Ari didn't even bother telling himself not to worry about her since he knew that would be impossible. With a frustrated sigh, he logged off Facebook and left the library. The newspaper reader had already gone, while the two older patrons were still too engrossed in their solitaire games to notice him or anything else.

Once outside he found a rare pay phone on the corner. He dropped in a quarter and dialed her cell. The phone didn't ring but went right to voice mail instead. A bad sign.

"Hi, this is Frankie," her cheerful voice said. "Sorry I can't come to the phone right now, but please leave me a message and I'll get back with you right away."

He hung up the receiver a little harder than he had intended, irrationally blaming the phone for Frankie not answering. Ari stood outside the library with the hot sun on his face while he pondered his next steps. It was a bright April morning with just a hint of a breeze, the temperature already cresting seventy degrees and promising a high of eighty. Above him jets of all types and sizes flew into and out of the Louisville International Airport based just a few miles away, their thunderous roar so loud it occasionally drowned out the traffic noise on the street beside him. Louisville was also a hub for UPS, so the area saw thousands of those flights each week. Even when he was home twenty miles away, he swore he could hear each and every jet as it passed overhead. He was not yet accustomed to it like the locals seemed to be. He envied them that.

Frustrated and concerned, Van Owen got into his pickup truck and drove back home. Once inside he warmed up some coffee from the night before. Ari purposefully walked past the small first-floor bedroom he used as an office since he was not in the right frame of mind to work on his research. The office desk was stacked neatly with several different piles of papers, notebooks, files, plus some odd handheld equipment that the average layman wouldn't have recognized. There were eight different maps pinned to the walls. All of them were of Central and South America, and each was marked up with different-colored felt-tip pens. They were filled with a rainbow of Xs and circles and dotted lines, and sticky yellow memos were pasted everywhere in what appeared to be a random hodgepodge. From the looks of it, he could have been planning the most comprehensive and confusing south-of-the-border trip ever.

He continued out the back door, across the gravel driveway, and to the detached, oversized garage behind the house. The long building appeared dilapidated and not in the least bit trustworthy, and in fact it canted about five degrees to the right, as if strong winds had battered at it for decades. The aluminum siding, once white, was faded and washed out, the gray metal underneath showing through in a dozen places. The main garage door was locked tight from inside, and the small side door was secured with a serious padlock and deadbolt. As insubstantial as the building at first seemed, it was actually quite sturdy and solid. It would have to be since it housed Ari's most prized material possession. He unlocked the door and stepped inside.

When he flipped the light switch, four banks of overhead lights hummed to life and rendered the interior in crisp, harsh light, the type only fluorescents could provide. He had chosen those lights since they mercilessly revealed every flaw, every blemish, and Ari needed that for this specific job. His eyes softened and a gentle smile warmed his thin face. Few things made him smile these days.

"So how you doing, darling? You're looking well today."

He reached out and ran his finger along the fender of his 1968 Pontiac Firebird convertible. It was the exact year and model that his dad had owned when Ari was a kid. Standing back and looking at this one brought back such wonderful memories of summer drives with his parents, the top down, and wind making water stream from his eyes. This classic car was about two-thirds through a complete body-off frame restoration and was finally taking shape. The body panels were once again painted their original Pontiac Verdoro green and were fitted in place, but the interior was still completely gutted and down to the steel flooring. It had been so long since anyone had made parts for that model and year that he was having a tough time finding everything he needed, especially the special custom interior that had been an option back in '68. That interior included an imitation wood center console, wooden steering wheel, and quite attractive swooping armrests instead of the rather chunky ones that were standard factory issue on most Firebirds and Camaros. The Internet and eBay had been a godsend for finding these odd parts,

6

but it was still proving quite a challenge to beg, borrow, or steal everything he needed. He wasn't overly concerned since he wasn't on anyone's time frame but his own, but he dreaded the possibility that he could come this far in the restoration and not be able to finish.

Right now the car was ignominiously up on four jack stands, and the special tires with the thin red sidewall stripes that had taken him forever to find were off to the side against the wall. He was replacing the standard drum brakes with disc brakes on all four corners of the car. It had been a difficult moral and ethical battle for him to move away from the original design of the Pontiac engineers, but the drum brakes had been so horribly inadequate that they'd been truly dangerous during hard emergency stops. Many a past Firebird owner could attest to that fact after finding the smashed, smoking front end of their car lodged securely in the trunk of the vehicle they'd been following, proving once again that two objects can't occupy the same space at the same time. Back in the early twentieth century, the automotive designer Ettore Bugatti had famously stated, "I make my cars to go, not to stop." That may have been fine in 1920s Italy, but Ari didn't share those same sentiments, not after all the sweat and heart he had put into this rebuild. Hubris was one thing; pragmatism was another. So disc brakes it was.

One of the few interior aspects of the Firebird that worked was the radio. It was a genuine ACDelco AM radio hooked up to two fairly inadequate factory spec speakers. At some point a previous owner had wired in a small Audiovox FM converter. Further tweaking of the original design still struck him as minor heresy, but since it had been there when he bought the rusty, beat-up wreck from a man outside of Athens, Ohio, he felt it was a fair compromise. He tuned into a classic rock station. *"Flirtin' with Disaster"* by the group Molly Hatchet crackled through the tinny speakers.

7

I'm travelin' down the road / I'm flirtin' with disaster,

I've got the pedal to the floor / My life is running faster…

Ari tried to concentrate on getting some work done, but his mind kept replaying his encounter with Butch and what the man had said. He idly spun a socket wrench round and round, thinking. Brubaker's reaction had come across to him as…weird. He'd seemed more pissed than concerned, Van Owen thought. He'd been almost furious to the point of blind rage. That was not the kind of reaction he'd expect from a man whose wife had suddenly gone missing. Worry and fear, perhaps, but not such anger. Odd… But Butch was an odd bird anyway.

He gave up trying to get any real work done. Frankie's apparent disappearance bothered him to the point where doing anything but the most menial tasks was out of the question. He considered calling in some favors to help find out what had happened to her. While he toyed with that idea, he meandered around the large garage and tidied up, putting tools away, wrapping up an air hose, making sure the big air compressor by the door was off. Next to the compressor was a propane heater that had proven more than adequate to take any chill out of the garage in the cooler months. He hadn't used it in a while and thought the propane tank, the same size and shape used by any gas grill in America, may be a little low, and he made a mental note to fill that later. When the other mindless chores were done, he checked his phone to make sure he hadn't missed a call from Frankie. He hadn't. The date and time glared at him impersonally, the service indicator showing four steady bars.

He ran a hand along the fender down to the huge chrome grill. His fingers left streaks in the fine dust. He turned off the radio.

"Sorry, darling," he muttered. "Just not in the mood this afternoon. It's not you, it's me."

8

He killed the lights and locked the door. Back inside the house he ignored his office again and went instead into the small utilitarian kitchen. He brewed a fresh pot of coffee and waited somewhat patiently until it was finished, pouring himself a large mug. He placed the mug in the microwave and heated it up another twenty seconds, then took a semi-cautious sip. It was just a few degrees shy of second-degree burns, perfect, just the way he liked it. He was getting settled at the small kitchen table when there was a knock on the front door. Ari sat up straight and a frown crossed his narrow face, a tiny cluster of wrinkles knotting between his brown eyes. He hadn't ordered any parts for the car lately and wasn't expecting any guests. Butch wasn't back for round two, was he? Curious, he went to the front door and opened it.

"Hi, Ari, long time no see."

Van Owen sighed. "Good afternoon, Hal."

Hal smiled warmly at him, as if at an inside joke. "How you doing these days?"

"Fine, thanks for asking. Would you like to come in?"

"Sure." Hal Hollenbeck was in his mid-thirties with short, sandy blond hair just starting to thin on top. He had a pleasant face that had just recently begun to go soft, the hard lines and sharp angles of youth blurring with age and inactivity. He was shorter than Ari, about five-ten, and solidly built, with a thick chest and a waist that was starting to swell, a process that would continue its slow, inexorable expansion due to limited exercise and nearly unlimited hours behind a desk. He wore khaki pants and a collared shirt with a light jacket even though the day was warm. Ari could just make out a slight bulge under his left arm. Gold wire-frame glasses were perched on his nose, glasses that he habitually took off and cleaned when he needed time to think. The overall impression of Hal Hollenbeck was that he gave no overall impression; he was a man who could walk through a crowd unnoticed, and no one, even the most attentive, would be able to give a consistent or accurate

9

description of him afterward. However, in an emergency, Ari knew, Hal would be the one person calmly directing the panicked masses to safety. The word that always came to Van Owen's mind when describing him was "unflappable."

"Is that coffee still fresh?" Hal asked.

"Just made it. Cream and two sugars, right?"

He smiled again. "You remembered? Yes, that's perfect."

They entered the kitchen, and Hollenbeck watched as Ari prepared his coffee. The man accepted the cup and raised an eyebrow as he read the side of it: there was a snarling Kodiak bear with the caption *I'm a bear until I've had my first cup.*

Ari shrugged. "It came with the house."

The two men sat at the table in silence. Hal took a cautious sip and flinched at the heat then blew softly across the top of the mug. Although his glasses were spotless he took them off and cleaned them against his shirt. He held them to the light in a quick inspection then slid them back on.

"So," Ari finally asked. "How'd you find me?"

Hal's only reaction was a slight grin. Besides that if he was pleased with himself it didn't show; gloating wouldn't have been like him. He was typically very careful about monitoring his expressions and body language. In all the time he'd known the man Ari had never seen him lose his composure.

"It wasn't easy."

Ari didn't say anything. He stared at him.

"Protocol dictates that I not tell you," Hal reminded him.

Ari set the mug down. "Fine, but you know I'll eventually figure it out anyway. Save us both the trouble, why don't you?"

He blew across his mug again and looked away, an obvious stalling tactic. "You must have taken a lot of precautions to stay off the grid this long."

"A few." Such as rent and utilities that he only paid in cash or money order, no Internet, a pay-as-you-go cell phone, no local bank

10

accounts, and his truck that was licensed in another state, just for starters. It hadn't been easy but he wasn't about to admit that.

Several moments passed before Hal nodded. "So how's the Firebird coming along? Still making progress? You've been working on that thing for what, a few years now?"

Ari thought furiously. In less time than it had taken to mix the cream and sugar in Hal's coffee, the light bulb went off. "The parts. You traced me through parts orders for the car. That must have been quite a task for your little worker drones. Well done, Hal. Whoever your Special Agent in Charge is should be very proud."

Hollenbeck held his hands out as if surrendering. "It's what we do at the FBI. It's tough to stay completely off the grid anymore, you know. For the most part even ultra-hermits like Ted Kaczynski can get located these days. We're scary good."

Ari didn't much care for the reference to the Unabomber when discussing his own circumstances. He wasn't laying low for any anti-government, terrorist reasons. He wasn't railing for or against any causes, hadn't committed any crimes, wasn't shaking his fist at the gods. His decision to fly under the radar of a so-called normal life was strictly a personal one. He had his reasons, only a few of which had to do with Hal Hollenbeck and the machinations of the outside world. Sometimes a person just wanted to be left alone.

Ari leaned back in his chair and crossed his arms. He knew the agent would pick up on the closed body language but didn't care. As a person he liked Hal, quite a bit actually. The man was very bright, intensely loyal, patriotic and dedicated to a fault, and would do whatever he thought was necessary to complete an assignment. Ari thought of him as an adult Boy Scout, a description Hal treated as a compliment since he had in fact been an Eagle Scout in high school. He was a friend of sorts, but one who could never be more than that due to his employment and his loyalties. That was a shame, too, as Ari didn't have many people he could call friends.

The man also possessed an almost surreal, maddening ability to stay clean and tidy no matter the situation. More than once Ari had wanted to throw a handful of mud at him just to see what would happen; he imagined it would simply slough off and fall to his feet in a pile, like an unwanted second skin.

"So let's cut to the chase, Hal," he said. "Why are you here? What do you want from me?"

"Ah, Ari, never one for small talk. You always go straight for the jugular." He cleaned his glasses again, for a second rubbing determinedly at a non-existent smudge. He held the frames at arm's length. "So how's the research going on that British explorer fellow, anyway?"

Ari was used to the way Hal jumped from one subject to another, knowing that there was always a final destination just over the horizon. The man rarely said something that didn't have either an overt or hidden meaning. He resisted the urge to look at his open office door.

"It's fine. Why?"

"What was his name? I can't recall."

Ari frowned at him. "Fawcett. Colonel Percy Fawcett. You know that."

Hal snapped his fingers. "Percy Fawcett, that's it. Disappeared exploring the Amazon, wasn't it?"

"What are you getting at, Hal? Yes, Fawcett, his son Jack, and a friend named Raleigh Rimmell vanished without a trace in 1925 while searching the Amazon for a fabled hidden city, what he called the Lost City of Z."

"Very Indiana Jones of him. How many trips have you taken to the Amazon searching for an explanation of what happened to him? Two?"

Two trips to the Amazon, both of which nearly killed him, especially the second one. That jungle was far and away the most dangerous, inhospitable place on Earth, much worse than the frigid lands of either pole, the oxygen deprived mountains, or the angry, impersonal oceans. For the most part those locales weren't actively trying to kill you, they were just inhospitable and deadly. The jungle was different. From the smallest microorganism to the largest predator the jungle and all its denizens simply wanted you dead.

The second trip he had been the only one of his party to emerge alive, and it had taken months and months in the hospital to recover. Yet despite all that, despite all the death and misery he had witnessed and endured, he had this terrible, conflicting itch to go back again. Colonel Fawcett himself had once said *"Civilization has a relatively precarious hold upon us and there is an undoubted attraction in a life of absolute freedom once it has been tasted. The 'call o' the wild' is in the blood of many of us and finds its safety valve in adventure."* Life in the Amazon was every bit of that, an adventure on a grand, deadly scale.

"Yes," he finally answered after what seemed like several minutes. His voice was flat and hollow in the small kitchen. "Two trips.

"Did you find what you were looking for?"

"No I didn't. You really need to stop asking me questions you already know the answers to. It's very annoying."

Hal smiled once and motioned for Ari to continue.

"Fine. The first trip was following the trail most people considered Fawcett's likely path. We based it on another trail using information discovered about a decade ago. Neither time did I find any concrete evidence of Fawcett's death, or the Lost City of Z, for that matter. They were both a bust."

"But you haven't gone back a third time. Why?"

"Good God, Hal, it's because the second trip almost killed me, that's why. Listen, hundreds or even thousands of people have gone off searching for Fawcett over the years, consumed with this thing many call Fawcett Fever. Few of them have ever been heard of again. They boldly and courageously head off into the jungle with porters and guides and modern equipment and think they're prepared, but they're not. The jungle doesn't give a shit who you are or how determined you are. The Amazon will always let you in, but it almost never lets you out. The only reason it tolerates us at all is that it knows it'll win in the end."

"And yet," Hal stated, turning toward Ari's office, "you still continue to try and figure out what happened to him. If I know you, and I think I do, I'd wager that room behind me is filled with notes and maps, all of it due to your own case of Fawcett Fever."

First the car parts and now this, Ari thought. I've become too predictable. Hal stood and walked into the office, flicking on the overhead light. Van Owen reluctantly followed behind, first setting the mug down since the contents had cooled too much for his liking anyway.

The FBI agent was bent over and looking at the first map on the wall, tracing the path of one of the dotted lines over the heart of Brazil with a clean, almost manicured finger. He read several of the many sticky notes that adorned the maps like square yellow Christmas tree ornaments. As bright as Hal was, and he was very bright, Ari didn't expect his cryptic notes and personal shorthand to make much sense to the man. He stood back while the agent absorbed as much as he could.

"Okay, I give. What does all this mean?"

Ari walked over and stood next to him. His thin frame was several inches taller than the agent's. "Careful, or you'll get Fawcett Fever too."

"Doubt it. I've got plenty of mysteries in my own backyard, thanks."

"I don't doubt that at all. Well, to really understand Fawcett you have to go back to the 1900s. The Colonel had been hired by the British Royal Geographical Society, or RGS, to map the vast, uncharted area of the Amazon jungle, a chunk of unexplored terrain the size of the entire United States. He made quite a few journeys

14

into the jungle and time and again he made it back alive. No one else could do that. No one. Between the insects, the predators, the dangerous indigenous tribes, and the diseases, almost nobody ever survived. And he kept going back and doing it again. He was quite a superman, really."

"Okay, the guy was pretty tough, I'll give him that. But what," he said, gesturing at the different dotted lines on the map, "does that have to do with all this?"

"You don't get it - he was more than pretty tough. He avoided sickness when all others succumbed. He talked his way out of being killed or held captive by native tribes dozens of times. The man was pretty much invulnerable. But above all he loved the attention and notoriety involved in all this. He adored the limelight of the day more than anything else, more than family, more than the RGS, more than country. Think of it this way: in today's world he'd be on magazine covers in every supermarket checkout lane and on every morning or late night talk show."

He gestured to the map in front of them. "But to win that limelight he had to be very secretive. Fawcett's one main goal, his driving force above all else, was to find that ancient city, the one he was convinced existed, the one he called Z. He was determined to discover Z and prove to the world that it existed, or had existed. But others were looking for Z too, so he typically gave false information of his whereabouts to throw them off track."

"He was afraid of someone claim-jumping him."

"Exactly. And to have someone else find Z before him would have been devastating. The RGS was his employer and even they didn't know where he was half the time." Ari pointed to a spot on the map marked with three initials: DHC.

"Dead Horse Camp was his last known official whereabouts, supposedly. Dozens of expeditions have looked for him starting right there, but according to rumors of what his wife said many years later he had no intention of heading there at all. It was just another ruse to throw people off his trail. Like I said, on his last expedition he set off with himself, his son Jack, and a friend of Jack's named Raleigh Rimmell."

"Only three people?"

"Yes. He determined that smaller parties had a better success ratio. They were more nimble and could run under the radar of the indigenous tribes easier. The entire world was watching this trip so he also employed some porters and pack animals and most importantly some Indian runners to relay messages back to civilization, but that was it. Sadly even those porters died or were killed, as were the pack animals. According to the final telegram sent in by his last surviving runner in the end it was down to just the three of them. But I'm sure his messages talking about his locations were all a ruse, more lies to confuse everyone. I don't think he was ever at Dead Horse Camp at all. I think he was well northwest of that before he disappeared."

"And you think that because?"

"Well mainly just a feeling in my gut, plus the fact my first two trips and everyone else's all around Dead Horse Camp were a bust. I don't have any solid clues, even with additional information that was recently unearthed at the RGS. Still, I just have this hunch people have been searching the wrong spot for years."

Hal stared at the maps for a minute in silence, finally taking off his glasses and absently cleaning them on his shirt again. He eventually turned away and walked over to Ari's desk. He picked up a complex brass instrument and turned it over in his hand.

"A sextant?"

"Very good, Hal. Yes, a sextant. Just like the one Fawcett used."

"He would've loved a modern GPS unit."

"Probably. But he was a wizard with one of these and could figure out his location very nicely, assuming he could see through the jungle canopy. I can't imagine how he survived all those years with this type of equipment, and so little modern medicine. How he never contracted malaria is beyond me. Like I said, the guy was nearly invincible."

"Not quite. If he'd been invincible we wouldn't be talking about him like this."

Ari shrugged. "Maybe so. But for all we know he simply put down roots in the jungle and died of old age with some Indian tribe. According to friends and relatives the older he got the more 'native' he was becoming anyway."

Hal gently put the sextant back on the desk. He gestured around the office. "So with all this, with all your newfound knowledge and modern technology, you still haven't gone back into the jungle again? I don't get it. You've got the money and the time, so that's not the issue."

"You're right. I've still got the trust fund to keep me going and I could probably scare up enough to put together another expedition if I wanted to."

"So why are you still here?"

Ari sighed and sat on the edge of the desk, suddenly looking tired, his shoulders slumping ever so slightly. "Besides the fact that my last trip nearly did me in, you mean? I don't know. I guess the fire has left me. I just don't care that much anymore. I can putter around here," he gestured at the office, "and play with my pet theories and work on my car. That's enough."

"The fire has left you? That's a crock," Hal countered. "You should see your eyes when you talk about this. They're more subdued then they used to be, sure, but they still twinkle when Fawcett's name comes up." He paused and tilted his head. "It's because of her, isn't it? It's because of Frankie."

Despite himself, Ari stood up straight and felt his face harden involuntarily. "I don't know what you're talking about."

"Right there. I can see it. I can't even bring up her name without you practically seizing up. This relationship you had with Frankie, it really screwed you up, didn't it?"

"We're not going to talk about this, Hal."

"I thought so. I knew you were a mess after that, but I didn't know how badly it affected you. Honestly, Ari, you don't even seem like yourself anymore. You're more serious, more...hardened."

Ari strode out of the office and back into the kitchen, his back ramrod straight. He couldn't think of anything better to do so he roughly put his mug back in the microwave and heated it up. After a few seconds the agent joined him at the kitchen table again. They sat in silence until the microwave dinged. Ari stared at the appliance but didn't make a move for his cup.

Hal stared at Ari. "So how long have you and Michelle been divorced now?"

"Over five years," Van Owen said eventually.

"Do you ever see her anymore?"

Ari shook his head. "Nope. She's living out West with her new husband. They've got a baby girl. I haven't talked to her in years. No reason to."

"That's too bad. I liked Michelle."

He laughed once, although it was humorless and a little sad. He inspected his opened, upturned palms as if they were new to him. "So did I. Ends up she just didn't like me enough. Or rather, she didn't like the Fawcett trips. I was gone for about a year that first time and she couldn't take the stress of not knowing if I was alive or dead. In hindsight I can't say I blame her. She filed the papers the day after I told her I planned on going back."

"That's a tough break, but I guess I understand. Extended trips like that are hard on a marriage, which is one reason I'm still single. I've seen a lot of agents go through the same thing. No thanks."

Ari was surprised. Truth was the agent had rarely related anything of his personal life before. He'd never seen a wedding ring on the man's hand but hadn't thought much of it. He also knew that Hal rarely said or did anything without a reason, so this sudden, miniscule glimpse into his life was probably not an accident. Was he trying to soften Van Owen up?

"So tell me, Hal, really, what do you really want?" he repeated. "You didn't come here to chit chat about our personal lives. I know you better than that."

Hal pursed his lips. He removed his glasses again and absentmindedly wiped them on the sleeve of his jacket, a gesture he probably didn't realize he performed so regularly. Ari would have considered it some kind of "tell", as in poker, but the agent did it all the time. He slid the gold frames back on and pulled a piece of newsprint from the inner pocket of his jacket. Ari caught the slightest glimpse of a black holster and the butt of a pistol tucked against his chest, under his arm. Probably a Glock .40 caliber handgun, he thought. Standard issue for field agents.

"Here," Hal said as he unfolded the paper. It was a headline from the Louisville Courier Journal. In large black print it read: *Delta Airline Fiery Crash – 77 Dead*. Below that in smaller type it said *Only One Survivor – longtime Flight Attendant*. The paper was dated the week before. Two pictures were embedded in the story, the first the skeletal, smoking remains of the 737, and the other a photo of an attractive blond woman in her mid-fifties.

"Yeah, I saw that," Ari said after taking a quick look. "It was all over the news. A terrible tragedy. But what's that got to do with me?"

Hal carefully folded the newspaper clipping and put it away. "The one survivor was a flight attendant named Alyssa Morris. That's her picture. She lived because she locked herself in the rear bathroom and it just so happened that section of the plane broke off and bounced to a stop in someone's backyard, well away from the fuselage. The rest of the plane caught fire and burned to the frame. It was so bad they may never be able to identify everyone."

Ari grimaced. What an awful way to go. There were not many good ways to die, granted, but that had to be one of the worst. Being in the plane and knowing it was going down and not being able to do a damn thing about it besides seeing the ground rushing toward you, waiting for impact... He shuddered.

"That's terrible, really."

Hal nodded. "Ms. Morris has been in the ICU ever since. She was very banged up with a whole host of broken bones, lacerations, and so many bruises she's purple and green all over. Looks like she pissed off SEAL Team 6, but she's alive."

"Amazing."

"What's amazing is what she told the police and the FAA after she was conscious and able to talk. Seems she wasn't even supposed to be on that flight. She got called up at the last minute and deadheaded from Brazil to Atlanta, then was the head flight attendant for the flight to Louisville. No problems the entire way until just as the plane began its final descent, then it got ugly."

"Ugly?"

"Yeah. When we talked to her about it she recalled several things that were odd, but not odd enough that it made her wonder at the time. Like neither the pilot or first officer got on the PA and gave the passengers any updates as they neared the airport. Or the fact that they didn't tell her to buckle up and prepare for landing, either. She just did it out of habit and didn't think much about it at the time."

"That's not so odd."

"No, it's not. But as they began their final descent it got worse. She felt the landing gear go down and lock, that much was still normal. After that things went downhill fast. The plane jerked and listed to port, to the left, she said, and the nose tipped down farther than it should have which meant the plane itself was picking up speed instead of scrubbing some off. Mrs. Morris tried to contact the cockpit but no one answered, even to the point where she got out of her chair and beat on the door. Still nothing."

"If the flight crew was having some type of problems I could see them ignoring her right then. It's kind of a busy time, you know. They'd have more important things on their minds."

"Yeah, until the cockpit door opened – a major breach of FAA protocol, by the way - and she saw the first officer on the ground and he looked, in her words, frozen. Bright red, like he had a raging fever, but paralyzed. The pilot was in the same shape but his hands were still on the controls. He was shaking so hard she was surprised he didn't snap off the yoke. He looked terrified but was unable to do anything about it. She flipped out then and for some reason ran to the back of the plane and locked herself in the bathroom. Best decision she ever made. The plane hit and cartwheeled about a half mile short of the runway but still on airport property, thankfully. The tail section snapped off and landed in the backyard of a Mr.," he pulled out his phone and opened a notes page dedicated to the crash. "In the backyard of a Mr. Robert Feldkamp. It stopped just short of their family room while they were watching Wheel of Fortune. Scared the hell out of them."

"I can understand that. It'd scare the hell out of me, too," Ari admitted. "I still don't see what this has to do with me, Hal."

"I'm getting to that. What I'm going to tell you now must be held in the strictest confidence, do you understand? No one outside several airline officials, the FAA, and the FBI have any knowledge of this."

Ari looked around at the otherwise empty house and his solitary life. "Really, Hal? Who the hell am I going to tell?"

"Point taken," the agent admitted after a few moments. "We've noticed a very disturbing physiological phenomenon among pilots and some flight crews over the past six to eight months. We're calling it sudden onset paralysis, or SOP. We don't know what triggers it or what causes it, but we've found about a dozen cases.

Until now we've only seen it on off-duty pilots and some grounds crew. If these two men were hit with SOP while in the air it's no wonder the plane crashed. From the previous cases we know it strikes suddenly with little warning and can last up to several days. SOP victims are almost completely paralyzed with only the most basic autonomic functions still operational. They seem to recover, but of course they're never able to fly again, not with that bogey hanging over them."

"The FAA and the airlines have to be shitting themselves over this."

"They are. If the public gets wind of SOP it would have a devastating impact on the industry and the economy."

Ari snorted. "Not to mention the lives of the people flying when it happens."

"That goes without saying, Ari," the agent admonished. "That's our first concern, of course."

"Hmm. Right. So you've checked the black box and all that stuff you normally do, I take it? And checked and cross-checked the victims of this SOP? Where they've been, who they've seen, all that normal stuff that you FBI guys are so good at?"

"Of course. The black box was recovered and is being analyzed, although at first blush it doesn't appear anything was mechanically wrong with the bird itself. Cockpit communications with the tower were nominal until right before the final descent, too. We won't know for sure about the rest of the data until later, but we're moving ahead on the assumption that it was human rather than mechanical error.

"So now we're looking at the human aspect," the agent continued. "We think we've found some correlation between the SOP victims. Here's where you come in."

Ari sat back in his chair, the shock on his face as clear as if he'd been punched. "Where I come in? What the hell do you mean, where

I come in? I'm not part of this. I'm just a simple researcher, that's all. And I'm not even that right now, you know."

Hal leaned forward, his arms on the table. He stared hard at Ari. "All of the SOP victims spent some significant time in South America within the last twelve months. More precisely, each one spent some time in either Brazil or Bolivia, countries that contain portions of the Amazon Jungle. We're trying to zero in on the locations more specifically, but haven't had much luck yet. Several of them spent some time in the jungle itself. Among other things that I can't go into now is that the Amazon seems to be the one big common factor here."

"And?"

"And the FBI wants you to go back to the Amazon and poke around a little, see what you can find. We want you to go back for a third time under the cover of another Fawcett expedition."

Chapter 2

Ari stared at him, masking his emotions. He was getting good at that today. *They wanted him to go down there again?*

"The FBI figures you of all people could easily insert yourself into the Amazon without raising any suspicion. You're not affiliated with any US Government agencies, you've been there before, and you have a valid reason for being there again. It's perfect cover."

Ari remained still. He figured that as long as he remained quiet the agent would feel the need to fill the silence with additional information, which would also give Ari the chance to think. Hal was no rookie and had to realize that, but obliged him anyway.

"We've given serious consideration to sending our own teams in, of course, but in our discussions with the local governments and the indigenous tribes we've been, ah, rebuffed. We could do it anyway and there are those in the agency that would rather we take that avenue, but it was decided that we approach you first."

"I should be flattered?" Ari finally said. He was still in shock that this was even under consideration.

"Perhaps," Hal replied with a small, knowing smile. "I'd like to think so. You're Plan A and we really don't have a Plan B, at least not at this time. Shy of sending in the Marines, that is, and if history is any indicator that tends to get messy and end badly. With the exception of taking out Bin Laden, those missions don't always go well."

Ari leaned back and crossed his arms again. His first inclination was to simply tell the agent to go pound sand, that there was no way in hell he'd consider going down there again. The damn jungle had almost killed him before, and the FBI wanted him to waltz back down there and give it another shot? The rational part of his mind was screaming at him to run away, to get off the grid again.

But the lure of the jungle was always there, that tiny, distant itch in his mind that Ari could never scratch. The itch would recede at times, would sometimes fade to a nearly imperceptible prickle, but would never disappear completely. It was that piece of dirt in your contact lens, that scratchy tag on the neck of your sweater: you could ignore it for a while, but during down times it always came back to nudge you closer to crazy.

Also more immediately there was the other visitor from this morning to consider. The vision of Butch sticking that yellowed finger in his face gave him an idea.

"Let me think about it for a few days," he finally told the agent. "And while I'm thinking there's something I'd like you to do for me."

Hal cocked an eyebrow. "Really? What do you have in mind?"

Ari told him about the surprise visit and what little he knew about Frankie's disappearance. He hesitated but then also told him about their continued conversations and communications on the phone and through Facebook. Hal didn't look surprised at that, which actually bothered Ari to a certain degree, although he didn't know why. The agent dutifully took notes in his phone while he asked about her job at the hospital, her husband Butch, friends, relatives, anything he could think of. Ari knew the answers to most. When the agent asked for a picture Ari said he couldn't produce one, but that all Hal had to do was go online and he could find one on her profile page.

"You realize of course that she may have just taken off, right? From your description this Brubaker guy doesn't seem like much of a catch. Maybe she just got sick and tired of him and decided she'd had enough?"

Ari shook his head in certainty. "No, she'd never do that."

"Really? Why not?"

He sighed and rubbed a hand over his face. "Because she's a devout Catholic, that's why. She'll stick with him through thick and thin no matter what. She'd never leave him, not unless the Church said it was okay – and she'd never even ask them to."

25

There were a few moments of silence while Hal worked through what Ari had just said. When he spoke it was as if he were answering a question nobody had asked, especially not Ari.

"And because she's a devout Catholic and married to this Butch guy, that means the two of you can never get together. Now I understand. Now it all makes more sense, finally."

Ari didn't say anything, just grunted.

"But why didn't you two become a couple before? I don't understand."

Ari sighed and inspected his hands some more. "Timing. Lousy timing, that's all." He thought about the lousy timing every single day. The phrase "if only" was always front and center in his mind. If only things had gone differently, if only they had met earlier, if only he hadn't already been married, if only he hadn't taken that last trip. Frankie was a huge believer in Karma and always blamed it on their predicament, even though he never understood why. It wasn't Karma, he knew, it was just bad luck. Or was that the same thing?

"Michelle and I had been married for a few years before my first trip. I never really was the person she thought I was, and I think we figured that out pretty fast. But things were okay, not great but okay. Probably like a million other marriages out there."

"So what happened?"

"What happened was the first Fawcett trip. I was gone and she was alone. When I got back and had to go into the hospital I met Frankie and I knew, somehow I knew right away, that she was special. During my rehab I started planning my next trip and it just freaked Michelle out. She filed for divorce and I signed the papers. Frankie was dating Butch at the time but broke it off and we started seeing each other instead."

Hal grunted. "No wonder he doesn't like you."

"We started dating but kept it pretty low-key since I was still going through the divorce. After that was final we stepped it up, but even then my next trip was right around the corner. I didn't want to go but couldn't back out, not then. Too much planning had gone into that and, well, I still had Fawcett Fever pretty bad. The trip went south in a big way and I was gone almost two whole years, laid up down there in the jungle with no way to communicate, no way to let her know I was alive. Some reports even said I'd been killed. Meanwhile Butch came back into the picture and they connected again, and finally got married. A few months after their wedding I made it back to the States but it was too late. They were married and I was screwed." He took a deep breath. Ari hadn't told that story out loud for some time, but even that telling didn't lessen the pain or the loss. "Now instead of sitting here talking why don't you get busy and find out what happened to her? Finding her would greatly enhance my decision-making abilities, if you see what I mean."

Hal saved the information in the notepad on his phone and tucked it into his jacket pocket. They both stood and walked toward the front door.

"I'll see what I can do, Ari. No promises, you understand. I'll try to poke around a little bit."

"Okay. Give me a week to think about your request."

Hal walked out the front door and looked around. His government-issue sedan was parked behind Ari's pickup truck. The blue on white license plates said US GOVERNMENT across the bottom.

Hal turned and shook Ari's hand. "It'll be nice to have you back on the team. You've been away too long."

Ari shook his head, the expression on his face a study in exasperation. "I never was on the team, Hal."

"Sure you were."

"No, I was a subcontractor you hired to do special research a few times, that's all."

"You sell yourself short, Ari. You have an amazing talent for figuring things out, for connecting obscure points in ways most of us can't."

"Whatever. Let's just say I'm lucky."

"Lucky? I don't think so. You have a gift."

Hal handed Ari a business card. In the upper left hand corner was the seal of the U.S. Department of Justice and the Federal Bureau of Investigation. To the right of that was Hal's name, address, office and cell phone, and a government email address. The card, made of heavy stock, was extremely official. He wrote down his own phone number on a scrap of paper and handed it to Hal.

"Or do you already have my number?" he asked sardonically.

"I could toy with you and say yes, but no, we don't. We just found out where you were yesterday." He pocketed the paper. "I'll be in touch if I find anything. And if we haven't talked before then I'll expect your answer in a week."

Hal walked back to the car. He looked around, up and down the road and across the street into the scrubby, weed-choked woods. Ari had no neighbors to speak of this far into the country and his road was relatively untraveled, bordering on abandoned. He wondered what the man was looking for, or if he simply did this all the time and it was the nature of the beast. A natural sense of suspicion was probably a healthy survival trait in his line of work.

"One week, Ari. Please think it over. We could use your help on this one."

Ari didn't say anything, just gave a half wave and watched as the agent pulled away. He shut and locked the door behind him.

Back inside he went into his office and sat at the creaky old desk. The maps of South America festooned with his yellow sticky pads and notes stared wordlessly back at him. He picked up the sextant and held the small telescope to his eye. He focused on the map across from him and carefully sighted on the western side of Brazil. Through luck or chance he happened on the two words *Mato Grosso*, one of the last known locations of Colonel Fawcett's party. He sighed and gently set the sextant down, careful not to jar any of the internal mirrors. From a neat stack of papers he took the top sheet. It was heavy bond parchment paper addressed to him from the Royal Geographical Society of Kensington, London. Their austere geometric logo was in the upper right-hand corner. It was dated the week before.

Dearest Ari,

As always I hope you are well. Per our recent conversation I have included scans of the information we discussed. This was all unearthed from the sub-basement of our old headquarters recently. You will see that in typical Fawcett fashion the devious chap was quite opaque about his location during his final expedition. Infuriating man. These will all be made public soon but I am forwarding them to you early in exchange for your fine work with us in the past. This should square us up now.

Should you truly desire to continue your Fawcett quest we wish you the best, but the Society has no plans on pursuing this on our own or assisting any parties, including yourself.

Fawcett Fever has claimed many lives so please plan your next moves carefully and with great consideration. I would not like to count you in the numbers of those lost to this folly.

As always, your friend,

Sir Alex Hanes
Honorary Vice President, RGS

Ari picked up several crisp white pages that were covered with handwritten notes in microscopic script. He spread them out on the desk and began looking them over again. The pages were scans of Fawcett's own notes and had been sent to his wife, Nina. Some were simple updates on his everyday life en route during his final trip, some were poems meant for his wife, others were drawings of hieroglyphics, maps, or other random objects. These notes had been saved by Nina, then filed away and forgotten decades ago at the previous headquarters of the RGS. On the surface they seemed quite ordinary, but Ari had a feeling there was more here than anyone thought. Van Owen enjoyed a good mystery but loved solving one even more.

However not right now - his head was still not in it. He tossed the papers back onto the desk where they landed in an untidy heap, the letter from the RGS fluttering to the floor. Five years ago receiving scans like those from the RGS would've made both his heart race with excitement, but no longer. Despite what Agent Hollenbeck had said, much of Ari's internal fire for solving the Fawcett mystery had dimmed. Were the flames completely extinguished? No, not yet at least, but the coals were cooling and covered with gray, powdery ash. He just didn't care much about anything any longer, not since Frankie. He hated that he felt so empty and vacuous but he didn't know how to shake off that heavy dark cloak of apathy. Ari leaned back and stared blindly at the flyspecked ceiling, unable to get Butch's visit and Frankie's disappearance out of his mind.

Thirty minutes passed while he sat motionless, neither asleep nor awake, his mind coasting in neutral. When he finally sat up he knew he had to do something. He shook himself and stood up, surprised when he noticed how much time had ticked off the little digital clock on his desk. Working on the car was out, he knew, and so was doing research on Colonel Fawcett. Instead he went to the other bedroom, which was actually a storage room for him, and pulled out his bicycle. It was an older Trek model, not at all up to date with the newest derailleurs or shifters. It was a road bike, which meant it sported very thin, insubstantial tires, and an equally thin and insubstantial seat. The bright blue frame was older and heavier than the newest models but it suited Ari's needs just fine. He wouldn't go as far as humanizing his bike and calling it a friend, but it had dutifully served him well for many years and thousands of miles and he appreciated it.

Ari changed into some suitable biking gear and a helmet. He checked to make sure the tires were pumped up around 90 psi and that the small kit dangling from the back of the seat was equipped with a spare inner tube and a pressurized inflation cartridge. Lastly he tucked his cell phone into the kit just in case something happened and he needed assistance. Ten years earlier he had wiped out fifteen miles from nowhere and had been forced to limp and carry the bike halfway back to civilization before a Good Samaritan had picked them up.

Once outside he locked the door behind him and headed out, snapping his shoes into the pedals. Non-bikers couldn't fathom how anyone could have their feet locked into the pedals, especially during a wipeout, but a quick twist of the ankle popped the shoe out easily. It was an equitable trade-off for not having to worry about slipping during hard riding, and with his feet securely locked in his legs could pull up on the pedals as well as push down, effectively doubling his power when needed, like on hills or when passing.

He turned right out of his driveway and started off. Ari's street was not much more than a one and half lane wide country road with little to no traffic. It was out of the way and didn't connect to any major thoroughfares, so there was no reason to be on it if you didn't live there. He rode on the right hand side and would've been moving with traffic had there been any. Two miles later he came to the end of his street and had to make a decision. Randomly he went left.

This was a State Route, which meant he had to be more careful. Half the time he felt as if he had a bright red bulls eye on his back when it came to motorists. Drivers were cautious around runners, but they certainly didn't give bicyclists the same courtesy. Most of the time cars were okay, but pickups and semi-trucks many times came so close they almost clipped his handlebars. Constant vigilance and awareness were necessary survival traits on these busy roadways.

The majority of his ride Ari was able to keep up a steady 15 to 19 miles per hour, making up time on downhill runs what he lost pedaling uphill. He was rarely out of breath and his legs felt strong and true. With the exception of under his helmet, sweat dried on him as fast as his body could generate it. He continued in a generally northern direction toward Louisville proper, always aware of the traffic building around him. At one point the number of cars and trucks got so thick he was forced to duck down a side street into a residential section of town. The only threats in the heart of suburbia were inattentive drivers backing out of driveways that somehow failed to see the bright blue bike and slender rider with a lime green helmet.

Another fifteen minutes passed before he looked up and noticed with a start that he was coming up on Louisville Mercy Hospital. The huge tan building was newer, only seven or eight years old, and didn't look much like a hospital. Had it not been for the ambulances parked to the side and the huge Emergency Entrance sign in front it could have been mistaken for a posh office complex, complete with a large pond where Canadian geese honked and floated peacefully. He stopped and popped a foot out of the pedals. Louisville Mercy was where he had first met Frankie, where she had helped rehabilitate him after the first Fawcett trip. It was also, according to Butch, the last place anyone had seen her.

Ari stared at the building from the road. He was not surprised that his seemingly random bike ride had brought him here. Over the years he had learned that his subconscious mind tended to direct him where he needed to be, sometimes even against his better judgment. He gave serious consideration to simply riding away and putting the huge edifice behind him, but curiosity and the need to actually do something was too strong. He glided down the long drive and into the parking lot, finally pulling up just outside the main front doors.

He clicked out of the pedals and leaned the bike against a pillar, out of the way, and sat down on a concrete bench. The sun was warm on his face and arms. When he removed his helmet his short brown hair was damp with sweat, giving it more of a tussled look than usual.

Anyone looking at Ari would see a thin, lean man in his early thirties. He had a runner's build, which meant he wasn't sporting much excess weight. His face was narrow and long with a wide mouth that used to smile much more frequently than it did these days. He had unruly brown hair that no amount of combing could conquer. He never really tanned, not even in the summer, his skin simply taking on a darker shade of reddish brown. His knowing hazel eyes seemed to absorb information wherever he was, and no matter what he was doing.

He leaned back against the bench and relaxed. For more than fifteen minutes people came and went through the main doors and didn't pay him much attention. Several doctors hustled in talking on their cell phones. A younger man in green scrubs pointed to the blue Trek bike and gave an energetic thumbs up. Ari smiled back at him, gathering that the man must be a cyclist himself. The big doors hissed closed behind him and Ari was again alone with his thoughts.

Five more minutes passed before the doors opened again. A woman in her late twenties or early thirties with straight, shoulder-length platinum blond hair and purple scrubs walked out. She was looking down at her phone and reading something. When the sun hit her she stopped and squinted at the now washed-out screen. She grumbled something harsh as she tried to read the tiny text. She had wide shoulders and narrow hips and had been a swimmer or athlete of some kind in her youth.

"Hi, Yvonne," Ari said from the bench.

Yvonne jumped a little and stared at him. Her blue eyes grew wide. "Ari? My God, what are you doing here?"

He stood and gave her a brotherly hug, one that took her a half second to return. She looked him up and down, checking out the

33

bike against the pillar. She glanced around to see if anyone else was nearby.

"You look good," he said.

"Yeah, right, you little liar. My hair's a brittle mess, my ass is getting wider and I'm pretty damn sure my boobs are losing their perkiness daily. But thanks anyways. And now I repeat my question. What the hell are you doing here? If Butch sees you here he'll shit. You know what a crazy bastard he is."

"Don't worry, he already paid me a visit today. He told me Frankie is missing."

"Really? So you decided to come over and poke the bear? He's been hanging around since Frankie went missing, you know."

Ari motioned for her to sit and after a moment's hesitation she did. Despite her self-deprecating comments she was still very pretty. Ari had always liked her, especially her no-nonsense attitude and a vocabulary salty enough to shock a Teamster. She was straightforward and blunt in an era of political correctness, and was the kind of girl who would push a shopping cart against the normal flow of traffic in a crowded grocery store just for the fun of it.

"Perhaps. But I'm just trying to find out what happened to Frankie. What can you tell me?"

Her face softened, some tiny lines around her eyes vanishing. There were only a few people in the world that knew the whole story of Van Owen and Frankie Brubaker, and Yvonne Peterson was one of them. The two women had been friends and co-workers for years and had lived together in a ratty apartment right after Yvonne's divorce. They still got together several times each week, usually when Butch worked late at UPS or was out of town.

She sighed. "You shouldn't get involved, Ari, you know that. We joke about how crazy Butch is, but I don't trust him. Neither should you."

Ari waved her objections away. "Thanks for your concern, really, but I'm not getting involved, not in a relationship way. I'm

34

just trying to figure out what happened. Help me out here, Yvonne. You of all people should understand all this."

She saw the pained look in his eyes and relented. She patted his thigh gently. "Okay, but I really wish you'd just stay out of it. For your sake and hers. I just don't want either one of you to get hurt again."

"Too late for that, I'm afraid."

"Yeah, I know, you love-sick bastard. I can't believe you haven't gotten over her after all this time. It's sweet, kind of, in a benign stalker kind of way."

Ari had no reply. He just shrugged, a sublime gesture that conveyed more than any words could.

"Alright," she relented, pointing a finger at him, her red nail polish bright in the sunshine. "Just remember that I warned you, okay?" She glanced over her shoulder at the building behind her. "We were both on duty a few days ago. Thursday, it was. Frankie had wrapped up all her work and was going golfing, a quick round at the driving range by herself. You know how much she loves golf, and with the season right around the corner she wanted to get a head start. Anyway, she was heading to that little range outside of town by the river. I was busy and didn't have any time to talk, but we were supposed to get together later for dinner or drinks. She left and I never saw her again. No one has."

"And her car was still here?"

"Yes, it was. Her scrubs were in her locker, so that means she changed into her street clothes, that much we know. A few people remember seeing her head out into the parking lot, and that's the last anyone saw her. She just vanished."

Ari thought for a second. "How about the security tapes? This place has cameras all over. There has to be a record of her somewhere."

"You'd think, wouldn't you? From what I heard that's the first thing the police checked, but something happened to the

35

surveillance system, according to the cops. The recordings from that time are all screwed up somehow. They're blank and useless. Some glitch in the system."

"A glitch in the system? That should be impossible."

"No shit. As new as this place is and with all the money they spent on stuff like that, you wouldn't think it could happen, especially as terrified as they are of lawsuits. You wouldn't believe how many people slip and fall at hospitals hoping to cash in. And the cops checked her car from top to bottom and didn't find anything. They had it all cordoned off and finally towed it away somewhere."

Ari stared out into the parking lot. "No one saw her out here, her car was untouched, and nobody's heard anything from her since?"

"That's pretty much it." After a second she added, a slight tremor in her normally confident voice, "I gotta tell you, Ari, I'm worried about her. I really am. She wouldn't just take off and leave without telling me. That's not like her at all."

"No, it's not," he agreed. He didn't tell her that he and Frankie still talked, and that she hadn't told him anything either. "So there's been no contact of any kind? No ransom notes or calls? Nothing?"

Her mouth dropped open in shock. "Ransom? No, of course not, not that I know of. Who in the world would hold her for ransom? She and Butch don't have any money to speak of. What would anyone want with Frankie? She didn't have any enemies either. Everyone loved her."

"I don't know, Yvonne. It doesn't make any sense to me either."

The concept of someone kidnapping Frankie and holding her for ransom had apparently not occurred to Yvonne. Her hands fumbled with her phone as if she couldn't figure out what to do with them. When she spoke again it was in a hushed whisper.

36

"Okay, Ari, thanks a lot. I was scared for her before but now I'm fucking terrified. What's happened to Frankie?"

"I honestly don't know. But I intend to find out."

"Shit, why did I know you'd say that?"

Ari leaned back and stared across the pond. Several more Canadian geese came in for a smooth, graceful landing, honking all the while. An ambulance pulled up to the Emergency entrance and two large men in white hustled out to help wheel a gurney inside.

"Yvonne, I need you to do me a favor."

"Hmm. What kind of favor?"

"I need you to find out who the security guard on duty was during the time Frankie vanished. I need to know who was in the surveillance room that afternoon."

Confusion flitted across her face. "What? Why do you need to know that?"

'I need to start somewhere, and that's as good a place as any. Can you do that for me?"

"I don't know, Ari."

"Please, for Frankie."

Yvonne sighed. "Dammit, Ari, I don't know. I thought you weren't going to get involved."

He smiled thinly. "Sorry, I think we're both involved now."

Ari's ride back home was uneventful, although so much was running through his mind during the trip that when he arrived back at the house he could barely remember any details of the journey. Once there he looked up a phone number and made a call.

"Louisville Metro PD, may I help you?" a pleasant female voice answered.

"Hi, yeah, I accidentally parked my car in a tow-away zone at Louisville Mercy Hospital and now it's gone. I think it got towed. Can you tell me where the impound lot is?"

"Certainly, sir." She gave him a phone number and an address on Bardstown Road, not too far from the airport and hospital. "And you'll have to pay any fines in cash and show proper ID and proof of ownership before it can be released."

He thanked her and hung up. He grabbed his wallet and truck keys then went outside and gently settled his bike in the bed of his pickup. Ari made the quick drive back to the hospital and parked the truck squarely across a red-striped area that clearly said NO PARKING – TOW AWAY ZONE near the Emergency Room entrance. He hefted the bike out and went around to the main doors of the hospital, right where he'd been only a short while earlier with Yvonne. He left the bike there and walked in the front doors to the main information desk. The air conditioning inside felt cool on his skin. Some barely audible Muzak drifted anonymously from hidden speakers in the ceiling and there was a faint, barely perceptible odor of rubbing alcohol in the air. As nice as the place was it was still, after all, a hospital.

The elderly gentleman at the information desk had a short, severe crew cut and precisely ironed white shirt with creases sharp enough to cut paper. Around his neck was a hospital name badge, white trimmed in red that he wore so proudly it could have been a Medal of Honor. The badge proclaimed that his name was Theodore Rust. Ari doubted anyone would have the guts to call him Ted, at least not twice. He had the look of a retired military man who demanded order above all else, which in this case suited Ari's needs perfectly. He looked up as Van Owen approached and made eye contact.

"May I help you, son?" His diction was crisp and perfect.

"Yes, sir. I noticed a pickup truck outside in a no-parking zone in the side lot. I think it's in the way of an ambulance trying to park."

Theodore's lips compressed and if anything he sat up straighter in his chair. Ari smiled inwardly. He imagined the phrase *Not on my watch* running through the man's head.

"Thank you, son, I'll take care of it right away. I appreciate your assistance."

"You're quite welcome. Have a nice day."

Theodore nodded and snatched up the phone and dialed with precise, stern jabs of his finger. In seconds Ari heard him demanding a tow truck. His conversation was brief and to the point, and he shortly hung up and nodded at Ari, who nodded back and strolled out the front door to his waiting bicycle. Within ten minutes a battered tow truck with the name Jake's Towing stenciled on the door rolled down the main drive to the side of the hospital. Several minutes after that it pulled back up the drive with Ari's pickup hooked behind it. As soon as he confirmed that it turned left out of the hospital and toward Bardstown Road he clipped his shoes back into the pedals and took off after it.

In very little time at all he rolled up to the address the policewoman had given him on the phone earlier. The impound lot was actually slightly off Bardstown, down a short lane and not visible from the main road. Behind a ten-foot tall chain link fence lined with coils of razor wire were visible several dozen cars and two tow trucks. A small brick shed was at the entrance with a sign over the top that proclaimed it was, indeed, *Jake's Towing*. The shed wasn't much larger than a single car garage and had a small, dirt-streaked window facing the street. As Ari pedaled up he looked inside and saw a large woman in her mid-forties. She had mousy hair that was mashed flat on one side, as if she had slept on it and had never gone to the trouble of locating a brush. She was watching a tiny black and white television. The picture jumped and fluttered and belted out a laugh track that blasted loudly through a small grill in the window's thick glass. Ari leaned his bike against the shed and knocked on the glass. After three attempts the lady finally noticed him.

"Help you?" she muttered. A cheerful Wal-Mart greeter she was not.

"Hi, yeah, my truck just got towed in from the hospital. I think it's here."

The attendant could barely pull her eyes from the show in progress. She grunted and pulled a stack of flimsy pink papers from a clipboard. She asked his name and the make and model of the truck. Ari complied, pulling out his driver's license and insurance card for proof.

"That'll be a hundred and twenty two bucks, cash."

"Ouch."

"Yeah, well, don't park in no tow-away zone next time, honey."

Ari paid and got a receipt. She hit an unseen button and the gate next to the shed buzzed. He pushed it aside and went in with his bike.

"All the way to the back, lot number 55," she yelled after him. "I'll open the main gate for you when you get here. Happy motoring." He lifted a hand in acknowledgement and she quickly went back to her show. He looked and saw through the shed's back window that she was once again ensconced in her seat, unblinking, staring at the little television as its meager light flickered across her slack face.

Ari quickly scanned the cars and trucks in the lot. His initial estimate had been too low: there had to be nearly a hundred vehicles tucked away all over the place, some of which had been here for quite some time given the amount of dust and dirt that had settled on them. The grime obscured their true colors and washed out even the most vibrant reds to a somber, dejected pink, and blues and blacks to a dirty gray the color of a hastily cleaned blackboard. His eyes tracked over each vehicle in search of Frankie's black Suburban. He figured he had ten minutes before the distracted lady in the booth would notice he hadn't shown up yet.

Two minutes flew by and he hadn't spotted it. The thick dust on so many of the cars and SUVs hampered him since it tended to homogenize the makes and colors of all the vehicles. He was beginning to wonder if he had guessed incorrectly about which lot it might be in, when he trotted behind a large Winnebago motorhome and spied another fenced-in area. This one was surrounding by a six-foot tall chain link fence sans razor wire, but with a battered yellow sign that quite clearly stated "Louisville Metro PD Impound Lot – NO Admittance". Inside were six or seven more vehicles. Frankie's Suburban was parked near the entrance, the imposing SUV towering over several Porsche 911s and a creamy white Bentley.

"Bingo."

Before making a move Ari looked around casually. Yes, there were two cameras aimed at the lot, both with tiny red lights indicating that they were on and functioning. Well, there was nothing he could do about that now. He simply had to hope that the pinnacle of customer service in the booth wasn't paying any attention to him, especially since he couldn't think of any plausible excuse for what he was about to do. He checked his watch. Six minutes had already elapsed.

He went to the gate and hoisted himself over. It clanked once but not so loudly that anyone would notice. He dropped down on the other side and quickly walked to the big SUV. Unlike most of its jail-mates it was very clean, the black paint just beginning to show an accumulation of dust. He grinned. Frankie always kept her Suburban very clean and tidy, both inside and out.

Nine minutes had passed and he knew he was pushing his luck. He circled the vehicle, alternating between crouching and standing as he inspected it from all angles. He didn't know what he was looking for. Careful not to touch it he peered inside and saw her golf bag lying neatly in the rear luggage area, black and white golf shoes lined up to one side. He moved around to the front, then to the passenger side, and finally to the rear. Frustrated that he hadn't found anything he was about to give up and collect his pickup truck when he looked sideways at the back tailgate. He knelt down and inspected an area near the keyhole. With a deep breath he got out his phone and carefully took a single picture, intent on holding the camera perfectly still in the fading light. The phone flashed and made a muted "click" and Ari checked to make sure it had captured the image correctly. He looked again at the tailgate. There, barely visible in the dust, was a hastily drawn design, a crudely rendered wagon wheel with eight jagged spokes. It was one of the universally known symbols for Karma. Frankie must have scribbled it on there with her finger, maybe just as she'd been taken. It had to be a message meant for Ari, a message to him that something was wrong.

If he'd had any doubts before that she was in trouble, now he was certain of it.

He hopped back over the fence, gathered up his bike, and loaded it into his pickup truck. He fired it up and drove back to the shed, honking his horn as he neared. The big gate swung open and he pulled out onto the narrow lane and then merged into traffic on Bardstown. His mind was working furiously as he drove back to his house. If she'd been surprised and unable to do anything else, if she'd felt threatened or frightened, she still would have had time to scribble that symbol. She could have drawn it on the tailgate even with her back to the car and nobody would've known what it was. His heart sunk as he wondered yet again what had happened to her.

Even though he had known these last few years that they could never be together he enjoyed the limited satisfaction that she was nearby and safe. He could have moved far away and stayed off the grid but he had chosen to remain geographically close by. He purposefully didn't dwell on her relationship with Butch and on where they might be or what they might be doing day to day, but the fact that she lived this close gave his heart some solace. He was learning to live with it. Most of the time that was enough since he understood it was all he was going to get.

But not now. This was different. He knew she was in trouble and that something had happened to her. He couldn't live with that.

He arrived back at the house and went to his office. Ari gathered up Hal's business card and dialed the agent's cell phone, impatiently drumming his fingers on the desk while it connected. After two rings Hal answered.

"Hal, it's Ari."

"Ari? Well that was fast. Do you have good news for me?"

"No, I don't, not really. Something's happened to Frankie for sure, I know it." He proceeded to tell the FBI agent what he knew so far about the likely abduction, the botched security tapes at the hospital, and the Karma symbol on her Suburban.

"You've been busy so far," Hal admitted with respect. "Still the old Ari, I see."

"Whatever," he snapped, his temper short, worry over Frankie overriding small talk and accolades. "There's no way I'm going anywhere until we find her. It's as simple as that. If you want my help then you need to help me first."

There was a slight pause on the other end. Ari could visualize Hal cleaning his glasses meticulously.

"I already contacted Louisville Metro PD and talked to them," the agent said. "They don't have any idea what happened and couldn't tell me much except the same news about the security tapes. And yes, before you say anything else, I find that odd, too. They've listed her as missing and have distributed her photo to all law enforcement agencies around the tri-state. They've questioned her husband, some friends, and hospital staff. I asked about next steps and they don't have any concrete ones. At least not now."

"We need to talk to the security guard at the hospital, the one in the surveillance room during the time she disappeared."

Hal sighed, the tired sound easily coming across the phone. "I'm afraid I can't do that now, Ari. Something else has come up. My assignment has changed."

His brow furrowed. "What do you mean, something else came up? Help me find Frankie and I'll go on your trip. That's my deal. Find her and I'll go back to the Amazon and see what's going on. I can figure this out, Hal, you know I can."

"I can't, Ari, not now. We've had two more reported cases of sudden onset paralysis, only this time it's not just airline personnel."

"What? Who is it now?"

"A freight handler for UPS at the airport, and someone else."

"Who?"

"A player for the Cincinnati Reds. Only this time it wasn't paralysis. This time it was worse. He died."

"Let me explain, especially since the media will only get a portion of the facts. We'll make sure of that." He paused. Ari wasn't sure if the agent was gathering his thoughts or worried about security on the line. After another moment of dead silence Hal continued.

"Do you know who Carlos Garrafon is? He was a young second baseman from the Dominican Republic. He'd been picked up by the Reds as a backup infielder. Don't know how much you follow baseball, but he was a very hot prospect a few years earlier with the Yankees. However after two mediocre seasons they released him. The Reds, like many of the smaller market teams, are always looking for cheap talent, whether it's new or someone else's cast off. They talked him into a one-year contract for substantially less than New York had been paying him. He accepted since the deal was better than a return to his native country or getting sent down to a triple A team. He'd also seen it as a chance to redeem himself."

"Garrafon? I've heard of him. I don't much about him but he's all over the papers. The guy's been on fire the last month or so," Ari said. "Most people in Kentucky are Reds fans since they're the closest Major League team. Garrafon's been hitting the cover off the ball lately, and his fielding has been tremendous."

"That's him. You're right, he's been tearing it up this past month. He was doing much better than in New York and in the pre-season. But this morning he was found dead in his apartment of an apparent heart attack. Further examination showed symptoms of SOP – the red skin, residual high fever, rigidity. We won't know for sure until the autopsy but we're moving ahead on this assumption for now."

Ari sat at this desk. Outside the early spring evening was closing in. He stared out the window and could just barely see the garage housing his Firebird. In a few minutes the security spotlight would click on, but for now the light was just enough to make out gray, indistinct shapes of trees and some hills beyond that. He took a deep breath.

"Hal, I'm sorry for Garrafon and his family, I really am. But he's dead and Frankie's still out there. Help me find her. You know as well as I do that the first 48 hours are the most important in cases like this, and 48 hours are already up. We've got to hurry."

"I'm sorry, Ari, I can't. Not now. This is getting bigger than we thought, bigger than anyone thought. It's not just happening to UPS and airline employees any more. The Amazon trip is on hold for a little bit while we work some of this out. For now I'm afraid you're on your own."

Ari swore and hung up the phone. *Fine.* If he was on his own, then so be it. He would take matters into his own hands.

Chapter 3

Ari woke up suddenly and looked at the clock next to his bed. The bright green digits read 5:01AM. He grunted and rolled over, facing away from the clock. For some reason he couldn't fathom he always woke up around 5:00 in the morning, and had ever since he'd started seeing Frankie. When the two of them had been together it was no big deal. She would snuggle up against him and lay her head on his shoulder, the down comforter covering them both, her soft breath on his cheek as warm as a summer breeze. He would smile and wrap his arms around her and she would mumble little nothings and press her body into his. She was always warm. Ari could lie like that for hours and not care, content that they were together. He had been happy. That was then.

Now waking up at 5:00 was empty, hollow, and made him miss her even more. Even drunk or exhausted his eyes would still pop open at that lousy hour. He hated 5:00 in the morning.

He stared sightlessly at the dark ceiling and debated his next moves. Nighttime sounds from outside the open window leached into his room: a distant dog barking, the chirrup of a cricket, another two or three UPS jets laden with cargo and mail, thundering by overhead. Typical country stuff.

His cell phone was next to the clock. Ari scanned his contacts and found Yvonne's number. Heedless of the hour he sent her a short text: *Any news on the security guard?* He hadn't finalized what he would do with the information when he got it, but he was certain that was his next move. Yvonne had called him a lovesick bastard. She knew him pretty well.

Despite his tumultuous thoughts he finally drifted off again, waking for good around seven o'clock. After a quick breakfast of coffee and toast he showered and shaved. The morning was still cool so he tossed on jeans and an old sweatshirt then went out to the garage, determined to get some work done on the car. He turned on the propane heater to help ease the chill. Once that was done he flicked on the radio and tuned it to a nearby NPR station. At one of the local news breaks at the top of the hour they announced the death of Garrafon, the reporter calling it an apparent heart attack. There was no mention of SOP or anything else, which didn't surprise him. They briefly touched on highlights of his short career and how well he'd been doing for the Reds, about how his loss would likely impact the team's chances of winning the Central Division and the Pennant. The story lasted about a minute before they moved on to a traffic report. So much for poor Carlos Garrafon, Ari considered. His life had been reduced to little more than a sixty second blurb on the radio.

Ari got back to work. He thought best with this type of multitasking, when his hands were busy and his mind could whirl away in the background unimpeded. He grabbed a handful of tools and began the careful disassembly of the drum brakes on the Firebird. The old corroded nuts and bolts gave him some trouble, resisting his attempts to loosen them at first, and although he was stronger than he looked a few proved too stubborn no matter how much force he applied. He moved to the big green air compressor, one of the reasons he'd rented this place, and switched it on. The electric motor thundered and echoed in the garage so loudly another plane could've crashed just outside unnoticed. After a minute of running the pump did its job and the big compressor tank shut down with a hissing sigh. He connected a long hose and an impact wrench and made short work of the stubborn hardware. He carefully put all the parts into an upside down hubcap at his side and stripped everything down to the bearings. He considered removing those as well but since he didn't have a machine press that pretty much settled that. For the next forty-five minutes he tinkered with the new brake assembly until he was satisfied that it had been installed correctly. Lastly he hooked up the hydraulic line, reminding himself that he would have to bleed the entire brake system when he was finished. That was a two-person job. Maybe he could talk Hal into helping him...

Ari genuinely enjoyed working on anything mechanical or electrical. Each and every part either did or didn't fit, either worked or didn't, with very little gray area. Even somewhat complex machines like the Firebird were orderly and logical, traits that he found appealing. Not for the first time did he wish life could be more like that. He re-tightened the visible bolts just for good measure. One down, three to go.

He took a quick break and checked his phone. Nothing from Yvonne yet. With a grunt he went to the right rear wheel and began tearing those brakes down next, perhaps using more force than was necessary. Two hours later he'd completed all four and surveyed his work with silent satisfaction. On the radio NPR had moved on to a news interview show that was recapping the headlines of the week. The genial female host covered the current trade imbalance with China, the sharp decrease in the value of the Euro against the dollar, and something about a spike in drug trafficking from South America. The guest speakers all weighed in with opinions that were little more than background chatter to him and so far removed from his life that none of it impacted him directly. A caller phoned in with a question about a story in the New York Times about a new drug he'd heard about, something called Ice, but Ari was bored with the news and spun the dial to a station operated by the University of Louisville, one whose playlist included all different types of music including Reggae, alternative, and classic rock. He was fond of the station since the student DJs had free reign to play what they wanted and weren't tied down to a specific genre. It was a nice change from the ho-hum, homogenous Corporate Radio that was typically heard across the country.

The garage was plenty warm now so he killed the propane heater, then hefted the tank and was surprised how light it was, a sure sign of an impending refill. He tidied up his tools, quietly pleased with the morning's work on the car. He was concerned that he hadn't conjured up a next step around Frankie's disappearance, but he knew that with him these things couldn't be forced. His intuitive leaps were like tiny seedlings; with proper watering, sunlight, and care he was confident something would blossom, he just didn't know what or when that might be.

The current tune on the radio was something by Bob Marley, a song he didn't know, and when it ended another came on without a pause. That was another reason he liked this station: it had limited commercials and almost no inane DJ chatter. This new tune began with a series of mellow acoustic guitar riffs accompanied by haunting lyrics, a song he had never heard before but which immediately grabbed onto his heart.

> *Honey you are a rock, upon which I stand.*
>
> *But I come here to talk, I hope you understand.*
>
> *But Green Eyes, yeah the spotlight shines upon you,*
>
> *And how could anybody deny you?*
>
> *I came here with a load, and it feels so much lighter now I met you.*
>
> *And honey you should know, and I could never go on without you.*
>
> *Green eyes…*

Ari was transfixed, rooted to the spot with a wrench held loosely in his hand like a forgotten appendage. *Green eyes*. Frankie had green eyes, sparkling jade eyes that could peer into his heart as if he were made of nothing but glass. It struck him anew that, over time, some of the tiny details of her face and mannerisms had faded and blurred, her image in his mind akin to an old photograph going grainy with time. He knew it was inevitable, like entropy, yet it still saddened him. But he would never, ever forget her eyes. He listened raptly to the final chords and hoped for once that the DJ would come on and announce the band's name, but they didn't, instead segueing into something by the group INXS. For the second time in as many days he reminded himself to call the cable company and sign up for broadband Internet, this time so he could look up the artist. After all, he thought, was effectively back on the grid now, so maintaining his self-imposed anonymity no longer seemed so important.

He finally shook himself and continued cleaning up, but no matter what he did the lyrics and melody of that song stuck with him. He locked up the garage and went back into the house, slightly shaken but more determined than ever to find Frankie.

Anxious about his limited ability to act, Ari got into his truck and started driving. His first stop was the library where he quickly checked Facebook on the off chance that Frankie had changed her own status to send him a message. She hadn't. He sat back in the hard chair and cruised around her Facebook wall but nothing new or out of the ordinary jumped out at him. He did look up a local Internet provider and called them to schedule a time to get hooked up at the house. They could be there in a few days between the hours of noon and four, they said, and thanks for calling your local cable provider.

Back in his truck he pulled into traffic. He wanted his destination to be as aimless as his bike ride the day before, but deep down he knew where he was going. Traffic was heavy in that part of town and he hit every single red light he came across. Fifteen minutes later he pulled into a subdivision on the east side of Louisville and drove slowly toward a two-story frame home down the street. The property was not as well kept as those surrounding it, with a yard that was overgrown and weedy, and bushes that were just beginning to need a good once-over with clippers. One gutter on the top left was loose and dangled drunkenly. He parked his truck on the curb a few houses away. He had never been this close to Frankie and Butch's place before, hadn't dared to in the past, but he knew exactly where it was and what it looked like thanks to a stalker's best friend, Google Maps and Street View. Brubaker's own pickup was in the short driveway. Ari had no idea what he was looking for but the urge to do something, *anything*, was too strong to permit him to sit at home and stew any longer.

Forty-five minutes passed. Several cars drove by but paid him little attention, the drivers intent on their own lives and destinations, kids' soccer games, and runs to the grocery store or dry cleaners. Ari considered giving up and moving on. Instead he pulled out his phone and brought up the picture he had taken of Frankie's car and the Karma symbol from the impound lot. He magnified the image and scrolled around it bit by bit. He got to the bottom of the wagon wheel shape and looked more closely, finally zooming in until the picture began to turn fuzzy. He hadn't noticed before, but the bottom spoke on the wheel was different than the rest. Instead of ending at the base of the rough circle it passed through and looked like a sloppy arrow pointing down. That was odd. Their shared symbol didn't have any arrows, it never had. What had Frankie meant when she had hastily sketched this? Why was it pointing down? Was there something else on the SUV? Had there been something on the ground in the parking lot? Surely the police would have seen an object left there.

Or was it pointing south? Like a compass.

Before Ari could consider that any longer a movement in his peripheral vision caught his attention. Butch's garage door had opened and Brubaker himself was walking out. He was in his UPS outfit, brown coveralls with his name stitched onto his breast pocket, a security badge on a lanyard around his neck. For some reason he stood in the garage and stared up and down the street, looking this way and that much like Hal had done when leaving Ari's house the day before. He was obviously looking for something or someone, or at least on the lookout for someone, and was acting as innocent as a fugitive in a witness protection program. Ari was thankful he had parked far enough away not to draw any attention to himself, yet even so he resisted the urge to drop down out of sight: he did *not* need Brubaker to see him now. After a few more seconds of this odd behavior Frankie's husband trotted out to his pick-up and jumped inside, pulled out of the driveway, and drove quickly up the tree-lined street away from Ari. When Butch had turned a corner Van Owen began to follow from a safe distance, always careful to keep him in sight without getting too close. He had never tailed anyone before and after ten minutes he realized just how hard this task was, especially with the heavy congestion and traffic lights. Twice he thought he had lost him completely and once he suddenly found he was so close he could see Butch talking on the phone almost right next to him. With a start and a chirp of his brakes he dropped back so quickly he was sure he'd been spotted, cursing this rookie mistake.

Brubaker merged onto the Watterson Expressway, then followed the posted route to the airport and the UPS Distribution Center. Ari found it was trickier here with fewer cars around but was saved any more shocks when Butch pulled into the employee lot where he flashed his ID and was waved in. Ari slowly cruised past the entrance and continued on farther ahead, finally easing to a stop on the side of the road several hundred feet away. Between cars and trucks he could catch glimpses of Brubaker's truck as the man searched for a parking spot. He finally saw him get out, look around again, then walk quickly to the monstrous main building, a huge UPS brown and gold logo on its side. His behavior still struck Ari as strange.

As he sat there ruminating over all this his phone chimed. He checked and saw he had received a text from Yvonne. *Nothing yet, toots. Still working on it.* Damn. He was hoping she'd have something for him by now. With nothing else to see here he drove

52

back to his house, his mind still churning in the background. For some reason when he got out of his truck he looked around, up and down the street and into the woods across from his house. With a thoughtful pursing of his lips he wondered why he had done that. Perhaps the suspicious behavior was catching.

When Ari Van Owen was a senior at a small Ohio liberal arts college, his parents were killed by an unknown intruder in their home, a mystery that had never been solved and had long since been allocated to cold case status in some dusty police basement filing cabinet. They had both been fairly well-off research scientists working for Procter and Gamble in Cincinnati, and unbeknownst to Ari had arranged for a healthy trust-fund, bolstered by life insurance policies, to care for their only child should anything happen to them. Ari graduated from college with honors in Political Science, and like many of his peers took a "gap" year to travel Europe, staying in hostels and backpacking across much of the European Union. He knew the trust fund was enough to keep him living comfortably for the rest of his life if he so desired. While that was tempting, his life took a different tack when he arrived back in the states. His college advisor, a man he'd always admired, contacted him and told him he should apply to the Martin Institute in Columbus, Ohio. Martin was a US Government-backed think-tank that specialized in alternative tactics in counter-terrorism from both domestic and foreign sources. No doubt at the urging of his college advisor, whom Ari later found out was on the board of Martin, the Institute hired him. While in Martin's employ a constant string of successes caused some to tag him as lucky, but sharper minds were aware that luck implied an occasional win, not multiple successes. Ari had been noticed, both inside and outside the Institute. He was now a bright blip on the radar of the Institute's main customers, the Intelligence apparatus, and more specifically the FBI.

It was around that same time that Ari first stumbled onto the mystery of Colonel Percy Fawcett's disappearance so many years earlier. With little but work to keep his attention he dove into the subject with a passion, to the point where his infatuation with the Colonel began to interfere with his employment. He soon found he could concentrate on little else. Less than a year after being hired at Martin he made a life-choice and resigned his position to devote himself to Fawcett full-time, much to the chagrin of many, including the FBI. He was suffering from the onset of Fawcett Fever.

During that period, an FBI field agent named Hal Hollenbeck visited him. After much cajoling and prodding Hal finally talked Ari into working on a special project for the Bureau, one their internal specialists had been unable to solve dealing with computer malware discovered lurking in Martin's own internal network. This was far from anything the young man had worked with before, yet within two weeks he had discovered the unlikely source of the malware – the US Government itself. It was a case of the left hand not knowing what the right hand was doing, and was quickly brushed under a red, white, and blue rug. But Ari was once again looked upon with admiration and favor in most circles.

Some months later Hal visited him again, this time with a different, highly sensitive request. The Bureau suspected one of their own agents was passing along sensitive information to the Pakistanis regarding terror targets along the Pakistan – Afghanistan border. Ari was married to Michelle at that point so was disinclined to get involved, but because American agents and soldiers had been killed and more were in danger he agreed to see what he could do. Ari had access to all the Bureau's records and information at Quantico, up to and including several trips to Pakistan itself. After less than a month he delivered an envelope to Hal with not just one name but three, one of whom was an Army full-bird Colonel. After that his standing with the Bureau was solidified. They wanted him full-time.

But it was not to be. Shortly after that Ari embarked on his first Fawcett mission to the Amazon. Unlike what has been known to happen in romance, time and distance caused him to eventually fade from their collective minds. He was gone and completely out of touch for almost a year and a half. After his return, his short marriage to Michelle imploded and his relationship with Frankie began. The FBI and their past requests diminished from his memory as other life events claimed him. Then came the second Fawcett trip and a two-year hiatus from the States. When he eventually returned he was stunned and heartbroken to find that Frankie and Butch were married. He purposefully retreated from life and the grid, or as the FBI would say, he had gone intentionally "dark". During that phase of his life he was despondent beyond his understanding. To call him a hermit would not be too far off the mark. He was a changed man, he knew. Where he had been happy with a curious, insightful nature and agile mind, he was now bitter and suffering, a shell of his former self. He hated what he had become but was powerless to change it.

It was then that he had moved to the house outside of Louisville. If he couldn't be with Frankie he could at least be geographically close with the calming knowledge that she was never far away. It was something, at least. He stayed off the grid and stayed dark so he wouldn't be bothered again, by anyone.

Now Frankie was gone and Hal had located him. He had a purpose again, there was renewed meaning in his life. He had to find her, not for himself, he knew, but simply to know she was safe. Like moving to Louisville this would have to do. It was enough. It would have to be.

Back at home he spent a little time thinking. He didn't like waiting for Yvonne to get him the information he needed. Instead of fretting at the house he drove back to the library where he got online and did a quick Google search. Right away he found what he needed and placed an order from a website in the Bahamas. It amazed him what could be purchased online these days. He put an overnight rush on the order and paid with his PayPal account so the funds would be pulled from his bank account out of state.

When he got home he went to the bedroom closet and perused his clothing, ultimately satisfied he had what he needed on hand. Sadly he couldn't proceed until his order arrived. The wait was killing him.

For the next two days he occupied himself with working on the Firebird and leafing through his Fawcett materials. The information from his friend Alex Hanes in Britain did manage to catch his fancy enough that he made some new notations and added sticky notes to the maps around his office. The colonel's cryptic notes to Nina, his wife, continued to convince Ari that the explorer's stated destination to the rest of the world was quite different from his actual one. Much of the correspondence between the two dealt with mundane topics such as where they had eaten dinner before he left and a theatre where they'd attended a play. He also talked *ad nauseum* about conditions in the jungle and how he worried about the health and fortitude of his third companion, Raleigh Rimmell. Raleigh had injured his leg somehow and was slowing the party down. Details were sketchy, but the consensus was that he'd gashed it and infection was setting in. Fawcett's son Jack was as solid and hardy as his father, but Raleigh was becoming a liability. He sighed and rubbed his forehead. There was something there that he didn't understand yet, something that he couldn't see, and he continued to have that undeniable feeling that Fawcett had been lying again. The man was crafty. Very crafty. *Where were you really going, Colonel, you sneaky devil?*

There was a knock on the door. Ari jumped up and looked out the window. Outside there was a white and green home FedEx truck idling in his driveway. His pulse kicked up a notch in anticipation as he threw the door open. The deliveryman jumped back in surprise.

56

"Package, sir," the man said, quickly regaining his composure.

"Thanks." Ari signed the electronic pad and accepted the small box. It was about the size of a hardback book, and heavy.

"Something from the Bahamas, eh?"

"Yep." Ari handed the electronic pad back.

The FedEx driver could tell there was no more conversation forthcoming. He told Ari to have a nice day and climbed back into his truck. Ari shut the door and walked purposefully back to his office, the small package weighty in his hands. With a sharp pocketknife he kept on his desk he cut open the brown wrapping and slid the contents out. He held up his rush order and inspected it in the light. He felt its heft in his hand.

"Not bad, not bad at all." His face held a look of cautious admiration. He could have been a connoisseur sampling an unexpectedly fine cabernet when he'd been expecting cheap table wine. "Pretty good craftsmanship. Thank you, Internet."

Holding back his excitement he went to the bathroom. He was in and out of the shower in ten minutes, fighting with little success to keep his unruly brown hair tamed and under control. He shaved and got dressed, donning black slacks, white shirt, a plain dark tie, and a tan sport coat. Ari surveyed himself in the mirror, convinced he was as unobtrusive as possible and succeeding in looking official without overdoing it. He snugged up the knot on his tie and tilted his head with a grunt.

"Not bad."

He picked up his new purchase plus a small notebook and pen and went out to his truck. In no time he arrived at a private car rental firm just off the airport grounds and rented a four door Chevy Impala, silver with a gray interior. It was the most nondescript, boring vehicle he could imagine and was perfectly suited for his needs. He told the rental agent he planned on keeping it for several days at least. Oh, and would it be okay if he left his truck there?

"Sure, whatever," the uninterested twenty year-old behind the counter told him, barely able to pull himself away from playing with his phone. "Just park it around back and leave us the keys in case we need to move it. No worries, dude."

Ari signed and initialed where indicated and was quickly back on the road. The inside of the Impala smelled like old cigarettes and burritos and there was a stain of indeterminate origin on the passenger seat. In a few minutes he pulled into the hospital parking lot and eased the Impala into a slot out back, far from the main entrances. A huge Hummer SUV was taking up more than its share of the space in front of him. No one could even see his car from the hospital. That was perfect, too.

He took a deep breath and walked the length of the parking lot and into the front doors. Ari was concerned that Theodore Rust, the retired military man from his previous visit, would be manning the information desk again, which could have been dicey, but he wasn't. Instead he saw an elderly woman with short gray hair and half-glasses perched on her nose. She was reading a thick hardback book, something by Danielle Steele, he saw. As he walked up she closed the book but saved her place with a finger. Her name badge said "Dot", which he guessed was short for Dorothy.

"Good afternoon. Could you direct me to the Security Office?" he asked.

Dot's old blue eyes widened just a fraction; apparently not many hospital visitors asked for that particular location. "Why yes. First floor, behind me and down to the right. You'll see the signs." She pointed with her free hand.

"Thank you."

"You're welcome, young man."

Ari marveled at the difference in the levels of customer service between the elderly and the young, such as the twenty-something at the car rental office compared to Dot. Society's demise would probably not be at the hands of external enemies, he mused, but more likely due to the disintegration of simple etiquette. He nodded his thanks and followed her directions. He quickly found a solid white door with the words "Security Office" in small print. Had he not been watching for it he would have walked right by. He squared his shoulders, shot his cuffs, and walked in. It was show time.

Inside the security room it looked more like a television studio control room than an office. The space was small, no more than fifteen feet square. Against the far wall were two banks of ten television screens, each with a time and date stamp and flicking through scenes of daily hospital life. Many showed hallways, lobbies, and waiting rooms. Three were focused on the parking lots, and two clearly showed the front door and main entrance where Dot was seated, her nose deep in the book. The pictures were bright and crisp, all digital now, not a fuzzy analogue screen in sight. To his untrained eye there were enough dials and switches to launch a space shuttle.

Two security guards turned to look at him. One was standing and drinking hot tea from a Styrofoam cup. He was short and a little chubby, his thinning hair slicked back over his head to hide a growing bald spot. Black framed glasses with thick lenses made his eyes look unnaturally large, like fish eyes. His name badge said Fred Armstrong. The other man was seated at the control desk with his feet propped up on another chair. He was thin and bald with just a ring of dark hair encircling his head. The thin man, his name badge proclaiming he was Neville Willard, sat up a little straighter.

"Can I help you?" Neville asked. His voice was quite deep for someone so thin. Both men looked mildly concerned that someone outside their fraternity was violating their inner sanctum unannounced.

"Yes, you can," Ari said. He pulled out his Bahaman purchase and held it toward them. It was a heavy gold-colored badge that read "Justice Department – Federal Bureau of Investigation". Underneath that was an identification card, complete with his picture and an official red stamp. Fred, the chunky man with the thick glasses, stood up completely and set his cup down. The two looked at each other warily.

"My name is Hal Hollenbeck with the FBI. I'd like to ask you a few questions."

Neville's feet fell off the chair with a thud. He looked to his partner.

"Um, sure. What's the FBI doing here?"

Ari gave the two of them a tight smile, one with just a hint of condescension, as if slightly pitying them their low status in the food chain of law enforcement. He had practiced that particular look in the rearview mirror of the car on the way over. The fact that he was impersonating a Federal officer didn't bother him. He was doing whatever he needed in order to locate Frankie, consequences be damned. "We're looking into the disappearance of one of your employees, a Francis Brubaker."

Fred Armstrong looked skeptical, his face screwed up as if he had been presented with a math problem and couldn't come to grips with the answer. He stepped forward and put his hand out, palm up.

"Okay if I see your ID?"

"Of course." Ari was honestly pleased that his hand didn't shake as he placed the badge and ID in the man's thick hand. He was not accustomed to field work, real or fictional. He was just praying that neither man noticed any subtle anomalies, such as his lack of an FBI issue sidearm.

Fred looked it over and compared Ari's picture with his face. He held the ID to the light and grunted before he was convinced. Either he had never seen an actual FBI badge or the fake was good enough. He gave it back to Ari.

"Why's the FBI so interested in a missing person from the hospital?"

Ari took the badge and ID and pocketed them, the test passed. "That information is confidential, I'm afraid. I just have a few questions for you."

The two security men looked at each other and nodded mutely.

"Okay, shoot," said Fred, the senior of the two.

"What can you tell me about her disappearance?"

Now that he had passed muster they were more at ease and open to questioning. Fred Armstrong took the lead and did all the talking. The air of tension in the small room eased, visible in the more relaxed postures of the two guards. They were all fellow lawmen, brothers in law enforcement.

"Not much, really." He relayed to Ari what was already known, that she had come to work, put in her shift in the Rehab unit, and announced that she was going to the driving range. She had changed into street clothes and left. He fidgeted a bit when he talked about the lack of security video and what had actually happened. Ari took notes in a little spiral bound notebook.

"This video snafu. Tell me about that. I don't understand how could that happen. Where were the security cameras?"

The two uniformed men looked both embarrassed and apologetic, reminding Ari of high school kids being questioned by the principal. The thin man, Neville, kept playing with his hand, his eyes down.

"We don't know," Armstrong said. "It shouldn't have happened. Hell, it shouldn't have been able to happen. We've got redundant backups that should've captured it all. For some reason about twenty minutes of our feed is blank and nothing but static."

Just then Ari's phone vibrated. It was a text from Yvonne. He excused himself and read the message. *Guard's name is Paul Paulson. No shit – Paul Paulson. What r parents thinking? Lives in Shelbyville. You owe me! ;)*

He pocketed the phone and made a quick notation in his notebook. Better late than never, Ari thought, glad to have the information.

"Sorry about that. Go on."

Armstrong nodded and continued. "No problem. We called the manufacturer and asked them about it. They said the only way that could happen was if someone manually erased it. Their rep couldn't give any other explanation."

"Who would have access and be able to do that?"

The two security guards exchanged glances. "Anyone in here that knows how to operate the equipment, I guess."

Ari glanced at each man in turn. "Do both of you know how?"

Neville nodded nervously. Fred's jaw muscles twitched, not liking the implied accusation. Ari kept his expression neutral. "Well?"

"Sure, we both could," Fred admitted eventually. "Any of us could. It's not that hard and there's no tracking that kind of action in the system, no signature who might've done it. There will be now, you can damn be sure of that."

Ari made a show of flipping through the blank pages of his notebook.

"The man on duty then, Paul Paulson, could he have done it?"

"Yeah, I guess so. Like I said, we all know how. It's not hard."

"Where can I find Mr. Paulson? Is he here today?"

Both men shook their heads, Neville in nervous jerks and Armstrong slowly: he could have been working a kink out of his neck.

"Nope. He's on paid administrative leave while we continue investigating what went wrong."

"Hmm. The police report says he lives in Shelbyville but it didn't have the exact address. I'd like that, please."

"Yeah, okay. Sure. I'll get that for you."

Paulson lived in an unattractive townhouse complex named The Fields of Shelbyville. There may have been fields in the area at some point in the past, Ari mused, but not in his lifetime. All the townhouses were dirty tan brick with stone trim and black shutters, an unlikely combination that was meant to look earthy but instead projected a tired, worn out feel. Several of the shutters were either missing or crooked, and weeds jutted boldly from crumbling sidewalks and parking lots. There were tennis courts in the center of the complex but there were no nets to be seen, and probably hadn't been for a dozen or more Wimbledons. To Ari it had a depressed, somber feel, a townhouse hospice, a place where once loved dwellings went to crumble and die. He parked the silver Impala at the end of the parking lot and walked until he found number 1004. One of the zeros was missing from the door so the address read 10 4 instead. Unless the inside of Paulson's townhome was something truly magnificent and wondrous and contrary to everything he'd seen so far, then this place would take a little nip out of your soul each and every day. He knocked on the painted steel door.

After a minute he heard shuffling inside and a muffled, tentative male voice said, "Yeah, who's there?"

Ari took a step back and held up the FBI badge so it could be clearly seen through the peephole.

"FBI, Mr. Paulson. I'd like to have a few words with you, please."

Ari heard a solid thud, like something – perhaps Paulson's head? - hitting the door, and an indistinct word that could have been "shit". But the young man that opened it grinned briefly and looked expectantly at Ari, as if they were sharing an elevator and he was waiting for Ari to tell him what button to push.

"You're Paul Paulson?"

"Yes, sir. And you are?"

Paulson was young, no more than twenty-five. He had a pleasant round face and blue eyes with wavy blond hair. His eyebrows were so blond that from ten feet away they'd be invisible. His nose was a bit bent and had been broken at some point in the past, probably more than once. He was shorter than Ari and thicker through the body, with an athlete's physique, not running or track, but perhaps a contact sport like football or rugby. He wore a sleeveless Louisville Cardinal's basketball T-Shirt and shorts.

"I'm Hal Hollenbeck with the FBI, Mr. Paulson. I'd like to talk to you about Frankie Brubaker's disappearance."

Paulson's expression didn't change. He stepped outside and began to shut the door behind him. Ari put his hand out to stop it.

"I'd like to talk to you about this inside, Mr. Paulson. Not out here. This is a private matter."

"Oh, um, sure. It's a kind of a pigsty in here. The, ah, maid hasn't been here for a few days. Sorry for the mess." He opened the door wider and let Ari in. When the young man walked he had a small but noticeable limp.

Ari stepped inside. Yes, the maid had *not* been here for quite some time, probably months instead of just days. He'd seen pictures of tsunami ravaged islands that hadn't looked this bad. There were beer and soda cans littered everywhere, and pizza boxes stacked fifteen high like a huge cardboard game of Jenga. He could barely see a flat area on the first floor that wasn't buried under clothes or dishes. The one bright spot was a huge Panasonic flat screen television that looked brand new. It still had stickers on the black frame, Ari noticed, and there were some cables coiled in a bag next to it. It was off, the screen empty and dark.

"Like I said, the maid hasn't been here for a few days. That or she ran away screaming, I don't know which for sure," he admitted with a sad laugh. Using his arm like a shovel he forced aside enough household debris from a section of the couch for Ari to sit. Paulson himself remained standing. He leaned against the wall with his hands in his pockets. Whether it was done purposefully or not, the young man had just put himself into a superior physical and psychological position, with him standing and Ari seated low on the couch and looking up at him. Interesting, Van Owen thought.

"So who'd you say you were again?"

"Special Agent Hal Hollenbeck with the FBI, Mr. Paulson."

"Just call me Paul, please. And aren't you too tall for a field agent? I thought they had height requirements that you couldn't be over five feet eleven, or something like that."

Uh, oh. Interesting. "That used to be the case, yes, but those requirements were rescinded quite some time ago as being discriminatory." At least he thought that was right. He was surprised Paulson knew anything about such a thing.

"Oh, okay. So what can I do for you?"

"As I said, I'm here looking into the disappearance of Francis Brubaker."

The young man nodded. "Yeah, I figured as much. You know Louisville Metro already questioned me about that, I'm sure."

"Of course, but we like conducting our own investigation."

"Yeah, I bet. So what can I tell you?"

"You can start by telling me how twenty minutes of the security recordings were blank. How could that happen?"

Paulson blew air out of pursed lips. "That's the million dollar question, isn't it? Wish I knew. During the day we typically have four men on duty, one in the room scoping out the monitors and the other three on their rounds. Not much happens during the day, really, but we like to have a visible presence, you know?"

"Understandable."

"More goes on at night, especially around the ER. You get your 3Ds then, your Dopers, Disorderlies, and Drunks. They make things a lot more interesting. That's the fun shift." He winked at Ari.

"That Thursday was like any other afternoon shift, as far as I can remember," he continued. "Nothing much happened. I wouldn't remember it at all if Ms. Brubaker hadn't come up missing, you know? I was in the security room the entire afternoon just watching the monitors and trying to stay entertained. My shift was over at four o'clock and I left. Didn't hear anything about her missing until a day or two later when her husband called in asking about her."

"And you didn't see anything wrong with the equipment? Nothing out of the ordinary?"

Paulson shook his head and kept his hands in his pockets. "Nope. Nothing, that's what makes it so weird."

Ari looked on a shelf above the new television and saw a picture of Paulson with a young, red-haired boy of about two or three. They were hugging and laughing on a small blue kiddy amusement ride of some sort, perhaps a pint-sized Thomas the Train. He gestured at the picture with his pen.

"Is that your son?"

Paulson twitched once, a barely perceptible movement, the same twitch anyone might have when they start to drift off involuntarily on a plane. He smiled quickly and looked at the framed photo. His expression softened.

"Yes, that's my son Taylor. That was taken earlier this year at the hospital's carnival days. We had a blast."

There was no ring on Paulson's hand and just the two of them in the picture. "His mother?"

"Ah, his mom and I are divorced as of a few months ago. They still live here in town, not too far away."

"Amicable divorce?"

He made a raspberry sound with his lips. "Amicable? No, not really. What's the exact opposite of amicable? That's what it was."

"Sorry to hear that. I notice you didn't name your son 'Paul'."

Paulson's expression couldn't have been more pained if he'd just been sucker-punched. "Good god, no. I wouldn't do that to him. I love him way too much for that. Don't know what the hell my parents were thinking. Maybe they'd been reading too many Marvel comic books with characters like J. Jonah Jameson, Peter Parker, or

Reed Richards. They were into alliteration or something. I don't know."

Ari leaned back on the couch but kept his notebook out. He visibly relaxed a degree and intentionally became less official, more conversational, a peer instead of a superior. "So, tell me a little about you. What's your background? How'd you get to be a security guard at the hospital?"

"My background? Well, you know, stupid kid right out of high school with no chance of paying for college. I signed up for a tour with the Marines and enjoyed several glorious months in Afghanistan. You know, a Jarhead. *Semper Fi.*" He tapped the side of his temple with a knuckle and grinned, fleetingly, before his face clouded. "Then one morning on patrol an IED went off next to our Humvee and I took a chunk of shrapnel in the knee. Wasn't bad enough for a discharge, but bad enough that I couldn't go back into combat. I can't run anymore which, you know, you kind of need over there."

"That's too bad about your injuries. But your son must be proud of you, being a Marine and now a security guard."

Paulson looked at the picture on the shelf and didn't say anything. After a few seconds he turned back. His face was tough to read.

"Yeah. Anyway my knee's bad enough that I can't pass the police physical. I always thought being a cop would be cool but I can't even do that. Had to settle for security guard. I can walk all day long with no problem, but running more than a short sprint is out."

Ari nodded and made some notes. "Is there anything else you can tell me about that Thursday afternoon? Anything that I should know or that would help? The longer she's missing the harder and less likely it is that we'll find her."

There was a pause while Paulson thought about it. When he spoke again he sounded quite sincere, more so than at any other time. "Sorry, Mr. Hollenbeck, wish I could help find her. I really do."

Ari levered himself out of the couch. He pulled Hal's business card out of his pocket and drew a heavy line through the cell phone number with his pen. On the back he wrote his own and handed the card to Paulson.

"Here's my contact info. Use the cell phone number on the back. Just had a change and haven't had new cards printed yet."

Paulson took the offered card and stared at it. The gold seal of the Department of Justice caught his attention and held it, perhaps making him realize for the first time that the man in front of him really was with the FBI, and this was serious business. He put it on the shelf by the picture of him and his son, well above the high tide line of the messy room.

"By the way," Ari said, snapping his fingers and jabbing a thumb out toward the parking lot. "I ran your car's plates before I came in and you've got about a dozen unpaid parking tickets you should probably take care of."

"What? No way, I don't have any parking tickets."

"Really? Don't you drive a blue Honda Accord sedan?"

Paulson shook his head. "Honda Accord? No, that's not me. I've got a BMW 325. A white one. It's parked right outside."

Ari checked some non-existent writing on his notebook. "That's odd. Okay, they must have run the wrong car. My apologies."

The young man grinned and put a hand to his heart. "Don't scare me. I can't have legal infractions, even parking tickets. My boss frowns on that sort of thing."

"Sorry. By the way, nice TV you've got there."

Paulson twitched again. "Yeah, thanks."

Ari saw himself out, saying he'd be in touch if he needed more information. Paulson shut and locked the door behind him quickly. Alone in the parking lot, Van Owen located the BMW. It was a newer model, only a few years old, and must have been very expensive when he bought it. He walked back to his Impala and climbed in. He tapped the pen against the steering wheel as he thought about his time in the townhouse.

"Now isn't that strange," he murmured to himself. "Here you have a guy who just got a nasty, expensive divorce, is probably paying child support, and likely has a healthy monthly car payment along with rent and everything else. He's strapped for cash, but goes out and buys a very expensive new television. Hmm."

He slid the car into drive and pulled out, still mulling it all over.

On his way home he drove past Frankie's house again. It felt weird after avoiding the place for so long. Butch must have been home because the pickup truck was in the driveway, but the rest of the house was buttoned up tight. The curtains were all drawn and several newspapers in yellow bags were scattered about the end of the driveway. The yard was a little overgrown and had tufts of weeds and taller grass sticking up randomly, as if they were sad, green hair plugs. The drooping gutter hung there swinging in its silent, almost eerie metronome fashion, keeping time in the breeze. Ari slowed but didn't stop this time. He thought that their house looked more and more like a candidate for foreclosure each time he saw it. He didn't think that Frankie would stand for it if she were around since she liked things neat and tidy, as did he. But she'd only been missing for a few days, and this level of neglect had taken weeks or months before it got to this point. To him that meant something may have been going on in the Brubaker household even before her disappearance.

When he got home there was a cable TV van in the driveway. He hurried up and parked the Impala and tapped on the driver's window of the white truck. The heavyset driver was busy talking on his phone and jumped a little. He rolled down the window and smiled.

"Glad you're here," he said in a pleasant voice. "I was just about to take off."

"Yeah, sorry about that. I got tied up in town. I take it you're here to install the broadband?"

"You betcha'. Let me finish this up and we'll get to it. Our records show this house had it before so this should be a piece of cake."

With a little rummaging in the woods down the street the cable installer found the nearest exterior junction box and reconnected the service. Once inside they located the jack in Ari's office behind the desk. It had been painted over some time in the distant past but with a little scraping it was pronounced hale and serviceable. The installer smiled again. He was a pretty happy guy.

"This where you want it?"

"Yeah, this is perfect."

"Great. Saves me from running new lines, and saves you from buying a wireless router or anything else. I love it when it works out like this."

He hooked up a new modem with its flashing lights and ran the blue Ethernet cable to his computer. He logged onto the Internet and checked a few random sites like Yahoo and CNN. They all dutifully popped up and filled the screen quickly with almost no waiting. Ari was impressed. It looked even faster than the connections at the library.

"That's it?" he asked.

"That's it. You've got a good connection and good speed. You'll probably notice a slowdown in the evenings or weekends when everyone's streaming Netflix, but that's to be expected. Capacity issues, you know. You're good to go."

Ari thanked him and the man got into his van and drove off. Ari sat himself down and logged onto Facebook to check Frankie's wall. There was no change in her status, not that he was expecting one. He stared at the picture on her profile page for a few minutes. Her green eyes gazed out at him wordlessly. No matter how hard he looked he found they weren't pleading or asking for help, they were just there.

"Where are you, Frankie?" he asked the empty room. His words sounded hollow and thin, distant, as if someone else were talking from several rooms away. Sometime later he clicked the X in the upper corner and closed the window. Her picture disappeared and he was left staring at the blank screen.

Chapter 4

Frankie was seated on a crude wooden bench before a small fire. It was nighttime and a deep Stygian black surrounded her, the fire doing little but illuminating the front of her with an oddly steady light. She looked thinner, Ari noticed. Yes, her face was definitely thinner, so were her arms. She was leaning forward with her elbows on her knees, her chin cupped in her hands. She had her light brown hair pulled back in a ponytail, blond streaks highlighted in the flickering flames. The firelight enhanced the green of her eyes and made them dance and shimmer like liquid jade. His heart swelled as he watched her.

"Frankie," he said softly.

She didn't reply or look up. She took a deep breath, her dirty white T-shirt snug against her small breasts.

Confused, he tried to move toward her but for some reason couldn't. It was as if he were both there and not there at the same time. He said her name again, louder this time. "Frankie?"

She looked up then, startled and confused. Her eyebrows knitted together in that cute way she had, and her hands fell to her sides. She sat up straight on the wooden bench. He could see that it was really just two tree stumps with a rough-hewn board on top of them.

She mouthed something then, his name.

"Yes, it's me. Where are you?" He began to wonder what was happening. Something was wrong. "I can't hear you."

She placed a hand over her heart then and her face softened. She mouthed his name again but no sound came. He knew then that this was just a dream, that he was asleep. The disappointment that this wasn't happening nearly crushed him. It had seemed so real!

"I'm sorry, Frankie. This is just a dream. We're not really together."

72

She nodded and he could see that her cheeks were wet. She suddenly had a stick in her hand and silently drew a circle in the black dirt at her feet. She scratched four lines into the circle, making eight spokes, their symbol for Karma. The middle spoke bisected the bottom of the circle and on it she drew an arrow pointing down. She pointed to the arrow.

"I know, sweetheart, I saw that on your SUV. What does it mean?"

Suddenly there were noises and flashing lights behind her, voices yelling, the sound of gunshots. Her eyes grew wide and she jumped to her feet. A dozen arms sprung from the darkness and began to roughly pull her away. She opened her mouth to scream but a huge hand as big as a catcher's mitt covered her face and yanked her into the blackness. The fire flared bright white with magnesium intensity then blinked out.

Ari shot up in bed, his heart racing, sweat coating his body. He roughly tossed all the covers off and looked at the clock beside his bed. It read 5:02 AM. He fell back onto the damp pillows and waited until his heart slowed. With a shaky hand he wiped sweat from his face. Crickets chirped outside his window.

An hour later he still hadn't fallen back to sleep so he got up and made coffee. He sat at the kitchen table with the warm mug between his hands and stared at it. When he finally took a sip it had gone cold and nasty. He washed it down the sink.

Later that morning his cell phone rang. Surprised, he looked at the number and saw that it was a Louisville exchange. He frowned, not in anger but confusion. Almost nobody had his number. He answered it.

"Hello?"

"Um, is this Agent Hollenbeck?"

"Yes it is. Who's calling?"

"Paul Paulson, sir. Can we, um, talk?"

He shifted the phone to his other hand and grabbed his small notebook and a pencil. His hands were quivering with excitement but his voice was steady.

"Of course. What can I help you with?"

There was a long pause on the other end. Ari could hear Paulson breathing but nothing else. Thirty seconds that felt like hours passed.

Paul cleared his throat nervously. "No, this is a bad idea. Forget it."

"No, no, wait! It's okay. Just talk to me, Paul. Really, it's okay."

The young man on the other end hissed air through his lips.

"Really, Paul, it's okay. Let's talk. Would you like to meet somewhere?"

"Um, okay, I guess. Damn. Somewhere public, I guess. Do you know the Cracker Barrel by the airport?"

He didn't but knew that he could find it through the magic of GPS. "Sure."

"Meet me there in a half an hour, okay?"

"You got it."

Ari made it there with four minutes to spare. He parked the rental near the Cracker Barrel entrance among big Buicks and the Toyota Camrys and walked in. He didn't see the white BMW anywhere in the parking lot. He'd done a quick shave and cleanup and had on a different sport coat, his second and only other one. If he kept meeting people in this FBI guise he'd have to go buy additional suitable clothing. The fake badge felt heavy and foreign in his jacket pocket. He straightened his tie and stepped inside.

He had forgotten, but Cracker Barrel restaurants all had a retail store right inside the front door. He wove his way through the racks of postcards, little plaques with cute country sayings, simple toys, and other bits of home décor and T-shirts. The hostess manning the entrance to the dining area was an older lady with gray hair and a smiling face, clutching some menus to her thin chest as if she owned them.

"How many this morning?"

"Two, please. And I'm looking for a young man with blond hair, but I think I'm early."

"I'll keep an eye out for him." She escorted him to a small table along the wall where he sat facing the entrance and ordered coffee. She handed him one of her prized menus and came back a minute later with a steaming white mug and two sets of silverware. "Suzie will be your server today."

He thanked her and she scooted off to her station at the entrance. Looking over the menu he found he wasn't all that hungry, especially not for the heavy offerings they seemed to favor there, entrees like biscuits and gravy, scrambled eggs with potatoes on the side, meals like that. He did find a fruit and yogurt parfait that looked like a winner so he mentally bookmarked that page. The coffee was actually quite good, he was pleasantly surprised to find. He quickly drained his first cup and waited for Suzie to come around, which she did just a few moments later. She was a cute blond of only twenty or so. She had a nice smile and quickly refilled his cup.

"Still waiting for someone else?"

"Yes, but it should only be a few minutes."

She smiled again. "That's great, no rush. I'll be back to check on you in a few." She hurried off to the next table where a party of four older adults was finishing up their meal. One of the men harmlessly flirted with her while his wife playfully rolled her eyes and gave him a soft slap on the arm. Suzie played right along and gamely flirted right back, knowing who in that group buttered her bread. For one so young she seemed to have this figured out, Ari thought with a grin.

Suzie had to refill his mug two more times before Paulson finally came in. He looked around the restaurant as wary as a blond fox in a room full of bloodhounds, jumpy and nervous. His eyes were dark and smudged as if he hadn't slept much. After a few seconds he spotted Ari and reluctantly walked over, taking the seat across from him. He hadn't shaved, his blond beard making his face look dirty.

"Hi, Paul," Ari said over his cup.

"Hi. Sorry I'm late. I, uh, well sorry I'm late."

Ari set his mug down, his motions smooth and easy. He stared at the young man across the table from him and could see that yes, he was anxious and nervous, but there was something else there, too. Paulson had trouble looking at Ari in the face. His eyes moved up and down and around the room at the people happily talking and eating, at the waitresses moving about, at customers coming and going, but they didn't seem to see anything.

"Can I order you something to eat? To drink?"

Paulson looked back at Ari as if surprised he was sitting across from him. "Um, some coffee, I guess."

Just then Suzie came over and her eyes widened happily. "Hi, Paulie, I didn't see you come in."

"Hi, Suze. How are you?"

"Oh, you know. Another day, so forth and so on. What can I get for you?"

"Coffee is all for me now, thanks."

She motored off with his order. Ari smiled at the young man across from him. "So you come here often?"

"Yeah, once in a while. Mainly when I'm too lazy to fix something or when I've got Taylor for the weekend. He likes Suzie and she makes a big fuss over him."

Suzie brought over his coffee and some cream and promised to be back soon. Ari thought he caught her giving Paulson a playful wink but wasn't sure. Paulson himself smiled, the first time he'd shown any positive emotion since he entered. The young man stared at her retreating form as she walked busily away.

"I'm glad you called, Paul."

Paulson snapped back to now. "Yeah?"

"Yeah, I am. So, what's up?"

Paulson stirred in some cream. The spoon made little ringing sounds as it tapped the sides of the mug. He exhaled loudly.

"You don't know me, not really."

"You're right, I don't. I think I have a pretty good idea of who you are but that's it. I only have my first impression to go on so far."

Paulson set the spoon down. "In high school I was a linebacker, probably one of the best our school had ever seen. I had pretty good grades, too, but after graduation I just didn't think I was ready for college. Not very mature, you know?"

"Sure. A lot of guys aren't ready at that age. The dropout rate for college freshman is about fifty percent, last time I checked."

"Yeah, no shit. That's why I did a tour with the Marines. I figured it would give me a chance to grow up, give me time to figure out what I'd like to do with my life. Plus the money from the GI Bill would help pay for college afterwards. My folks didn't have much and I didn't want either of us going deep in debt for me, really."

"Actually that's very mature. More teenagers should consider that option."

"Yeah, maybe. That's where I figured out that I'd like to go into law enforcement. I even checked out the FBI. I like things orderly and right, you know? Probably the German side of me coming out. Think. Plan. Act. That's what I like to do. And it was all moving along according to plan, too, until I took that shrapnel in my knee. That screwed up everything. When I got out of the service I still wanted law enforcement but couldn't pass the physicals."

Ari nodded. "Bad break, Paul."

"Yeah it was. It sucked. So then I was planning on college but screwed up and got my girlfriend pregnant by accident and we had to get married. That put an end to school like right then. No way I could go to college and take care of a family. That's why I took the job in security at the hospital." He sighed and stared at his untouched coffee. "Then the divorce came and everything went into the shitter. It was ugly and expensive and my ex did all she could to screw me over. Not just with Taylor, but in every way she could. Divorce does something to people, you know?"

Ari nodded again and kept quiet. Paulson was on a roll.

"She took everything, furniture, TV, everything, and now I've got to pay child support and alimony on top of that. Plus I've got the BMW payment. It's killing me. I'm close to getting kicked out of the apartment 'cause I'm behind on the rent, too."

Suzie came by and checked on them. Seeing they were fine she trotted off to her other tables. Paulson watched her go and his face softened just a fraction, a lessening of the tension around his eyes. A line that had appeared on his forehead nearly vanished. After a moment he pivoted his gaze back to Ari.

"I need you to promise me something," he finally said, gravely serious. "I can't say anything more unless you promise that what I say from here on out stays between us. I can't put my job on the line, I just can't. It's not much but I've got to be able to take care of my son."

Ari waited just a split-second before he nodded. A real FBI agent wouldn't make any such promises, he figured, but at this point he didn't care. He was impressed how Paulson had given him just enough information to effectively reel him in without actually admitting to anything.

"I can assure you that whatever you say stays with me and won't make it any farther up the FBI chain of command. My goal is to find Ms. Brubaker, not go after you."

"Good. I feel terrible that she's been taken, I really do. That's the only reason we're talking right now."

"So you know she's been kidnapped?"

"Oh, yeah. I saw it happen."

Ari's heart began to race. This was the first real lead he'd had so far. He took a deep breath and tried to remain calm, as befitting an actual FBI agent.

"You saw it happen?"

"Yeah. I was manning the security room that Thursday when the door opened and a guy came in. Not too many people come in, but some do. I didn't think that much about it."

"What did he look like?" Ari took out his notebook and pen.

"I didn't get a very good look at him. The lights were low in there like always so I could see the monitors better, and he was wearing a dark hat, like the one Indiana Jones wears. And a black suit with a white shirt and tie."

"A fedora?"

"Yeah, a fedora. That's it. It was pulled down low so I couldn't see his eyes. But he had a dark complexion and spoke slowly with a really thick accent. Spanish, I'm pretty sure. He talked very softly, almost in a whisper, so it was hard to tell for sure."

"What did he say?"

"Not a whole lot, really. He pulled an envelope from his pocket and tossed it on the desk and told me to open it. It was filled with money, more money than I'd ever seen at one time. It was all hundreds, too. I about shit."

"How much?"

"Five thousand dollars. Five thousand dollars!" A couple at the table next to them looked up from their own conversation at his outburst. Paulson lowered his voice and they went back to their meals.

"Five thousand dollars," he repeated earnestly. "I just held it in my hands and thought of all the problems it would solve, you know? The back rent, months and months of BMW payments, some fun stuff for Taylor, child support. I couldn't believe it. All I had to do, he said, was turn off the monitors for twenty minutes and erase everything for that same time period. He said if I did that I could expect another five grand within two days as a final payment."

"So you did it." Not a question, a statement.

Paulson picked up a napkin from the table and began shredding it in methodical, precise strips. Ari could tell what the young man had done was killing him, was eating him up inside and had likely been gnawing at him since last Thursday. He laid the napkin strips down side by side in their exact order as if he were trying to reassemble them.

"I did it. Well, not exactly. I kept the cameras on and followed the guy as he left, jumping from monitor to monitor. He moved fast through the hospital and out into the parking lot, back to where most of the employees park. I saw Ms. Brubaker come out and walk out to her Chevy, where the guy was waiting for her. They talked for a minute or two, tops. Her back was to her Suburban and she was kind of leaning against it. She tried to walk away but he grabbed her arm. She, uh, struggled for a second before the back door of the Caddy Escalade next to her opened and this huge dude got out. And by huge I mean he was freaking enormous. I've never seen anyone so big. Professional football player big. Incredible Hulk big. He just grabbed her by the arms and dragged her to the back of their Caddy and tossed her in like she didn't weigh a thing. They got into their Escalade and just drove away. The whole thing couldn't have lasted five minutes, probably less than that."

Ari found that his hands were quivering. Paulson had *watched* Frankie being taken, had in essence been an accomplice! He had to restrain himself from reaching across the table and grabbing Paulson and violently shaking him. His reaction didn't surprise him, but he was amazed at how even his voice sounded when he spoke. Maybe he was getting better at this fake FBI thing.

"Then you erased the all the information."

Paulson continued shredding and trying to reassemble the napkin. "Yes, I did. I erased it and stuffed the money into my pants and kept on working like nothing had happened. My shift ended a few hours later and I went home."

Ari took a deep breath. He locked his hands in front of him on the table in an effort to keep from doing something rash. His jaw was locked so tight his back teeth hurt.

"Then?" The word came out almost as a hiss.

"Then I went out and bought that stupid TV as a treat to myself. But I haven't even been able to turn the damn thing on. I hooked it up but that's been it. I can't even bring myself to watch it. It just stares at me like a big black accusing eye."

"Did you get the second payment? I'm guessing that you didn't."

He looked up. "No I didn't. And I'm not going to, am I?"

"No, I wouldn't expect it."

Paulson nodded as if he expected as much. "Probably just as well. All the rest of the money's still in the envelope. I can't even bring myself to touch it. I'm such a fucking moron."

Ari almost felt sorry for the young man, but not quite. Maybe later. Right now it was still all he could do to remain calm and in his seat. Just then Suzie bopped on over and asked if they were ready to order. They both demurred again, which didn't faze her in the least,. She smiled and said she'd be back, a seasoned pro.

Paulson seemed to deflate, his shoulders slumping, as if by confessing his sins they had actually left his body and made him physically smaller. He took a cautious sip of his coffee and either didn't notice or care that it had gone as cold as Ari's expression.

"So what's next?" he asked.

"What's next is this: you and I are going to sit here and you're going to tell me everything you can about the man who talked to you and everything you remember about that day. We're not going to quit until I'm sure you've told me every single thing you remember. Got it? And I'm going to need that envelope for analysis."

"Yeah, I got it. But I may need something stronger than coffee for this."

Paulson couldn't recall much more since the encounter had all happened so fast, he said, but there were a few things that stuck in his mind.

"His accent, like I mentioned. His English wasn't very good, and he had that accent. He only said a sentence or two to me, and it sounded like it'd been rehearsed or something."

"What else? What did he look like? Specifically. Nose, hair, ears, complexion, body shape, height? And his hands. What did his hands look like? People can easily change their hair and some facial features, but not things like hands."

Paulson screwed up his face in thought, his eyes shut. At this distance his eyebrows were shockingly blond, bordering on white. Suzie came by again and this time his appetite seemed to have kicked in. He ordered a full breakfast of eggs, toast, and waffles with strawberries. Ari wasn't hungry at all. Suzie smiled and wrote it all down, ending with a pop on the pad with her pen, giving the period a final flourish. She darted off toward the kitchen. Paulson stared at her retreating form.

"She's nice," he said to no one, as if his thoughts had accidentally leaked out.

"The man, Paul. Focus. What did he look like?"

"Oh, like I said the fedora kind of hid his face but he was a pretty good looking guy. And he had high cheekbones and a narrow chin. His hair was black and went over his collar a little bit. Kind of creepy, really. And you're right – his hands, there was something wrong with the skin on his hands. It was all scarred up, you know, different colors and smooth and shiny in places. It was not pretty."

He reiterated his recollections of the man's clothing. Black suit, white shirt, and a black tie. "With that outfit he looked like one of those guys from a Men In Black movie," he said. "Oh, and he had a funky tie-pin."

"A funky tie-pin. How so? What was funky about it?"

"I only noticed it because I was sitting down and it was at eye level, you know? It looked like a silver tiger head, or some cat like that. It was about the size of a thumbnail, with black stones for eyes and an open, snarling mouth. I've never seen anything like it before. It had to be expensive as hell."

Ten more minutes of talking garnered no additional useful information, at least none that he could recognize. Then his food came and they took a break while he shoveled everything into his mouth as if he were on the clock. It was obvious he was starving and Ari figured he hadn't eaten much in the last few days. Only now after his confession was his appetite back. When he had scooped the last remnants of the eggs onto toast and gobbled it down he sat back and exhaled in honest satisfaction. There were some toast crumbs in the corner of his mouth.

"Okay, that's better. I needed that."

"Let's talk about what happened in the parking lot. Go over that for me."

Paulson looked tired now, drained, as if the telling of his part in this had exhausted him. He pushed away the plates and rubbed a hand over his young face. He began arranging the shredded napkin into neat lines again.

"I already told you what I saw. The guy with the hat went out to the parking lot about the same time Ms. Brubaker went out. He met her at her Suburban and they started talking. She tried to leave but he grabbed her arm. That's when the big guy got out of the vehicle next to them and tossed her into theirs."

"That's it? That's all you saw?"

"Pretty much. It was on the monitors so I couldn't make out much detail, you know? They were only out there a few minutes, tops."

Ari made a few notes, his script tight and precise. "Tell me more about this big guy you saw."

"He was huge, enormous. Had to be at least seven feet tall. He had on black pants and a white shirt with a collar. His hair was long and black, down over his shoulders. He picked her up like she didn't weigh a thing. Definitely not a dude you'd like to meet in a dark alley, or any other alley for that matter. A guy like that could lose at Russian Roulette and demand a rematch."

They talked for several more minutes. Ari was a little calmer now, his initial anger at Paulson's hand in this having decreased from a boil to a simmer. There may come a time when he could forgive him for his actions, he knew, but it wasn't yet.

Paulson looked at his phone and said he had to get back home. His supervisor at work was supposed to call him in a little while to discuss what had happened. He pushed his plates and the pieces of paper away from him. He looked at the shredded napkin as if seeing it for the first time.

"Remember, you promised. Not a word to anyone about this. I'm only telling you so you can find Ms. Brubaker. I need my job, Mr. Hollenbeck. I feel like total shit about this, but I need my job."

He pursed his lips and nodded to the young man. "I won't tell anyone. But you know how bad this is, right?"

Paulson looked sick again, his pale complexion blanching even further. "I know. Believe me, I know. You don't have to remind me. It's all I think about."

Ari signaled to Suzie for the bill, which she quickly brought over. She placed it on the table and rested a sympathetic hand on Paulson's shoulder. She kept it there longer than was probably necessary, but the young man didn't seem to mind.

"Glad you could come in, Paulie. You sure you're okay? You don't look so good."

He thanked her and assured her he was fine. Then the men stood and Ari picked up the check. Suzie smiled brightly and waved goodbye. As they walked to the register out front he looked hard at the young man beside him.

"Paul, I should demand the money back from you as well, you know that, right? And I will, unless you're going to do something good with it, something positive. What are your plans?"

He shrugged, his shoulders lifting just a fraction of an inch, as if his guilt was simply too heavy to budge. "God, I don't know. Give it to some charity or something. I can't even look at it."

Ari was not feeling very sympathetic. "You do that. If I need anything I'll be in touch. Don't go anywhere."

Paulson laughed once, a monosyllabic cross between a bark and a grunt. "Go anywhere? Really, where the hell would I go?"

Ari got into his rental and texted Yvonne. *A quick favor. Are you at work? Can you check and see if Theodore is at the front desk now?* It was getting warm outside so he turned on the air conditioning and slowly pulled out into traffic. He was right down the road from the airport and planes came and went with amazing frequency, especially those from UPS. Their planes were mainly white and brown with their signature gold logo clear on the tail. He wondered idly if any of the flight crews up there were going to suffer from sudden onset paralysis. He was glad he didn't have to fly anywhere soon.

A few minutes later his phone buzzed and at a traffic light he read the text. *As a matter of fact he is. U know Theodore? U r full of surprises, stud. Ha!*

Ari was already on his way to the hospital. He pulled in the main entrance and parked near the front doors. Pleasantly warm air washed over him as he opened the car door and got out. He adjusted his tie and smoothed his shirt to lend him the most official look possible. Theodore Rust would expect nothing less from a Federal agent.

When he walked in he saw the older man at his post behind the desk. He was dressed as before in a crisp white shirt and his hair hadn't changed a millimeter. He probably cut it himself every few days, Ari imagined. He was more fit than most men half his age. He stared at Ari as he approached.

"Mr. Rust?"

"Yes? May I help you?"

Ari deftly pulled his fake FBI badge from his pocket and held it purposefully in front of him. After a second he snapped it shut.

"My name is Hal Hollenbeck with the FBI. Can we talk for a few minutes?"

Theodore squinted and looked Ari up and down, displaying no emotion at seeing the badge. He thought for a second then held out his hand.

"May I see that identification, please?"

"Certainly."

He handed it over and did his best to look impassive as the older man inspected it very closely, verifying the photo was indeed Ari. After a minute that dragged out longer than he thought possible, Theodore handed it back to Ari.

"You were here the other day. You told me about the illegally parked truck."

Ari nodded. "Yes, that was me. I was just visiting someone. Today I'm on official business. Can we talk for a few minutes?"

"Of course, sir. In private?" Ari nodded and Theodore picked up the phone and dialed an extension. "Marge, can you relieve me for a few minutes? I have a matter I need to attend to. Okay, thank you." He hung up. "Marge will be here in a minute. Where would you like to go? The snack bar is right around the corner if that will work."

"Perfect. Thank you."

The two waited in silence until Marge came. She was a short, rather dumpy lady in her sixties with a number of silver bracelets around her chunky wrists that jangled like a bag of coins as she walked. She smiled warmly at Theodore and took the seat that he held for her. She could barely take her eyes from the older man. It was obvious she had a crush on him.

"Thank you, Marge. I won't be more than ten or fifteen minutes." Ari could swear that she giggled.

The two men walked away, Theodore the Alpha dog and clearly in the lead with Ari a few steps behind him. Theodore never looked back but just assumed that the younger man was keeping pace, which he was with a little difficulty. Mr. Rust walked very fast indeed. After rounding a few corners they came to a small shop that served snacks, donuts, and assorted pastries. Ari offered to buy him something to eat or drink, and he accepted a Coke. The two sat at a small, round table near the back and out of earshot of anyone else. Ari kept his back to the corridor in case Yvonne walked past and saw him. That could get interesting quickly and it would at the very least be very tricky to explain. Theodore stared at him blankly. He would be one hell of a poker player, Ari decided.

"How may I help you?"

"I'm here looking into the disappearance of Francis Brubaker."

"I assumed as much. What does the FBI care about Ms. Brubaker?"

"That's classified, I'm afraid."

Theodore nodded, accepting the explanation.

"Before we go on, if you don't mind my asking, which branch of the military were you in?" Ari asked.

"Career Army. Full Colonel, 82nd Airborne."

"Several tours of duty, I assume."

Theodore nodded again. "Yes, sir. Several, including the first Iraq war."

"Thanks for serving your country."

Theodore allowed the briefest of smiles, but from his lack of expression it was clear that, like many career soldiers, he didn't particularly care to talk about his time in the service. "You're welcome. Now what can I do for you in this matter of Mrs. Brubaker? Very odd, her disappearance."

"Yes it is. I was wondering if you were on duty or around the hospital the day she disappeared."

"I was. I was on duty at the front desk. If you're going to ask if I saw anything the police have already talked to me about that, which you probably know."

Ari didn't, but assumed as much. "Of course. But we like to conduct our own investigation into these matters, as you can understand. I've talked to a number of people here at the hospital as well as her husband and friends. We have no new leads to speak of, with one exception. Did you, by chance, notice a man with a black suit, white shirt, black tie, and a fedora that day? He may or may not have come in the front door, but at the very least you may have seen him."

Theodore didn't even pause to think. "Yes I did. I remember him distinctly."

Ari sat up straight in his chair and nearly dropped his pen. "You did? Why was he so memorable?"

"Because of his shoes." He said it very matter-of-factly, as if it should be clear to anyone. "They were very, very expensive, probably Italian."

Ari tilted his head sideways. "Why would you notice his shoes?"

"Sir," he explained patiently and leaning slightly forward, a polite and patient teacher imparting wisdom to an attentive student. It was obvious he put a lot of stock in this. "When you've been in the military as long as I have, you tend to notice well-maintained shoes. His were in excellent condition. Ankle high and polished to a high gloss. You can tell quite a bit about a man by his shoes." He leaned forward. "People may pay a lot for a suit or a jacket, a haircut or jewelry, but many times they'll skimp when it comes to shoes. He didn't. This was a well-to-do individual who cared very much for his footwear and appearance. Quite admirable."

Ari was impressed. He realized he was beginning to like Theodore Rust.

"Anything else you remember?"

"No, not really. He walked behind me at the desk but I turned around by chance and saw him. I didn't see him return but as I recall we were busy that day, so that's not out of the ordinary. Average height, dark complexion, black hair. The fedora was a nice touch even though he was inside. A hat should never be worn inside."

The two talked for several more minutes while Ari took notes. They finished up by Theodore sharing his contact information in case Ari needed to get in touch with him later. It ended up that he lived south of town, not too far from Ari's house out in the country. Ari gave him his cell phone number as well and asked him to call if he thought of anything else. Theodore said he'd be happy to do so. They stood and shook hands.

"Thank you for your help, Mr. Rust."

"You're quite welcome, Agent Hollenbeck. Always happy to help out civilian law enforcement, especially when it comes to someone like Mrs. Brubaker. After so many years in the service doing time behind that desk is a bit tame. A little intrigue like this is just what a man needs to put some spring in his step, although not at the expense of Mrs. Brubaker, you understand."

Ari nodded. "I do."

"Good. Let me know how I can help. Thank you for the soda." He looked at his watch. "I have a few minutes before I need to get back. I may as well patrol the area. You can find your way back, sir?"

"Absolutely. No problem."

"Excellent. Enjoy your day."

Ari resisted an irrational urge to salute as the older man turned and walked away. Even the back of his shirt was ironed to perfection and tucked precisely into the narrow waist of his slacks. His shoes, though not Italian and more likely from Target or some other department store, flashed and winked in the hallway lighting. They were so shiny they could have been wet.

He took a minute and cleaned up the table then retraced his steps to the main desk. Marge was still there and appeared mildly disappointed when she saw that Theodore wasn't with him. Ari gave her a small wave and smiled inside at the schoolgirl crush she obviously had on Colonel Rust. He wondered if the older man knew, and suspected that he did. He was a bright guy. He doubted much got past him.

For once he was feeling rather light-hearted as he walked through the main doors. He wasn't any closer to Frankie but at least felt as if he had made some progress. However that feeling crashed headlong into reality as he looked up and nearly collided with someone. He started to excuse himself when he realized it was Frankie's husband, Butch.

Ah, shit, he thought.

The man had been crystal clear concerning his feelings for Ari and what he would do if he saw him again. He steeled himself for the verbal and likely physical onslaught that was certain to come.

Chapter 5

For a second Butch didn't see him. He was looking down and not paying attention to where he was going. His black hair was parted on the side and framed a squared-off face and dark eyes that were spaced far apart, almost unnaturally so. He and Ari were about the same age but right now Butch looked the senior of the two. There were new and pronounced crow's feet around his eyes, and his mouth was an unforgiving horizontal line, like something drawn on a whiteboard with a Sharpie. His cheeks were pinched and pale. He could have been hung-over or coming down with the flu, but either way he looked stressed and not well. Frankie's disappearance must really be eating at him, Ari thought.

He stepped aside to let him pass. Perhaps they'd both be lucky and he wouldn't notice him? Butch mumbled an apology then did a double take when he saw who he was sharing the doorway with. He stopped dead, his dark eyes flashing wide in shock. *Damn.*

"Hey, Butch."

"Van Owen. What are you doing here?"

Ari was prepared for some type of attack, some show of anger or aggression, but was surprised when Brubaker just stood there with that shocked look on his face. Ari shot a quick glance over his shoulder toward the main desk and saw that Marge was there, which meant that Theodore must still be making his rounds, thankfully. He did *not* need the Colonel to get involved in this, since his FBI persona would crumble in a hurry. He wondered again how anyone could do this undercover crap for long.

"Just here on business. You?"

Butch nodded toward the hospital. There was still no sense of a threat about him, just a nervous twitching in his hands, like he had trouble keeping them still. He was acting nothing at all like he had at Ari's house just days earlier, which overall was a good thing.

"Picking up Frankie's personal stuff from her locker."

"Oh. Any news on what happened?"

His eyes narrowed and the horizontal line that was his mouth compressed again. After a split-second it eased but the ensuing more neutral expression appeared forced and manufactured. His hands continued to twitch nervously at his sides as if he were shooing away flies. Butch shook his head.

"No, nothing. The cops don't have any leads. Listen," he took a breath and settled himself. "I'm, uh, glad I ran into you here. I wanted to, um, apologize for what I said at your place the other day. I was upset. I shouldn't have said anything at all, you know?"

Now Van Owen was shocked. The last thing he had expected from the guy was an apology. They had never had any love for each other, granted, but just days earlier Butch had threatened to kill him. That was something not easily forgotten or dismissed, not when the threat had been delivered with such vehemence. Restraining orders had been issued for less.

But now Ari had to take a mental step back. When it came right down to it he didn't know Frankie's husband that well. For the most part he was relying on interactions they'd had years ago when Ari had stolen Frankie away, and of course none of those had ended well between the two of them. But people change, people grow. Perhaps Butch had moved beyond that and was now a guy able to apologize, to see beyond himself. He wouldn't have believed it possible, but here he was.

"Come on," he said, more insistently. "No hard feelings?"

After a second's pause Ari forced a half-smile. He hoped it didn't look as false as it felt. "Sure, Butch, no hard feelings. I understand what you must be going through."

Brubaker exhaled loudly. "Thanks. Yeah, it's been a bitch."

"I don't doubt it. Good luck with everything. I hope you find her soon. She's a great girl." He almost added, "Let me know how I can help," then thought better of it. Yvonne had warned him not to poke the bear.

Butch nodded once stiffly, his mouth still grim. "Yeah. Thanks."

The two men stood there in an awkward moment of silence, neither one sure what the proper protocol was at this point. Finally Butch ducked his head once and moved on into the hospital, his posture and shoulders stiff, like a man expecting to be shot in the back at any second. Ari saw him go and exhaled in relief.

"Well that was damned peculiar," he said softly. There were many scenarios he had envisioned should they encounter each other again, but this had not been one of them. Not even close. He watched as Butch rounded a corner and was gone, then smiled and sketched a wave to Marge at the desk. As the doors hissed shut behind him he walked to his car and got in, then sat there and thought about the last few minutes. Maybe Brubaker had changed after all this time. Maybe he really was worried about his wife and was sorry.

In the end it didn't matter, Ari didn't like him and likely never would. After all, the guy had ended up with Frankie.

On the way home he picked up a newspaper and flipped to the sports section, curious if there was any more public information about Garrafon, the Reds player that had died. He had to believe that in this day and age of information exchange and instant news dissemination there would have to be a leak sooner or later about what had actually killed him. A story that juicy just couldn't be contained forever. He leafed through the entire paper but didn't see anything, at least not yet. Hal and the FBI must really be locking this one down. It was both impressive and scary at the same time.

Back home Ari fixed a quick bite to eat, a turkey and Swiss sandwich on whole wheat. He took his lunch and iced tea into the office and fired up his computer. Without any real hope of a change he logged onto Facebook and checked Frankie's page. Nope, nothing. Her green eyes still stared out at him from the screen without a plea, just impersonal, multicolored pixels arranged in the shape of her face. He looked at her profile picture for a minute before exiting the site, then glanced at the turkey sandwich he had made, suddenly not hungry at all. He pushed the plate away and drank some of the tea instead.

Halfheartedly he pulled the Fawcett folder over and idly leafed through the pages. That new information from his friend Sir Alex Hanes at the Royal Geographic Society was potentially explosive and should have had his head buried in the writings like a paleontologist over a fresh fossil find, but he could barely manage to give them more than a cursory glance. New papers and information on the elusive Percy Fawcett that nobody else had seen before? Penned in the Colonel's own hand? In his circles that was big, big news. So if that was the case then why wasn't his pulse and mind racing? Truly, he was pissed for not being able to pick himself up and move on any more than he had, but it all seemed so out of his control. He didn't like what he had become but felt powerless to change.

He forced himself to look through the info from the RGS. Colonel Fawcett's notes to his wife were some of the same musings that anyone today would have posted on Facebook or Twitter. Most were no more than observations of his health or that of his companions, recollections of events that he and Nina had enjoyed together, or conditions in the jungle itself. Many barely made sense to him since they were almost a hundred years old, and times and language itself had moved on since then. Worse yet were those notes those that referred to places and events that no longer existed. Fawcett was a nut for dates and dating events, Ari noticed, especially in this batch of documents. He'd have to put all those down in a timeline eventually, he guessed, just to make sure everything jibed. He made himself vow that he would at least get that done.

But not now. He powered down the PC and sat at his desk. The only window in the room faced east and the afternoon sun had long since moved to the front of the house. The little light from the window was just strong enough that he could see the yellow post it notes on the maps adorning the walls, but the yellow was pale and indistinct, just washed out blobs with no more color than daisies after the first frost of winter. One of the notes had lost its adhesive and had fluttered to the floor unnoticed. The vertical blinds on the window threw regular patterns of vertical shadow on the opposite wall as if the office were a prison cell. Ari sighed but made no effort to move.

Some time later his phone chimed. It felt heavy in his hand when he picked it up. He had a new text from Yvonne. *Busy tonight? Hope not. I'm bringing Angelo's pizza over at 6:00. Beer is on you. Not optional!*

He considered declining her offer but knew she'd ignore it and just show up anyway. He shot her a quick message back: *Okay. See you then.*

Yvonne didn't bother to knock, just walked right in. True to her word she had a large pizza box in her hand, the name *Angelo's* in bright red script across the top. A little grease had seeped through the edges of the cardboard.

"Pizza delivery! Get yer fresh pizza here!"

Ari walked into the living room drying his hands on a kitchen towel. Despite his foul mood he managed a grin. She was smiling broadly at him and holding the pizza box in front of her like a revered gift. Her long blond hair was pulled back into a ponytail and she was wearing an orange and white striped cotton V-neck shirt with half sleeves and very short denim shorts, Daisy Duke style. The V-neck revealed a considerable amount of cleavage. Typical Yvonne.

"Hi, there. Thanks for coming over. Come on into the kitchen. I was just cleaning up."

"Hi, to you, too." She walked up and gave him a quick peck on the cheek, then sauntered past him and into the kitchen. She set the pizza box down and began to methodically open cupboards until she located the plates. Ari grabbed two beers from the fridge and handed her one.

"That smells great. I can't believe you remembered that Angelo's is my favorite."

"You're welcome. Truth be told any pizza is my favorite, but this is a pretty good pie."

She flopped open the lid and deftly dished out two hot slices. It was topped with pepperoni, double-sausage, green peppers, mushrooms, and banana peppers. The mélange of smells hit him with an almost physical force and his mouth watered as if he'd just been rescued from months on a deserted island. He was glad now that he hadn't bothered with the bland turkey sandwich earlier in the afternoon. Her good mood was infectious, and despite himself he felt his own mood lighten a few notches.

Yvonne was diving into her first piece like it was her job. She deftly popped her beer open with one hand and washed down the first bite. He did the same. Those first slices were gone in mere seconds.

"So what made you decide to come over?" he asked.

She shook her head. "Uh, uh. More eating, less talking."

He wasn't going to argue. They had been friends long enough that there was no need to fill silence with needless chatter. With two slices gone he got another pair of beers from the fridge. Five minutes later nearly two thirds of the pizza was history and they were each tucking into their third and then fourth beers. Ari began to realize how little he'd eaten in the last few days as he felt the alcohol start to hit him, a faint, pleasant buzzing in his head. He thought about slowing down but Yvonne plunked another can in front of him.

"Try to keep up," she chided playfully.

He muffled a belch. "I don't think I can. I'm out of shape."

"Nah, it's like riding a bike. Unless you have too many and you crash the bike, of course. That can't be good."

Soon enough there was nothing left in the box but a scrap of crust and a smear of greasy sauce. He'd seen coyote kills that had left more behind. They both leaned back in their chairs and stared at the vanquished meal. Yvonne took a sip of her beer and exhaled noisily.

"Oh, man. Here come the meat sweats," she lamented.

The slight buzz in Ari's head had intensified. He reached for his can and almost knocked it over. He squinted and managed to get a handle on it on his second attempt. She laughed at him.

"You really are out of shape." She handed him another beer.

Ari considered refusing for about half a second. *Oh, hell, why not?* He gulped the last of the one in his hand and carefully began stacking the empties in a pyramid on the table. It was an impressive construct considering there were just two of them providing the building materials.

"Yeah. Haven't had much reason to practice lately." His words were slightly slurred.

Yvonne took another sip then hiccupped once. She giggled and put a hand to her mouth.

"Sorry. Bubbles tickled my nose."

Ari couldn't help but laugh at her. His elbow hit the table and the pyramid of cans wobbled and almost toppled. They both held their breath as the top can danced back and forth dangerously before settling down. He carefully tidied up their masterpiece. It took more concentration that he thought possible.

"Got any more beer?" she asked.

"Um, no. We killed that twelve-pack already. I may have a bottle or two of booze around here somewhere." He stood a little unsteadily and opened a cupboard above the refrigerator. He pushed around some paper plates and random kitchen items and found a nearly empty bottle of gin and another of tequila. The tequila had never been opened. He really didn't remember why he had it. Ari held up both bottles.

"Pick your poison."

She wrinkled her nose at the gin bottle. "Gin? No thanks. Tastes like Pine-sol. By all means bust out the tequila." She intentionally pronounced it *tay-kill-ya*.

"Your wish is my command."

He rummaged around one of the cabinets and finally found a shot glass. A nearby Indiana casino had their name and logo embossed in faded yellow on the side. He slid it to her across the kitchen table. His judgment was off and it almost flew off the end, hitting the pizza box instead.

"Whoops."

"Whoops is right," Yvonne laughed. "Fill 'er up, cowboy."

Ari plopped back into his seat and broke the seal on the tequila. He unsteadily poured two fingers of the amber liquid into the shot glass and nudged it her way.

"Ladies first."

She buzzed her lips and laughed. "Find me a lady and we'll talk. In the meantime, bottoms up." She tossed the tequila back then slammed the shot glass down on the table. She visibly shivered as the alcohol coursed through her.

"Smooth," she wheezed.

Ari laughed and managed to pour himself a shot, only missing the glass twice and slopping it on the table. *Wow.* He really was getting drunk. This wasn't like him.

"So tell me, Yvonne," he said, trying to sound sober and failing quite handily. He had a hard time pronouncing her name. It came out *Eee-von*. "Why are you here? Not that I don't appreciate the company – 'cause I do, honest – but really. Why're you here and why're you trying to get me wasted?"

Yvonne leaned forward. She rested an elbow on the table but it slipped off and she almost tumbled out of her seat. After she regained her composure she carefully leaned toward Ari again. She had to work hard to maintain a serious expression. Her scowl looked forced and exaggerated and more than a little comical. She pointed at him.

"Because, mister, I need to talk to you and I know you wouldn't listen to me if you were sober, that's why."

"Really? I don't know. I like you, Yvonne. I'd probably listen."

She wagged a finger at him. "Oh, probably not. Not about this."

Ari tried very hard to appear serious and sober. It wasn't working that well. Good thing she was drunk, too, and didn't notice. "Go ahead, hit me."

She punched him in the shoulder, then laughed loudly at her own joke.

"That's not what I meant, goofball."

"Ha! I know, sorry." She sat up and swayed a little. "Whew, that last shot is kicking my ass. Okay, ready? It's about you and Frankie."

"I figured as much. What is it?"

"How long has it been since you and she were together? Years, right?"

He nodded, his head wobbling side to side as much as up and down.

"And she and Butch are married, and because she's got that Catholic thing going that's never going to change, is it? She'd never ask for a divorce."

He did not like where this was going. "Pro'lly not, no. What's your point?"

She slid the shot to him. "Drink this first."

He was having a hard time focusing, both with his eyes and his mind. "I really don't think I need it, thanks. What's your point?"

"Drink first."

"Fine, bossy. Whatever." He tossed back the tequila and felt it burn all the way down. He suddenly remembered that he didn't even like tequila. He shivered, a full body shiver that actually vibrated his chair. "There. Happy?"

"You betcha'. Okay, here goes." She took a deep breath and tried to look serious again. It was difficult because she kept swaying like seaweed in a gentle current. "This is going to be tough, but it needs to be said. What I want to tell you, Ari, dear, is that you need to move on. Not just for your sake, but for hers as well. Having you around, knowing that you're living out here and that you're just a phone call or short drive away, is not helping her at all. She's almost as miserable as you are, my friend, and it's never going to get better as long as she knows you two are still even a distant 'maybe'." She hiccupped again but didn't snicker this time. "She can't get on with her life. Ari, you need to be the one to move on. You need to step up. As your friend, and as Frankie's friend, I'm telling you that's what you need to do." She grabbed the bottle and poured herself another shot. "There. I said it. Damn the torpedoes."

Ari stared at her as she tossed back another shot. Yvonne poured one for him and slid it his way. He didn't take it.

"I know staying here is wrong," he finally admitted. "And I know keeping in contact with her isn't helping either. And you were right – I wouldn't probably talk about this if you hadn't gotten me trashed."

"Here's a deep thought. Maybe you let me get you trashed so you could talk about it." She tapped her temple with one finger. "Pretty good, eh?"

"Yeah, maybe, Dr. Phil. Who knows? She's been with Butch now for more than two years and will be forever. I'm fucking miserable without her, but I'm afraid I'd be more miserable if I cut her out altogether, you know?" Ari tapped the side of his temple. "In here, in my head, I know this is all pointless, but my heart keeps telling me something different all the time. It keeps telling me that maybe, just maybe, some weird twist of fate will happen and Frankie and I can be together." He suddenly rubbed his face with both hands vigorously, like he was trying to wipe off an unseen stain. When he looked at her again his eyes were haunted and pained, more pained than if he had just lost something dear. "I'm scared to think she won't be in my life somehow. Shit. I'm so screwed up I don't know what to do. What a fucking mess."

Yvonne stood unsteadily. Weaving, she walked behind him and put her hands on his shoulders. She began to knead them, her strong fingers unlocking tight, bunched up muscles. Dimly Ari remembered that she was in the Rehab unit at the hospital, too. Of course she'd have strong hands.

"Yes, you're right, it is a fucking mess. And your back is all knotted up. Good lord, man, are you always this tense? Getting drunk's supposed to loosen you up."

His head drooped as her fingers dug into his back and shoulders. The touch of her skin on his bare neck felt warm and delicious. Ari couldn't remember the last time he had felt the touch of a woman. His eyes drifted nearly shut and what few sounds there were in the kitchen faded into a distant, indistinct hum, becoming little more than noises from some faraway place.

"Ari?" she whispered.

All he could do was offer a light grunt.

"Do you want me to stop?" Her face was down by his right ear.

He turned his head and her lips were right there, only millimeters away. Her breath was hot on his face. He reached behind her neck and pulled her close. Yvonne offered slight resistance. The kiss was gentle, tentative, the kiss of two people unsure of what was happening, but the skin on his face was warm and his body twitched, almost as if a minute electrical charge was running through him.

Then suddenly they each took a deep, shuddering breath and the kiss became more passionate, more immediate, lips open and tongues thrusting in and out, exploring, discovering. Yvonne groaned.

Ari's mind blanked, became something more primitive, more basic. With a quick motion he shoved back his chair and grabbed her around her waist. Almost effortlessly he picked her up off the ground and set her down hard, straddling his lap. Her back banged into the table and the pyramid of cans clattered to the floor. Neither noticed or cared. He had his hands in her blond hair and wondered fleetingly when she had taken the ponytail out, or if he had somehow done it himself.

She pulled away, her hands on either side of his face, holding it tight. Her cheeks were bright red and her breath was fast and shallow, coming in short, hot gasps. Yvonne's breasts were straining against the thin fabric of her shirt. Their faces were so close together her eyes looked almost crossed. Their foreheads touched.

"This is prob'ly a bad idea." It came out as a throaty, breathy whisper.

"Yeah," he admitted. "It probably is."

They attacked each other again, only this time it was even more frantic, lips sliding over lips, lips to neck, hot, musky breath on each other. Without even realizing what he was doing Ari pulled at her orange and white striped shirt, almost tearing it. Yvonne lifted her arms and he finally tugged it off, tossing it in a heap onto the floor by the oven. Her thin white bra was bright in the kitchen light and contrasted starkly with her tanned skin. They pulled away from each other long enough for him to see that the bra's clasps were on the front instead of the back. His head was so full of tequila and beer that he had to genuinely concentrate to undo the hooks and fleetingly considered simply tearing them off. When he finally unclipped the final clasp the bra almost popped open, revealing her large, full breasts. Her areolas were surprisingly small, no bigger than quarters, but her nipples were firm and tight. A single drop of sweat glistened between her breasts and he couldn't help staring and following it as it gently rolled down to her stomach. Her chest quivered and heaved in expectation.

Then his mind flashed white with primitive, drunken lust, and they were upon each other.

Chapter 6

He awoke with nothing on but a sheet draped haphazardly across his midsection. Ari looked at the clock and wasn't the least bit surprised when it said 5:02 AM. It was dark outside but the light next to his bed was on, the shade cocked sideways and throwing an oblong puddle of light across the floor and wall. He stared at the ceiling of his bedroom and had no recollection of how he got there or what had happened. His tongue had the texture of old stucco and his head hurt. No, it didn't just hurt, it felt like the Macy's Thanksgiving Day Parade had just walked right over it, bands, floats, and all. His left bicep ached too, which sort of made sense once he looked at it and saw teeth marks.

Teeth marks? Damn.

Eventually, Ari looked to his right and saw the naked, hourglass shape of Yvonne's back, shoulders, and ass. Her blond hair was in a tangle across her head and face. Her breathing was deep and steady. Regardless how she lamented about pushing thirty, she was in terrific shape and still very trim and pretty.

He turned away and stared at the ceiling again. Dribs and drabs of the night before began to trickle into his mind, drip, drip, drip, a spigot of memory just barely turned on. He remembered the pizza and beer, and the tequila. *Damn, never should've dug out the tequila.* After that, events got fuzzy again, but he had blurred images of him and Yvonne tearing at each other's clothes and going at it right there on the kitchen table. Then they had stumbled to the bed. Oh, lots of positions on the bed, with Yvonne screaming as she came again and again when he was on top of her, behind her, then with her on top of him. He was pretty sure they had taken a break after that, sweaty and hot, until, giggling and still quite drunk, he had lifted her onto the washing machine and set the cycle to spin-dry. Between the vibrations of the machine and his own oral machinations he was pretty sure he had brought her to climax again, although at this point his memory fuzzed out to the point where he didn't know what was real and what was imagined. He thought they had ended up on the bed again, too tired and spent to do anything but pass out. Somewhere in there she had bit his arm hard enough to bruise.

Slowly, as to not wake her, he eased himself clumsily off the bed and padded, naked, into the kitchen. Beer cans were scattered on the floor and the pizza box was crushed in the corner. His boxers were inside out on the counter and he slipped them on. He'd attended frat parties that hadn't been this messy. He made a note to thoroughly clean and disinfect the kitchen table before eating there again.

Ari dug some Advil from the cupboard and downed three tablets with a tall glass of water. The quick influx of liquid partially renewed his buzz and he had to hold onto the counter to keep from falling over, vomiting, or both. As soon as the queasiness passed he tossed down another glass. He was dehydrated, he knew, and wouldn't feel better for quite some time. He made another mental note to throw out whatever was left of the tequila since he knew he wouldn't want any more for a long, long time. Even the thought of it made him almost puke.

He poured himself a third glass and sat at the kitchen table. Now what in the hell had *that* been all about? Why in the world had he and Yvonne attacked each other like horny teenagers? It had been a long time since he'd been with a woman, granted, but he had never gone at it like that before. He felt pangs of guilt hit, as if he had just been caught cheating on Frankie, which was stupid. She was with Butch and had been for years now. Neither one had a hold on the other, and neither had vowed celibacy in any way. Regardless he still felt like he'd been unfaithful to her. He sipped the water and sat with his elbows on the table, thinking.

Several minutes later he heard a rustling and Yvonne walked unsteadily out of the bedroom with the sheet wrapped around her like a toga, furthering his image of the frat party. Her hair was still tousled around her face and her eyes oozed red.

"Good morning," he said.

She held up a quieting hand. The sheet slid partially off and displayed one of her breasts. She absently tugged it back up, not overly concerned.

"No yelling, please," she whispered. "Have pity on a poor hungover girl."

Ari got her three Advil and her own glass of water. She expertly tossed them back and drank the water, holding the cool glass to her forehead. She wobbled over and sat across from him with a thud. She winced as the chair squeaked on the floor.

"Good lord I'm going to walk like a cowboy for a week," she mumbled. "I don't know if that's what you're always like, but man oh man that was quite a time."

"Hm. Sorry, I don't know what came over me."

"Sorry? Ari, dear, never apologize for that. It was one for the record books."

Embarrassed, he walked to the sink and refilled his glass. His stucco tongue was beginning to morph into a texture only slightly less annoying, like heavy grit sandpaper. Ari sat back down with his chin in his hands. Yvonne looked at him through the tangle of her blond hair.

"Do I look as shitty as I feel?"

He smiled thinly. "No, of course not. You look terrific."

"Ha. Liar, but thanks anyway." She looked around the kitchen and squinted at the small clock on the stove. "Six o'clock? What the hell are we doing up at six o'clock?"

"Sorry. I'm kind of an early riser most of the time. Can't help it."

"Ugh. You're a sick man, Ari Van Owen. I'd go back to bed but I'm afraid if I lay down I'll hurl. Think I'd better take a shower, if that's okay."

"Sure. Go right ahead. Towels and everything are in the bathroom."

She stood and began a slow walk to the bathroom. She passed by the laundry room door and briefly paused, then turned back to Ari. There was a cute smirk on her face, a knowing look as of a shared secret.

"The washing machine. Did we, ah, play around on the washing machine last night?"

"Yes we did. At least I think so. I thought maybe I imagined it but apparently not since you remember it, too. We were pretty drunk."

"Hmm. Very imaginative, my dear Ari. Bonus points for you." She winked at him over her shoulder as she walked away. When she got to the open door of the bedroom Yvonne rather gracefully unwrapped the sheet and tossed it onto the bed. Naked, she slowly sauntered into the bathroom and eased the door shut. Ari recognized an invitation when he saw one, although this morning he was able to resist the temptation. He heard the water turn on and the shower curtain swish open and closed. Pretty soon a melodic humming came from the bathroom, a catchy tune he couldn't immediately place but could've been something from the band Journey.

With a deep sigh he made a full pot of coffee, figuring they'd need it. He stuck his head in the bathroom door and almost couldn't see the shower due to the thick steam. Her humming was loud in there, the harmonics echoing oddly off the hard tile. Yes, it was a Journey song, for sure.

"Want some breakfast? I can whip up some pancakes or something."

"No thanks!" she yelled over the water. "Just some coffee. Maybe some toast?"

"Will do."

Ten minutes later she was back in her clothes from the night before with her long blond hair wrapped expertly in a towel, turban-style. She gratefully accepted the coffee and the toast, butter only. She munched it in satisfaction, careful to catch any crumbs on the plate. She motioned at the table.

"You did clean this up, didn't you?"

"You bet. While you were in the shower."

"Good man."

Ari sat back down across from her. A strand of her blond hair had escaped the towel and was curled around her cheek. The wet lock looked brown instead of blond. She absently tucked it back in and kept eating. He cleared his throat.

"So. We going to talk about what happened last night?"

"What about? My choice of pizza parlors?"

He pursed his lips, his eyebrows knitting together in a bunch. "No, not that. You know what I mean."

"I know. I'm just yanking your chain."

"Thanks. So what was that all about? Why the hell did we do…all that?"

She finished her toast and wiped her mouth with a napkin. "Ari, dear, when I got here last night I had no intention of doing anything but talking to you about Frankie. Really. My goal was to loosen you up so we could just talk about it. Guess things just got out of hand."

"Yeah, I guess so."

"And our discussion still stands. Please tell me you'll drop this crazy thing you've got for Frankie. It's not good for you, and it's certainly not good for her. She's married to Butch and that's how it's going to stay. You need to move on."

Ari leaned back in his chair and stared at the ceiling. She was right, of course. He knew it, had known it for years now. But knowing it and being able to do something about it were totally different. She had been right about one thing: talking about the two of them, about him and Frankie, had been easier last night after all the beer and booze. Now all he could think about was what he would do if he moved on, if that part of him that was still connected to Frankie was no more. He was certain it would leave him less than he was now. He looked back to Yvonne and found her staring at him, waiting for an answer.

"I don't know if I can."

"But can you try? Just tell me you can try. For Frankie."

Seconds passed, seconds that could have been a lifetime. She was still staring at him and waiting for an answer. Finally he nodded, a fractional, tiny head movement so slight that it would have been easier to catch it with time-lapse photography.

"I can do it, I think. I know I should, I've known it for a long time, I guess. But not until she's safe and sound. I have to make sure of that first."

Yvonne pursed her own lips and stared at him some more. After a few moments she nodded assent. When she moved the turban suddenly toppled and came apart, falling about her shoulders. She tried fixing it but had little success without a mirror, finally giving up.

"I guess that's the best we can ask for right now," she admitted. "One step at a time, right?"

"Yeah. One step at a time."

"Oh, and all that fun stuff last night?" Her cheeks flushed pink, a demure side of her Ari had never seen before. "I think we both needed that, honestly. Let's just call it a night of friends with benefits, okay?"

For some reason Ari wasn't completely convinced, but he didn't know what to say. He was still stunned it had happened at all, shocked that he had acted like that. Finally he agreed and she smiled at him warmly, then ruffled his messy brown hair and went back to the bathroom to finish getting cleaned up. The hair dryer hummed for five minutes, and when she came back out her hair was in a ponytail again. Ari had busied himself by cleaning up most of the kitchen and was at the sink rinsing off the last of the dishes. Yvonne stood in the middle of the floor, her hands locked in front of her. She looked small.

"I guess I'd better be going. I've got to be at the hospital in a few hours, and I probably shouldn't have the same clothes on as yesterday. Looks bad."

"Thanks for coming over, and for the talk. And for everything else, too, I guess."

"You guess? I'm going to remember that for a long, long time."

He walked her to the door where she gave him a long, lingering hug, her breasts pushing into his chest. Her hair smelled clean and damp, the ends not yet dry. She looked up at him and gave him a kiss on the lips, a kiss that he barely returned.

"Damn. Drunk Ari was a shitload more fun," she chided, patting his chest. "Maybe he can come out and play again sometime." Her tone was light but with a trace of an edge, like a warm fall breeze with just a hint of winter. She hugged him once more, fleeting and fast, then walked out to her car, her ponytail swaying in time with her strides. She waved to him over her shoulder.

He stood there in the door thinking again what Journey song she had been humming. He couldn't dredge up the name or all the lyrics verbatim, but one line went something like *When your lover, he hasn't come home, cuz he's lovin', he's touchin', he's squeezin' another.*

Her car pulled out of the driveway and she didn't look back.

Yvonne had only been gone a few minutes when Ari heard his cell phone ringing from the bedroom. It had rung five or six times before he found it buried in the covers at the foot of his bed. He didn't remember putting it there, yet another byproduct of his drunken night. He looked at the number.

"Hello, Hal," he said.

"Impersonating a Federal officer is serious business, Ari." Hal Hollenbeck's usually easy tones were clipped and short.

Well, shit – that hadn't taken long.

"I'm sure it is." He thought furiously for a moment, connecting some mental dots. "So Theodore Rust called and checked up on me, did he?"

If Hal was surprised at Ari's guess he didn't let on.

"Yes, Theodore Rust checked up on you. Let me tell you, I had to do some pretty quick thinking and lying to cover for you, too."

"You want to know what I found out?"

"No, dammit, I want you to stop pulling this kind of stunt, that's what I want. You can't go around impersonating an FBI agent."

Ari continued as if he hadn't heard. "There's something going on here, Hal."

"I don't care," Hal said, enunciating his words slowly and clearly. "We've got bigger problems and I can't keep an eye on you, too."

"Frankie was kidnapped from the hospital. Someone fairly well off paid one of the security guards five grand to look the other way and erase the security tapes. The same guy and one of his thugs, a huge man, the muscle, abducted her from the parking lot. She's been taken somewhere south of here, probably out of the country. Maybe Central or South America, but that's just a gut feeling. And since there's been no ransom demand she's being held for some other reason. I don't know why, but it wasn't for money – at least not directly."

There was a moment's silence from the other end. Ari could hear Hal shift the phone from one ear to the other. Some papers rustled.

"And you got all this in just a few days, did you?"

"I'm serious, Hal. There's more to this than we think."

"Yeah? Why's that?"

Ari sat on the edge of the bed. "I don't know why, at least not yet. Just a feeling I've got. I do know one thing – we need to find the man that bribed the guard. Find him, find the man in the fedora, and we'll find Frankie and get to the bottom of this."

There was a long pause where the only sound from the other end of the phone was Hal's breathing. Ari imagined the agent cleaning his already spotless glasses. When he finally spoke again his voice was a harsh whisper.

"Ari, what did you just say?"

"I said, find this man in the fedora and we'll find Frankie. Why? What's wrong? Why is this so important?"

"Dammit, Van Owen, I can't believe it."

"Believe what? Talk to me, Hal."

"No. Not over the phone. Your line's not secure. I'm leaving in five minutes from my office. I'll be at your door in less than two hours. Don't go anywhere, got it?"

The line went dead. Ari stared at the phone, bemused. He had struck a nerve with the agent, that was for sure, and it had something to do with the man in the hat and the strange tiger tie pin. He had no idea why Hal had reacted so strongly, but that didn't matter. What did matter was that he had the FBI's attention again, and that was a good thing. At this point any action was good action.

True to his word Hal Hollenbeck arrived from his Cincinnati office in just under two hours. Ari opened the door when he heard the government-issue sedan's tires crunch on the gravel driveway. When he walked in the house he handed the agent a fresh cup of coffee with the requisite cream and two sugars. Hal took it.

"Thanks."

The two men sat at the kitchen table. Hal was dressed similarly to his previous visit, but a dark sport coat had replaced the tan jacket. The bulge was still visible under his arm. He looked tired, the corners of his eyes pinched with stress. He held out his hand.

"Hand it over."

Ari didn't bother to ask what he meant. He pulled the fake ID from his back pocket and gave it to the agent. Hollenbeck inspected it carefully before putting it into his jacket pocket.

"Pretty good craftsmanship," he grudgingly admitted, "although the number sequence on the badge is wrong. Where'd you get it?"

"Online. I was impressed, too. And the turnaround time was amazing."

"Can I have the website, please? We need to shut it down, or at least monitor it."

Van Owen had anticipated this request and handed him a slip of paper with the website address on it. Hal folded it over and put it with the fake ID. This specific website would likely be gone later today, although he was equally certain it would pop back up somewhere else. There would be ways to get another from a different site in the future if necessary.

Hal sipped from his mug and stared at Ari. A muscle in his cheek twitched. "I am in no way condoning what you did, and in fact I could take you into custody right now if I wanted. You know that, right?"

He stared at the agent and didn't say anything.

"But of course you know I won't. In your own particular way you've stumbled onto something, something big, bigger than Frankie Brubaker's abduction. Tell me everything you know."

Ari figured he owed Hollenbeck that much at least, so he obliged and told him everything, only withholding the identity of Paul Paulson. It would be a simple matter for the agent to figure it out, but he didn't think he would bother. He told him about finding Frankie's car in the impound lot, the traced Karma symbol with the arrow pointing down, his time with the two security guards, his multiple meetings with Paul, and his talk with Theodore Rust. He even shared his dream about Frankie in the jungle. Lastly he described his chance encounter with Butch. He omitted his time with

113

Yvonne since it wasn't exactly pertinent information, but also due to embarrassment: this wasn't college, and despite her praise of his performance he wasn't proud of what he had done.

"And her husband wasn't belligerent to you this time? That seems strange after he drove all the way out here just a few days before and threatened to kill you."

"I know, I thought the same thing. He's all torn up about Frankie, I guess. He wasn't acting like himself."

Hal made some notes in his phone before he put it down. He stared hard at Ari as if measuring him up, as if determining how much he should or could say. His glasses came off and he vigorously cleaned them using a napkin from the table. His eyes were red and tired, and reminded Van Owen of dad whose infant child had kept him up all night, screaming and crying.

"What I'm going to tell you stays right here. Do you understand?"

Ari's mouth compressed. He leaned back and crossed his arms. "Of course, you know that. Haven't we had this conversation before?"

Even with his reassurance it was hard for the agent to continue. Hal sat there and drummed his fingers on the table while he watched a thin wisp of steam rising from his cup. It was the same one he'd used before, the one with the Kodiak bear on it. He wasn't amused by the cartoon this time. As close as the two men were Ari was afraid Hal wasn't going to share. Finally he took a deep breath.

"We've been busy, as you can imagine, and we've made some progress in the Garrafon case. There is so much going on and so many departments involved that it's hard to keep up. The autopsy came back this morning and he probably did die due to what is officially now known as SOP, sudden onset paralysis. Blood work initially came up empty. No pathogens, no known drugs, no recognizable toxins. However one of our forensic teams did a very deep, very complicated and expensive dive and stumbled on

114

something strange, a trace chemical we've never seen before in relation to a death. It was virtually undetectable and only the best forensic team out there was able to find it."

"Never seen before? What was it?"

The agent continued unabated. "Here's where thing's get more complicated. Ever hear of a new drug called 'Ice'? It's very exotic, and very rare."

Van Owen thought back. He knew something about this, but didn't know how. It took him a second to recall. "I have, actually, maybe on the radio. But I don't know anything about it, really. What is it?"

Hal was silent for a moment. When he spoke his tone was both apologetic and a little angry. Not having all the answers bothered him. "I wish I knew. It's so new we know almost nothing about it. Not what it is, where it's made, the distribution channel, nothing. It's too new. But I can tell you this - it's powerful, virtually undetectable, and very expensive. It's such a designer drug that the average Joe will never be able to afford it. It's strictly for the upper crust, that top 1% of the population that people talk about."

"The top 1%, eh? Someone with a lot of disposable income, like a professional athlete? Like maybe Garrafon?"

His eyes behind the glasses were hard. "Exactly like Garrafon."

"So what's it do?"

"We don't know that for sure either. We think it acts like a performance-enhancing drug, a PED, sort of like a hyper-steroid. But we think it also has mind-altering capabilities, like cocaine or amphetamines. If that's the case the combination of those two characteristics may explain why Garrafon was doing so well on the field the past few months."

"Until it killed him, you mean."

"Yeah, until it killed him. We don't know much, but we've never heard of an Ice overdose before, at least not one that killed someone. This is a whole new angle."

Ari got up and poured another cup of coffee. He looked a question at Hollenbeck, who declined by placing his hand over the Kodiak mug. Several thoughts were rambling around Ari's mind.

"So Ice is virtually undetectable and it's killing people. You know about Garrafon but there could be others, right?"

"Right. We're of the same opinion. There could be more. Probably are."

"So it's a killer. But if it's also a new performance enhancing drug it's got to have everyone in the sporting world worried as hell, assuming they know about it. I mean, hell, look at the Lance Armstrong debacle. PEDs do not play well with the public. So besides the fact that you've got pilots crashing planes and killing people because of sudden onset paralysis, now you've got the potential for athletes all over the world to be, in essence, using Ice and cheating, and maybe dying, and there's almost no way to catch them. Wow."

Hal nodded. "You're starting to get it. It would seem that SOP and Ice are related somehow, and that means we've got huge problems. The safety of the airways and the general population are our top priority here, but the secondary issue of an untraceable performance enhancing drug killing athletes doesn't help matters."

"Not to mention when athletes cheat like this they're screwing with bookies and the big money types in Vegas. When they use drugs to cheat the system it has the potential to hit those types hard, right in the wallet. They don't like that. And we haven't even mentioned collegiate sports yet. This isn't good for anyone."

"No it is not. You're right."

Van Owen stared at his mug. He had a momentary flashback of him and Yvonne on the table last night but he tried to clear that image from his mind. He was not ready to think too much about that yet.

"You said your forensic team found a trace chemical in Garrafon's blood. What was it, and why do you think it's related to SOP and Ice?"

"You know as well as I do that there's lots of stuff out there we know nothing about, we just don't like to publicize it. Fortunately we recently hired, for lack of a better term, a forensic entomologist, someone I think you know. Does the name Dr. Carrie Fox ring any bells?"

Ari blinked twice rapidly in surprise. "Carrie Fox works for you? Sure, I know her. She was the lead entomologist working for UC Berkley, last time I heard. I ran into her at the start of my second Fawcett trip. She's very good. I didn't know she'd come back stateside."

"Seems the urge to settle down and have a family trumped living in the jungle. No shock there as far as I'm concerned."

Ari was impressed. "You're very lucky to have her. She's excellent at what she does, and very bright."

"I agree. I doubt we would've caught this without her. She's the one that recognized something that everyone else missed. Do you know what *Paraponera clavata* is?"

Ari rolled the name around in his head for a minute. "Paraponera clavata. Para…Wait, I know that. Isn't that the name of the Amazon bullet ant?"

"Give the man a star. Yes, bullet ant it is. They're named so due to their sting that, according to something called the *Schmidt Sting Index*, is equal to the pain of being shot with a gun. Dr. Fox recognized a trace of something that looked a lot like a neurotoxin peptide called *poneratoxin* that comes from a very specific type of bullet ant, one only indigenous to a particular area along the Bolivian, Brazilian border, deep inside the northwestern Brazilian state of Mato Grosso. Don't ask me how but she found it in Garrafon's blood, but she did."

The name Mato Grosso caught Ari's attention. It was one of the possible final locations of Percy Fawcett. "If anyone could find it, Carrie Fox could. And I know about bullet ants on a personal level. They're exceptionally nasty, and a single bite can cause temporary paralysis in humans and animals. I was stung before, on the arm. Damn, that hurt. It was dead and completely paralyzed for almost 24 hours. I've never been shot so I can't compare it to that, but I'd rather not go through either, thanks. Male natives in the jungle have been known to use these bites as a test of manhood." He rubbed his left arm absently, keenly remembering the searing, throbbing pain. "So this toxin is found in a single type of ant, and you know where these ants are from?"

"That's what I've been told. There are several hundred strains of bullet ant, apparently, but only one that matches this exact poneratoxin. And here's where things get even more interesting." He leaned forward with his hands locked on the table in front of him. "Carlos Garrafon was a citizen of the Dominican Republic, just like we've all been told. That's all perfectly legit and his paperwork and passport check out. However we drilled deeper into his family history and found that he's originally from much farther south."

"South of the Dominican Republic is the middle of the ocean."

"Funny. That's not what I meant. His family is originally from Bolivia, a tiny village on the Bolivian – Brazilian border called *Boca Andreas*, not too far from Mato Grosso. He moved to the Dominican Republic when he was eight or nine years old, but he still has a lot of family back in Bolivia. A lot of family." He took a sip of his coffee and glanced sideways at the mug. He still didn't smile.

Ari stared at him. "Can you get to the point, please?"

"I'm getting there. During our investigation into his death we talked to friends and teammates, anyone we could think of, anyone who may have had contact with him. Nothing extraordinary surfaced. Nothing. He played baseball, lived with some other young Latinos from the Reds in an apartment in downtown Cincinnati, and did little outside the ballpark except play video games. Nothing at all out of the ordinary popped up, that is until your phone call earlier today. You mentioned a man involved in Frankie Brubaker's disappearance, a very well-dressed man in a fedora."

Now Ari was interested. He leaned forward too. His pulse quickened and his gaze was laser-focused on Hal. "As a matter of fact I did."

"Several of Garrafon's roommates mentioned a man they started seeing a few months ago hanging around with our young ball player, a man who said he was Garrafon's uncle. None of the guys knew anything about him except that he was always dressed to the nines and seemed pretty well off. They rarely talked to him but several times they saw Garrafon getting into his car and heading out. He spoke Spanish with a South American accent. They knew him as Uncle Roberto. And he always wore a fedora. Always."

Holy shit. "That can't be a coincidence."

"I don't believe in coincidence, and you shouldn't either. If we look back at Garrafon's performance this is also when he started doing well on the field. He and this Uncle Roberto are linked to SOP and Ice, I just know it, and somehow, directly or indirectly, Frankie Brubaker is, too."

"Wait a minute," Ari said, bristling at the accusation, the hair on the back of his neck standing on end. "Are you saying Frankie is involved in some drug trade? No way. There's no way she'd do anything like that."

"No, I agree. From what I know of her I can't imagine she would be. I said either directly or indirectly, but somehow she's involved."

Ari's pulse quickened more. He was putting the pieces together and they matched what the agent was saying. "Okay, I can't argue with your assumptions just yet, but it's certainly indirect and involuntarily. So we have a performance enhancing drug called Ice that's probably related to or even causing sudden onset paralysis, and this SOP is somehow linked to a specific strain of bullet ant and the chemical *poneratoxin* that's indigenous to one particular area of the state of Mato Grosso in western Brazil. Am I right so far?"

Hal nodded. "That's it."

"So correct me if I'm wrong, but I'm thinking that our next step is to head south to Mato Grosso, and by 'we' I mean 'me'. I'll find our bullet ants which will hopefully be the source of all this, and then maybe I can locate this Uncle Roberto. Find Uncle Roberto and maybe I can find Frankie. And the Ice drug. Am I still on track?"

"Exactly."

He stood quickly, anxious to get busy. "So what are we waiting for? Let's get busy and get to Mato Grosso. I guess I'm going back to the Amazon after all."

"I figured you'd say that."

Chapter 7

He was so pumped that if he'd had his way Ari he would've left that instant, ready or not. Fortunately the agent belayed that by holding up a hand and gently motioning him back to his seat.

"Whoa, now, not so fast. Yes, the FBI wants you to head south and check this out. But we've got some serious planning to do first, you know that. First thing we need to do is assemble our team and get our supplies all set."

Ari looked hard at Hal. "Team? I don't need a team. Plus I don't have anyone lined up for this type of trip. Something like this typically takes months to plan. We don't have that kind of time."

"Really? No one? How about me for starters?"

He cocked his head at Hal, appraising the agent before shaking his head. "You? Sorry, but if I'm going to take anyone it's going to be experienced men, guys used to the jungle and the kind of adverse conditions down there. But I repeat, we don't have that kind of time."

"Ari, think about it. You've said before that a small squad is what works best, not just a single guy or a huge group. I figure we'll need four or five men. You and I are two. Who else comes to mind? Anyone? I won't let you go by yourself. That's suicide."

The rational part of Ari's mind agreed, although the emotional side was bitterly against how long it would take to put a qualified group together. It was clear that Hal just didn't understand.

"And besides," the agent continued with a raised eyebrow. "I might surprise you. I'm pretty hardy."

Ari looked dubiously at the agent's thickening middle and soft, rounded edges, wondering how long it had been since he'd done anything more physical than mow the lawn. People in the Amazon died being just "pretty hardy."

"No offense intended, Hal, but I don't think so. You're not cut out for this."

"Okay, let's put it this way, *Arjen*. I'm coming along and you don't have any choice. Now who else can you get to round out our team?"

His eyes narrowed. "Don't call me Arjen. You know I hate that name."

"So who else do you have in mind? I'm serious here."

Ari stared at the agent and their eyes locked for a full ten seconds, like two boxers in the ring just prior to the bell. Neither man looked away, the thick, uncomfortable silence dragging on. Eventually Ari's eyes softened.

"You could die out there, Hal. I mean it," he said, suddenly sincere.

He nodded. "I understand, but give me some credit. I've been stationed in both Pakistan and Afghanistan. I've been in heated gun-battles with insurgents and the Taliban. I've had a bullet whiz by my ear so close I felt the heat and had it singe my hair. I've dug shrapnel out of my vest more times than I can count." Hal took off his glasses but for once didn't clean them. He stared at them blankly and rolled them around in his hands, his mind thousands of miles and a lifetime away. "I had to clean blood and brains up after a soldier from Missouri next to me got hit with a .50 caliber round that took his head off at the neck. The doctors had to pick pieces of his skull from the side of my face." His eyes locked with Ari's again. There was a haunted, aching look there that Ari had never seen before. "So don't tell me I'm not cut out for this. I'll be fine. And like I said, I might just surprise you."

Ari stared at him another moment before nodding. There was no way around it, he understood. Hal was coming with him.

"So," Hollenbeck continued, "do you have anyone else in mind that you can get on short notice? Anyone you can trust?"

"Hmm, perhaps. You?"

He nodded. "I figured you might. I've got someone in mind, yes. Let me do some checking and I'll get back with you. I'll call you tomorrow from Cincinnati. I've got to get back to the office so we can get moving on this. Deal?"

"Fine. Deal."

Both men stood and Hal walked to the door. He patted his pocket to make sure he still had the fake badge and website address with him.

"Oh, Hal, by the way – what did you tell Theodore Rust about me? How'd you cover my, ah, identity?"

"Theodore is ex-military. I told him you were doing undercover work on a matter of national security and that it was top-secret. He's a good soldier. He understood." Hal squinted at him. "You're not thinking of taking him along, are you?"

"What? No, no way. I was just curious in case I run into him again."

"Good. Theodore Rust at age twenty-five would be great, but the current AARP version is out of the question."

"I know. Too bad."

The agent nodded again and walked out to his car, Ari following. Once inside the plain sedan he rolled down the window. The sun was in his face and turned his glasses into mirrors that shielded his eyes and nearly blinded Van Owen.

"I'll need a list of the supplies for the trip. The Bureau will pick up the tab for all that. Don't scrimp on what you may need, and get whatever you have to. Cost is not an object here."

"Fine, thanks. Some of that we'll have to get once we're down there. Hope your budget can stand it. And bring cash. Lots of cash. Some stuff we'll only be able to buy with American dollars."

"We'll be okay unless you ask for an Apache helicopter, trust me."

"Is that an option? I'd like to put a reservation for one, please."

He grinned then rolled up the window and drove off. Ari wasted no time and dug his cell phone out, quickly scrolling through the recent call history. When he found what he was looking for he hit Send. It rang three times before a voice answered.

"Hi, it's me," Ari said. "Where are you now? Okay. Can you meet me at the hospital in thirty minutes? No, I'll explain when we get there. Meet me at the snack bar, okay? Good, see you then."

He grabbed his keys and locked up the house, then jumped into the rented sedan. This route to the hospital was becoming second nature to him.

Van Owen parked the rental in the main lot this time, near the entrance. He walked in the front doors, the now-familiar antiseptic smell tickling his nose. Theodore Rust sat properly at the information desk and nodded curtly at him as he passed by. He really was a good soldier, Ari thought, still resisting the urge to salute.

He got to the snack bar a few minutes early and ordered a Coke, which he took to a table in the rear. He sat with his back to the wall and watched as people came and went, some hospital staff in their requisite colorful scrubs, but mainly visitors just passing by. No one paid him the least attention. He wondered idly when scrubs had changed from white or blue to the rainbow of colors he saw now, and why. Were the hot pinks and pastels meant to cheer up the patients, or the medical staff? Either way it was a nice change.

Five minutes later Paul Paulson eased in and looked around, spotting Ari in the back. He pointed at him and sat down at the small table. His blond wavy hair was bright in the dim lighting of the coffee shop and contrasted with the black Nike T-shirt he was wearing.

"Hi, Paul."

"We've got to stop meeting like this," the young man quipped.

"Yeah. So how's it going?"

The young man shrugged. "Not bad, I guess. I'm still on administrative leave so meeting here's a little awkward. I feel sort of like Bill Gates at a Luddite convention, if you know what I mean"

Ari forced himself not to grin at the rather oddball statement. Despite what Paulson had done and his complicity with Frankie's abduction, it was hard not to like the guy. He was eminently personable, even if he'd had a lapse of good judgment that day in the Security Office.

"Paul, I've got to tell you something, and then I'm going to ask you something that cannot go any farther than here."

"Sure, I guess."

"You can't guess, Paul. This is serious."

Paulson's blond, almost invisible eyebrows arched. "Okay, sure. No farther than the two of us."

"First of all, my name's not Hal Hollenbeck, and I'm not an agent for the FBI. My real name is Ari Van Owen, and while I've done work for the FBI in the past I'm not directly employed by them right now."

Paulson's eyebrows arched even higher but he didn't say anything. His hands were flat on the tabletop. His blue eyes were bright in the white light.

"I really am looking into the disappearance of Frankie Brubaker, and the FBI knows this. In fact I've teamed up with the real Hal Hollenbeck to find her. We're working on that right now. We've got some leads that we're following up on."

Paul leaned forward. "So what, you lied to me about all this?"

"Yes, yes I did. I'm not going to apologize because I'd do it again if it would help me find Frankie Brubaker."

Paulson's face was turning red. "But I opened up to you, told you all that personal stuff. What the hell?"

Ari nodded, afraid for a moment that he might be losing him. "You did, yes, and because you told me so much we were able to piece some additional valuable information together that may help us find her." He motioned Paulson to move closer. Initially it looked like he wouldn't, but after a moment's hesitation the young man leaned in.

"What?" The word came out short and harsh, more of a bark.

Ari's voice was lower and more intense. "Paul, I'm sorry if you're angry, but you need to get over it. When we first met, there in your apartment, you said you wished you could help find her. You felt terrible about what you'd done. Well, this is your chance. I need your help, Paul. *We* need your help. I'm afraid we don't have much time. The longer we wait the less chance we'll have to find her."

Paul sat for a minute before getting up and buying a bottled water at the counter. When he came back he drummed his fingers on the tabletop and stared at Ari.

"What'd you say your name really is?"

"Ari Van Owen."

"Ari? What kind of name is that?"

"It's short for Arjen."

"Arjen Van Owen. What is that, Dutch?"

"Very good. Yes, it's Dutch."

Paulson set the water down in front of him and spun the bottle around slowly, staring at the label. It portrayed a mountain scene against a blue sky, very peaceful and serene. "So why are you trying so hard to find Ms. Brubaker, anyway? Especially if you're not with the FBI or the cops? I don't get it." He took a pull on the water. "You know, we used to toss around an acronym when I was going through security training: WIIFM, or What's In It For Me? Or, in your case, What's In It For You?" He looked up then and locked eyes with Ari. "What's in it for you, Arjen?"

Typically any question about Ari's relationship with Frankie would slam shut his emotional gate, just as it had when Hal Hollenbeck had asked. But staring at Paulson he knew that to get his buy-in he'd have to be more forthcoming, surrender a little more. He'd have to push open that heavy gate a little, as difficult as it was.

"Fine. First, don't call me Arjen. I hate that name."

Paulson smirked. "Don't blame you for that, although 'Ari' isn't much better."

"Second. Well, ah, Frankie and I have some history together from before she was married." His eyes unfocused and he stared over Paul's shoulder. His voice became softer. "We were pretty close at one time. If I hadn't been out of the picture for so long I think we'd still be together. Instead...now she's with her husband, and will be forever, and I'm screwed."

Paul raised an eyebrow. "How long ago was this?"

He snapped back to the present. "A few years. Why?"

"And you're still burning the torch for her?" He whistled. "She must really be something."

Van Owen allowed himself a small, wistful smile, a rare curving of the lips that was gone as quickly as it had come. The song *Green Eyes* came to him then, a brief snippet of the music and lyrics: *Honey, you are a rock, upon which I stand...*

"Yes, she is," was all he would say, his throat unexpectedly tight.

Paulson had stopped spinning the water bottle. "Well, I'm no expert but I can see what she means to you. And by the way, if you were trying to hide how you feel about her you suck at it." He sat up straight in his chair, his expression uncharacteristically serious, his blue eyes narrowed. "And you're right - I did say I wanted to help, so now's the time to man up. Especially considering how I...screwed up earlier. I think it may be the only way I can live with myself." He sat up straight in his chair and exhaled heavily. "This is something I think I have to do."

Ari looked expectantly at him. "So you're on board?"

Paul smiled grimly. "Aye aye, captain. Count me in."

"Good. I'll have the real Hal Hollenbeck call your boss and work out the details. Getting you a leave of absence shouldn't be a problem."

Paulson snorted once and took a swig of his water. "Yeah, they still don't know what to do with me right now, so that's probably a good thing. I doubt they'll miss me."

"We'll tell them the truth – that you're helping out the FBI, and that we don't know how long you'll be gone. That should help you regain some credibility, too." Ari could see the young man's eyes light up as it suddenly dawned on him that he really would be working with a true law enforcement organization. He thought back to their earlier conversation, that it was Paulson's dream to work with such a group, something much more than just hospital security. There wasn't much higher law enforcement than the FBI.

"But hold on a minute," Paul said, a finger raised, "let's talk about this. You haven't given me anything to go on. How long will I be gone? And where the hell am I going? I could use some details here, you know."

Ari nodded assent. "You're right, of course. I can't tell you everything just yet, but here are the basics." He began ticking points off on his fingers. "You'll probably be gone for several months at least, out of the country, and into some of the most inhospitable jungle wilderness you'll ever see. It's going to be brutally hard, so hard in fact that the last time I went the rest of my party didn't make it."

"What do you mean, didn't make it? They died?"

"Yes, they did." Ari stared hard at the young man's mildly shocked expression. "Still sure you want to do this? I'm not going to sugar coat it. This will be the most difficult thing you've ever done, and I'm counting your time in the Marines overseas."

Paulson took a few moments to think, his Adam's apple bobbing up and down as he gulped several times. Van Owen knew that terrible things had likely happened to him and his buddies in Afghanistan, horrific things that could haunt his nights and dreams forever. He could see that Paul was wondering how much worse it could be than that. He finally motioned for Ari to continue.

"For Mrs. Brubaker. Yeah, I'm still in. I gotta pay back my debt. When Taylor gets older I want to be able to tell my son about how I helped someone out, that I did the right thing. Go ahead, keep talking."

"Okay. Like I said we'll be gone for a while, a few months at least. I don't know for sure. But if we're successful we'll find Frankie *and* stop some other major shit from happening. This could have national implications, maybe even greater than that. You've got a passport?"

Paulson stared at him with his blue eyes wide. "Sure."

"Good. So, you still in?"

"Yeah. But suddenly I feel like I'm in so deep it'd take a week of climbing just to reach ground level."

"Yep, that sounds about right."

For the most part, Ari was good at reading people. He'd been pretty certain Paul would say yes, which was why he'd asked him to meet at the hospital. With Paulson's acquiescence their next stop was the Rehab Wing, ironically right where Frankie worked. He asked around a few minutes before they found Yvonne just wrapping up an appointment with a patient down the hall, a teenage soccer player with a recently repaired ACL. She looked up, mildly startled, when Ari knocked on the door.

"Ari, what are you doing here?" She was still sporting her blond hair in a ponytail that contrasted with her bright blue scrubs, a nice summertime combination. There was a pencil tucked behind her ear. She winked at him and said in a low voice, "No time for round two, if you know what I mean. I've got patients now."

Van Owen looked at the teenager lying on the bed, his bum knee smothered under a bag of ice. He had a despondent expression on his young face that went beyond the simple pain of his leg, and Ari imagined he was reliving the play that had cost him his season. Van Owen felt Paulson right behind him as he peered warily into the room. Other hospital staff members were coming and going, laughing, talking, speaking in hushed voices with dire news. Overhead the PA requested that a Dr. Ness contact the main desk. Ari ignored her comment about round two.

"I've got a quick favor to ask you."

Yvonne patted the shoulder of the soccer player and told him she'd see him next week, and to make sure he performed his stretches.

"And no cheating," she admonished him, her lips pursed tightly as she wagged a finger.

The young man clumsily got his crutches under him and made his way out the door, wincing as his bad leg hit the ground. They could hear the clanking of the crutches as he hobbled down the hall. Yvonne watched his retreating back before turning to Ari.

"I'm pretty backed up here, stud. What do you need?"

Van Owen stepped aside. "Yvonne, I'd like you to meet Paul Paulson. Paul, this is Yvonne Peterson. She's a friend of mine."

Yvonne's eyebrows lifted momentarily when she heard the name, remembering it from before and his association with Frankie's disappearance. Paul sheepishly stepped forward and held out his hand, almost as if he were asking the prettiest girl at the prom to dance.

"Nice to meet you," he said, his voice low, eyes down.

Yvonne grinned and took his hand. "Charmed. Nice to meet you too, Paul."

"I'd like you to check him out," Ari said. "He took some shrapnel in his knee while with the Marines overseas. He says he can't run for long distances, but I want your opinion on whether or not he can walk a long way and how bad it really is."

"You want me to check him now?"

"If you could. It's important, Yvonne."

She saw the expression on his face. "So is this about...you know who?"

"Yes it is. He's volunteered to help, but I need to know if he's physically able or not. We're headed into some extremely hostile and inhospitable terrain, places that'd take down a lot of healthy people, much less an injured one."

She exhaled noisily and picked up her clipboard, leaning her butt on the edge of the examination table. She plucked the pencil from behind her ear and used it as a pointer, poring over the schedule. Finally she made a few notations before excusing herself and crossing the hall to the girl on duty at the main Rehab desk. Ari heard her tell her to shuffle some appointments around, that something had come up. The girl started to protest but Yvonne waved away her objections. A minute later she was back in the room.

"Okay, but I'm only doing this for you, and for her."

"I understand. Thanks."

Yvonne motioned to Paul. "Come on in, soldier, and let's have a look at that leg. And you," she pointed to Ari, "you go sit in the waiting room. I'll take care of this." He tried to protest but she waved him away. "Shoo. Go read some old fishing magazines or something. Give us 30 minutes or so. He's in good hands."

It was more like an hour before they summoned him back to the room. Paulson was sitting on the end of the examination table while Yvonne was looking at some x-rays clipped into the wall-mounted viewer. There were several different shots of Paul's knee, all rendered in amazing digital clarity.

"Okay, here's the scoop," she began, completely professional now, her flirtatious manner curbed. She pulled the pencil from behind her ear and used it as a pointer again. "The shrapnel did some pretty extensive damage to our boy's knee, here and here, but it's not as bad as it could've been. He's got a hefty amount of scar tissue, and it shredded these two ligaments which either the VA or Field Hospital repaired, albeit a little clumsily. The problem, as far as I can tell, is that he didn't receive the correct rehabilitation after the fact."

"So what's that mean, in layman's terms? I need him to be able to walk a lot, and running is probable, too. I can't have him breaking down on me."

She sucked some air between her teeth and inspected the x-rays in more detail, tapping her pencil on the clipboard. "He's not some antique car, Ari," she scolded lightly, her pretty face in a scowl. She knelt down again and inspected Paulson's knee, massaging around and poking here and there gently. Paul involuntarily winced once or twice. "Anyway, physically there's nothing here that says he can't, it's more a matter of how much pain he can handle if it comes to that. I don't think anything is liable to break, if that's what you're asking. If he pushes himself it'll just hurt more and more. It's a pain threshold thing more than a physiological thing."

"So you'll sign off on him."

She held up an imperious hand. "Not so fast. I'd like to see him on a regular basis, two or three times a week, until he's improved. I doubt he'll ever be at one hundred percent, but I'd like to get him as close as possible."

Ari shook his head. "Sorry, but I doubt you're going to have that much time. We'll be shipping out soon, maybe within the week. Two at the most."

"Then he can come in everyday and I'll do what I can. Every little bit helps."

He turned to Paulson who had been staring at Yvonne in rapt silence. Van Owen had to tap him on the shoulder to get his attention.

"Huh?"

"So you've been cleared to go. Still up for it?"

The young man didn't say anything, just nodded fast. He had a hard time tearing his eyes from Yvonne, which hadn't gone unnoticed by her.

"Perfect. Hop down from there and let's go. Thanks, Yvonne."

Paulson got down off the examination table and held out his hand again, the picture of formality. "Uh, thanks, Yvonne."

Yvonne laughed once, more of an earthy chuckle, and took his hand warmly. "You're welcome, Paul. My pleasure."

Paul walked stiffly out but Ari hung back for a moment. "Thanks for doing this on such short notice. I appreciate it. When do you want to see him again?"

"Tomorrow morning at 8:00, right here, and every morning after that until you leave. And what's his story, anyway?" she asked with mild curiosity, watching the young man's receding form. She rested her hand on Van Owen's shoulder.

Ari just grinned and walked out.

Chapter 8

The dream was back, and as much as he loved seeing her again these visions were tearing him apart. Frankie was sitting by the fire like before, everything around her dead and dark and without form, without shape, as haunting as the description of the earth in the first chapter of Genesis. The fire was an eerie orange glow that did little more than illuminate her face and a small patch of ground around her. If anything she looked even thinner, her white T-shirt still dirty and wrinkled. Her green eyes shone bright in the light of the fire. One addition was a bright yellow flower she cradled in her hands.

"Hi, Frankie, it's me. I'm back again."

She sat up straight, her gaze tracking all around, but just like before couldn't see him. Their Karma symbol was still scratched into the ground at her feet. She pointed to the eight-spoked wagon wheel, focusing on the downward pointing arrow. Her eyes were wide, the whites so bright they glowed like twin full moons. Ari could tell she was terrified and it tore at his heart to see her like that and not able to do anything. It didn't matter that it was nothing more than a dream: he felt himself choking up. He couldn't help it.

"I know, sweetheart. I'm coming as soon as I can. I'm coming to the jungle to find you. Just hold on."

Then as before flashing lights and the cracking sounds of gunfire erupted around her and rough hands burst from the darkness, roughly dragging her away as she screamed soundlessly. But this time a single object was left behind on the ground by the fire. He wasn't sure what it was for a moment, then saw that it was a hat, a brown fedora with a black band, its brim just beginning to smolder as the fire spat a spark on it. The rim of the fedora burned sedately for a few seconds before it flashed magnesium white, then the whole scene was gone.

Ari gasped and woke up. He wiped sweat from his face and looked at the clock. It was 5:00 AM on the nose. His bedroom was pitch black save for the green glow of the clock. He roughly kicked off the covers and rolled away from the abnormally bright glow, facing the wall, while he waited for his heart to slow. After ten minutes of staring sightless into the darkness he relented and got up to make coffee. These goddam dreams were killing him.

His cell phone rang several hours later.

"Hi, Hal."

"Ari? Good morning. How's your team shaping up?"

"I got my guy, so I'm all set on my end. You?"

"Really? Already? I'm impressed, but then I guess I shouldn't be. Look who I'm talking to."

Ari grunted. "Whatever. You said you had someone in mind, right?"

"I did, and I do. I'm in the car on my way over. I'll be there with my man in about two hours so we can meet and plan our next move."

Ari nodded, equally impressed. He considered asking who it was but understood that if Hal wanted him to know he'd have told him already. Chances were he didn't know the guy anyway, and it was probably another field agent. "Good. The sooner the better. I've got my list of supplies ready. I'll probably be in the garage working on the Firebird. Just come on in when you get here."

Hollenbeck hung up and Ari headed outside. The morning was cool and clear, the only sounds were the crunching of his feet on the gravel driveway and several jets straining for altitude far overhead. The faint contrails they left behind slowly thinned and grew wider, like white watercolor brushstrokes painted on the blue backdrop of the sky, pretty in their own, ephemeral way. He unlocked the garage door and flicked on the lights. With a muted hum they lit up the inside with their unforgiving, soulless light.

Van Owen felt his face loosen in a small grin as he surveyed his project. The old Firebird was covered with a light patina of dust, just enough to mute the dark green and make it appear nearly matte black instead. He ran his finger along the huge chrome bumper.

"Hi, darlin', how are you today? You're looking well, as always."

He checked the pressure on the big compressor by the door and saw the gauge still read 150 psi, more than enough in case he needed it. For the next few hours he gratefully lost himself in working on the car, mainly tinkering with some of the mechanicals of the brakes and manual transmission linkage, but truly taking this small window of time to lose himself. Ari had a gut feeling that in the near future he'd be looking back on this relaxing, rather empty time with envy. Focusing on the car he had earlier noticed a hitch in that linkage when he shifted quickly from first to second gear, and finally found where it was binding up. A little tweaking and some elbow grease cleared that up to the point where each shift was clean and smooth, just the way it had been, straight off the manufacturing line in Michigan back in the mid-60s. Forward progress was still being made, which gave him a small measure of satisfaction. He stood and stretched out his back, hands on hips, cracking sounds running up and down his spine.

"Not bad," he observed of the morning's work so far.

He checked the time on his phone and was surprised to see how late in the day it was already, almost noon. Figuring Hal would be along shortly he began to clean up, placing each tool precisely where it belonged after wiping away any grease or dirt. He performed this task thoroughly but absently, his mind clearly elsewhere. Anticipation over the upcoming Amazon trip was beginning to set in, which typically meant there was so much to do, so many preparations to make – and almost no time to get any of it done. This was *not* the way to survive a trip to the Amazon. He especially didn't like leaving so much of the preparation to someone else, even if it was Hal, one of the most trustworthy people he knew.

He set the last wrench down in the drawer of the toolbox, lining it up next to its neighbor where it gleamed in the bright lights.

He dimly heard a car pull up and two sets of doors clunk shut. He continued putting tools away and a few moments later heard footsteps on the gravel outside the garage. In typical Hal fashion he didn't yell out for Ari or draw attention to himself. He was just too careful for that. He peeked his head into the garage and saw him arranging his work area.

"Good afternoon, Ari."

Van Owen grabbed a white rag and wiped off his hands. He nodded toward the agent. "Hey, Hal."

Hollenbeck walked in. As usual he was in khakis, a button down shirt, and a cream-colored jacket that was doing a pretty sound job of hiding the ubiquitous bulge under his arm. In his right hand he was carrying a black plastic case about the size of a kid's lunchbox. His thinning blond hair was slightly mussed from being outside in the breeze.

Ari motioned to the box. "What's that?"

Hal set the plastic case on the hood of the Firebird. He looked over the car and nodded with appreciation. "It's looking pretty good. You've made some progress. The paint job is perfect. Did you do that?"

"No, I hired that out. It's outside my skill-set." Van Owen carefully picked up the black case from the hood and set it on his workbench. It was heavier than he expected. "And let's not hurt the paint, please. It's still very susceptible to scratching and will be for a while yet."

"Sorry." Hal moved around the Firebird and made positive murmuring sounds. He ran his finger along the large chrome bumper, much as Ari did each time he came in. He leaned over the driver's door and checked out the inside, still nodding. Ari peered out the door trying to spot the second person, but couldn't see anyone.

Finally Hal straightened up and wiped the traces of dust from his hands. "So you got your man lined up already for the trip? Who is it, if I may ask?"

"Paul Paulson, the security guard from the hospital."

The agent's eyebrows arched. "The young guy who took the bribe? Really?"

Ari had expected this reaction and was ready for it. "Sure. He's an ex-Marine who saw several tours of duty overseas and likely knows how to handle himself in a fight. He feels terrible about what he did and is looking hard at some way to atone for his part in it. Plus he sees this chance of working with the FBI as the fulfillment of a dream of his, too. He's always wanted to be a part of a serious law enforcement team. I can't think of anyone better."

"That may be so, but the kid took a bribe once already. He's shown that he can be had. Do you really trust that?"

"I do. I think he's perfect."

"And physically? Wasn't he wounded in action? Something with his knee, I think. Can he make it?"

Ari nodded. "I think so, yes. I had my friend Yvonne from the hospital check him out. It's not as bad as he thought, or at least we don't think so. He's going to work with her until we take off. He'll be fine." Van Owen really hoped he would be but didn't admit that. Deep down he was concerned the knee injury could cause problems at some point in the future. He just had to hope the young man could take it. It could be very bad for him if he couldn't.

Hal's silence conveyed his thoughts, that he was dubious and unconvinced. He smoothly removed his glasses and cleaned them on the hem of his jacket.

"Trust me, Hal. The guy will be fine. So," he said, changing the subject, "who'd you get? I gather he's out there right now? I didn't see him."

"I want to show you something first." He opened the black case he'd brought with him and slid it on the workbench toward Ari.

138

Inside was a black handgun nestled in thick grey foam. Two separate clips were tucked alongside it.

"What the hell is this for?" Ari asked warily as he eyed the pistol.

"It's for you, for protection. You know how to shoot one, right?"

"Well, yeah. I had to take all those classes at Quantico when I first started helping you out. But, Hal, I'm not a gun guy. I don't even like them, you know that."

"But you still remember everything?"

"In theory, sure, but I doubt it's like riding a bike. I'm a pretty good shot but I haven't used one in years." He pushed the black case back toward the agent. The plastic made a crunching sound as it slid over the gritty top of the workbench. "I don't need one, thanks."

"I disagree. We're getting deeper into this now, and like it or not you may need protection and I can't be around all the time. These people are serious. Take it. If not for me, for Frankie – you can't help her if something happens to you. Please."

Hal's reference to Frankie was an overt and transparent tug on his heartstrings, Ari realized. However in the end, even though he knew the agent was more concerned with finding the source of the Ice drug than Frankie, it did what the agent had intended. Van Owen grunted and scrutinized the weapon more closely. As with most things mechanical he admired it for its craftsmanship and near-flawless engineering. Decades of research and untold millions had gone in to the development and refinement of this and other guns like it, he knew. He didn't much care for the ultimate reason for its very existence, but he couldn't help but appreciate it on a more basic level. He stared at it warily, in no hurry to touch it.

"What exactly is it?"

Hollenbeck lifted the handgun from the foam with practiced, comfortable ease. "It's a Glock 22, a .40 caliber. The clip holds fifteen rounds. You remember how to load a round into the chamber?"

"Sure. You slide the top back to load and cock it."

"Right. Then you can fire just as fast as you can pull the trigger, until the clip is empty that is. Test question: where's the safety?"

Ari considered for a moment, thinking back to his training in Virginia. "This is a Glock, so there isn't one, not really. It's built into the trigger, and pulling the trigger disengages the safety automatically. But listen, Hal, I really..."

"That's right," he said, interrupting him. "This model is the same one I use. It's strong enough to punch a hole right through both sides of a car if necessary. It's much better than the old .45s we used to use. Easier to handle, lighter, low recoil, and virtually jam proof." He held it out butt-first to Ari. Its flat black surface seemed to suck up the light around it.

"No, thanks. Really, I'll be fine. I don't need to play with it."

Hollenbeck stared at him for a few moments. Finally he nodded and tucked the weapon back into the foam. He left the lid open.

"The clip's full and there's a bullet in the chamber right now. The other two clips are full, too. If you ever need more rounds than that..." He trailed off, the unspoken meaning clear. If Ari needed more rounds than that he'd be in so deep that a thousand bullets wouldn't help matters much. He had to agree.

"Hal, I really don't see why this is even necessary. There won't be any trouble."

"You never know. Now, just promise me you won't lose it – it's registered to the Bureau and that could get awkward, especially if word got out to the press. Okay?"

"If you took it back we wouldn't have to worry at all."

Hal ignored him and flipped the case closed, but didn't latch it. Sitting there on the workbench it looked like any other power tool case inhabiting that tidy and organized area. It seemed the matter was closed.

"So you're ready to meet the fourth member of our Amazon team?"

"Yeah, sure. Let's get going. I keep telling you that the more time we spend up here the harder it's going to be to find Frankie. We've wasted too much time already." Ari reached into his pocket and handed the agent a piece of paper. "Here's a list of the supplies I took on my last trip. I've checked off what I already have. Use this as a guide when you're putting our stuff together."

"You're right, of course. Now that we've got our personnel lined up things should move pretty fast." Hal leaned back against the workbench, his hands resting on its rough surface. If he was worried about getting dirty he didn't show it. Van Owen swore that the man was Teflon coated. "Like you, Ari, I had someone in mind when we began considering who to take. We needed a person with an intimate knowledge of the situation, and someone fit enough to not be a detriment to the group. None of us have your unique knowledge of the jungle and how to survive down there, of course: we're counting on you for that. But I wanted someone with a stake in all this. I asked, and after he had a day to think about it he accepted."

"Okay, fine. Who the hell is it?"

"But I also need you to promise that you two will get along. It's a long way to Mato Grosso. Finding the source of the Ice drug and SOP is too important."

"And finding Frankie. That's why I'm in this, Hal. To find Frankie."

"Right, I understand that. However I have a feeling that if we find one of them we'll find the other. But I need your word on this."

Ari was getting impatient and the edge to his voice showed it. "Fine, whatever. You've got my word. Let's get going."

"Good." Hal pushed himself away from the workbench and walked to the open door. He raised his voice a bit and yelled, "Okay, come on in."

Two seconds later Butch Brubaker walked into the garage.

Chapter 9

Ari felt his face freeze, as if all muscular control had seized. He'd had more Butch sightings in the last week than he'd had in years, but that didn't change how he felt when seeing him. His eyes narrowed involuntarily and his pulse skyrocketed. The two stood there silently, staring at each other, two gunslingers ready for a shootout in a dusty western street. All that was missing was the eerie, haunting soundtrack.

"You of course know Butch Brubaker."

Van Owen nodded curtly, a single jerk of his head. His mouth had suddenly gone dry, Sahara dry, surface of the moon dry. His tongue was no more than a piece of driftwood.

"Good. Butch has agreed to help us," he said, referring to him in the third person even though the man was standing in the doorway. "At this point I've only filled him in a little bit, just enough so he can make a decision. He's agreed to help so he can find his wife. Right, Butch?"

Brubaker nodded back, his expression neutral, like something he'd practiced in a mirror. All traces of the anger he'd evinced days earlier were still nowhere to be seen.

"Excellent," Hal continued. "Now I know there's history between you two, but this is all bigger than that, so I expect both of you," he looked pointedly from one to the other, "to get along. Our goal of finding Ms. Brubaker and completing the mission is too important to be jeopardized by any lingering personal issues. I'm not going to have you shake hands like you've just had some middle-school playground dust up, but I won't put up with any infighting either. We can't do that." He swiveled his head back and forth between the two silent men, his eyebrows arched in a question. "Do we have a deal?"

Butch was the first to respond. "Sure, yeah, no problem. I'm just here to find my wife. That's all," he said, his voice flat but sounding sincere.

Hal looked at Ari. "And you?"

Van Owen forced his jaw to unclench and manufactured an expression as passive as possible. He blew air slowly through pursed lips but stopped as soon as he realized he was doing it. A smile was out of the question.

"Yeah, I'm good. You asked me to help, and that's why I'm here. No worries."

Whether or not the agent believed either one of them was impossible to know. Regardless he plowed ahead, all business. "Great. Now that we've got our Kumbaya moment over with we need to get to work. Ari, how soon can you be ready?"

"Right away. As soon as you get the supplies and equipment on the list I gave you. That's in your court. I've got a lot of my stuff all ready to go. "

"I'm working on that now. Butch, how about you?"

Butch jerked a fraction, as if his mind had wandered elsewhere. "Um, as soon as you need me, I guess. You've already cleared this with my boss, right? I guess I can go anytime. There's nothing else going on here that I need to worry about."

"Okay, that's great. Please head back out and wait in the car and I'll be there in a minute. I'll give you some more details on the drive back to your place."

Brubaker left without another word. As soon as he was out the door the tension in garage began to dissipate, as if a lit fuse had been pinched out. Hollenbeck stared at the door for a moment before turning back to Ari.

"That went better than I expected," he said finally, taking off his glasses and inspecting them in the fluorescent lights. "Well done."

"Well done? What the hell? Was that really necessary?" Ari snapped, his ire bubbling over. "Why in the world are you bringing him along? Butch being in our little gang of four isn't going to change my mind about going, but it won't make it more pleasant."

Hal buffed the lenses on his glasses then slid them back on. "Yes, it was necessary. I needed to see you two tossed together to make sure you could get along. And he knows Frankie better than you do, if you think about it. He may have insights along the way that you or I would miss." He took a step toward Van Owen, his head angled downward, voice lowered as he argued his case. He sounded both genuine and determined. "Think about it, Ari – he's been married to Frankie and living with her for years. Years. He knows her intimately and recently. You can't discount that. Take a step back and you'll see it's the right thing to do. We'll need him."

Grudgingly Van Owen considered the agent's reasoning, and as much as he hated to admit it Hal was probably right. By his own admission his memory of her was beginning to blur and fade, whereas Butch's was fresh and personal. He was still stuck thinking with his heart instead of his head, something he'd have to be wary of during their upcoming journey. It was coloring his judgment. But this was for Frankie's sake, he reminded himself.

"Okay, fine. I get it, he should come."

"I don't expect you two to become best buddies or anything," Hal admitted. "But you never know when he'll come in handy. Trust me. And he told me he's been a sportsman his entire life. An avid hunter. Having someone else that knows how to handle himself can't hurt either."

"I said fine. Let's change the subject, okay?"

Hal smiled briefly and walked to the door. "I'll be back in touch the next day or two. You and Paul Paulson get ready to go. If he needs anything, just charge it and I'll reimburse you. How much have you told him about this?"

"Not much. He didn't ask and I figured less was better in this case."

"Good. Get him what he needs in the way of clothes and personal supplies and be ready. Once I have everything lined up on my end we'll be out of here pretty fast. Five or six days, tops. Leave the flights up to me."

Ari nodded at him. "I'll be all set."

Hal allowed a small smile, one that softened his expression and showed a few laugh lines around his mouth. "Yeah, you will. That's never been a problem for you." He pointed to the workbench at the back of the garage. "And don't lose my gun."

Van Owen gave the black case a little impatient shove away from him. "Don't worry. I'm just going to lock it up in here. You know me, I don't like those things."

Later that afternoon Ari gathered up Paul Paulson and together they went shopping. Their first stop was an outdoor outfitter store near the Oxmoor Mall on the southeast side of Louisville. It was a warm afternoon, the sun shining brightly and reflecting off the windshields of the hundreds of parked cars, SUVs, and trucks in the massive parking lot.

"So why are we here?" Paulson asked as he shut the pickup's door. He walked around toward the front of the truck, a slight limp evident. "And I mean here at the mall, not in the more biblical sense."

Ari pointed toward the young man's bad leg. "How's the knee?"

Paul steadied himself on the hood of the truck and flexed it. "Sore, right now. Yvonne is really working it hard. We've only been at it for a few days and I think it hurts more now than before." He winced a bit as he continued moving it around.

Van Owen gave him a pat on the shoulder. "Don't worry about it. She's as good as they come. If anybody can fix you up it'll be her. Just keep doing what she says." His warm words belied what he really thought, that maybe he'd chosen poorly and Paulson wouldn't be able to make it. But it was simply too late to make any changes now.

The big box outdoor outfitters store wasn't crowded this time of the day. Some gentle Muzak played over hidden speakers, punctuated now and then by announcements concerning sales in such and such a department. The burbling of water from an enormous fish tank, easily as big as a small semi, worked to promote the sensation of being outside. The inside air was bordering on chilly. Paulson shivered.

"Damn. Shouldn't have worn shorts, I guess. So what are we getting here?"

Ari directed him around a wall of guns and fishing gear, over to the footwear and hiking shoe section. "Remember when you said you like to Think, Plan, then Act? We're in the planning phase now. We've got to pick up a few things for the trip, starting with boots. Then some appropriate pants and some long sleeve shirts."

"Um, I already have some boots and jeans. And won't it be hotter than hell down there? No shorts?"

"Nope. No shorts, and no short sleeve shirts, either. Way too many things down there that can sting, bite, slither and ooze. We always wear high leather boots, long pants, long sleeves, and hats. And jeans are too heavy, especially if they get wet – which they will. There are better choices." He stood in front of a long rack of ankle and calf-high leather boots. There were some high-tech looking hiking numbers constructed of leather and nylon. Ari skipped over those and went right to the section housing all leather models that laced up high, well past the ankle.

"Not the fancy ones?" Paul asked, picking up a green and brown nylon and leather pair. "It says they're waterproof and good for any conditions."

"They're light and comfortable, yes, but that nylon around the ankle area won't always stop a snake bite, or half the other nasty things down there. And good leather ones are waterproof, too, and can generally take more punishment." He picked up a dark leather pair that laced high. "What size for you?"

"Twelves, usually."

Ari looked the shorter, stockier man up and down dubiously. "Twelves? Really? I only wear elevens."

Paulson grinned. "Yep, twelves. Hey, know what they say about a guy with big feet?"

"Hmm. I have an idea, yes."

"He wears big socks," Paul replied with a wider smile, pleased at his own joke.

"Funny. Here, try these on and let me know what you think."

Still grinning, he sat and pulled the new boots on then laced them up. "Hey, these feel pretty good. They might be a little tight through my foot, though. A little narrow."

Ari found a salesman, an older gentleman with short gray hair and a name badge pinned to his store-issued plaid shirt that proclaimed in bold type that his name was MAX. Max agreed that Paul needed a wider version and walked briskly into the back room to locate a different pair. As they waited Paul leaned against the rack of shoes and looked at Van Owen.

"So, is it time to tell me what's going on here?"

"What do you mean?"

"Come on, you know what I mean. All this. Getting me out of work, buying me stuff, the whole trip thing. This can't all be just to find Mrs. Brubaker."

Ari was impressed that the young man had picked up on this so quickly. He'd been hoping that finding Frankie would be cover enough for now, but apparently that wasn't going to be the case. Even with the role Paulson had directly or indirectly played in

Frankie's disappearance, he decided that he deserved to know precisely what he was getting into. He nodded.

"You're right, this isn't all about finding Frankie," he admitted. "There's a lot more at stake than you can imagine."

Paulson set the poorly fitted boots down. "Yeah, I figured as much."

Just then Max the salesman hustled back with several green boxes cradled in his arms and they stopped talking. Paulson tried on two different versions of the same boot, finally settling on a slightly wider version of the original. Ari thanked Max for his help and accepted the oversized box.

Paul checked the price tag on the boots, his blue eyes wide. "Three hundred bucks for boots? That's crazy."

"Worth every penny. You can't imagine how important dry and comfortable feet can be. And don't worry, I'm getting reimbursed for everything."

Paul arched an eyebrow. "Oh, really. By who?"

Ari began walking toward the clothing department, Paul beside him. "Let's just say we've got a rich uncle taking care of us."

"We've got a rich uncle? Like Uncle Sam, perhaps? Is this our tax dollars at work?"

Van Owen just raised his eyebrows at him, his face otherwise expressionless, and stopped beside a long rack of men's outdoor pants and shirts. He rummaged around until he found the general style he was looking for: a tough nylon blend with lots of Velcro pockets and zippers just above the knees.

"What's your inseam?"

"Thirty or thirty-one, depending on the pants."

He pulled out a pair of dark tan ones and unclipped them from a hanger. He handed them to Paul. "Here. Go try these on."

"And then we'll talk some more?"

"Yes, and then we'll talk some more."

He was gone only a few minutes. When he returned he came out, spinning slowly in front of Ari like a runway model, his bad knee barely evident. The fabric made a muted swishing noise when he walked.

"Got lucky this time. Perfect fit right off the bat."

"Good. And they've got a drawstring inside?"

Paulson checked. "Yes. Why?"

"In case you lose weight. You don't want them to fall off if you get skinny."

The young man's eyes opened wide for a moment as it dawned on him again just what he might be getting into, that this expedition was going to be more rigorous than most anything he had done before - perhaps even tougher than his tours of duty overseas. He changed back into his street clothes and handed the pants to Ari.

"Only eighty bucks for these. Now what?"

Van Owen grabbed another pair to have as backup on the trip. As he folded the clothing up he glanced around to make certain they were alone before he started talking again.

"You're right. There's more to this than simply saving Frankie, although that's my main reason for going."

"I figured as much. What's really happening here?"

Ari asked if he'd read or seen anything on the plane crash. Paulson had, noting that it had gone down not far from his house and had kind of freaked him out.

"And did you hear about that Reds' player suddenly dying? That infielder named Garrafon?"

"Yeah, sure. That was a bummer, and weird, too. Professional athletes don't usually drop over dead of a heart attack."

"You're right, they don't. Those events and about a dozen others that haven't gone public yet are what this is all about." Ari proceeded to fill him in on everything he knew so far: that other episodes of sudden onset paralysis had been discovered; the flight attendant Alyssa Morris' tale of the pilot and first officer and how

150

they had appeared frozen by SOP; how Garrafon had likely died of the same thing; that the newest performance enhancing drug on the streets, Ice, was now chemically linked to SOP but was still virtually undetectable; and lastly, how the man in the fedora had been connected to both Frankie's disappearance and Garrafon's death. He didn't omit anything vital to the case, even covering the karma symbol on Frankie's SUV at the impound lot. The one thing he didn't talk about was his recurring dreams of Frankie in the jungle. Those were too deeply personal and probably not relevant.

During all this Ari had been sorting through long-sleeved shirts that might be appropriate. They were of the same basic material as the pants and festooned with many pockets, zippers, and tabs. He held several out to Paul.

Paulson was staring at him with wide eyes, his mouth a little slack. Van Owen had to nudge him to get his attention.

"You okay?"

"Um, yeah, I guess. This is a lot to take in, you know? You weren't kidding when you said before that other stuff was going on that could have huge implications. This is some serious shit." He took the offered shirts.

"Yes it is. Go try those on and let me know how they fit."

The younger man walked off in something of a mental fog to the fitting rooms, Ari staring at his receding back. At heart he figured he was a good kid, albeit a desperate one that had screwed up. He just hoped and prayed that Paulson was up to this, both physically and mentally.

Five minutes later he returned, still looking slightly dazed but resolute, his mouth set in a harder line than Ari had seen before. He may have been a little pale, but that could have been the lighting in the store.

"They fit?"

Paulson nodded. "Yeah, fine. That materials a little funky, but it's okay."

"Good. The fabric is a nylon cotton blend that dries fast and is tough as Tyvek. It won't rip or tear and it's almost impossible to cut. It's perfect for our work down there."

Van Owen waited for him to say something else, but when he didn't the two of them went to the cash register and checked out. The bill was over six hundred dollars, which, Ari knew, was a bargain in the long run. He pocketed the receipt.

"I need to get more stuff for you but I can do that on my own later. This should do for now." Together they walked out to the parked car. The afternoon sun was still warm, the sky nearly cloudless. It was another beautiful spring day in Kentucky. Traffic on the nearby Watterson Expressway was flowing well, a thousand tires hissing along the asphalt lanes, each driver only nominally aware of anything happening outside their small rubber and steel universe. Finally Paulson spoke.

"This is going to be a real bitch, isn't it?" he said, his voice uncharacteristically soft. Ari almost couldn't hear him. "This trip. It's going to be a bitch."

He nodded. "Yes, it is. You can still back out, you know. There's no shame in getting out."

They had reached the car. Paulson was on one side, Ari on the other. They looked at each other over the roof, their images ever so slightly blurred by the heat radiating off the silver paint. The young man was as serious as Van Owen had ever seen him, his blue eyes hard and focused, unblinking. Ari imagined this is what Paul looked like in battle, all humor and levity smashed to bits and swept aside, the Marine in him showing through.

"No, that's where you're wrong, Ari. I couldn't live with myself if I didn't go. How could I? And how could I face my son again?"

Ari didn't say a word. He didn't have to. He unlocked the doors and they both got in, then drove in silence back to Paulson's condo.

Chapter 10

With the trip in the immediate offing Ari was finally in a better frame of mind. He spent several hours in his office that evening poring over the Fawcett papers he'd received from his friend Sir Alex Hanes at the Royal Geographic Society. As Sir Alex had noted in his letter, these recently unearthed documents at first blush seemed to confirm conventional wisdom and known facts about the Colonel's whereabouts on his final trip. The final entries from Fawcett talked about being at Dead Horse Camp, right when they were supposed to be there. Ari ran his fingers through his permanently unruly brown hair. He was bouncing back and forth between his maps and the scanned documents in a fact checking frenzy, plotting coordinates and dates and stated locations from previous assumptions. From what he could see everything checked out when compared to previous assumptions. But still it didn't feel right.

"You crafty old dog," Van Owen muttered in restrained admiration. "What were you really up to, I wonder…"

After another few hours of making notes and observations he moved online, thankful that he had finally gotten broadband access at home. He was also beginning to understand how very useful Google and the other search engines could be at uncovering stray facts and oddball information, much of which would've taken him days or weeks to uncover at a large library – if he could've found it at all. The days of searching through dusty old tomes, periodicals, and microfiche were becoming passé. A small, traditionalist slice of him mourned that passing, but the eminently practical side of him was ecstatic.

The sections of scanned documents pertaining to Fawcett's notes and missives to his wife were of particular consideration to Ari. They were a combination of love letters, daily journals, and scribbled observations. It was clear as he pored over them that the Colonel had been enamored with his wife, what with all the times he used phrases like "My dearest Nina," and "My lovely darling." It was sweet, actually, that two people separated by so much distance and who saw each other so rarely still had such strong feelings for each other. Delving into the scans there were dozens of references to places they had gone and activities they had enjoyed together, such as plays and concerts, dinners out, lectures, and visits with friends - all of the things expected of an upper middle-class couple in early 1900s England. There were specific events mentioned as well, such as the time the two of them attended a play in London by a certain J.M. Synge called "The Playboy of the Western World", which had caused some unrest and ruckus at its debut in Dublin several years before. Most of the plays and other mentions of theater weren't familiar to him, even if some of the playwrights themselves were, such as George Bernard Shaw and Noel Coward. Ari continued reading and rereading the scanned images well into the night and making notes, most of which consisted of little more than question marks and arrows pointing here and there to different pages and corresponding locales on the maps. Staring at everything he just knew there was something there, he was sure of it. If only he could see it…

At some point later in the evening he woke up with his head on the desk and a mass of yellow sticky notes stuck to his face. A string of drool stretched away from his mouth as he lifted his head, and the corners of his eyes were crusty with sleep. The clock on his desk read just after two in the morning. Van Owen silently wiped the yellow Post-its from his face and pushed himself away from his messy desk, trudging heavily to the bedroom and flopping into bed with all his clothes on. He was back asleep in an instant, not even bothering to turn off the light.

At 4:59 in the morning Ari gasped and shot upright in his bed, covers flying off, his body covered in sweat. His eyes were wide and his heart was banging in his chest harder than a straining diesel engine. The Frankie dream hadn't made an appearance, not this time, not that he could remember at least. But he had this sudden sense of dread, of loss, that was impacting him in a physiological way. He continued sitting up in bed while his breathing and heart rate slowed, finally getting up and stripping off his clothes and sliding on an old pair of running shorts and a T-shirt. Awake now, he padded back to his office and powered up the PC. While he waited for it to get up to speed he tidied up some of the loose papers and yellow sticky notes littering his desk. His fingers idled next to the keyboard, drumming quietly, until he finally fired up his Internet browser and opened Facebook. He expertly navigated to Frankie's page, not expecting to see any changes, and wasn't surprised when there weren't any. Ari stared at her profile picture for a full minute, her bright green eyes seeming to look into and through him, just like before, just like always. He browsed around her personal information for a few minutes and checked out some older pictures, some just of her, others with her and Butch. He clicked through those quickly. There was nothing else to see and he was beginning to feel a bit too much like a cyber-stalker, so he clicked off the monitor and went back to bed. He wasn't even aware that he was rather tunelessly humming Green Eyes under his breath.

Later that morning, after a quick breakfast and a little more time reading and rereading the Fawcett scans, Ari tossed all the papers onto his desk and decided to work on the Firebird for a while. He needed to let his mind wander, to rearrange the complex jigsaw puzzle pieces of notions and vague concepts he had rattling around in his head. He knew himself well enough, knew from experience, too, that by not concentrating on the problems and questions at hand that he had a much better chance of them crystalizing into something useful. He hoped so, at least, because nothing good was coming of his time in the office.

It was about ten o'clock in the morning when he unlocked the small garage entrance and went inside. The garage itself was bigger than most and had likely been used as a shed for farm equipment in an earlier age. It was easily as wide as a typical residential two-car garage, but was so long he could've parked at least two Firebirds end to end and still had room left over for a dinner party of eight. There was always the underlying scent of petroleum products coupled with wet earth, like an old-fashioned, dirt-floored cellar that housed a fuel oil furnace. Van Owen ambled around the forest green car, running the tip of his index finger along the huge chrome bumper and doorsills, admiring the clean lines of the classic ride. He figured he was over seventy-five percent done now, and not for the first time wondered what he would do when it was finally finished. Sell it? Drive it? Find another wreck and begin again? He truly didn't know, and was a little scared to think that far ahead, to consider that another chunk of his being would be empty and vacant when this very special project was done. He could drag out the restoration for many more months, he was sure, through the summer at least, but at some point it was going to be finished. And then what? What would he do then?

He'd once had an Army surplus blanket that he'd picked up for a few bucks at a garage sale. The dark green wool blanket was so heavy and thick it felt capable of deflecting a knife thrust. But when he'd covered up with the damn thing it was so heavy it felt oppressive, suffocating. In the end he couldn't use it and gave it away. Looking at the Firebird and his progress there, and thinking about Frankie and the impossibility of their relationship, everything suddenly came to a head and a thick depression settled over him. It was as if he could feel the dark green blanket drawing tight around him, could feel its stifling, overwhelming weight bearing down on him, covering his head and face, making breathing difficult…

Ari shook himself and momentarily put his face in his hands. He had to lean against the car. He stood that way several seconds or minutes, he didn't know how long. Only the thought of finding Frankie, of making sure she was safe, brought him back from that dark, empty place in his mind. He stood there for another few minutes and listened to his now steady breathing and the soft humming of the fluorescent lights. Outside he thought he heard a gentle thud, that unique sound of a car door carefully shutting, but he wasn't sure and no other noises followed. Because he didn't know what else to do but felt the need to do something, anything, he turned on the car radio, hoping that some music might shake off this sudden funk. The radio was still on the college station and the song came on louder than he had planned. It was something pretty mellow by the rock band Green Day. Ari knew the song, "21 Guns", but not well enough to understand or follow the lyrics. For this band it was a pretty melodic tune, not at all head-banging, with plenty of acoustic guitar and piano. After a time he felt his more traditional calm, steady self slowly returning, the suffocating sensation of the heavy blanket dissipating. It wasn't completely gone, not by a long shot, but for now it had receded to little more than a dark line in the horizon of his mind.

He took a deep breath and exhaled noisily through his lips, his arms crossed protectively across his chest. The Green Day song continued but Ari wasn't paying attention any longer. He wandered over to his tool bench to unnecessarily tidy it up. He grabbed a towel and mindlessly wiped off the countertop, brushing nonexistent dirt and grit into his palm to be thrown away.

As he turned towards the trashcan the door at the other end of the garage opened and a man walked in. He was short with very black hair slicked back and a complexion the color of light chocolate. His face was wide with dark eyes set far apart. He had puffy, heavy cheeks, like a chipmunk with a peanut jammed in either side. The man saw Ari and smiled, a friendly and confident smile that showed very white, evenly spaced teeth. He was wearing jeans and boots, a tan T-shirt, and a dark jacket. Van Owen placed his lineage as Mexican or Central American, definitely somewhere south of the border.

"Hi, good morning," the man said cheerfully, no accent of any kind evident. "My name is Ronaldo and I'm looking for Arjen Van Owen. Can you help me?"

As usual Ari involuntarily bristled at the use of his full first name. "I'm Ari. What can I do for you?"

"Oh, good. I've got someone who wants to meet you." He turned and yelled outside, "Está bién. Él está aquí."

Van Owen started to ask what this was all about when Ronaldo stepped back inside a few more paces. Seconds later a huge, enormous man entered. He was so tall he had to duck low just to clear the doorway. When he stood to his full height Ari guessed he was over seven feet tall, taller than most professional basketball players but husky and thick, muscular through and through. He had black hair parted down the middle and falling almost to his shoulders, hair that served to obscure most of his features. Ari could just make out a thick, heavy brow over black eyes and skin that looked pocked and scarred, as if he had suffered horrible acne earlier in life. A deep purple scar ran down his left cheek. He towered over Ronaldo. Something inside, something primitive and raw, made Ari take a cautious step backwards. He sucked in a quick breath as he made a mental connection.

Holy shit, it was him. The man who had taken Frankie, he knew. This was the giant that Paulson had described. It had to be.

Then a third man entered and stood next to the giant. Standing by himself he would've been considered rather tall, well over six feet, but next to the big man he looked downright ordinary. He was darker-skinned as well, but thin, almost emaciated, with hollow cheeks and wide, bulging frog eyes. The sides of his head were shaved to the scalp but he sported a long, braided ponytail that fell nearly to the center of his back. It was an odd combination that normally would have captured anyone's attention, but Ari only had eyes for the huge man, the man that had to be one of Frankie's abductors.

Van Owen continued to stare, then took another step back and groped around on the tool bench until his right hand stumbled on something heavy and substantial, a large wrench. He picked it up and cradled the heavier end in his left hand, not hiding his actions from the trio that stood about twenty feet away. He had no idea what was happening but he suddenly felt trapped; sweat beaded up on his forehead faster than condensation on a cold glass, and the hair on the back of his neck was standing at full attention.

"What's all this about?" His voice sounded calm and even, which surprised him. He didn't feel that way at all.

The giant spoke in a foreign language softly toward the third man, but his eyes were locked on Ari. It sounded like Spanish, but he wasn't sure. The third man didn't wait for the sentence to end but began speaking immediately.

"You are Arjen Van Owen. My name is Señor Gonzalez. You need to come with us now. We want to discuss some important matters with you. Please put down the tool and come with us."

Ari didn't drop the tool. In fact he gripped it more tightly although the cool metal felt slick in his sweaty hands. "No, I don't think so. You want to talk, then talk, but stay where you are."

The translator spoke at the same time Ari did, his voice low but distinct. Again, it sounded like Spanish, but he couldn't be sure since he only knew a smattering of the language. Gonzalez compressed his lips at Ari's refusal and began talking. The third man spoke without hesitation. Despite himself and the surreal situation, Van Owen was very impressed with the instantaneous translation that was going on in front of him. It was a rare individual who was capable of doing that.

"That is not acceptable. You will come with us, or we will make you come with us."

"Sorry. That's not going to happen. And you, Gonzalez" he said, pointing at the giant with the wrench, "what have you done with Frankie Brubaker? You took her in the parking lot of the hospital. Where is she?"

The big man drew himself up to his full height and growled something low and threatening. His dark eyes flashed. Ari never would've guessed that he was in charge of this group. As large as he was he figured he'd be the muscle, not the leader.

"You are clever, that much is certain, and you have just given us more reason to talk. However, there are three of us, and one of you, and you don't strike us as much of a fighter. This is your last chance to come along quietly, otherwise…" He paused. Ronaldo, the first man in, lifted his jacket and showed a holstered pistol of some sort, something black and mean-looking. The translator reached behind him and brandished a handgun as well. He waved it in Ari's direction before stuffing it back into the waistband of his pants.

"You see," he continued, still translating Gonzalez's words, "you can make this easy, or you can make this hard. It is your choice. Now come with us."

Ari stared at the trio blocking his only way out. The heft of the wrench in his hands felt both comforting and useless at the same time. They were right: he'd never been much of a fighter, not really, and honestly couldn't recall the last time he'd had to defend himself with anything more than words and his wits. He would never be able to do any real damage to these three before they subdued him – or worse. Especially the giant. He couldn't get over the sheer "immenseness" of the man.

But Frankie was still out there, and she needed him, and these three knew something about it. Ari was probably the only person that could help her. He couldn't let them take him to God knew where, to do God knew what. He had to help himself so he could help her. He had to, for both their sakes.

A strange inner calm settled over him then, a calm that was both physical and mental. As he began a slow movement to put the wrench back on the tool bench he understood that passion, sometimes, could make people perform acts they never thought they'd be capable of doing. The intruders saw him putting the big wrench back and relaxed, just for a second.

As the handle of the tool clunked on the wood surface he reached beyond it to the black plastic box. He quickly flipped open the lid and grabbed the Glock 22, pointing it with both hands at the giant, directly at his chest.

The two men on either side of Gonzalez jumped back a step, startled, then quickly recovered and expertly snatched out their own weapons, training them on Ari with practiced ease. They were not new to this business. The giant never moved, only lowered his massive lion's head and shook it side to side in apparent disgust at the situation, perhaps saddened at the sour turn their encounter had taken. He spoke and the translator immediately began talking, his voice an octave higher and strained, tension showing through.

"This is foolish. You are foolish. Put down your weapon. You might be able to shoot one of us, but then the other will shoot you in the leg, or the arm. Nothing mortal, at least not right away. Then of course you still have me to contend with. We have orders to take you, but you don't have to be in one piece."

Ari was impressed at how steady he held the pistol. He had never done anything like this before, didn't know he had it in him. He shook his head.

"No, I won't put it down. Now, last chance – where is Frankie Brubaker? Tell me that and you can leave now and no one gets hurt. Tell me now, and everyone walks away. I mean it!"

Ari looked behind the men, to the left of Gonzalez and down around their knees. He wished they would cooperate, he really did, but he was sure they weren't going to.

"Where is Frankie Brubaker?" he repeated. Each word was said slowly, individually, with perfect enunciation.

"Idiot," the translator continued. "We will take you, whole and in one piece, or bloody and broken. It's your choice. You can't take us all out." Gonzalez took a step toward him and Ari knew then that they weren't going to tell him anything. He lowered the pistol a few inches and remembered his training. Sight down the barrel, squeeze the trigger slowly…

"I don't have to take you all out," he said, bracing himself for what was to come. This was going to be messy. He couldn't bring himself to look at the Firebird. "I only have to hit that. Oh, and don't call me Arjen. I hate that name."

The giant squinted at Ari's Glock and followed the barrel. He turned his massive head and looked down and spotted the old white propane tank against the wall directly behind them. Comprehension dawned and he grabbed the translator by the arm and flew for the open door. He was fast, lightning fast, Olympic sprinter Usain Bolt fast. Ari had never seen anyone move like that before, especially not someone so damned big. He was moving and almost out the door as Ari gently pulled the trigger and the striker snapped home.

The pistol's report in that enclosed space was deafening, tremendous, louder than he thought possible. He'd been close to a semi-truck once when a tire blew, and the single shot from the pistol rivaled that sound. But his shot was on target and a split second later the propane tank exploded and made the pistol's report sound like a child's cap gun. The tank blew up and a fireball expanded outward at least ten feet, roiling and churning upwards, mindless and consuming. Ari was already throwing himself to the ground behind the Firebird as the blazing heat lashed out and singed most of the hair on the right side of his body, the concussive wave tossing him back at least five feet. Red hot shards of the propane tank zinged past him and peppered the walls, the ceiling, bouncing and ricocheting off everything, including the unprotected car. The first intruder screamed then stopped, cut-off like a blaring stereo with an abruptly cut speaker wire. The door to the garage was torn off its hinges and careened past him, spinning wildly and smashing into the back wall where it clattered to the ground, smoldering. In seconds it was all over but for several more hot pieces of shrapnel pinging as they continued bouncing off walls and clattering to the ground all around him. Thick black smoke filled the upper half of the garage. The remains of the tank itself resembled a huge, nightmarish, black and white orchid in bloom. It teetered in place for a moment before falling over with a metallic crash, rocking back and forth on the gritty, charred floor.

Ari stayed supine on the garage floor for a few moments, his arms over his head. Different smells filled the thick air, the combined reek of singed hair, burning wood, and an odd, metallic stench. His ears were ringing something terribly and felt filled with cotton. He slowly levered himself to his feet and carefully looked around, the Glock dangling from his right hand and now nearly forgotten. His right arm was bleeding from several small cuts and his elbows were scraped up, but nothing seemed too serious. The hair on that arm was black and curled. Thank God the propane tank had been almost empty, he thought. He stumbled around and turned his attention to the Firebird, expecting the worse, and his heart sank.

It was bad, really bad. The front of the car had taken the brunt of the explosion. The windshield was shattered and gone, diamond-sized pieces of glass littering the inside of the car and the floor. The hood and grill of the car looked like they'd been peppered by multiple shotgun blasts, with huge gashes raking the hood from front to back. Of course the pristine paintjob was completely ruined. The massive chrome grill, the signature piece of the car, was twisted and destroyed, hanging down drunkenly. In an instant, with the single pull of the trigger, he'd undone three or more months of work. His jaw clenched at the sight. Then he looked beyond the car, to the figure crumpled near the door, and he suddenly felt weak and nauseous.

The first man in the door, Ronaldo, had been only feet away from the exploding tank. What was left of him could hardly be called human and was barely recognizable as a person. He looked, at least to Ari right then, to be little more than scorched, shredded meat and bone covered in ripped and smoldering clothes. There was blood, oh so much blood, puddling and pooling around the crumpled form. All the previous smells were quickly overwhelmed by a thick stench of badly cooked meat, like a cheap hamburger left too long on the grill.

Oh my god...

Ari felt his bile rising, his stomach flip-flopping and clenching. His knees nearly gave out and he had to grab onto the Firebird to keep from falling over. *He had to get out of the garage right now!* Legs trembling he stumbled past the bloody mess on the floor and out into the bright morning light, where he leaned against the garage wall and breathed heavily of the clear morning air. Van Owen leaned down with his elbows on his knees, his back still against the garage. He belatedly thought to look to see if Gonzalez and his translator were anywhere around, and fortunately they weren't. All he saw were some deep grooves in the gravel of the driveway from where their vehicle had left in a hurry. He hadn't heard anything, but his ears were still ringing so loudly he couldn't have heard a UPS jet flying twenty feet overhead.

He stayed that way for what he was certain was only a few minutes but felt like days, a lifetime. He made himself breathe – slowly in, slowly out, slowly in, slowly out – until his stomach had settled and he could straighten up without fainting. When he did stand he still felt queasy and shaky, woozy, like when as a kid he'd tried to inhale a cigarette for the first time and nearly puked. His face was as grey as fireplace ash.

For a moment he had no idea what to do. Finally, with a shaky hand, he dug his phone out and dialed Hal's number. After a few seconds he heard a dim voice on the other end and realized he couldn't make out a thing Hal was saying. He plugged his nose and blew hard. His ears popped and his hearing came back a little, just enough.

"Hal? It's Ari."

"I said, I figured as much," he heard, the man's voice still muffled. "What's up? In case you're wondering I'm almost ready."

"Hal, I'm at my house. I need...I need a cleaning crew here." He racked his brain for the right thing to say, thinking back to his training. "I need Mr. Clean right away."

There was a long pause, long enough that he wasn't sure the agent had heard him. Finally Hollenbeck, to his credit, simply said, "Okay, right away. I'll have someone there in less than an hour. Where, exactly? In the house?"

"No, in the garage."

"Okay, listen to me. Listen carefully. Go in your house and lock all the doors, you got that? Don't answer the door for anyone but me. Take that gift I gave you and go inside. I'll be there as soon as I can. Stay away from the windows and doors. Understand?"

Ari's first inclination was to jump in his pickup and just drive, drive and keep going, to get as far from the garage and the bloody mess in there as he could. However he nodded and finally agreed.

"Yeah, okay, I will. And, Hal...hurry."

"I will. I'll be there in less than two hours." Then, belatedly, "You alright?"

Van Owen nodded again before he realized the agent couldn't see that. "Yeah, I'm okay. Just a little shaken up, I guess."

"Go inside now, Ari. We'll take care of everything."

The phone went dead and he stood and quickly trotted to his house. Once inside he did as instructed and locked all the doors and windows, pulling the blinds. For what seemed like forever he nervously paced from room to room, peeking out the windows periodically, unable to sit still. He realized the Glock was still on the floor of the garage, but there was nothing to do about that now. In just over forty-five minutes he saw a white panel van cruise slowly up his street. On the side of the van was a smiling bald man with large biceps and a big smile, a clear rip-off of the Mr. Clean ammonia products. Underneath were the words in a flowing script "Mr. Clean – No Mess Can Best Us!" The van backed into his driveway, all the way up to the garage. Three men in white uniforms with the Mr. Clean logo on their backs hopped out and carefully peeked into the garage before easing inside. After a few minutes they opened up the back of the van and carried in several pieces of equipment, much of which he couldn't recognize, and dim noises could be heard. An hour after that Hal pulled up in his sedan and the agent joined them inside. He was only out of sight for a few minutes before he emerged and walked up to Ari's back door. He knocked and Van Owen opened it. He motioned to the garage, his expression that of a parent checking on the well-being of the child who had just wrecked his bike.

"Wanna' tell me what happened here?"

Ten minutes later, Ari's recounting of the incidents complete, Hal stood from the kitchen table. He'd cleaned his glasses so frequently that Ari was amazed he hadn't worn right through the lenses. He started to say something, then thought better of it and closed his mouth with an audible click. He paced around the small kitchen while Ari looked on, a hot cup of coffee on the kitchen table in front of him and cradled between his hands, the warmth welcome. The nausea had finally passed but he was still a little shaky. The horrific vision of the dead man in the garage, Ronaldo, the man he'd killed, refused to leave him. It was there, in front of him, light a bright light always in his eyes. Finally the agent stopped and turned toward him.

"Damn, Ari, I'm sorry. I never should have left you here alone. I had no idea your life would be in danger." He started pacing the floor again. Every time he took a heavy step the coffee in the cup bounced and formed concentric rings, like when the tyrannosaur in the movie Jurassic Park was stomping towards the kids in the jeep. Ari watched the rings, transfixed. He felt as if he should be furious at Hollenbeck for what had happened, but he was oddly devoid of emotion. The anger would come later, he figured, after the shock wore off.

"So why'd you leave me the gun? I mean, if you had no idea, that is."

Hal winced like he'd suffered a gut cramp. The expression was likely involuntary and gone in a second, just a quick grimace. "Okay, fine, so I figured there was a slight chance. But it was just that, a very slight chance. I never imagined this would unfold so fast. I figured we'd be out of the country and in the jungle before anyone got wind of anything."

After a few seconds of uncomfortable silence Ari got up and walked to the window. He looked out and saw that the Mr. Clean van was still there. He also noticed that the door that had been blown off its hinges was re-hung. It was scorched and burned along the edges but otherwise appeared intact. He motioned towards the garage.

"What about...what about that?"

Hal went and stood by him, easily half a head shorter than Ari but thicker through the shoulders and middle. There was a small patch of whiskers on the agent's cheek that he had missed while shaving, as if he'd been rushed. It somehow made him appear more human, even fallible. Van Owen considered that revelation and wasn't sure how that made him feel.

"You mean the body? We'll take that away for an autopsy and identification, if possible. Hopefully we'll be able to determine who he was and how he was connected to this. If he's got any priors at all we'll be able to ID him, either here in the US or abroad. Since 9-11 we've got lots of different avenues to do that." He was silent for a moment, staring out at the faded white building. "I'm sorry about the Firebird, Ari."

Van Owen didn't do or say anything. Finally he shrugged, a tiny movement that belied its actual importance to him. "It's just a car. I fixed it once. I can do it again."

"The Bureau'd like to help cover the costs."

"Okay. Fine."

As they watched two of the men came out of the garage carrying a long, heavy black bag with a full-length zipper on top. They struggled a little with the weight as they duck-walked to the back of the van before rather unceremoniously tossing it in the back, then made their way into the garage again. Ari winced at how cavalierly they handled the corpse.

"You did the right thing, Ari. If they'd taken you you'd probably be dead by now, or would be shortly. You know that, don't you?"

"Yeah." He did know that, but it didn't make it any easier. He had never killed anyone before, had never even considered it.

"The cleaning crew will be done in a little while. They're thorough. When they're finished nobody will be able to tell anyone died in there, not even a forensic team. This is what they do. They make incidents like this go away, and it'll be as if nothing ever happened."

Ari nodded and didn't say anything, just stared out the window. It was a bright sunny day but that barely registered. A few cars travelled up and down his road, their occupants oblivious to the mayhem and death that had taken place here just a short while ago. Van Owen envied them their ignorance.

"The big guy, Gonzalez, was the same one who took Frankie. It had to be," Ari finally said.

"Yeah, I know. You figure he's injured?"

"I don't know. Maybe. He may have gotten out in time. He was fast. I've never seen anyone move like that before."

Neither man spoke for some time. They could hear noises coming from inside the garage, the sound of equipment running, no doubt cleaning equipment or high-pressure chemical sprayers of some kind. Hal didn't look away from the scene.

"We need to leave now, of course. Today."

Ari blinked once, twice, as if suddenly waking up. "Today? No, that's not possible. We're not ready."

"It doesn't matter. We have most of what we need, and we have our team. I can get us on flights. Whatever else we don't have we can buy down there. It's no longer safe here for you."

"Of course it matters. If we're not ready and equipped properly we'll just die down there and save them the trouble. We can't go yet."

Hal was adamant and wouldn't be swayed. "Nope. I'm taking you with me today, right now. Gather up what you need and let's head out. You've got an hour."

As badly as Van Owen disagreed he knew deep down that the agent was right. They had to go. He nodded then finished the now cool coffee. It was bitter and nasty, a fitting taste for his mood.

"Fine. Let me gather up my papers. I'll get my passport and everything else and I'll be ready to go. There's nothing for me here now anyway. Not anymore."

He turned away from the scene outside the window, but the bloody vision of the dead man refused to leave his sight.

Chapter 11

"There is no foreign land; it is the traveler only that is foreign."
- Robert Louis Stevenson

The next day they arrived in Brasilia, Brazil, on a standard commercial flight, but shadowed by an undercover air marshal in their section just in case. Ari was fidgety and nervous about so much of the trip, not the least of which was his prolonged proximity to Butch, something he doubted he'd ever get used to. Paulson on the other hand was chatty and in good spirits, happy to be doing something, and if he noticed any tension between Frankie's past boyfriend and her current husband he didn't show it. Hal for the most part kept to himself, which was a little out of character for the normally affable agent. After a brief layover they boarded a puddle-jumper to the Brazilian city of Cuiaba, where they landed at the relatively modern Marechal Rondon International Airport, deep in the heart of the Brazilian state of Mato Grosso, their last taste of what many Westerners would call civilization. From there they secured passage on a well-used and mechanically suspect bus filled with locals, families, day-workers, and children, plus several chickens and a small pig, all headed northwest. After two days of bouncing around on increasingly poor roads in the beat-up bus, tired and short-tempered, they pulled into the small, sleepy frontier town of Carrabas, not too far from the western border of Brazil and nearly on the Bolivian border. Here they bedded down for the night at the tiny Hotel Del Carmen. It wasn't much of a hotel in the conventional Western sense, but it had beds and running water, luxuries that they would soon sorely miss. Ari had stayed there before on both of his earlier Fawcett trips and knew it would do. It would have to since it was the only game in town.

In Carrabas they used Ari's past connections and Hal's ample supply of US dollars to purchase on old Toyota Land Cruiser. It was the color of a bleached Band-Aid and had mismatched tires and rusted floorboards. The power steering didn't work and one of the headlights pointed straight up, but the four-wheel drive was still serviceable and the engine was virtually bullet-proof. It was one of Van Owen's favorite vehicles for this kind of trip and he was happy to have it. Right away Paul christened it Betty for some reason they could never figure out, and despite their initial reluctance the name stuck. Betty held all their supplies, including dried food, canned goods, six big jerry cans of water, five more of gas, and still had room left over for the four of them. On the rear tailgate was an aging, wrinkled bumper sticker that read *I lost my heart and my virginity in Gatlinburg.*

"I hope you didn't pay more than a hundred bucks for this bucket of bolts," Butch observed, standing with his arms crossed next to Hal and Paulson as they all inspected their newly acquired transportation. "I'll be surprised if the damn thing makes it out of town."

Paul rested a hand on Betty's hood. "Are you kidding? Betty's perfect. I've got total faith in her."

Hal took no offense at Brubaker's opinion of his purchase. "It's the best we could get on short notice, and Ari thinks it'll be fine. Right?"

Van Owen was inside the Toyota checking out some of the controls. "Yep. It may not look like much, I agree, but they're pretty much indestructible."

Hal refused to allow any porters or guides to come along, which Ari had already figured would be the case. For several days in Carrabas they met with locals and secured more supplies. Van Owen was both antsy to get moving and wary that they wouldn't have everything they needed. It was never possible to have everything, but not being prepared went against his very nature.

One of Ari's past contacts in town was a small, compact local man named Raul. They met daily in the dark lobby of the Hotel Del Carmen. Raul smoked thick black cigars nonstop, always wore oversized white shirts with broad collars, and spoke English with a moderate accent. He had moved to the US as a child but had returned to his home in Carrabas as a teenager. He was, as Van Owen described him to the others, a buyer's guide. The native knew everyone in the small town and had a knack for locating hard to find items that they still lacked. Ari had found him indispensable in the past and was happy to pay the nominal fee for his services.

"So you were able to get everything on the list?" Ari asked. He was in the hotel lobby on an old leather couch so shabby that Goodwill would've passed on it as a donation. It smelled of dust and damp towels.

Raul expertly clipped off the sodden end of his cigar with a black plastic cutter. The damp, chewed end plopped neatly into the ashtray. He puffed a few times and thick smoke momentarily obscured his square face. He looked over the list.

"Sí, yes. The rifles were a bit of a problem, but I got them this morning. They are in pretty good shape. You certainly want a lot of ammunition."

"Better safe than sorry, you know that. Once we're out there we won't have access to more."

The small man nodded and kept puffing away. With a small stub of a Number 2 pencil he drew lines through the items on the paper.

"What are these here? I can't read this."

Ari looked at the paper. "Trinkets. You know, things we can easily trade with the natives in case we run across any. Costume jewelry, small knives, things like that. Do you still have any of those tiny glass beads from Azerbaijan? The ones you can thread into bracelets and such? Those have been a big hit in the past."

Raul thought for a moment and tapped the paper. "I don't know. I'll have to check on those. For the rest of it let me see what I can do. There's a man in town that may have something unique, too. Anything else?"

"Just the usual, really. Oh, throw in some of those tough flip-flops. I've used those to my advantage in the past and they've been huge hits. They love flip-flops. I guess that's it unless you can think of anything I missed."

"Not really, no. I should be able to have everything tomorrow or the day after, although you're not giving me much time. But, as you Americans say, this is not my first rodeo." He puffed a few more times on his cigar but it had gone out. He frowned and pulled a large ornate silver lighter from his pocket and flicked it on. An intense blue flame powerful enough to weld steel shot out, and he soon had the stogie going again. He drew on it thoughtfully.

"Truly, Ari," he said finally, neatly folding the list into his pocket and leaning back in the chair. "I continue to be surprised that you are here again. After last time, I mean. I never thought I'd see you again after that. You swore you were done chasing this Fawcett person, this *fantasma*."

Van Owen sat still on the old couch. Raul and most of the people in Carrabas knew all about Ari's second trip to the jungle, the one that had nearly claimed his life. In fact Raul had helped transport him to the small hospital where he had been laid up for so many months afterwards. Ari eventually forced a smile that he hoped looked genuine.

"Guess I've still got Fawcett fever, Raul."

The small man rolled his dark eyes. "Everyone here thinks you're crazy, muy loco. You know that, right? They think you're just another crazy American. I hope you have more success this time. Try not to get killed, okay? It's bad for my business."

"I'll do my best. Just find me the rest of the stuff, okay?"

Raul gave him a bemused look that clearly mirrored his thoughts, that he believed Ari was crazy, too. But in the end, businessman that he was, he agreed he would do his best. He left, the smelly smoke from his cigar gradually dispersed by the slow-moving ceiling fan overhead. Ari stared after him, not so sure that he wasn't crazy after all.

The next morning the four members of the team met in the lobby.

"Raul has done all that he can," Ari began, seated again on the worn leather couch. He sunk so low on the cushion that getting out each time was a bit of a chore. "I think we're as ready as we'll ever be."

Paul was standing next to him, almost bouncing on the balls of his feet, anxious to be on his way. He rubbed his hands together briskly. "Good. I'm ready to go. Let's do this thing."

"Me, too," Butch Brubaker groused. "This place is a dump. I'm ready to get out of here."

Ari sat back and looked around the lobby. To describe it as merely shabby would have been charitable, and finding anything approaching charm would've been next to impossible. "Trust me. I doubt you'll think it's much of a dump in a few weeks."

"Yeah, maybe so," Butch said. He turned and lifted his shirt, showing several dozen little red splotches across his back. Several more were on his chest and stomach. "But there's something in my bed that's eating me alive. I can't think the jungle will be any worse."

Hal checked out his back and looked at Ari. "Got anything for this?"

"Yeah, some Benadryl and anti-bacterial cream should help. I've got some in my room. Just remember, everyone – any kind of skin irritation needs to be taken care of right away. That goes for any cuts or abrasions, too, since infection sets in very quickly down here. If you don't take care of it it'll only get worse in a hurry, and there's no doctors out there, or none that you'd want to treat you. Understand?"

The three men nodded their assent, although Brubaker was barely listening as he rubbed his irritated back on the wall. Ari stood and pointed next door.

"Let's all get one last meal under our belts and then we'll head out. Agreed?"

Butch said, "Then you'll tell us the real reason we're going out there? I know it's not all about Frankie. We wouldn't be going to all this trouble for one person, no matter who it is."

Van Owen turned to Hal. "How much did you tell him already?"

"Not much, really. He didn't need to know. We're here to find his wife, as well as investigate an additional matter of serious national importance."

"Well I've already filled Paul in on most of it, except what happened in the garage." He turned to Butch. "Once we're on the road we should probably tell you everything, if that's okay. Hal?"

Hollenbeck wiped a nonexistent speck of dirt from his glasses. "That'll be fine. Up until now it's been on a need to know basis. That all changes when we head out. You both will need to know everything."

Butch's lips compressed to a thin line, not happy at being put off, but he didn't push the issue. Together the four of them went next door to a small restaurant to fill up one last time. Over a lunch of deep-fried chicken tacos, diced fruit, and syrupy, South American Coca-Cola, Paulson decided out of the blue that their foursome needed a name.

"Fantastic Four? How about that?"

Between bites of what he hoped really was chicken in his taco, Ari said, "We don't need to name our group, Paul."

"Come on, why not? Fine. How about the Fab Four? The Four Horsemen?"

Butch ignored him and concentrated on his food. Hal looked slightly amused. Ari had to admire the young man's enthusiasm.

"Keep working on it, Paul."

After lunch they all met back in the lobby. Hal checked them out and paid the very reasonable bill out of his stash of American dollars. Now that the time had come to leave, both Butch and Paul were a little nervous, unable to stand still in one place for long. Ari looked them over. He knew there was no way they could ultimately be prepared for what was out there - he just hoped they'd be able to handle it. Especially Paulson. Despite what the young man had done Van Owen found that he was becoming quite fond of him, and he hoped nothing would happen. He was just such a likeable guy.

They stepped outside into the heat of the early afternoon. Betty, their newly-christened Land Cruiser, was so loaded down with supplies and equipment it looked like its shocks might pop on the spot. Jerry cans were strapped all around it and on top, along with dozens of plastic bins stuffed with food, gear, ammunition, tarps, tents, and more. Four rifles were mounted upright inside, cop-car style, against the dash where the radio should have been. Hal opened up a small suitcase-sized plastic box that was on the passenger seat and withdrew four matte-black handguns in black holsters. He handed one to Paulson and Brubaker who looked momentarily surprised but began to strap them on, neither man a stranger to weapons; Paulson from his time in the service, and Butch from years of hunting everything from deer to moose to prairie dogs. Hal looked at Ari.

"Here. Consider it a gift from the FBI."

Ari didn't take his. It was a Glock, just like the one he had used to blow up the propane tank and kill the intruder, the man named Ronaldo. It might even have been the same one. He recoiled a step.

"I don't want that thing."

Hal stared at him. "Take it, Ari. You don't know when you might need it again."

He crossed his arms and stood his ground. His face was cold and hard, set so firmly it could have been chiseled from stone. "No. I don't want it."

The agent continued to stare at him, as if by force of will he could change Ari's mind. He thrust it out to him again. The Glock's flat black finish seemed to suck in light like a miniature black hole. Ari couldn't pull his eyes away.

"Take it."

The bloody image of the dead man was vivid in Van Owen's mind. He couldn't think of any circumstance where he'd ever use a gun again, no matter what. Hal held it out until his arm was tired and eventually let it fall to his side. With a sigh he put the pistol in the Betty's glove box and slammed it shut.

Raul the buyer jogged around the corner of the hotel with a heavy canvas bag in his hands, a wide smile on his dark face. Slightly winded from his run he presented the bag to Ari, obviously pleased with himself. His eyes were dancing.

"What's this?" Van Owen asked.

"Why it's your trinkets, of course. You asked for trinkets so I found you trinkets. I think they will do the trick for you."

Ari grinned thanks. "Well done, Raul. How much do we owe you?"

"No, no, this is one is on credit. When you return to Carrabas you can pay me then. Okay? I think it will mean good luck to you on your journey if you are in my debt here."

"Okay. Deal. Thanks."

He shook hands with his friend. Ari grabbed his brown canvas and leather backpack, the same one he'd had for the previous two journeys. It was worn and frayed, threadbare in more places than not, complete with a burn hole on the side where, on his first trip, he'd passed out from too much local *pulque* while smoking a cigar.

The cigar had burned a hole clean through and almost destroyed some very valuable papers tucked away inside. On these trips that tattered backpack was his best friend and companion. The four men then climbed into the Toyota and Betty obediently rumbled to life when Van Owen turned the key.

"Smells like an old gym bag in here," Paulson observed.

Hal was riding shotgun in the front passenger seat while the other two got settled in the back. There was little traffic to speak of as he pulled out onto the dusty, poorly maintained road in front of the hotel. He waved to Raul, gunned it and they bounced their way down the few blocks of downtown, quickly putting the small business district of Carrabas behind them. Houses and the odd neighborhood store passed by in a pastel blur until they too thinned out and were gone, with just the occasional shack or small shed left to break up the roadside scenery.

"Next stop, Wally World," Paulson quipped. Despite himself Ari grinned again, just a little. He had to admit that it was good to be back on the road once more.

Here we come, Frankie, he told himself, trying to somehow throw his thoughts into the jungle. Here we come.

They drove for several hours along the rutted road. The sketchy pavement had vanished miles earlier and had devolved into gravel, then into straight dirt, rutted and riddled with potholes. Their kidney-jarring forward progress slowed to speeds of single digits much of the time. They came upon few people and even fewer vehicles, and for a while saw more scrawny horses and mules than locals. Several times they passed loose clusters of tin shacks with blankets for doors and cisterns on the roof. Skinny, dark-skinned children ran along the road when they passed, waving and smiling. Mounted outside several of the shacks were huge black satellite dishes, completely anachronistic and out of place in what were little more than groups of hovels. In these huts he could see the blue glow

178

of TV screens. No toilets, but they did have TVs, he marveled, not for the first time. Paul would wave out his open window at the kids as Betty trundled past, yelling greetings in a language they couldn't understand but which was universally understood.

Late in the afternoon they pulled off the side of the road in a small clearing. All four men climbed out of the Toyota and stretched, groaning a little and working the kinks out of their backs. Paulson limped around for a few minutes but didn't complain as he loosened up his stiff knee. The afternoon was warm and so thick with humidity they felt as if they could peel it away like a second skin, and it only took seconds for a multitude of bothersome flying insects to zero in on them.

"Damn, these roads suck," Butch grumbled as he twisted his torso back and forth. They were all wearing cloth hats with full, floppy brims. Brubaker took his off and swatted at bugs that were bombarding him.

"Okay, dude, this isn't what I thought the jungle would look like," Paulson finally said, looking around at the low brush and scrubby trees all around them. There were only a few trees taller than ten feet, and even those were scattered thinly here and there, several more fading into the rolling distance. Ari had to agree that it wasn't impressive.

"This? No, we're not there yet. A few decades ago this was all thick and dense jungle, pretty much impassable without a machete. But there's been a lot of deforestation and people moving here, trying to turn this land into farms and ranches. Loggers are the biggest threat in Brazil and surrounding countries. Loggers and oil drillers. After loggers clear out the land people always follow. It never fails, even though the soil isn't any good for farming. Once they quickly burn out a patch of land by over-farming the locals just move on to the next clear-cut area and start again."

Hal had finally decided he didn't need his jacket and it was okay to display his sidearm in public, what little public there was.

He looked around with his hands on his hips, surveying the area with interest. He was still his clean-cut and tidy self, with some sweat stains under his arms the only indication that he was even slightly uncomfortable.

"How far until we get to a good place to stop for the night?" he asked Ari.

Van Owen pulled a laminated map from his tattered backpack and laid it on the faded hood. He consulted their GPS unit and pointed to a spot just northwest of Carrabas.

"We're about here." He moved his finger fractionally up the red line that was their current road. "We need to get to here. It's only another few hours."

The agent motioned at the GPS unit mounted to their windshield by a suction cup. "Not sure why you use a map instead of this, but either one beats the hell out of a sextant, doesn't it? Okay, I think it's time we filled everyone in on what we're doing. See any reason we shouldn't?" This question was aimed at Van Owen who shook his head, surprised that he'd even been consulted. The four of them gathered around Betty's hood, which was warm from the engine and ticked softly as it cooled. Insects continued to buzz around their heads and they all swatted at them unconsciously, like cows flicking their tails. Hal took charge of the conversation.

"Butch, I want to thank you for taking this leap of faith and coming with us, considering how little information I gave you. We are indeed on a search for your wife, be assured of that, but there is much more to it. Much more.

"So far we've told everyone we're here to find what happened to an explorer from the early 1900s called Percy Fawcett, someone Ari here has tried to find twice before without success. In fact the last time he was here it just about killed him. This trip is great cover, one that no one would suspect. It helps us fly under the radar, which is just what we need."

"Percy Fawcett? Never heard of him," Butch said.

"Not that many people have, at least not anymore," Hal continued. "Searching for him was very popular in the past, I've learned, and a lot of people who've looked for him have died doing it. It's legitimate cover for what we're really doing here. Not only are we looking for Frankie, but we've got an even bigger goal. You've never heard of this before, but you've heard about what it can cause. There's a new drug on the street, one that's killing people and could kill a lot more. Remember the name sudden onset paralysis, because it's going to come up again and again."

For the next ten minutes he told the three of them everything he knew, beginning with SOP and how their search had been stymied from the start, and how little they knew.

"We had no idea what was causing it, but we'd seen it in some flight crews in different parts of the country, including the UPS hub in Louisville. But always when they were on the ground. Nothing had happened to anyone in the air, at least as far as we knew. We didn't know if it was caused by some unknown insect, an allergic reaction, something they ate or drank, or what. The final straw was the commercial flight that crashed in Louisville just outside the airport. For that one we had a witness so we knew SOP was behind it. Thank you, Alyssa Morris, our gutsy flight attendant."

Ari had heard all this before, and for the most part so had Paulson. Regardless, they were all listening raptly as the agent continued.

"We finally got a break when that Cincinnati Reds ballplayer, Carlos Garrafon, died. From what we can tell he overdosed on a new drug on the street, one called Ice, a very expensive performance-enhancing drug that we know almost nothing about. This was the first Ice overdose we'd seen, and his symptoms were virtually the same as a death by SOP, which was something new to us. We determined then that they were connected."

"Damn, that sucks. He was pretty good," Butch said, shocked.

"Yes he was, at least when he was pumped full of Ice. An FBI forensic biologist did some additional digging during his autopsy and found out the Ice overdose that killed him was chemically very similar to the toxin of something called an Amazon bullet ant, one specific to an area of Brazil in the extreme northwest corner of the state of Mato Grosso, where we are right now."

"Impressive work, detective," Paulson told him with admiration.

"Thanks, Paul. It's taken a lot of work from a lot of people, but we've made some progress. When we need to we can work pretty fast, like when the Boston Marathon got bombed. Look how quickly we all figured that one out." He made eye contact with each man, one by one, before continuing. "And here's where it gets tricky and perhaps just a little fuzzy. Paul here was approached by a man in a fedora with a Spanish accent when Frankie Brubaker was kidnapped." Ari tensed, waiting for Hal to go into detail on how that had gone down, how the young man had accepted cash to look the other way and destroy the security tape. He wasn't sure how Butch would react but suspected it wouldn't go over well. He kept his eye on Frankie's husband just in case. Paul himself was pale and looked a little sick. "This is the same man, we think, that people saw hanging out with Garrafon several times before his death and said he was his uncle. The descriptions match. What we never realized was that Carlos Garrafon always said he was from the Dominican Republic, but it turns out he was born and raised in a small town in Mato Grosso, a place called Boca Andreas. He moved to the Dominican Republic later, when he was a teenager."

Brubaker's eyes went wide. "So you're telling me that Garrafon and this other guy are probably related, and they're both from this Boca Andreas place?"

"That's right. It all ties together: the bullet ant toxin, Boca Andreas and Mato Grosso, a chemical tie between SOP and Ice, and now this uncle. Mainly what we don't know is why your wife was kidnapped by him, but I just bet if we find him we'll find her and the source of SOP and Ice all at the same time. And that, gentlemen," he said, standing up straight and tilting his head north, "is why we're here and why we're heading into the jungle. It's a reconnaissance mission for the most part, but our secondary goal is to find Ms. Brubaker. Ari, why don't you tell them what happened in your garage, if you don't mind. They need to know how serious this really is."

In reality Van Owen minded very much. Some would insist that the retelling of what took place in his garage would prove beneficial, even cathartic, but not to him. He shook his head. "No thanks, Hal."

The agent didn't miss a beat. "Okay. Right before we left Ari had three men visit him at home. For some reason they were intent on kidnapping him. In fact one of the men was likely the same one who helped abduct your wife, Butch. From Ari's description he was huge, over seven feet tall, and either didn't speak English or didn't speak it very well."

Paul turned to Ari. "Damn, man. What did they want?"

Ari shrugged, finally finding his voice. "Besides me? They never said, but they knew about Frankie. They pretty much admitted to that."

"Thanks to some very quick and clever thinking our man here was able to escape relatively unharmed, but in the process one of the trio was killed. Had Ari not done what he did I'm sure he wouldn't be here with us now."

Paul looked him up and down the way a fan checks out a favored athlete. "Way to step up. Didn't know you had it in you."

Van Owen didn't share his enthusiasm and said nothing. Butch was trying hard not to be impressed, but with this new information both men were looking at him in a new light and likely reassessing him. Before this they had seen him as a bookish researcher, rather quiet and unassuming, but now their opinions had been altered. Ari didn't much care for it, and in fact hated that he'd been tagged as a man willing and able to kill. He wasn't that guy.

"So now you're all up to speed. I think it would be helpful, Ari, if you filled us in on Fawcett as much as you can, but I think we can save that for an evening around the campfire or something like that. Agreed?"

"Yeah, sure. I can do that." His voice sounded distant and detached.

"Great." The agent slid off his glasses and for once had something to wipe away; the lenses were coated with a thick layer of brown road grit. "Let's get going again. We probably want to get to our first stop before it gets dark, wouldn't you think? Where did you say that was?" he asked Ari.

His mouth twitched into a small grin. "You'll see," was all he would say.

With no more information forthcoming they all clambered back into Betty, Ari's backpack slung into the rear. The suspension squeaked and groaned under their combined weight as Ari fired her up and they moved off. All four men were quiet now, subdued, running everything through their own heads. Ari focused on navigating the rutted road as they pushed on, heading northwest, always northwest, deeper into Mato Grosso.

The poor road conditions persisted to the point where they were lucky to make it to their first destination before nightfall. They'd been asking Ari for the last few hours where they were going, but he would only give a small wave and tell them to hold tight. When he finally pulled over they all clambered out moaning and feeling like they'd been on the wrong side of a street brawl. They twisted and stretched, various body parts cracking audibly over the sounds of the cooling engine and the abundance of squawking, singing birds flitting in and around the trees.

184

"Christ, that damn piece of crap is going to kill me," Butch hissed, slowly swiveling his trunk back and forth with his hands on his hips. "Does it even have shock absorbers?"

Ari wasn't too sore except for his arms and hands from fighting the steering wheel for the last several hours over Mato Grosso's liberal definition of a road. He cracked his knuckles with satisfaction and motioned back toward the Toyota.

"Okay, everyone, grab a blanket and some water. Some food wouldn't be a bad idea, either, just in case."

Paulson walked past Betty and stood next to him, peering around with wide blue eyes. The two others stood behind them. Either consciously or not Hal's hand had drifted near his holstered Glock. Butch hadn't stepped away from the four-wheel drive yet, suddenly seeming much more attached to it than just moments earlier.

Paul continued to look around them. "Um, where are we?"

They were in a small village of some sort. Clustered around them were several small stucco huts with thatched roofs. At some point in the distant past they had been painted in pastel pinks, yellows, and blues, but the colors were now dull and lifeless, little more than promises that had faded with time. The huts were for the most part simple structures consisting of one door and a window, maybe two, usually with towels or rags hanging in the open frame in lieu of glass. The village was less than a city block long, and at the end of the dirt street there sat a squat blue building that was a church or chapel. It had a dark wooden door and a stubby steeple, complete with a black cross perched on top that was listing slightly to the left. A few chickens pecked in the dust of the street, and a thin dog, black and white with a mainly white face, stared at them from the shadows of one of the huts. Its tired eyes tracked them without emotion. Dust filled their nostrils.

"This is Villa de San Pedro el Justo."

185

Paul looked warily around like a white suburban kid suddenly dumped in the ghetto. "Big name for such a little place. Not much to it, you know?"

"No, there's not much. But thanks to the Conquistadors and their Jesuit friends in the fifteen- and sixteen-hundreds you'll find places like this all over South America. What you're also likely to find are priests willing to put you up overnight. Hopefully Father Ed is still here."

Hal stood beside him and wiped at his glasses. Under the brim of his hat his eyes tracked everywhere, up and down and side to side, taking it all in. Ari figured he was looking for threats even when there were none. As before, back in Louisville, Van Owen thought being suspicious must come with the job. "Where is everyone?"

"I'd say the men are still out hunting and tending to what little crops they can grow out here. The older boys are probably with them. The women and children are likely in their homes, watching us. We just can't see them. They're not used to having strangers here." He cupped his hands to his mouth and yelled, "Hey, Father Ed! You here?"

The chickens scattered at the noise, clucking nervously. The dog lifted its head an inch, its mouth now open and panting. Ari waited a moment then started walking toward the blue chapel. Behind them the sun was dipping low, throwing their shadows before them like malformed giants.

"Come on," he said. "Let's find Father Ed. And let's hope he's hammered."

Paulson was walking beside him. "Hammered? You mean drunk? Why?"

"Oh, he's just a lot easier to get along with if he's drunk, that's all."

"What do you mean?"

Ari didn't answer, just motioned them all to follow and walked on. The black and white dog stood and shook, dust flying off its short fur. It fell into step ten feet away from them, looking almost expectantly up at Paul. He reached toward it but the dog shied away at the friendly motion, skittering sideways like a startled crab. They continued on and the mutt shadowed them, still a few feet to the right.

"Wonder whose this is?" Paulson asked to no one in particular. "He looks like he's in pretty decent shape, considering."

Ari looked down at the black and white dog. "Just a stray, I'd say. Probably doesn't belong to anyone."

"Looks kinda like a border collie mix, or something. Maybe Australian shepherd."

They got to the church and walked up the two shallow steps. The stone treads of the stairs were worn down and bowed from so many years of the penitent shuffling in and out. Ari rapped on the heavy wooden door. The sound was muffled and barely audible, the door so thick he could have been knocking on a brick wall. The dog sat at the foot of the steps and stared at them. Its tail twitched once.

"Father Ed? You in there?"

He knocked again with the same lack of effect.

"Nobody home?" Hal ventured.

Van Owen shook his head. "No, he's probably here. Come on."

He pushed and the heavy door groaned open. The still air inside was heavy and smelled of old candles and something else, something sour and a little foul. Ari was pretty sure he knew what it was. Inside the dim sanctuary there were only four sets of pews on each side of the narrow aisle. They were straight-backed with their black finish worn through to the blond wood below, a testament to the many decades of devoted usage. The only light was from stained-glass windows on either side of the small sanctuary. The image depicted in the colored glass was of Christ bleeding from his hands and feet, a long bloody gash on his side.

"Father Ed? It's Ari Van Owen."

Ari walked down the aisle and around the pulpit, to a narrow door barely visible in the gloom. On the door the word *Sacristia* was etched into the nearly black wood. He pushed it open and looked down.

"Well, good evening, Father."

The others clustered around behind him. Inside the tiny sacristy was a small army cot on which slept a huge man, his bare feet dangling well off the end. He had on dirty shorts and a black, wrinkled shirt, unbuttoned and revealing a large hairy stomach so big it threatened to overbalance the cot and pitch him to the floor. His white collar was on the ground buried under several empty Coke bottles. The sour smell they had all noticed from before was so strong here it overpowered all others. The huge priest grunted and shifted in his sleep then farted, a long drawn-out rumble that vibrated the cot and was easily loud enough to be heard outside.

"Real nice," Butch commented.

Father Ed mumbled something incoherent and may have smiled. Ari knelt down next to him, putting a hand on his shoulder and shaking it.

"Father Ed, wake up. It's time to get up."

The man feebly swatted his hand away and tried to roll over. The cot moaned ominously, the frame pushed nearly to its engineered limits.

"What the hell is that smell?" Butch asked, his face twisted up in disgust. He waved his hat in front of him in a vain effort to blow the stench away. If anything it disturbed the still air and made it even worse.

Ari knew it was a combination of the local mango-based alcoholic drink the locals brewed and delivered in the Coke bottles scattered about, the dirty sacristy, and most of all Father Ed himself. He shook the big priest's shoulder again, a little harder this time.

"Time to get up. There are souls to be saved and I've got a fifth of Maker's Mark with your name on it."

Father Ed didn't crack an eye, but he worked his mouth a moment before he said in a deep, rumbling voice, "You wouldn't be lying now, would you, son? Lying's a sin against God and man, and neither one of us would appreciate it."

"Nope, that's no lie. Paul, run back to the Toyota and open the blue crate on top. The one marked First Aid. Grab the bottle of Maker's Mark and bring it here, please."

Paul hurried off, his footfalls loud as they slapped on the stone floor of the quiet church. Father Ed slowly sat up and put his head in both hands. He had long brown hair in a ponytail that ran a foot down his broad back.

"Kentucky bourbon? You know how to please an old priest, my son. And Maker's Mark to boot, bless you." He made a sloppy sign of the cross with two fingers in Ari's general direction. "Whatever local concoction my children put in these things," he mumbled, kicking at one of the empty Coke bottles at this feet, "does the trick, mind you, but it's no Maker's Mark, that's for sure. Oh, damn my blasted, aching head."

Ari grinned briefly at the priest, happy in his own way to see him again and equally pleased he was in a decent mood. "Glad we could help. Now I've got a favor to ask. Would it be okay if we spent the night here in the church? It's getting dark and we'd rather not have to bed down on the side of the road."

Father Ed lifted his huge head. His eyes were red-rimmed and bloodshot, but his smile was sincere. He placed a big, meaty hand on Ari's shoulder.

"My son, for a fifth of Maker's Mark you can bunk down here all year."

Half an hour later they were all on the steps of the church outside, Hal and Butch leaning against the blue walls and the other three sitting down and relaxing. The sun was quite low in the sky but Father Ed had materialized a small oil lamp and it threw a warm puddle of light around them. He was peeling little bits of the red wax seal from the bottle of bourbon with a dirty fingernail. He poured a hefty portion into a chipped water glass and held it at arm's length, gazing at it in wonder, the expression on his face mirroring that of a lotto player possessing a winning ticket.

"I'd give one of Gabriel's testicles for some ice right now."

He lifted the glass and took a small drink, sucking in air afterwards, his face beatific and peaceful. An angelic chorus and beams of light from the heavens would have completed the scene.

"Looks like he just healed a leper or something," Paul whispered to Ari.

Father Ed came back down to Earth and rather reluctantly offered the bottle to the four men clustered around him, but much to his obvious pleasure they all declined. After several more sips he turned to Ari with a stern, overcast expression, his thick eyebrows knotted.

"You're not Catholic, are you son?"

They'd had this identical conversation years before, several times, actually. "No, Father, I'm not. I don't really practice any religion, but my folks were Lutheran."

"Lutheran? Protestants? Damn that Martin Luther and his cursed Reformers. They did more to screw the Catholic Church than anyone should've been able to." He turned to look at the others. "How about the rest of you? Any good Catholics in the group?"

Butch sat up straighter. "I'm Catholic, Father."

"Good for you. Been to mass lately? Confession?"

Brubaker glanced around at his travel partners as if for support. "Ah, no, not for a while, Father. I've had some, ah, personal issues lately."

"Personal issues? All the more reason to go to mass. We'll do something about that before you leave. And confession, too. Good for the soul. Trust me." He sipped at the bourbon. "So, Ari, what in God's grace are you doing out here again? And don't tell me you're still looking into that explorer fellow, are you? Thought you'd be done with that after the last time."

"Yes, I'm still looking."

The big man shook his head. "Stupid, just stupid. Damn fool quest, son. It's going to be the death of you, you know."

"I hope not, Father."

He sighed heavily, his ample gut lifting and dropping expansively. "Well you're welcome to spend the night here, of course. You've got your own water, I see, which is wise. I'll have some of my flock bring you something to eat. Or perhaps a little celebration? It's the least I can do in exchange for your gift." He tapped the side of the bottle, which dinged musically. He was still idly peeling the red wax off the neck and rolling it into little red balls that he dropped at his feet.

Paulson was sitting to Ari's right. The black and white dog had warmed up to him a bit and was cautiously allowing the young man to scratch between its ears, although it continued to keep a wary eye cocked in his direction. Paul looked at the priest.

"Father, if you don't mind my asking, what are you doing out here? This is one heck of a long way from nowhere, you know?"

The priest raised the glass and sloshed more of the amber liquid down his throat. He shivered as if chilled, then coughed once then motioned vaguely to Ari. "You tell him." His deep voice was momentarily hoarse from the liquor.

"You sure? Well, okay. Father Ed, shall we say, got caught up in the child molestation scandal that rocked the Catholic Church a few years back. So instead of going somewhere, um, unsavory, like jail..."

"Or Rome," the priest interjected.

"Yes, or to Rome, his superiors sent him here to do penance. And here he stays. Have I summed it up pretty well?"

"A crock and an injustice! Damned Philistines. It was all political, that's what it was." The booze was beginning to take hold. His gestures were becoming more animated and exaggerated, but even so not a single drop of the bourbon splashed out of the glass to stain the shallow stone steps.

"And now that he's here, he decided he doesn't want to go back. Is that still the case, Father?"

"Damn straight. I can save more souls here than I possibly could back home. I mean really save souls, not just minister to a bunch of suburban, BMW-driving, snooty sycophants. And I don't have to put up with all the political nonsense, either. I'm never going back. Never."

Butch looked around him in bewilderment and distaste at the run-down hovels, dusty street, and scrawny chickens scratching at the ground. The village was not much of a vacation destination. He shook his head.

"Really, Father? You wouldn't rather be somewhere more, well, civilized than this?"

The big priest narrowed his eyes at him. "My son, don't confuse wealth with happiness. The people of this village are God-fearing, unpretentious, honest folk. There's more goodness here than in all of Rome. I wouldn't trade a thousand red-frocked Cardinals of the Vatican for a single man, woman, or child here."

Brubaker looked a bit offended and was about to argue the point when they heard some distant conversations drawing closer. In no time a small group of men and boys, probably no more than twenty in total, rounded the corner and walked toward the church. With the sun at their backs it was hard to make out features, but they looked small with broad shoulders, blocky frames, and short, stout legs. Several of them wore dirty, tattered shirts replete with American slogans and names like Hollister and Nike. They all came to a halt when they saw the four strangers sitting with Father Ed.

One of them came toward the priest, while the big man stood and scratched his impressive stomach.

"Stay here," he genially said to the four of them. "I'll be right back."

He wobbled down the steps and spoke to the lone villager for no more than a minute. Whatever their language was, Ari mused, it wasn't straight Portuguese or Spanish. It seemed like a combination of those two languages and something else, perhaps a local Indian dialect. He couldn't understand a word of it. Father Ed tottered back to them and refilled his glass.

"We're all set. You can bed down in the sanctuary while the villagers get a meal together. Look alive, weary travelers, this should be a fun night!"

In less than thirty minutes the women of the village had a fire going with a huge pot boiling above it. The smell of the food, whatever it was, sent Ari's mouth to watering as they got set up inside the church. Soon they were all sitting around the stone steps with wooden bowls full of something filled with vegetables, broth, and some meat they couldn't identify. Coarse, homemade flat bread was passed around, as was the local mango-based drink they'd seen in the Coke bottles earlier. It was fruity and pulpy and delivered a kick like moonshine. Father Ed waved it off and thoroughly savored his Maker's Mark instead. Hal and Butch stayed to the rear of the festivities while Paul tried to mingle with the villagers; he couldn't understand a word they said, but his voice rose in volume as he laughed and kept trying to make himself understood. Soon he had a group of smiling partiers around him as he talked and laughed, grinning wider as the alcohol took effect. Ari watched him and allowed a grin as well, enjoying and envying the man's youth and exuberance.

As the night wore on and darkness claimed the village, the locals began to drift away. Van Owen sidled up next to Father Ed. The big priest was standing in place and weaving dangerously, but somehow managed to keep his feet planted and himself upright. It was an impressive accomplishment.

"Father, can we talk for a few minutes?"

"Absolutely, my son. What's on your mind?"

"We're heading deeper in Mato Grosso, but a different direction than my other trips here. We're going more northwest this time."

Father Ed's eyes crossed once before he could focus on Ari's face. "Northwest in Mato Grosso? Why the hell would you want to go there? That's not a very hospitable place, you know, and not in the direction of that Dead Horse Camp you always ramble on about."

"Yeah, I know. I've had, ah, no luck before and I've got a hunch Fawcett may have headed this way instead. Have you heard of anything from that part of the jungle?"

The big priest's eyes squinted in thought. "No, not really, my son. Nobody goes there, not really. It's dangerous, as you know; there are still tribes in there that have no contact with white men and aren't as friendly as this bunch." He sloppily waved a hand at the villagers. "There's no law to speak of, and fewer morals. No Christians either."

"So you haven't heard or seen anything out of the ordinary?"

Father Ed scratched his head with his water glass full of bourbon. "Out of the ordinary? Well, not sure how you define that, son, and not sure what you're looking for. No, nothing…except there was a young priest from the States that wandered through here earlier this year, a Father Sean from somewhere in Iowa. Can't recall. Young stud, full of God he was and hell-bent on meeting up with some of the tribes to spread the gospel of our Lord. I was hoping he'd be back through here by now by, but we haven't seen hide nor hair of him." He hiccupped once. "Besides that? Just the normal scuttlebutt of illegal loggers and oil drillers, murderous ranchers. You of all people know what it's like out there."

He did indeed. "Yeah, it used to be survival of the fittest. Now it's more like survival of the most ruthless, or of the best armed. I'm sure it hasn't changed." He looked away, into the distance. It was common knowledge that there wasn't a native tribe who could directly compete with Western civilization's wealth or brutality. Ari knew that when the ultimate goal was religious conversion, land, or other natural resources, the indigenous tribes were never the ones that ended up writing the history books.

"So why in God's grace would you want to go out there in search of your explorer again? And do these other men," he bobbed his head toward Hal, Butch, and Paulson, "know what they're getting into? Is this Fawcett thing so important they're ready to die for it? Or are you here for something else, my son?"

Ari squirmed a little. This is why he'd waited until Father Ed was half bombed; the man could be incredibly perceptive when he needed to be, and even though he wasn't overly devout Van Owen was very uncomfortable lying to a man of the cloth. Ari looked down at his boots and then squinted out into the dusty street that was now nearly dark. He could see Paul tossing a stick to the black and white dog who was happily chasing it without making a sound. Ari realized he hadn't heard it bark once.

"It's all very important, Father. Trust me."

The big priest stared at him with red-tinged eyes. The smell of bourbon was thick in the heavy, humid air. Finally he looked away and belched. "Hmm. I can see that. Well whatever this quest of yours is about I wish you God-speed and good luck. I hope you don't come back this way in the same shape you did last time, I'll tell you that. Surprised you lived through it." He raised himself up to his full height and smoothed his wrinkled shirt. "Now if you don't mind, I think it's time to call it a night. Why don't you gather up your flock and I'll gather mine."

"Thanks, Father. We'll bed down in the church sanctuary so you can have your cot in the sacristy."

The big priest waved that suggestion off. "No, no, no need to worry about me. I'll sleep elsewhere tonight. You can have the whole church." He stood up straight and yelled something in that polyglot language that made no sense to Ari. The native women stopped whatever they were doing and quickly gathered up their cooking utensils and doused what remained of the fire, leaving a damp, sooty stench in the air. The men and children left them to this chore and headed back to their homes, all the while murmuring happily amongst themselves. In less than a minute the street was nearly vacant except for a few women and the dog. Father Ed walked unsteadily towards one of the younger women, a girl really, probably no more than sixteen or seventeen. He spoke briefly to her before reaching down and playfully slapping her on the ass. She giggled and together they went into the last hut on the left, the girl taking off her top and revealing small petite breasts before she even reached the door. The four Americans were left standing on the steps of the church.

"Never met a priest like him before," Paulson commented, his words slurred and thick, staring after Father Ed. He swayed back and forth and had to catch himself more than once.

Butch stared at the door where they had disappeared. "Me neither, kid. And I'm Catholic. What the hell?"

Ari turned and started into the church. "Let's go, guys. I'd like to get a good night's sleep before we head out tomorrow."

The four men went inside and shut the heavy door with a clunk. The dog paused for a second before trotting up the steps and lying down outside the door, curled into a tight black and white ball.

Chapter 12

In the morning they were up and moving at first light. The men of the village were gone and the women had already been busy cleaning and cooking for some time. There was no sign of Father Ed.

They packed up their few belongings and loaded the Land Cruiser. A young girl of no more than ten shyly brought them a large green leaf filled with something like tamales, still hot and steaming. She had a pretty smile and a dirty face, her black hair pulled back in a ponytail and secured with a stick and scrap of leather. She paused next to Paul and tried not to stare at him. He knelt down to her eye level and took the tamale, bouncing it gently in his hands.

"Wow. Damn thing's hot." He looked up at Ari. "Uh, why does she keep staring at me like that?"

"Your blond hair and blue eyes, I'm sure. I doubt she's ever seen anyone like you before. There are no blonds out here."

Paulson turned back to the little girl and thanked her for breakfast. She smiled and scampered away, her bare feet kicking up dust as she ran.

Hal cinched a strap on the Toyota and turned to survey the village. "I don't see your Father Ed anywhere."

"Yeah, and you probably won't. He's not much of an early riser, especially after the night he had last night. Plus, when he's sober he gets awfully damn preachy and a little mean. We said our goodbyes last night."

Ari made sure he had his backpack, then they piled into Betty. In the rearview mirror he saw Paulson looking back and forth as if he'd forgotten something. His eyes were a little bleary, but if he had a hangover he masked it well.

"I wonder where that dog is. You think he'll be okay?"

Ari turned the vehicle around in front of the church. Some of the children came out and waved at them as they passed, running alongside and smiling, yelling what were clearly goodbyes. One of the boys of about five or six had a dirty red Liverpool Football hat on. The brim was frayed.

"I'm sure he'll be fine, Paul," Ari assured him. "Someone will take care of him. Somebody has been, you can tell."

Paul didn't look convinced, but before he could say anything or protest they accelerated and Villa de San Pedro el Justo was quickly lost behind a copse of trees.

The day wore on as Ari fought the wheel on the rutted dirt road. Their progress was again limited since they couldn't hit speeds much higher than a few miles per hour, and at times simply trundled along at walking speeds. They passed several more villages that all appeared much like San Pedro el Justo. Once in a while another vehicle would chug towards them and they would slow to squeeze past. Toward noon they had to pull over so far to let a big pickup truck pass that Ari banged the passenger mirror on a tree, and from that time on it hung down at a crazy angle showing only the road as they motored along. The heat and humidity by this time were nearly stifling, and even with the windows rolled down the inside of the Toyota was murderously hot.

Lunch on the side of the road consisted of the leftover tamales from breakfast and some fruit that they needed to eat before it went bad. All four of them quickly realized that as uncomfortable as the Toyota was it was better than when they were stationary and the flying insects rediscovered them. Butch began scratching at his chest and back again since his skin was still inflamed by whatever had feasted on him back at the hotel in Carrabas. They took turns smearing Benadryl from the first aid kit on his splotchy back, then sprayed insect repellant over all their exposed skin. They were all swatting at bugs with their hands and hats, but a single or even a dozen kills meant there were still millions poised to take their place.

The meal over, they were just heading out again when Paul looked backwards and yelled at Ari to wait. He clambered out of the Toyota before it had come to a stop, hopping a little on his bad leg. Thirty feet behind them they could see the dog from Villa de San Pedro el Justo trotting up behind them. Paul knelt down and the black and white dog ran up to him, tongue out and panting heavily. It laid down in exhaustion while Paulson happily scratched behind its ears.

"Hey, buddy, what the hell are you doing here?" he asked the tired mutt.

Van Owen killed the engine and got out. The dog tracked him with tired, cautious eyes, but was either unwilling or unable to get up.

"Come on, Paul, we've got to go."

The young man didn't look up. "We're going to take him with us, right?"

"No, we're not. The jungle is no place for a dog. He'll die out there."

"What? We can't just leave him. He'll die if we leave him."

Hal leaned out the window. "He's right, Paul. We're not equipped to handle a dog on this trip."

"No! We can't just leave him here."

Butch got out of the Toyota and stretched, scratching at his aggrieved skin as if he were covered in ants. Several small spots of blood had leaked through his shirt from all the abuse. "Come on, kid. He's just a damn dog. Let's go."

Paul would have none of it. "No! I'm not leaving him here. I won't do it."

The four of them argued for ten minutes, but even with the three older men against him Paulson refused to relent. Ari was both impressed and annoyed at his stubbornness. In the end they grudgingly agreed the dog could go, but its food would have to come from Paul's rations if it got to that point. The young man scooped him up and together the five of them continued on, the nameless and silent dog eagerly lapping up water from Paulson's cupped hands.

Later that afternoon the road improved enough that they could make some good time. The Toyota's speed crested about forty-five miles per hour on the combination asphalt and gravel surface, fast enough that the breeze whipping in the open windows made it difficult to talk. The dog sat on Paulson's lap with its head out the window in the classic dog pose: mouth open, ears flattened back by the wind, tongue hanging out the side of its mouth and flapping in the breeze. Short trees and green ground cover flew by in a welcome blur, and the occasional settlement or village was there and gone in a blink. There was still not much oncoming vehicular traffic, just the stray pickup truck or horse-drawn cart filled with produce or palm leaves. Around four o'clock they came to a curve in the road and Ari pulled over and killed the engine. He referred to the GPS system and pulled his laminated map from the backpack, examining one then the other. His finger landed on a spot on the red line that was their road. He turned in his seat to look at his passengers.

"Okay, guys, here's where it starts to get really interesting. The road we're on bends northeast and heads toward a city called Nova Mutum, and then about sixty miles east of that is Dead Horse Camp, the last known supposed whereabouts of Percy Fawcett. Up until now all Fawcett missions have begun there since that was where his last letters to his wife were from."

"But?" Paulson asked, sensing there was more to come. The dog was now asleep on his lap, sprawled across him in an untidy heap.

"But that's not where we need to go. The bullet ant toxin that the FBI's Dr. Fox discovered in Carlos Garrafon, the toxin that we think Ice is derived from, is from an area north by northwest of here. That's our real destination now." He pointed to a tiny, almost invisible red line on the map that diverged from their road and headed north and west in a squiggly, zigzag pattern, more like a piece of spaghetti dropped on a plate than an actual road.

"So why are you telling us all this?" Butch asked. "Let's go."

Ari turned and looked at him. The man's wide-set eyes were narrowed and a little defiant. It was still strange as hell to have him this close and he doubted he'd ever get used to it. His natural inclination was to snap at him but he managed to keep his voice level.

"Because my two previous missions also started at Dead Horse Camp, that's why. It's familiar territory for me, but I know very little about anything northwest of here. The terrain, tribes, customs – everything is going to be almost as new to me as it is to you. I just wanted to warn you, that's all. Normally I would've studied up on the area for months before a trip like this, but we didn't have time."

Paul craned his neck to look at the map. "So it's going to be real jungle now?"

"Well, not exactly. That comes farther on, probably in a few days, depending on our progress. When you see the hills and the taller trees begin you'll know we're close."

Hal also did his best to inspect the map, not that it did any good; everything here was new to him, too. "So let's find a place to bed down for the night, and we can prep for tomorrow."

Van Owen smiled at the ever-practical agent. "Good idea. Hold on, everyone – the road is likely to get lousy again really fast."

It did. As soon as they pulled off the main road it deteriorated into little more than a goat trail with vegetation arching into their path, creeping in as if determined to reclaim its turf. Large, thick leaves slapped against the Land Cruiser as it bounded and shuddered its way along. The humidity picked up again to the point where their shirts were heavy and wet and they doubted they'd ever be dry again. The sun was still high overhead but was just beginning to dip down into the west. They drove on for several more hours in silence as Ari manhandled the wheel, for the most part dodging the worst of the potholes. Once in a while he miscalculated and hit a kidney-jarring trench that tossed them so high it felt like their supplies would fly off and the Betty's suspension would disintegrate. After an hour of this abuse they came to a small river, no more than a creek, with brown water that flowed sluggishly by. Ari came to a halt and climbed out of the vehicle.

"What are you doing?" Butch asked. "It's only a few inches deep. Let's just drive through it."

Ari didn't say anything. Instead he just waded carefully out into the brown water in his waterproof boots, testing the depth. Satisfied that there were no surprises lurking beneath the surface he got back in and drove slowly, the four-wheel drive Toyota splashing through and easily cresting the bank on the other side.

"It only takes four to six inches of moving water to lose traction. There's no AAA to help if we get stuck or float away. Out here it really is better to be safe than sorry."

Brubaker gave a derisive grunt, which clearly conveyed his opinion, but otherwise kept to himself. The dirt road leveled out again and they were soon going almost twenty miles per hour. The dog had had enough of the leaves smacking its face and was back to laying on Paulson's lap, its eyes closed. The young man stroked its head gently. Each time they hit a bump it would crack open an eye to make sure all was well with the world before drifting back to sleep.

Soon after that they arrived at another water crossing, although this one had a rickety bridge of sorts spanning the twenty-foot gap, and the slow-moving black water looked much deeper. The bridge could have been designed by grownups using adult-sized Lincoln Logs and Tinker Toys, and by unanimous silent vote they deemed the sturdiness factor very low. By this time the sun was lower in the sky and long shadows crossed their path and the bridge, lending it an ominous feel. Ari looked at his watch as he got out.

"Let pitch camp here for the night. I don't feel like crossing that thing now, not with night so close."

He walked onto the bridge. It was little more than rough timbers lashed together with vines and a few scraps of rope, the driving surface made up of rough-hewn two by six boards, some newer and others splintered and rotting. It wasn't much wider than six or seven feet, or just wide enough for the Toyota to ease across. Maybe.

Hal joined him on the span and tested it by stepping here and there, with some of the planks bowing and groaning under his weight. He bent down and lifted one of the coarse boards, and quite unexpectedly it came up easily in his hand, not even secured. He dropped it back into place with a clunk. The look on his face was open and comical, and Van Owen imagined this was the expression the agent wore when interrogating a loud, protesting suspect that everyone knew was guilty, even the suspect himself.

"Really? We're going to cross over on that thing? I barely trust it to walk on."

Ari stomped here and there, all the way across to the other side, and jumped with his full weight from end to end. He had to admit that the old wooden bridge didn't look like much, but he was satisfied with its overall integrity.

"We don't have much choice, do we? Not a lot of other options since that river's probably too deep to go through. And trust me," he assured Hal with a sideways look, "we're going to see a lot worse the farther we go."

Butch and Paulson got out of the vehicle and joined the others. They were in a small clearing where it appeared many other travelers before them had made camp. The ground near the narrow river was flattened down and the thick vegetation was worn away. To Ari's mind it was as good a place as any to call it a night.

"Paul, you and your furry friend look around for something to burn. Palm fronds, sticks, whatever. But don't go far – no more than shouting distance away, please. I'll be surprised if you find much but do your best. We'll pitch the tents and get some dinner ready." He reached into one of the many pockets of his pants and pulled out a few rubber bands. "Here. Put these around the bottom of your pant legs and on the cuffs of your shirt."

Paulson took the rubber bands. "Okay, sure. But why?"

"Remember how I said how things like to slither and crawl around here? This will keep them from getting up your pant legs and into your boots. Trust me. And wear your hat, too."

The young man was accustomed to following orders in the Marines and did as he was told, rolling on the rubber bands and gathering up his hat. He then began a systematic hike around their campsite, moving in ever-widening circles. Ari saw the dog as it trotted behind him, sniffing around and marking this new territory eagerly. Soon they were both out of sight but could be heard crashing and stomping around in the brush.

Butch looked at the bridge for a second. "Sure we don't want to keep going? We've got plenty of daylight left and I'd rather get over this rickety thing now and have it behind us."

Ari was half-tempted to agree with him, eager to have this risky crossing behind them as well. But he shook his head, waving the recommendation away. Was he acting contrary simply because Frankie's husband had made the suggestion, or did he honestly feel like they'd gone far enough for the day? He wasn't sure himself, really, but he was pretty sure it was Butch. And besides, he knew better than to rush anything here in the wilderness.

"No, we've done enough. Let's get camp ready."

The three of them busied themselves setting up their small, two-man tents on some ground that was slightly higher than the rest, and in a matter of minutes they were ready to go, the green tents partially blending in with the surrounding foliage. Paul returned with an armful of sticks and twigs, apologetic that he couldn't find more. Ari assured him that was okay, and in short while they had a small fire popping and crackling nicely. Dinner was the last of the warmed up tamales and a little more fruit, washed down with water from the jerry cans. Hal leaned back against a thin tree with striated bark and sharp pointed leaves, and put rubber bands around his pant legs, too. He motioned to Ari.

"While we've got time, why don't you give us a little more insight into your Colonel Fawcett? It'd be helpful for all of us, I think, and since it's our cover the more we know the better."

Ari looked around the three of them illuminated in the firelight and didn't see any obvious objections. "Okay, sure. Now's as good a time as ever, I guess."

"Horror stories around a campfire? Awesome," Paul joked, batting away bugs that were dive-bombing his face and neck. He sprayed more insect repellant on his exposed skin and passed the can around. Everyone else did the same. "Does it have a guy with a hook for a hand in it? That's a classic."

Ari grinned. "No, no hooks, no horror stories. As I've said already Percy Fawcett was a British explorer back in the late 1800s and early 1900s. He was charged by a group called the Royal Geographic Society of London to survey the Amazon Jungle, which at the time was a largely unknown territory roughly the size of the entire USA. It was an impossible job for one man, but he made a go of it.

"He'd been in the British army and was a decorated soldier. He was battle-hardened and tough, and honestly I believe he thought himself indestructible. Fawcett went on a bunch of these expeditions with different goals in mind, such as finding the source of the Amazon River, or charting paths across the continent, or befriending tribes that had never seen a white man before." Ari poked a stick into the fire and watched sparks leap up into the darkening sky, forming little stars that twinkled before winking out, their incandescent lives quick and fleeting.

"But to Fawcett the most important thing was his search for what he called the Lost City of Z. Some people have called it El

Dorado, the fabled city of gold. Others had different names for it, some even thinking it was the home of The Fountain of Youth. Regardless, that was his one overarching goal; he was desperate to find Z and bask in the fame and fortune that would have been his if he'd been able to find it first."

Butch was scratching at his skin through his shirt again, almost absently, like it had become a nervous tic. His brow was knitted, the flickering light from the fire throwing confusing shadows across his broad face. His black hair was nearly invisible as it blended into the night behind him. "So how come I've never heard of this guy before all this? If he was so famous, I mean."

Van Owen shrugged, the gesture nearly lost in the orange glow. "I don't know. In school everyone studies famous explorers like Lewis and Clark, Daniel Boone, and of course Christopher Columbus. I hadn't heard of Fawcett until well after college. I've started thinking it's because he was British and didn't have anything to do with exploring North America, but that's just a guess. What matters is that on his last trip he headed back in with a small party, much like ours. He took along his son Jack, a young man very much like himself, tough as nails and hardy, and they talked one of Jack's friends into going too. His name was Raleigh Rimmell. He wasn't quite as tough and got talked into going at the last minute. He was young and more happy-go-lucky, and likely accepted the challenge on a lark, not really sure what he was getting himself into. Somewhere on their journey he injured his leg, maybe even to the point where they had to leave him behind. We really don't know. They told the world they were going to Dead Horse Camp and work their way north from there, thinking that was the location of The Lost City of Z.

"But at that time other parties were also searching for Z and Fawcett was terrified that someone would use this information to find it first. He couldn't allow that. My first two journeys began there too but didn't end well; I didn't find Z and I didn't find any trace of Fawcett, not really. All I ever got were some confusing and contradictory stories that had been passed down in tribal lore. Now, looking back and after a lot of research, I think he probably never went to Dead Horse Camp at all, and probably headed off in a different direction entirely. Whatever the truth is, after that he vanished and was never heard from again."

Paul plucked a leaf from a bush that was a mottled red and brown color and was inspecting it absently, rubbing it between his thumb and finger. "Even though other people have tried since then? Not including you, I mean."

"Oh, yeah, lots of people have tried to find the Colonel, and a lot of people have died, too. Hundreds, maybe thousands. There was even a huge, well-funded expedition in the 1970s that gave it a shot and failed miserably. It included pontoon airplanes and high-powered speedboats. Most of those people died, too."

Brubaker slowly stopped itching as this talk of failed missions and death began to sink in. Ari figured all these tales of dying had been more abstract before, but now that they were here in person the man was beginning to worry. Good, Van Owen thought. He should be worried. They should all be worried. The man's eyes, spaced so far apart, were squinted in thought, his mind somewhere distant and foreign.

"So just what the hell kills everyone out here?" he finally asked, squinting into the darkness, his eyes shaded and deep. "This hasn't been bad so far. I've been on hunting trips in Canada a lot worse than this."

A thin lizard about ten inches long inched toward the campsite. It was a light green with a yellow and black stripe down its back. Ari absently tossed a stick at it and the lizard jumped up and sprinted away on its back legs, into the brush, amazingly fast. Paul and Butch stared after it. Neither of them had expected that.

"So far, no, it hasn't. But the closer we get to the jungle everything changes. Just about anything can do you in: snakes, quicksand, insects, wild animals, heat, starvation, thirst, disease, exposure, and most of all the indigenous tribes, many who've never seen a white man before. You name it. Any one of those could kill you. Tell you what," he instructed, "next time you're online pull up Google Earth and pan over the Amazon rainforest. It's nothing but one huge mass of green, black, and purple, a swatch of dark colors so huge and uncharted it nearly covers the continent, and it's almost completely lawless. Kind of makes our Wild West seem tame in comparison. Whatever you do, just don't forget that."

During Van Owen's talk the stars had slowly vanished and the sky was now covered with a thick layer of black, churning clouds. Deep within the heavy mass lightning flashed and flickered, followed by deep, distant peals of thunder. It was beautiful in a primitive sort of way, Mother Nature strutting her stuff.

Hal stared at the heavens, mild concern written on his usually calm features. "We'd better call it a night. I think we're going to get wet pretty soon. Ari, we can talk more about this later, but this gives us an idea. Deal?"

By mutual consent they retired for the night, Paulson and Ari in one tent, Brubaker and Hal in the other. Ari was relieved that the agent had opted to bed down with Frankie's husband. The tent flaps were zipped up tight against the night, and whatever nocturnal predators or dangers prowled the area were outside their campfire's meager light. Each man in turn reapplied bug repellent to their faces and any other exposed flesh just as a precaution, then turned in for good. The dog scratched at the tent so Paulson lowered the zipper enough for it to squirm in. It curled into a tight ball at the foot of the young man's sleeping bag, barely visible.

Ari wasn't in the least bit cool in the warm, humid air, but liked having a thin blanket covering him regardless; he felt safer, more secure that way for some reason. The sounds of unfamiliar birds and other animals and insects outside the tent were just as he remembered, but would be at the very least strange and new to the others. It was so noisy at night it was sometimes hard to sleep until you were used to it. To him it was almost comforting. He had grown up near train tracks, and hearing a late night train whistle in the distance still eased his mind and comforted him. This was almost the same thing. Just as he was nodding off Paul shifted next to him.

"This is going to suck, isn't it?" Paulson didn't sound particularly worried. He was simply stating what he thought was a fact. Van Owen remembered him asking this same question before they had left, back in Louisville. "This trip. It's going to get rough."

Ari didn't want to lie to him, not now, not here. They had already come too far, and besides, he found he was becoming fond of the young man. And anyway, Paulson had been through tough times in Afghanistan during his stint in the Marines, and was likely a lot hardier than any of them gave him credit for, with or without a bum knee.

"Probably. What was that motto of yours?"

"What motto? Oh, you mean Think, Plan, then Act? Yeah, why?"

"Just don't do anything rash and always follow my lead. Acting or attacking without thinking and planning can get you killed fast. Just do as I say and we'll get through this."

Paulson grunted and seemed to accept the suggestion, even if it did sound more like a thinly veiled order. Van Owen heard him roll back over, facing away from him. The dog sighed and repositioned itself at the end of the small tent, its nails scratching lightly on the nylon floor.

"By the way, you plan on giving that dog of yours a name? You're pretty quick to name everything else. I figured you'd have one for him by now."

"Working on it. Kind of waiting for inspiration, you know? Nothing seems to fit yet."

Van Owen nodded in the dark, and in seconds they were all asleep, too exhausted to notice the huge storm that blew in and drenched their small camp, tearing and snapping at their tents. The diminutive fire hissed and smoked and went out under the deluge, stinking of wet, sodden coals.

Five o'clock came and Ari jerked awake in the tent. Like so many times before there hadn't been any dreams that he could recall, just an uncomfortable, leaden feeling, as heavy as the stifling, humid air inside the tent. He'd never been able to understand why he woke like that every night, snapping awake as if he were primed and ready to attack. He was burning hot and sweating so badly his head hurt and he felt nauseous, and he was afraid he might vomit. He kicked away the single blanket and tore off his shirt, aware but not caring that he was leaving his bare skin open to attack by a host of insects. Then he forced himself to lay back and relax, his eyes unfocused on the roof of the tent only a few feet above his face. At Paulson's feet the dog lifted its head and stared at him curiously before resting its chin on the young man's foot and closing its eyes once more.

The storm had passed several hours earlier and the roof of the two-man tent was soaking wet. There was almost no breeze to speak of outside. The nighttime was still full of sounds; birds calling back and forth in a pre-morning mating ritual, the rustling of nocturnal creatures nearby, the howl of a monkey. And – he sat up straight, his head brushing the tent – a very distant growl. Perhaps a jaguar, or maybe some other feline predator? He knew he was being hypocritical, but while he still had no desire to carry a firearm he was reassured that the other three did.

He settled back down and slapped at a mosquito that had infiltrated the tent. He doubted he would fall back asleep now and he was right. He listened to Paul's easy breathing and envied the young man his sleep.

At daybreak Ari was the first man up and about. The area around their campsite was a muddy, boot-sucking mess, the slop a deep rust color that reminded him of Georgia clay. There was also a swampy, rotting smell that came from everywhere and nowhere at the same time. But through good fortune or unconscious planning, the tents had been pitched on slightly higher ground and were just wet. He heard a grunting, snuffling sound about twenty feet away and saw a dark grey peccary, a pig-like animal about three feet long and with short legs, nosing through some of their dinner scraps. Paul stuck his head out of the tent and saw it too, his eyes wide.

"What the hell is that thing? A pig? Christ, what's a pig doing out here?"

"Close. It's a peccary, native to most of South America, and even though it looks like a pig it's really related to a hippo. And I'm glad it's here since it means there's no other nasties around."

Butch crawled from his tent and stared at the animal. Its crusty grey fur was bristly and rough and its snout was definitely pig-like. He was looking it up and down as if considering whether or not it would make a good meal. "Nasties? Exactly what nasties are you talking about?"

Ari stretched and began walking toward the bridge. The animal took notice of them with beady, alert, tiny eyes like black ball bearings. "Jaguars, mostly. Peccaries are a favorite snack for jaguars. And I may have heard one last night as we went to bed." Butch's hand moved quickly to his sidearm and he looked around as if one of the big cats were just outside their campsite, ready to pounce. He clearly was a hunter at heart, Ari noticed with mixed feelings. "They probably won't bother us now. We'll only have a problem if we surprise one or mess with its young."

The peccary apparently didn't care for the attention of the group. It snorted at them once, then with a dismissive head-flip it trotted in a bouncing gait into the brush, effortlessly gliding through the grasses as easily as a fish through water. Ari watched it go as Hal joined him and together they made the short walk through the thick, cloying mud to the bridge. They both saw that what had once been a slow-moving creek was now anything but; it was twice as wide and probably ten feet deep, with brown, churning water crashing against the banks and sticks and branches spinning and tumbling in the fast current. There was no going through that, no way.

"If you had a notion of crossing through the creek and avoiding the bridge, I'd say you lost your window of opportunity," the agent observed, stating the obvious. He slathered on bug repellant and tossed the can to Ari, who sprayed it all over, even onto his clothes. His skin glistened in the morning sunlight.

Van Owen grunted assent and walked around and then onto the bridge itself. He carefully paced off the width of the span and then went over to the Toyota and measured it. Then he prudently went ahead and did it again, just to make sure he'd been correct the first time; any mistakes at this point would be disastrous. His boots made sucking, popping sounds in the red mud as he walked.

"I'd considered it, but you're right; no choice now. It looks like we've got about six inches of clearance, three on each side," he told Hal. "Not much, for sure, but we should be okay if we take it nice and slow. You want to drive while the rest of us guide you across?"

"Me? No, not really. You and Betty have become pretty close these last few days. You'd better do it."

"Thanks loads." He stared at the bridge and back at the Land Cruiser. "Okay, let's get packed up and move out."

Their small fire pit was filled with water and floating coals so there was no chance for coffee or hot food, which was a disappointment. Ari grabbed an energy bar for breakfast instead and together they bundled everything up and packed the Toyota as well as they could, considering how wet and sloppy their gear was. The thick red mud was caked on their boots, which in turn made each one feel at least ten pounds heavier. Bungee cords were lashed across the top of Betty to keep everything in place but it wasn't nearly as neat and tidy as it had been before; the Land Cruiser had a top-heavy, awkward look, as if a stiff breeze might topple it over. When they were finished and ready Ari instructed Butch and Hal to cross over and help guide him. As they crossed to the far side they left dark red footprints and mud clods on the bridge. Paul was left behind to keep an eye on things back there.

"I'm going to go very slow and easy," he told them from the driver's seat, the window down and the engine purring softly. "I'll have my door open so I can watch this side, but shout out if I'm getting too close or something's wrong. Don't be shy, okay?"

Everyone nodded and took their positions. Ari wiped his hands on his pants and slipped it into four-wheel drive low and began to ease forward. All four tires spun and slipped before grabbing at the sloppy muck, and it took him almost five minutes to get it lined up properly with the bridge. Finally he had it positioned properly and began inching ahead.

"Here we go!" he yelled.

The front tires inched onto the primitive span and he began carefully easing it toward the other side, Hal and Butch standing on either corner and monitoring his progress. The back tires were almost on when the ass-end of the vehicle slipped and the Toyota pitched sideways, the right rear tire spinning off the bridge. They all shouted a warning as the vehicle jerked and the undercarriage banged hard on the wood, splintering the rear post. Ari cursed and carefully backed up, then repositioned himself and tried again. This time he managed to manhandle all four tires onto the rickety span and once again began slowly rolling across under minimal power, so slow it could've been measured in feet per hour. He had the front door open and was leaning low to keep an eye on his progress, watching with mounting concern as the bridge sagged and creaked ominously under the weight. He was nearly across when he heard a loud cracking sound, a bang like a single firecracker, followed by several more menacing pops. The back end of the Toyota dipped dangerously, almost as if it had fallen into a deep pothole, and he heard and felt a heavy crunching noise.

"We've got a problem, Ari!" Paul shouted, his voice loud and frantic. "Go, go, go!"

Ari didn't wait to figure out what was wrong. He gunned the four-wheel drive as gobbets of red and brown slop went flying ten, twenty feet in the air as the engine whined and all four tires spun in unison. He was still aimed almost straight ahead and he bounded and crashed off the bridge and onto the other bank. He quickly realized he was going too fast, so in desperation he spun the wheel and slammed on the brakes. Hal and Butch both dove to the side and away from the out-of-control vehicle. The filthy Toyota slid past them both and spun sideways in the mud before slamming into a small tree, bringing it to a jarring halt. With a quivering sigh of relief Ari leaned back in the driver's seat and exhaled noisily. His grip was tight on the steering wheel. Finally he reached out a trembling hand and killed the engine. Paul ran up to the driver's window and looked in, his cheeks flushed red in panicked excitement.

"Damn that was close! Check it out. Some of the boards back there just snapped in two."

Van Owen got out and walked shakily around the vehicle. There was now a two-foot gap in the span where several of the planks had simply broken in half and tumbled into the river, leaving a wide, dangerous gap. It was big enough for an unwary man to fall through, and easily big enough to stop any more vehicles from passing over. The broken boards had already fallen in the muddy torrent below and rushed out of sight.

Butch inched to the edge and looked down at the fast moving water. He kicked at a clump of mud and watched it plop into the current and vanish. "Hope to hell we don't have to come back this way. We're not crossing that thing again, not driving at least."

Paul stood beside him. "Somebody's gotta call the highway department. This is unacceptable."

Ari walked back to the vehicle and leaned against the muddy bumper. He knew how close to disaster they had just come. Not only could they have lost the Toyota, but all their supplies as well. Hal appeared at his side.

"You okay?"

"What? Yeah, I'm fine." He sighed deeply, still feeling shaky. "That was close."

"Yeah, I know. We can't afford to lose our main mode of transportation, and we can't afford to lose you, either. Let's be careful out there, okay?"

"Trust me. I'm doing my best. We've still got a long way to go and a lot to do."

He called the others back. They kicked as much mud off their boots as they could before getting in and heading out. Away from the river the road was in pretty good shape and he was able to hit double-digits, sometimes going nearly twenty miles per hour. The mud that had been caked on his tires thudded on the undercarriage as they picked up speed. The green landscape outside their windows blurred past them. Small rodents and larger animals that looked like raccoons with long tails scampered out of their way. Ari knew they were called *Coatimundis* and were really quite friendly, at least the ones he'd had interactions with before. He took great pains not to hit any with the Toyota as he buzzed along.

"Next time," he told everyone, "if it looks at all dangerous let's carry all our supplies on the other side of the bridge before crossing. That way if anything happens to our ride we won't lose it all." They all nodded in admiration at his after-the-fact wisdom, but secretly he was chastising himself for not remembering that ahead of time. He knew better but had simply forgotten, having been away from the jungle too long. A mile or two down the road Paul leaned forward.

"So who's going to fix that thing? Nobody can cross it the way it is now."

Ari didn't take his eyes from the road. "Someone will. Someone always does. Locals, probably."

"Locals? What locals? I haven't seen a soul."

"Just because we don't see them doesn't mean they're not around. This place conceals all kinds of secrets."

Paul lifted his blond eyebrows in mild surprise and leaned back in his seat. The dog crawled onto his lap and began to lick the cloying stuff from its paws with limited success. The wet, heavy smell of mud and near disaster was pulled out the open windows as they drove.

As the morning gave way to afternoon they stopped for lunch. They hadn't seen a single soul or village all day, but had noticed the trees and bushes getting taller and thicker the farther northwest they travelled. While they munched on some dried fruit and tough, chewy bread from one of the bins, Ari pulled the map from his backpack and spread it out on the hood.

"As far as I can tell by the map and the GPS we should be right about here." He pointed to a spot on the red squiggly line. "See how the color on the map changes from light to dark green? That means we're getting into some real jungle soon. We'll keep going until dinner and find a place to stop for the night."

Paul tore at a piece of bread and pointed with the crust at the map. "So what are we waiting for? Let's get going."

"Well what worries me is this." Ari moved his finger fractionally to a dark line that bisected their road up ahead. "This is a serious river. Let's hope the bridge is better than the last one we crossed."

They drove another two hours over the rutted road, the potholes so bad that they couldn't count how many times the Toyota's suspension bottomed out with a body-jarring crash. More than once the bumping was so extreme the dog flew off Paul's lap and into the air. The third time it happened it bared its teeth and Paulson had to calm it down, petting it and whispering soothingly.

Ari didn't take his gaze from the road. "Sorry about that. You figure out a name for that dog yet?" He had to yell to be heard over the noise of the engine and rough road.

"Nope. Not yet." He tapped his temple. "Working on it."

The road opened up a bit and was now almost two full lanes wide, and a few miles farther on they noticed that it began to slope gently downwards, a sure sign they were approaching another water crossing of some sort. Ari downshifted and slowed to less than ten miles per hour.

"What's up? Why are we slowing down?" Butch asked from the back seat. He was leaning forward between the two front buckets, his head between Ari and Hal. Ari involuntarily shifted away a few inches, still not used to having Frankie's husband so close to him. Van Owen followed a gentle curve in the road and pointed ahead. All four of them could now see a river directly in front of them, a very broad expanse of muddy water with the far shore a long way off. Ari's heart sank. There was no bridge, none at all, and in fact it looked like there had never been one.

"Ah, shit," Butch muttered, leaning back hard.

Van Owen pulled up about ten feet short of the water's edge, then killed the engine and got out of the vehicle. Hal and the others followed as he walked to where the dark green water met the land. It was a gentle, almost imperceptible slope, more like a beach, complete with rocks and pebbles in lieu of sand. The river there at the edge was only a few inches deep and lapped softly at the shore.

"How could there not be a bridge?" Butch asked to no one in particular. He spun around and stared at his companions with a look of open disbelief, his hands outstretched. "What kind of fucked up country is this anyway?"

217

Nobody had an answer for him. Ari stared at the expanse in front of them and pondered the crossing. The river was easily a hundred feet across, but midway through was a small hump of land, basically a speed bump laying lengthwise in the water. Some short grasses could be seen growing in tufts on the low island. The grass was flattened out in the direction of the slow current, evidence that there had been much higher water rushing through here in the recent past. He turned to the group.

"This really isn't out of the ordinary around here. I've got a feeling this is pretty shallow, at least right now. It probably fills up fast during a storm, but fortunately for us we haven't had one yet today and whatever rain we had last night has already gone. I'm going to try to walk across first and find us a path through this. Just stay here."

Without preamble he left his three companions and headed straight out into the murky water. For the first twenty feet or so it was only inches deep, not even coming up to his ankles, and he was able to easily walk through it. He saw small, brown fish darting around his feet, none any longer than his hand. As it got a little deeper Ari began to put each foot down more carefully, making sure he had solid purchase before taking another step. He was feeling cautiously optimistic when he stepped forward a little too casually and his boot slid on a rock. He slipped and nearly fell, waving his arms to keep his balance, the water suddenly up to his thigh. He cursed under his breath and backed up, then moved to his left and tried again. This time the rocky bottom was more forgiving and the water once again shallow, only up to his calf. He had to perform this ritual three more times before he finally waded up onto the island. His boots squished and made loud, sucking sounds, as if he were pulling a suction cup off glass with each step. After about twenty sloppy strides he was through the muddy grasses, to the other side of the island, and then he was back in the water again. He had to correct his course a few more times but this water remained no more than a foot deep and he finally made landfall on the other side. As he was stepping onto the rocky ground he heard a splashing to his left and saw a large, slick animal about the size of a collie slip into the water. Then he saw two more. He recognized them as capybaras, one of the largest members of the rodent family. He stared at the black creatures for a few moments as they swam off and away from him, barely making a ripple in the water despite their girth. When he was sure they were headed away he carefully retraced his path, his pants soaked nearly to his crotch.

Apparently Butch and Hal had seen the animals as well, as Hal had his Glock in his right hand and Butch had secured one of the rifles from the Toyota. He had the gun trained on the spot where the capybara had been. Ari waved them away.

"Nothing to worry about with the capybaras," he told the two of them. "They're harmless unless antagonized. We don't mess with them and they won't mess with us. At least they weren't caimans. The good news is we should be able to cross here without a problem. That's why there's no bridge. The locals must know there's no need for one."

"What are they, big-ass rats?" Paul asked, staring at the vanishing ripples where the capybaras had melted into the water. "They look like something you read about in New York City sewers."

"That's pretty much what they are." He turned to Hal. "Why don't you drive this time, okay? Follow me precisely and we'll get through this no problem. I've got our path mapped out."

The agent took off his glasses and wiped them on the hem of his shirt. Ari was impressed how clean and tidy the man could remain through all this, especially since the rest of them were covered with so much grime and filth they could have spent the day working in a New York City sewers alongside the giant rats. Hal's face held an odd, embarrassed expression, as if he'd let slip a loud belch in a posh restaurant.

"Ah, I'd rather not, thanks."

"Why not?"

He sighed. "Because I can't drive a stick shift, that's why."

"Excuse me? You never learned to drive a stick?"

"Nope. Never did. Government cars are all automatics, and that's all we had growing up, too. I never learned. Sorry."

Ari raised an eyebrow and looked towards the other two. "How about you guys? Either one of you know how to drive a stick?"

Paulson shook his head and put his hands up. "Nope. Sorry, I've always driven automatics, just like God intended."

Van Owen appraised them with pursed lips, looking each one of them up and down. "You know, this would've been good information to know ahead of time."

Butch took a step forward. "I can drive one. I haven't for years but I can."

Van Owen stared at Brubaker, considering. Damn. He was the last man Ari wanted behind the wheel, not only because by his own admission he hadn't driven a manual in a long time, but because Ari considered him too impetuous and impatient for the delicate touch the job called for. One slip with the gas pedal, one botched turn, and their transportation would be stuck, or worse. But neither did he trust the others to guide the Toyota through the river, not when he was the only one who knew the correct path. He couldn't be in two places at one time. He mentally flipped a coin.

"Can you do this?"

"Of course I can," Butch responded, clearly annoyed that Ari doubted his ability. "You lead the way and I'll follow."

Still apprehensive Van Owen stepped back into the river and began retracing his exact path. He looked at the other two. "You guys want to cross with me or ride over?"

Paulson looked to where the capybaras had just vacated and opted for the interior of the Toyota, still apprehensive about the huge rat-like creatures. The dog hopped in after him. Hal and Ari exchanged a quick look and the agent climbed back into the passenger seat and grabbed onto the handle. Ari nodded at him, thankful he had chosen to ride along and help Butch out. Finally he looked back at Brubaker.

"Keep it in four-wheel drive low and just go at a snail's pace. No faster than me. Got it? And no jerky moves or sudden acceleration."

Butch waved him away and climbed into the driver's seat. He fired up the engine and let out the clutch too fast, killing the Toyota with a jerk that snapped his passengers' heads forward. He muttered under his breath and tried again, and this time the big land-cruiser eased forward into the river, a little too fast at first but then slowing down to what Ari considered a safe speed.

The going was easy at first, flat and predictable, the water not even up to the Toyota's rims. Ari followed his prior path and angled left when he came to the drop-off that had soaked him before. He motioned Butch to do the same and noted with satisfaction that Hal was talking him through this too. Even if Brubaker couldn't or wouldn't take advice from Ari, he at least listened to the agent.

"A little more to your left, then straighten it out!" Van Owen shouted.

Butch corrected his course a fraction and kept close to Ari, only feet behind him. He was revving the engine more than necessary, but that was to be expected under these tough and unpredictable driving conditions. He bumped over an unseen rock and the Toyota popped up before it crashed down hard in water that was now mid-way up its tires.

"Easy! Slow it down a little. It's going to get deeper here right before the island."

Butch didn't acknowledge the order, his hands gripping the steering wheel and his nose mere inches from the windshield. But he did slow down a fraction. The water was now lapping at the floorboards and would soon start to seep inside. They moved ahead and Ari watched with concern as the vehicle suddenly listed dangerously to the right.

"More to your left," he yelled at Butch. "Easy does it."

Brubaker corrected some more but gave it too much gas. The back end of the Toyota kicked sideways and the right rear tire splashed into deeper water. He panicked and gave it more gas and cranked the steering wheel hard, all four tires spinning and tossing river water high into the air. Ari cursed and saw Hal grab onto the handle above his head with both hands as the back of the four wheel drive suddenly dropped into even deeper water. All four tires were still spinning crazily and the engine was revving higher as Butch fought to keep the big Land Cruiser steady. His eyes were wide and rimmed with white.

Van Owen splashed through the water as fast as possible and jumped behind the flailing Toyota. He put his back against the black bumper and pushed as hard as he could. He strained, his boots losing purchase on the slippery, rocky bottom. The Toyota's exhaust pipe was underwater and belching out a torrent of grey smoke and angry froth. Finally the tires bit into something substantial and the four-wheel drive careened toward the grassy island, throwing up four equal rooster tails of water. It plowed up and onto the small spit of land and spun sideways, mud and grass flying, its tires leaving deep ragged gashes. The engine revved once, coughed, then shuddered and died. Ari splashed heavily through the river and up to the passenger window, totally drenched and mud splattered, his brown hair dripping. The water that ran down his face couldn't quench the fire burning in his eyes.

"You call that taking it easy?" he barked at Butch across Hal. "What the hell was that?"

Brubaker wrenched his hands from the wheel and stared daggers back at him. "I got us here just fine," he snapped, his wide face slightly pale. He had a lock of black hair dangling down, partially obscuring one eye. There was sweat on his upper lip and broad forehead. "So just back the fuck off!"

"No, dammit, next time I say take it easy, I mean take it easy. You could've pitched our only means of transportation into the damn river, and then what?"

"But I didn't, did I? So take it easy, *Arjen*."

Ari flushed and his eyes narrowed to slits. He knew Brubaker was baiting him with the use of his proper name. Anyone else saying it was annoying, but to have Butch do it… He felt heat rising to his face and his hands clenched onto the side of the Toyota. His arms were straining as if he were trying to rip the door clean off its hinges. Years of frustration and dislike boiled to the surface. He wasn't thinking clearly and was poised to dive across Hal to get at the man.

But both Hollenbeck and Paulson saw the trouble that was about to explode across the tiny island. Hal quickly opened the door, effectively pushing Ari farther away from his target. The agent hustled out of the vehicle and interposed himself between Ari and their vehicle. Paul stayed inside but looked ready to grab Brubaker should he make a move to get out.

"What do you think you're doing?" Hal asked, his voice low but strong.

"That dumb bastard could've screwed everything up," Ari snapped, dodging from side to side to keep Butch in his line of sight. His breath was coming in fast gulps.

"Give the guy a break, Ari. He did the best he could and we're fine. You think that was easy, driving an unfamiliar car through a damn river?"

"He didn't listen! He panicked and didn't do as I said."

"Cut him some slack, will you? Everything considered, I'd say he did just fine, okay? We're safe and sound and so's the Toyota. So he panicked a little bit. I bet any one of us except you would've done the same thing."

Ari stopped his agitated moving and stared at the agent. Amazingly, there were specks of mud on his glasses that he hadn't bothered cleaning off yet. Van Owen knew he was right, knew he shouldn't have blown up, but the fact that Butch was the culprit irked him more than he thought possible. He took a deep breath and stared up at the sky overhead. Here in the middle of the river the blue expanse above them was clear of trees. A large bird of some sort, probably a harpy eagle, glided against the deep blue, its shape black and sleek, a true hunter.

"And besides," Hal went on, hands now resting on Ari's shoulders. His voice was low, meant to travel only to Ari's ears. "We need him. He can help us find Frankie, and isn't that what you really want?"

Ari recognized the intentional reference to Frankie for what it was, but it did serve to calm him down. He took another deep breath and nodded that he was better.

"Good. Now let's get back into Betty and get moving. We've got a long way to go yet. Okay?"

A whisper of a smile passed over Ari's face at Paul's unconventional name for their transportation. "Yeah, okay."

Together they slogged back through the mud and Hal got into the passenger seat. Only then did he remove his glasses and clean off the mud, inspecting them as well as he could in the confines of the Toyota. Ari fought through the slop and took the lead again. He forced himself to speak evenly.

"From here to the other side is pretty easy. Nice and slow and straight and we'll be okay."

Without a word Butch turned the key and the Toyota obediently rumbled to life. He slid it into first gear and eased out the clutch. All four wheels spun briefly in the mud before gaining purchase and they moved slowly over the weed-filled island and back into the water, leaving a dirty trail in the water that was soon washed downstream. The capybaras were gone, as was the eagle. Van Owen splashed ashore with Betty following behind him like a huge leashed dog. It rolled up onto the rocky ground and came to a halt. Without a word Brubaker took his original seat in the back and Ari got behind the wheel. He pulled away and quickly the river was behind them as they moved out. Ari could feel Butch's eyes on his neck as he drove. They were companions on this journey, Ari knew, but that was all they would ever be. That was fine with him.

Chapter 13

Two more days of travel, three blinding afternoon thunderstorms, and four more uneventful river crossings brought them to a tiny village that wasn't on any map. Ari wasn't even sure it had a name, although with the dusty, deserted roads, the sun beating mercilessly down on them, and a general air of despair, something like Tombstone or Deadwood would've fit perfectly. It was only lacking tumbleweeds and a saloon with swinging doors. The village consisted of a crossroads, a handful of thatched huts, and two adobe buildings, one of which turned out to be an ancient gas station of sorts. There was no signage indicating it was anything other than another decrepit building, just a lonely and battered white gas pump from circa 1950 that was connected to a rusty tank out back, and operated by a hand crank. The lone employee, if he could be called that, was an older teen-ager in a red Adidas T-shirt who didn't speak but managed to get his point across by taking about a hundred of Hal's American dollars and stuffing them in his pockets before motioning for him to go ahead and fill up. He was drinking a bottle of Coke absently, taking a sip every few seconds, each small sip followed by a loud smacking of his lips. Empty bottles littered the floor behind him. There was a battered old Coke machine against the wall, its light off and the cord lying limply on the floor, as lifeless as a flattened snake on a highway. Wherever he got his supply of soda, it wasn't from that relic, Ari thought.

"I think I just got ripped off," the agent said, scrutinizing his empty hand thoughtfully. "How do we know he even works here?"

"We don't," Ari said as he cranked the handle. The pump screeched louder than a car with bad brakes, one where the pads had deteriorated to just metal on metal. "Let's just hope he does. Man the nozzle, will you?"

Butch and Paul were outside the filthy Toyota as Hal began to fill it up. Ari noticed that Hollenbeck had strapped one of their machetes to his side, the evil-looking black blade nearly two feet long. Paul's dog trotted over and peed against the wall of the station, leaving a dark stain on the tan adobe, then happily lapped up water from a bowl Paul had found in their supplies. There were a handful of dark-skinned natives sitting in the narrow shade of the nearby buildings but none of them bothered to make eye contact with the travelers, or even seemed to care they were there. An ancient and wrinkled lady in a tattered shawl and who looked every bit of a hundred years old was squatting on a milk carton next to the station. She was busily husking sad little ears of corn that were even more fossilized than her. The old woman never raised her head from her task, just mumbled under her breath and pulled at the dusty husks with strong, gnarled hands.

"Not a very friendly place, is it?" Paul observed in a low voice. "Why's it even here?"

There was no automatic shut-off on the pump so when the tank was full some gas spurted out and ran down the side of the Toyota. Hal pulled the nozzle out and started on their jerry cans. The dog spotted a stray, scrawny orange cat ambling down the road and the fur on its neck stood on end, its head low to the ground and its rear haunches up in the air. If it growled at all it was too low for them to hear. Paul whispered an urgent order to it and the dog reluctantly hopped back into the Toyota. The cat acted like cats everywhere and paid no attention to them, haughtily strolling away.

Ari finished cranking the pump and stood up while the agent continued filling the last of the cans. "I don't know. My guess is that it's here to service illegal loggers, illegal oil drillers, drug smugglers, or all of the above. Impossible to say. So we're not going to spend any more time at this garden spot than we have to. We fill up and we're outta here. The quicker the better, no matter what they charge."

"Agreed," Hal stated. He was looking around almost casually, but his eyes were alert and dancing in all directions. Ari did the same but couldn't spot anything out of the ordinary. He either sucked at it, he conceded, or there wasn't anything to see. He hoped for the latter.

Just then three men he hadn't noticed detached themselves from the shadow of the farthest hut. They shuffled toward the Americans, walking side by side with an air of high school seniors striding imperiously through the freshman wing. The three were dressed in ratty jeans and tennis shoes, their once bright T-shirts now dirty and faded. The middle one wore a green ball cap pulled low, so low his eyes were hidden in black shadows. None of them could have been more than eighteen or nineteen years old. With their fists balled at their sides and their backs stiff there was a clear air of menace in the trio.

No, thought Ari, reconsidering. Not seniors in high school, but rather bullies on a playground, thugs used to getting their way through muscle and intimidation. He looked around to get Hal's attention but to his surprise and chagrin the agent was no longer there. Ari cursed under his breath then hissed at Paul and Butch to stay put. He straightened up and walked a few paces toward the threesome, hands open and arms extended in peace, all the while smiling broadly.

"Hi, there. How are you today?"

The newcomers stopped short at Ari's friendly advance. The center youth, the one with the ball cap, muttered something to his cohorts and continued on until he was just a few feet from the still smiling Van Owen. He peered up from under the brim of the hat. His left eye was clear and white, normal, but his right eye was blood red. Not just bloodshot, but so bright and bloody it could've been sliced open with Hal's machete. The eye was so unnatural that Ari nearly jerked back in shock. His smiled faltered for a split second before he managed to paste it back in place.

228

The native said something fast that Van Owen didn't understand, pointing up and down the road. It sounded like Portuguese or Spanish but with a thick local accent.

"Sorry, friend, but I don't understand a word you just said. Do you speak any English?"

Red-eye frowned and spoke again, louder and slower this time, as if by doing so he could be better understood. He gestured at the road once more, stabbing at it with his index finger, then pointing to his chest.

Ari kept his forced smile in place and looked at Red-eye's companions. "How 'bout you boys? Do you speak any English?"

The two looked at their de facto leader and the one on the left mumbled something in obvious frustration, ending his sentence with an angry shrug of his shoulders. The other didn't say anything, just coughed once then spit in the dust. The Coke drinking attendant who'd taken Hal's money stood in the open doorway with a neutral expression. his arms crossed. He said something that Red-eye didn't seem to like very much, since he barked a command back at him, the tone dark and menacing. The attendant smirked once and walked back into the station with a short, dismissive wave. Ari heard a shuffling behind him but didn't look away from the trio. He was praying that none of his companions were doing anything rash, like going for their guns or making a run for it. Keeping the game show host smile on his face was proving harder with each passing second.

"Nobody make a move," he hissed at Butch and Paul. "I mean it. Just act friendly, okay? And where'd Hal go?"

Red-eye took an angry step forward and shoved Ari's shoulder. Van Owen stumbled backwards and as he did so the leader's other hand suddenly brandished a long knife. He pointed the tip toward Van Owen, still gesturing heatedly up and down the road with his free hand. He heard Paulson and Butch gasp from behind him, and recognized that this was spiraling out of control in a hurry. He had to talk his way out of this now, before someone did something stupid. Ari knew the trio facing him could see that Paul and Butch were armed, and yet their leader was threatening him with nothing more than a knife? That didn't make any sense. Then an old adage came to mind: *never bring a knife to a gunfight.*

Oh, shit, he thought, quickly putting two and two together. They've got someone else out there.

"Guys," he said, his Jack O' Lantern grin never faltering. Sweat was beginning to run down his back, tickling as it soaked into the beltline of his pants. "Whatever you do, don't draw your weapons. They've got to have someone else in the shadows with a gun trained on us. I'm sure of it. Just let me work something out here…"

Red-eye took another step forward. He was shorter than Van Owen by a few inches, but he was wiry, his arms thin and stringy, with taut muscles and tendons under dirty brown skin. Their inability to speak each other's language was a problem, but Red-eye's underlying message was simple to decipher: that he was in charge, that this three-on-three matchup was no contest. His unmatched eyes were wild and alive as if he were not just anticipating but actually relishing an upcoming fight, a contest he figured would be theirs to win. The blade he waved around was specked with brown rust and was at least eight inches long, likely an old hunting knife. The cutting edge was notched and scratched as if it had seen plenty of use in the past. Then before Van Owen knew it, the point materialized under Ari's chin, the tip lightly pricking his skin. Behind Red-eye his two friends were grinning and laughing under their breath, elbowing each other.

Ari's hands went slowly up in the air to shoulder height, intentionally sending the clearest, most passive message he could. His natural instinct was to take a step back but he didn't think Red-eye would appreciate that.

"What do you want us to do?" Paul whispered from several feet behind him.

Ari didn't know, not really. In his prior trips he'd been confronted with angry natives, loggers, and oil drillers many times, but had never been in quite this situation before. If only he could communicate with them somehow! Talking and mutual respect had been his mainstays in the past. He'd always been able to sweet-talk his way out of danger, usually with a few trinkets greasing the skids first.

"Hold on," he said through a smile whose sincerity was no longer fooling anyone. He slowly tilted his head toward the Toyota.

"You don't happen to have another bottle of booze, do you?" Paul asked.

Van Owen didn't, much to his dismay. He looked at the four-wheel drive again, motioning with his head toward the vehicle. He slid his foot through the gritty dirt toward it and stared at Red-eye. He pointed at Betty with one of his upraised hands.

"You want something we've got? Come on, let's take a look. We've got all kinds of goodies with us." His voice was still smooth and steady, belying his true state.

He eased toward the vehicle while the tip of the knife stayed at his throat, shadowing his every move. Heartened that he'd gotten this far he kept moving slowly until he was standing at the rear of Betty. Red-eye's two companions stopped sniggering and watched them warily. Their hands were still at their sides with no weapons visible, but Ari knew that didn't mean they weren't bristling with hidden arms.

He began to open up the back to show their supplies when he noticed Hal leaning casually against the other side of the Toyota. His face was slightly flushed and he was breathing a little heavily, but he otherwise appeared relaxed and at ease. One flap of his shirt was untucked from his pant, and his hat was nowhere to be seen. He smiled at Ari and winked discretely.

Red-eye jerked at the sight of the agent and the knife moved in a flash from Ari's neck to a point equidistant between them.

Hollenbeck smiled genially at him and held his arms up, palms out in evident surrender.

"Ready, Ari?" the agent asked, his eyes still locked on Red-eye.

Van Owen started to ask, "Ready for what?", but in that instant Hal ducked low, pivoted on his left foot and lashed out with a wicked kick at Red-eye's knee. The young man screamed as Hal's right boot crunched into it with the sound of someone stomping on a bag of pretzels. His knee buckled, bending in an odd, gut-wrenching angle that nature never intended. He grabbed at his leg and toppled over sideways, the knife hitting the dusty road with an audible thud. Red-eye rolled onto his back and cradled his shattered knee with both hands, his back and sides covered in orange and brown road dirt as he thrashed on the ground. Spittle ran down his chin and between his clenched teeth as he howled in pain. Ari was both surprised and impressed; he had no idea Hal could move that fast or that viciously.

Red-eye's wingmen growled in shock and made a lunge towards the agent, but Hal's Glock appeared in his hand and was aimed squarely at the pair, the muzzle steady and unwavering. The two skidded to a stop, dust kicked up by their shoes. Their hands went up fast.

"Paul," Hollenbeck snapped, "the attendant!"

Paulson snatched out his own sidearm and sprinted into the station's open door in three long strides, moving quite well even with his bum leg. In less than twenty seconds he marched back out, the attendant in front of him with his hands laced behind his neck. The attendant looked over the tableau in front of him, humor crinkling the corners of his eyes.

Red-eye's companions were looking around them as if expecting something to happen, some hammer to fall, but nothing did. The old lady continued shucking her corn as if this sort of thing happened daily, and the rest of the locals simply peered quietly from the shadows. Ari's eyes darted around the huts, ready to duck or hit the ground if necessary.

"Hal!" he shouted, "be careful! They've got to have somebody else out there."

The agent never took his eyes off the two in front of him. "I already took care of that," he said softly. He took a step forwards and curtly motioned them to their knees with the Glock's barrel, nonverbal communication they both understood. They were whispering in hissed sentences to each other and still looking around as if they expected the cavalry to come charging over the hill at any moment. They slowly fell to their knees as Hollenbeck stood behind them. One of them began to say something and Hal rapped him on the back of the head with the gun barrel. He yipped in pain and fell silent, massaging the fresh bump on his head.

Paulson had his gun in the attendant's back and walked him over to Hal. The agent motioned him to the ground as well, but to their surprise the man spoke.

"Please, no," he said in halting English, the accent so thick he could barely be understood. "I am a friend."

Hal didn't look away from his charges. "So you speak English? Why didn't you say so before?"

The man nodded at the three men on the ground. "Because of them. They do not like it when I speak the English since they cannot."

Ari was finally coming to grips with the fact that the drama was over, at least for now. Butch had his pistol out but wasn't sure where to aim. He held it at the ready but had no target in mind, his eyes jerkily tracking everywhere. His face was pale but composed. Ari was impressed; he himself was a nervous wreck and could barely control his trembling hands.

"So who are they?" Hal continued.

"Bad men," the attendant said simply. *Valentões*. Bad men who do bad things. They work for El Quemado. How do you say? The Burned One."

"The Burned One? Who is that?"

The man scrunched up his face in concentration and frustration. "Sorry. I do not have the words. In the jungle. They work for him."

Ari stepped up to him and motioned for Paul to lower his gun. The man saw this and slowly put his hands down, nodding thanks.

"Where did you learn to speak English?" he asked, not unkindly.

The man smiled widely at Van Owen. His teeth were straight but stained yellow, perhaps from a poor diet and a lifetime of Coke consumption. "From priests and from TV. I try very hard to learn the English."

"You speak it very well," Ari commended, and the man puffed his chest out in pride, pleased at the compliment.

"Thank you very much. I try hard."

"What did those men want from us?" Ari asked, keeping his sentences simple.

"Money, to pass. I know there is a word for it…"

"A toll? Did they want us to pay a toll?"

"A toll?" the man repeated, rolling the foreign word around in his mouth. "I do not know that word. But they wanted money for you to pass, to use the road. They do that to all who come through here. They make them pay. El Quemado permits this. They work for him."

Hal turned to his three companions. "We need to go right now. I took care of the two shooters in those other buildings but someone else could come by any minute." He focused his attention on the attendant. "We'll take care of these men for now. Will you be safe?"

He shrugged. "Yes, I think so. I did nothing bad. I just work here. I collect the monies for gasoline."

234

Hollenbeck told Butch to get some rope from the Toyota and together they tied the hands of the thugs who were still on the ground. Paulson kept his gun trained on them while the agent went into the other buildings and came out a few minutes later with two more men, both of whom were holding their heads and moaning, staggering a little as they walked. They lashed their hands together with rope as well, then used more to secure them together, chain-gang style. The end of the rope was tied to Betty's sturdy rear bumper. Under Hal's concise directions they completed all this in less than five minutes. Butch motioned to Red-eye who was still moaning and holding his wasted knee, a knee that was now swelling visibly.

"What do we do with him?"

Hollenbeck didn't hesitate. "Help me pick him up."

Together they hauled him up on his one good leg and roughly draped him across the hood of the Toyota. Then as Brubaker held him Hal lashed him snugly in place with several red bungee cords. The wounded man barked out several painful cries but stayed put. His eyes were screwed tightly shut.

Ari walked to the attendant. "What's your name?"

"Ernesto. My name is Ernesto."

"Thanks, Ernesto. I don't think they'll bother you for a while."

Ernesto smiled his yellow smile at them again. "Thank you," he said. "And be careful. The jungle is bad. El Quemado is bad."

The four of them hustled back into the Toyota, eager to be clear of the place. Ari fired it up and slowly moved out, the four men walking unsteadily behind them and mumbling what were certainly curses and threats.

"We are not going to be on their Christmas card list," Paul said to no one in particular, his hand on the dog's head.

They drove like this with their captives stumbling and tripping along for nearly four miles into the thickening jungle before stopping and cutting the rope from the bumper. Bright flowers were scattered along the edge of the road, flowers with colors so vivid they left an after-image in their eyes when they looked away. One that caught Ari's attention was a bright yellow bloom about five inches in diameter with inner petals that were streaked with thin, wispy brush-strokes the color of blood. Red-eye was no longer moaning in pain but was glaring at the four of them, hatred radiating from him in nearly physical, palpable waves. His knee was swollen tight against the fabric of his filthy, dusty jeans. Hal grinned once and unclipped the strap holding his holster closed and calmly slipped the Glock out. Without preamble he gently placed the end of the barrel on Red-eye's forehead with no more emotion than if he were opening a refrigerator door for a snack. Red-eye's breath caught and his eyes comically crossed as they stared in horror at the black barrel pressed to his skull, and any measure of guile or anger was instantly vanquished, replaced by open, blind horror. Hollenbeck snapped his fingers twice and got the man to look away from the gun and at Hal's face. The agent shifted the point of the barrel to one side and pulled the trigger. The blast thundered through the jungle and made all of them except Hal jump. Red-eye flinched backwards so hard he nearly tumbled off the hood. Brightly colored birds burst from the trees overhead and wheeled away, squawking their displeasure. The young man was shaking as sweat poured down his face, rolling down his cheeks like tears, and a dark stain appeared in his crotch where it spread wetly. Hal pointed the gun at him again as a faint wisp of smoke curled from the hot barrel. He pointed to his own eyes, then at the gun, and then at Red-eye. The young man nodded rapidly, the agent's meaning clear: *If I see you again I will kill you.*

They roughly slid Red-eye off the hood and left them all there, deep in the jungle and still lashed together. As the Americans pulled away there were no sounds from the stunned men behind them. All they could hear was the noise of the Toyota's engine as they drove along the dirt road, the village growing more distant with every passing second.

After a few minutes on the road Ari broke the silence. "So can you please tell me what the hell happened back there? How'd you know there were other men? And what was that business at the end with your gun?"

"Yeah," Paul chimed in from the back seat. "And that kick? Where'd you learn that move? Impressive."

Hal was watching the road, his right hand holding on to the overhead handle for support as they put as much distance as they could between them and the village. He had tucked his shirt back in and was pretty well tidied up, his short blond hair brushed back and no outward sign that anything untoward had happened. His hat was in his lap. But Ari could see that his mouth was a tight line and his eyes behind his dirty glasses were hard and unblinking, little more than cold dark marbles. To Ari he looked like someone altogether different, not at all the Hal Hollenbeck he'd known for years. For a minute he thought the agent hadn't heard them, but when he finally spoke his voice was odd, almost mechanical, like he was relaying the incident to his superior during a standard debriefing.

"The village felt wrong, I'm sure you all noticed that. As I was filling up the car I thought I spotted some movement in one of the huts. Not much, just someone in the shadows. That was bothersome enough, but as soon as I saw those three make a move toward us I thought I had it all figured out. Turns out I was right."

"Good thing, too," said Paul with admiration. He patted Hal on the shoulder, a gesture that evinced no reaction. "Keep it up."

"I ducked behind the Toyota and hurried around the huts, coming at them from behind. The two shooters weren't expecting anything and it was a simple matter to temporarily neutralize them." He didn't sound at all proud or pleased. His voice was still flat and monotone, the highs and lows clipped off. Ari didn't understand

237

why he was acting like this. After all, he thought, Hal likely had just saved all their lives.

"By the time I got back to the car the one with the ball cap had his knife at your throat, Ari. I'm sorry that happened; it should've never gotten that far."

Van Owen glanced away from the road for a split-second to look at Hal. "Sorry? I'm not sure what happened but I'd say you did great. You saved our butts and no one got killed. What's to be sorry about?"

Hal grunted and stared ahead, his face still impassive. He could have been nothing more than an animatronic replica of a man, like something from Disney World's Hall Of Presidents. "You don't understand. My job as an FBI agent is to protect American citizens no matter where we are. I should've permanently neutralized the leader right away, the one in the hat, and probably the other two as well."

It took a second before that completely sunk in, and even then Ari couldn't believe what he was hearing. He slowed the vehicle and stopped before staring at Hollenbeck, his mouth open. "What do you mean, permanently neutralize? You mean you should've killed him?"

"That's exactly what I mean. Contrary to what you see on TV we don't yell 'freeze' or give an aggressor time to act. If an American citizen is in imminent danger we use maximum force without warning. It's how we're trained. We shoot, and we shoot to kill."

"I can't believe that."

"You should. If an FBI trainee can't agree to that he scrubs out. And besides, now all five of those men know we're out here, which direction we're heading, and that we're no push-overs. That could be very, very bad in the future." He stopped and blinked once, still clearly deep in his own mind. "I hope we don't regret my inability to do what needed to be done..."

Ari was shocked. To him Hal had always been the consummate agent, a man always on his game and ready to follow protocol and orders without question. Now Van Owen was seeing him in a new and different light, like a sculptor who carefully chisels away at a perfect block of stone until his vision is revealed – only to find out that the rock itself is flawed. In all the time he'd known him Ari had never been privy to this side of Hal, and he wasn't sure he liked seeing this fallible, human side. Paulson and Brubaker were quiet in the backseat but he doubted they were picking up on any of this. Ari stared at the unmoving agent for another few moments then put the Toyota into gear and continued on. If Hal Hollenbeck was worried, he wondered chillingly, what should the rest of them think?

Chapter 14

After their encounter at the village they all agreed to put as many miles between them and Red-eye's group as they could. They drove until dinner, grabbed a bite from their supplies, then pushed on until it was getting dark. Darkness, they all noticed, was coming sooner each day – not because the sun was setting any earlier, but because the trees were taller and thicker and the canopy overhead was becoming denser and blocking out the sun. In fact it never seemed like full daylight any more, just constant shade with only random sluices of sunlight knifing through the heavy blanket of leaves. More often than not howler monkeys screamed and scolded at them from high in the branches, and birds of all sizes and colors, some with blues and reds as bright as neon, darted in and out of the shafts of light. They spied anacondas and other snakes that were easily fifteen or even twenty feet long that dozed in the patches of sunlight or dangled from low branches, silently eyeing the travelers as they passed by, their ancient reptilian minds considering the travelers' potential as a meal. For men more accustomed to neat and tidy air-conditioned homes, a Starbucks on every corner, and amenities like hot water on demand, this land had shifted to a place completely foreign and strange. This was the jungle now, and they all keenly felt its raw, primordial nature. With his prior exposure it impacted Ari to a lesser degree, but the rest of them were so far out of their element they could have been on another planet.

The road now was little more than a rutted trail through the trees, peppered with potholes big enough to swallow less hardy transportation in a single gulp. The speedometer rarely registered over ten miles per hour and at times they were forced to such an agonizingly slow crawl the red needle jiggled near zero for miles at a stretch. They passed two or three locals walking along the road coming from the opposite direction, but no one gave them more than a passing glance or even a wave. They hadn't passed another vehicle in hours. The sense that they were virtually alone in this vast wilderness was pressing upon each of them. Their GPS only worked when they came to a clearing and had a clear view of the sky. It still showed them on the squiggly red line, which was heartening as it meant they were headed in the right direction, deeper into Mato Grosso. Ari's hands and arms were aching from fighting with the Toyota over the increasingly poor road conditions, but none of his companions would or could spell him. They were all feeling sore, tired, and filthy, their nerves beginning to fray.

Perhaps worst of all was how they smelled. After so many scorching, humid days without a proper shower they all reeked. The stench reminded Ari of the time he'd left his gym bag full of sweaty clothes in the trunk of his car for a few weeks during a heat wave. The four of them smelled just like that, he admitted, and he could barely stand himself. A bath or shower would've done wonders for their spirits and morale. They rarely spoke to one another, and when they did it was only in short, terse sentences. Ari talked little, his eyes glued to the dimly lit path ahead of him.

About an hour before dark they noticed the road slanting down again, which they all recognized by now meant an imminent river crossing. Paulson shifted in his seat to get a better view up ahead. The dog had its head out the window to catch what little breeze there was at such slow speed, its tongue lolling out the side of its mouth as it panted heavily. They were all staring ahead through the tunnel formed by the overhanging trees and saw what looked like a bright, nearly incandescent light farther down the road. Ari kept the Toyota creeping forward as he tried to figure out what he was seeing. As they approached it the bright light grew in size and intensity until they realized it was nothing more than daylight at the end of the jungle canopy. When they reached it the road terminated at a wide, nearly desolate, colorless sand flat. For what must have been miles in either direction there was no jungle at all, just a swath of sand and rock at least a hundred yards wide, maybe more. On the other side of the expanse they could see that the jungle began again, a solid wall of black and green that looked as impenetrable as the hull of an aircraft carrier.

"Okay, I give. What the hell is this?" Paul asked from his perch on the back seat.

Ari shrugged. "I don't know. I've never seen anything like it before."

Across the sandy expanse were large rocks scattered about in random patterns, huge bocce balls tossed out and worn smooth by thousands of years of flowing water. Puddles and small ponds littered the open area, most small and inconsequential, others with a footprint as big as a house and reflecting the dark grey sky above. Ripples were visible on the larger ones, a sure indictor of things living below the surface. Tall thin birds like marlins strutted around stabbing at underwater prey, their feathers fluttering in the cool wind that was starting to kick up. More harpy eagles wheeled overhead.

"Didn't expect to see something like this here," Butch commented. "What the hell is this place?"

"I'd say it's a riverbed," Ari conjectured. "Just a dried up riverbed. It shouldn't be too hard to cross."

Brubaker continued staring straight ahead at the odd sight. "That'd be a nice change, considering what we've seen so far."

Hal was looking around at the dense jungle on either side of them. He removed his glasses and polished them on his shirt. Of the four of them somehow he remained the cleanest, although even he was beginning to show the effects of so many days without fresh clothes and a shower. Ari didn't feel the need to verify it, but he'd bet good money that the agent smelled better than the rest of them, too. He didn't look much worse for wear than an average Joe mowing the yard on a warm summer day.

"You want to cross now? So close to nighttime?"

Ari joined him in looking around. He deeply wanted to keep going toward Frankie and couldn't imagine stopping now if they didn't have to. "Not really, but there's no good place to set up camp for the night on this side, that's for sure." A few drops of rain spattered on the windshield. "I was busy watching the road as I drove. Anyone notice anywhere behind us where we could set up camp?" The three of them shook their heads. No one had.

"I'm not too keen on pitching our tents in the middle of the road here. And I definitely don't want to sleep in this thing," Ari stated, waving his hand in front of his face as if to ward off the stink.

"Good God, no." Paulson wrinkled his nose in disgust. "Smells like road-kill in here. Sorry, guys, but it does."

Nobody could argue with that. Ari got out and walked twenty feet into the open expanse. Huge dragonflies buzzed over his head, their gossamer wings nearly invisible in the fading light. The sand and scree were loose under his boots and with each step he broke through a thin crust, then sank a few inches into the gritty, damp surface. He probed some more with the toe of his boot while rain patted the top of his head. When he was satisfied that it was nothing Betty couldn't handle, he got back in.

"Last chance to sleep in the Toyota. Any takers?"

"I sure don't want to," Paulson admitted passionately. The other two agreed.

"I thought not." He dropped it into four-wheel drive low. "If we hurry we'll have plenty of time to find somewhere to set up camp on the other side. Hold on, here we go."

He eased out the clutch and moved ahead. The going was easy at first but he had to take a roundabout path across in order to dodge the larger ponds and huge boulders in his way. Rain started coming down heavier now, still little more than a sprinkle, but the drops were big and fat, pinging on the Toyota and leaving quarter-sized, muddy splotches where they hit its dusty surface. He turned on the wipers but they did little besides smear thin, creamy mud across the windshield in uneven streaks.

They were making decent, albeit slow progress. Ari had to back up a few times and try a different tack when he came across other ponds or rocks too big for Betty to handle. They were halfway there when he came to six large boulders blocking his direct route. Several dozen mid-sized ones, too large for Betty to traverse, were also in his way when he tried to go around them. To avoid going even farther out he decided to forge through what looked like a small pond only thirty feet across that was in-between two of the largest rocks. As he eased into the shallow water no deeper than two or three inches deep he felt Betty suddenly sink, as if they were on a malfunctioning elevator that had dropped a few feet unexpectedly.

"What the hell was that?" Butch exclaimed. "That wasn't right."

"No, that wasn't right at all," Van Owen admitted, his stomach sinking nearly as far as Betty had. He gave the Toyota more gas and it obediently ground forward a few more feet before stopping with a thud, all four of them jerking forward with the impact. He knew he'd run into a larger obstacle under the surface.

"Hold on," he ordered through gritted teeth. "I'm going to back up and try a different way."

His hands were slick on the wheel as he dumped it into reverse and gave it some gas. Betty moved a few inches before the rear end dropped again, almost as if they'd driven off a shelf. As the others watched in growing concern he tried rocking the four-wheel drive vehicle back and forth. Each time it would move a few inches before bumping into something firm and unyielding. Finally he sat back hard.

"Dammit, we're stuck."

"That's just fucking great," Butch snapped. "Nice going."

Ari ignored him. "Sorry, but everyone's going to have to push."

Hal, ever the calming influence, opened his door and stepped into water that was up to the middle of his calves. He motioned the other two to do the same. "Come on, folks, this stuff happens," he said. "If this is the worst thing we do today we can count ourselves lucky. Let's just get this done so we can get out of here."

Brubaker and Paul splashed into the water while the dog looked on curiously. It tried to jump out but Paulson gave it a pat on the head and shut the door before it could make a move. Thunder rumbled somewhere behind them as the three of them, at Ari's direction, moved to the front of the Toyota. The sky was getting darker and the wind was picking up. The tops of the trees behind them danced and fluttered, the leaves turning upside down and twirling in the gusting wind. The dragonflies had vanished.

"I'm going to rock it back and forth, but my plan is to back out of here and try a different way. Everybody ready?"

The three moved to the front and put their collective backs against the bumper. Ari gunned the engine and began moving forward then backward as fast as he could shift gears. The engine revved and dirty water sprayed up in all directions and mixed with the rain that was coming down even harder now, until all three of the pushers were soaked, water dripping off their faces and hair. The tires spun and thrashed but they made no progress, and if anything they quickly realized they were doing little but digging themselves deeper into the riverbed.

Just then they heard a tremendous crash as lightning struck near the edge of the jungle behind them. A towering tree exploded at the base as the lightning danced there, sparks and flames shooting in all directions. It moaned and toppled backwards out of sight, noisily taking out several of its smaller brethren with it. More thunder crashed around them in almost physical waves and the dog jumped down onto the floor behind Ari's seat where it trembled in fear. The rain suddenly began pounding down in earnest, thick, heavy sheets like undulating waterfalls that connected the sky to the ground.

"This isn't working, Ari!" Hal shouted over the downpour.

"I know!" he yelled back. "Get behind me and push. Let's try going forward again!"

245

The sand-flat was quickly filling up under the torrent of water. The pool where they were stuck was already twice as large now and it was becoming hard for the men to walk. Ari imagined dozens, perhaps hundreds of tributaries upriver feeding this main trunk, the whole thing quickly filling up as the rain poured down. The three men splashed and fought their way to the back of the Toyota and began pushing anew, cursing as their boots slid on the uneven, rocky bottom. Paulson's feet went out from under him and he fell completely underwater, jumping up and sputtering.

"Dammit!" he shouted, spitting and wiping water from his face. He could barely be heard over the roar of the engine and the pouring rain.

"Keep pushing!" Ari yelled back at them. "If we don't get out of here soon we're gonna be in serious trouble!"

The three men managed to get back into position and push again, all of them grunting with the strain. Paul's young face was red with the exertion. Whether the deeper water made Betty slightly more buoyant or because adrenaline was shooting through their systems, they felt the SUV inching forward. The engine was screaming so loudly it nearly drowned out the driving rain, a high-pitched roar like some wounded beast. One of the front tires finally found traction and the Toyota leapt forward – then the front end fell nearly a foot and it slammed to a halt. Ari cursed and tried rocking it again, but this time it wouldn't budge. All four tires spun uselessly in water so deep even the exhaust pipe was underwater. He swore again and turned off the engine.

"Why'd you do that?" Hal shouted, his voice barely audible above the storm.

Van Owen pointed to the hood as he opened the door and got out. "The water's getting too deep. It's going to get into the engine and seize it up for good. Turning it off might just save it. We're too stuck to move anyway!"

Hollenbeck nodded in understanding. "What now?"

Ari clambered onto the roof and ripped off bungee cords, freeing up their supplies. He tossed the first bundle, one of the tents, to Hal and motioned him in the direction they'd come, back toward shore. They all looked at him in confusion.

"We get everything off here now!" He grabbed the other tent and heaved it at Paulson who caught it with both hands. He staggered backwards but didn't fall over. "We may lose it and we need the supplies. We've got to work fast! We don't have much time."

The torrent continued unabated as the men formed a ragged assembly line. The sand flats were submerged and they could see that it really was a river now. Agitated water was everywhere, flowing fast and getting deeper by the second. In no time the flow was up to the bottom of the Toyota's doors and Ari felt the heavy vehicle shift dangerously under him. He picked up the pace and threw more supplies down to Hal, who passed them along to Butch, who in turn handed them off to Paulson. The young man was panting as he splashed through the turbulent water to the shore where he threw everything in an untidy heap beyond the reach of the rising water. The river was up to their knees.

Suddenly Betty shifted again and slid sideways, canting dangerously to one side, and Ari nearly flipped off the roof. His grip on the roof rack was the only thing keeping him place.

"Get down from there!" Hal shouted as he fought to stay upright.

"Yeah, forget the rest!" Butch yelled. "We're going to lose it any second!"

Ari grabbed his backpack and reluctantly jumped off into the water and ripped open the back gate. He tossed more crates and plastic bins out, faster than either Hal or Butch could handle them. Some fell through their hands and began rushing down the river, including one bright blue container the size of a small suitcase. Brubaker swore loudly and tried to go after them but the supplies were gone in an instant, bobbing and spinning away. He stopped and looked toward the far shore. He impatiently slapped water from his face and squinted through the driving rain.

"Hey!" he yelled over his shoulder, pointing at the opposite shore. "What the hell are those things?"

Ari paused long enough to see what he was talking about. Through the downpour he could just make out shapes, long, narrow, knobbly shapes filled with yellow teeth, slipping into the river and swimming towards them.

"They're caimans," he yelled, staring in open disbelief.

"Caimans? What the hell are those?" Butch yelled.

"Alligators," he said, loudly enough to be heard. "Amazon alligators. Shit."

He couldn't tell for sure but there had to be a dozen or more of the dark green reptiles swimming quickly towards the Toyota. Most were no bigger than ten feet long, but several of the larger brutes were at least fifteen feet of ridged, armored skin. All four men had stopped hauling supplies, frozen in place by the sight. Finally Hal grabbed Ari's shoulder.

"This may be a stupid question, but should we be worried?"

Van Owen wiped water from his face and nodded. "Yes, we should. I don't know if they've got some young close by or if they're just hungry. They may be spooked by the storm. Whatever it is we need to hurry. You should probably get your guns out just in case."

Just then Betty slid five feet and listed more to one side, the constant pressure of the water pushing it sideways. It was shuddering and pitching as if in death throes and they could tell it was going to flip over any second. Ari grabbed a few more random bundles and threw them at Hal and Butch, rushing now and not thinking clearly. Paulson was lugging some bins to the shore and was the farthest away. Another bolt of lightning hit somewhere behind them and they heard the tortured wail of another tree going

248

down. Then the Toyota bobbed upwards for a moment before it slowly, almost serenely, tipped over with barely a splash. It floated fifteen feet then bumped and wedged itself against one of the large rocks, the oily, rusty undercarriage now facing them. The back tire spun slowly, water dripping from it as it turned. The bumper sticker *I lost my heart and my virginity in Gatlinburg* was flapping and only stuck on by a corner, the force of the water about to tear it off completely.

The group of caimans slowed and several veered toward the floundering Toyota while the rest were still aimed squarely at the trio. Butch pulled out his pistol, gripped it with both hands, and sighted down the barrel. He squeezed off a shot that splashed just right of the lead caiman, a huge beast nearly fifteen feet long. They didn't slow.

"Time to go!" Hal yelled urgently. Paulson was screaming something from shore but they couldn't hear him over the storm and the torrent raging around them.

All three began quickly slogging through the river that was now waist deep in places, with a current that threatened to knock them over any second. Paul was pointing and splashing toward them in a hurry, his face wide and panicked. He was jabbing his finger at the capsized four-wheel drive. They all turned to look and Ari gasped. Paulson's dog was standing on something inside Betty and had its head out the open side window, looking around wildly. Rain had matted down its black and white fur and its eyes were wide and terrified. It saw the three of them and clambered out the window, preparing to jump toward them into the swift current. Paulson was frantically splashing toward the Toyota. He reached them in seconds.

"We've got to get my dog!" he shouted, his voice laced with panic.

Van Owen grabbed his shoulder and pointed at the caimans that were now only a dozen yards away. Paul roughly shook off his arm and surged ahead. Ari snatched at his shirt but couldn't hold him back.

"No, Paul! Don't! It's too late!"

Butch growled something low under his breath then shoved Ari aside and took off after Paulson. The dog saw Paul and its ears pricked up. It scrambled onto Betty's side and stood there unsteadily as the vehicle shuddered and bucked underneath it. Hal had his Glock out and began taking shots at the oncoming caimans. He hit one just behind its head and it spun once, snapping at the air before rolling onto its back and drifting away in water that was momentarily tinged a foamy red. He pulled the trigger again and again, more often than not hitting his intended target. The lead caiman's head exploded in pink and red mist and two others fell upon it, ripping viciously at the twitching carcass.

Butch and Paul were less than ten feet from the Toyota when the dog jumped. It splashed into the raging water and luckily bumped back up against Betty's undercarriage just as its head broke the surface, paddling madly. Paul dove forward and grabbed its tail as it was about to get swept around the vehicle and carried away. Two caimans were almost upon it when Butch began firing rapidly, so fast the individual shots sounded like one long explosion. Two more hungry reptiles thrashed in agony and began flopping around in the red, surging water. Paul reeled the dog in by its tail and scooped it up in both arms. He began struggling against the current and away from the Toyota when he stumbled against the undercarriage and yelled out in pain, his face contorted. He hobbled toward them limping heavily, wincing, the dog still cradled protectively in his arms.

Hal yelled at Ari who pushed through the rising water and grabbed the young man's arm. He half pulled, half supported them as they fought their way back towards the shore. There were more rapid-fire shots behind him that were muffled by the downpour and claps of thunder. Together they struggled twenty or more steps and before he knew it the water was growing shallower, not quite knee-deep, and walking over the rocky bottom became less treacherous. He glanced over his shoulder and could see both Hal and Butch following them, both men still firing at the few remaining caimans. The rest of the creatures were either dead, wounded, or devouring what was left of their kind. Thunder crashed in the distance, rolling like a living, angry being across the turbulent water.

The four of them struggled the rest of the way to shore and collapsed in an exhausted, drained heap. Paulson lay on the ground with his hands wrapped around his right leg, just below the knee. Blood welled through his fingers. The dog leaned against him and shivered, looking thin and ragged. It licked Paul's face then settled next to him, still shaking.

Ari levered himself to his feet and gathered them around, panting heavily with his hands on his knees. Water poured unnoticed down his face. "You two grab our supplies and pull everything to higher ground. Paul, let me check out your leg."

Hal and Butch were both exhausted but slowly nodded assent. They holstered their weapons and got to work, moving slowly and unsteadily, stumbling about as if half-dead. Ari began to kneel down next Paul at the same time a slight movement caught his eye. The water level was still rising and now almost completely covered Betty. With no sound at all the nearly indomitable Toyota bumped up against its anchoring boulder, then slowly spun away and began floating and bouncing serenely down the river. It noiselessly flipped upside down and turned around a few times, then drifted downriver like a huge fishing bobber. Oily bubbles trailed after it. In under a minute it was gone from sight with only a greasy slick on the choppy river to show it had been there at all.

Butch looked up from where he was dragging supplies to higher ground. Rain matted his dark hair down so flat he could have been wearing a skullcap.

"Hey, kid," he yelled at Paulson. The young man looked his way, pain etched in new lines across his pale face. At that moment he appeared much younger and vulnerable than his actual twenty-five years. Plastered to his head as it was, his blond hair was nearly invisible.

"Yeah?"

"I got a name for that dog of yours." He hefted two jerry cans of water, grunting with the effort. He walked away, toward the pile of supplies far from the water's edge. "After all it's been through you should call it 'Lucky'. What d'you think?"

Paul wasn't looking as Ari began tending to his wounded leg, didn't see his blood dripping down onto the wet rocks and puddling there, nearly black in the fading light. His eyes were far away in thought but at least some color was returning to his cheeks.

"Yeah, I like it," he finally agreed as the dog pressed up against him. He pulled it close and rolled the name around in his mouth. "Lucky. Yeah, that's perfect."

The rain finally diminished to a light shower, then tapered off to a drizzle as Ari worked on Paulson's wounded leg. The young man had suffered a large gash on the outside of his right calf from something sharp and nasty on the underside of Betty when he'd stumbled against it. There was a three-inch flap of skin that at the very least needed stitches and antibiotics.

"But here's the problem," Ari told him. "The medical kit was in the Toyota."

"Yeah, and the Toyota now sleeps with the fishes, I know."

"The good news, if there is any, is that I don't think it did much muscle damage. It looks more superficial. Ugly, but superficial. And it's going to leave one helluva scar."

Paulson watched as Ari continued inspecting it. "Hey, that's okay. Chicks dig scars, right?"

"So I've heard."

Van Owen cleaned it as well as he could with some of their water. Paul hissed each time he touched the wound and openly blanched when water was poured over it. He used some cloth strips ripped from a towel they found in one of the remaining boxes and tied up his leg, which finally succeeded in slowing the bleeding. Paulson wanted to stand and try putting some weight on it, but Ari kept him down with a gentle hand on his shoulder.

"It's really not that bad, guys," Paul reassured them. "I'll be fine. Really."

All three men looked at his hopeful, positive expression dubiously. Ari patted his shoulder then motioned Hal over to one side, out of Paulson's earshot. Hal lifted an eyebrow and joined him several yards away as Butch started sifting through their remaining supplies.

"We don't have any medicine," Ari whispered urgently to the agent. "The blue bin that held our first aid kit is probably several miles downriver by now. He ripped open that leg in the dirty river on a piece of rusty old steel. There's only so much I can do with water and a towel. He's going to need antibiotics or it's going to get infected."

"You're sure of this? Not every cut gets infected."

Ari glanced side to side. "Not at home, no, but here it's a different story. Here an injury like that gets infected, and it happens fast."

"So what are you going to do?"

Ari watched for a moment as Butch continued going through what they had salvaged out of Betty. From what he could see they still had both tents, thankfully. They also had some nutrition bars and three jerry cans of water; at least they wouldn't starve or die of dehydration anytime in the very near future. Among the other random boxes left there were also some green metal tins of ammunition.

Ari pinched the bridge of his nose between his thumb and index finger, thinking. "Um, you and Butch set up the tents. I don't think there's any way we'll start a fire in this slop, which is too bad since it would do wonders for our spirits." Daylight was slipping away and was edging toward darkness in a hurry, even with the storm clouds moving out. If he was going to do this he only had a brief window of opportunity. "I'm going to look for something. Get started and I'll be right back."

Hal looked like he'd just been ordered to let a convicted killer go free. "What? You can't go out there, Ari. Not you, and not without a gun."

"I appreciate your concern, I really do. But I'm not going far. If I can't find what I'm looking for right away I'll be back right back. Honest."

He moved out quickly before Hollenbeck could muster a response. He knew what he was looking for. He went down to the river's edge and waded in until he was ankle deep in the brown water. Picking a direction at random he went to the right, walking with the current, thinking that while he was there he might run across some of the lost supplies from their capsized vehicle. Right this moment, however, he was looking for a specific plant he'd used in the past. It was called *Trapaeolum majus*, more commonly known as the Flashing Flower, because at dusk the bright orange petals seemed to actually emit small flashes, or sparks. He'd seen them earlier beside the road while they'd been driving, so knew they were in this region of the country. They were terrific at preventing infection and had been used by indigenous tribes all over the Amazon for that very reason. It would be just what the doctor ordered, if they'd actually had a doctor...

As he splashed through the brown water he kept a wary eye out for more caimans, but they weren't what worried him most: snakes were what scared him and were the bigger threat. They were everywhere down there, and not just the big boas they'd seen hanging in trees or lazing in the sun. The really large ones such as the anaconda were bad enough, he knew, but it was the small, stealthy ones that made him twitchy-nervous. Coral snakes were the worst. The bright red and brown snakes were highly venomous, and with their first aid kit still joyriding down the river there'd be little hope for a victim now. His concern mounting, he nearly stumbled across a four-foot long stick floating up against the shore and picked it up. He hefted it in his hands and felt a little better with this defensive weapon, limited as it was. It would have to do.

Trapaeolum majus, he remembered, liked sun and water both, so if he had any hopes of running across the orange flower it made sense that it'd be in this vicinity. Still scanning all around him, he continued splashing along the shore, stick at the ready. A piece of a long green leaf came toward him in the current and for a second it looked so much like an emerald tree boa that he almost jumped out of his boots. He took a deep, nervous breath and moved on. A line from the movie *Raiders of the Lost Ark* came to him: "Snakes, why did it have to be snakes?" Yeah, it'd been a lot funnier in the movie.

Before long he'd gone much farther than he'd planned, not to mention farther than he'd promised Hal. Disgruntled and more than a little anxious for Paulson, he turned around and made his way back. When he got to the road he continued on past it, the sun now behind the trees and setting fast. He upped his pace. Back towards where the tents were being set up he heard some shouting and, oddly, laughter. He almost gave up and went back right then but was determined to locate his quarry. Unsurprisingly, the mosquitos had zeroed in on his location and were attacking with a vengeance. He prayed they hadn't lost their bug spray since that was almost more vital than food at this point. Mosquitos clustered to the underside of the brim of his hat like bats hanging from the roof of a cave.

Thirty more paces along, and he still hadn't found anything. Disheartened he turned and began splashing his way back toward the road. Out of the corner of his eye he swore he saw something, a spark, no more than a muted flash, several yards inside the tree line. He peered into the shadowy brush and was convinced he saw it again. Carefully using his stick, he pushed away some thorny vegetation and spied three orange blooms, each about the size of his hand. The orange petals were streaked with darker red and were quite beautiful, but it wasn't the flowers themselves he was interested in. He eased in his hand and plucked a handful of the plant's large leaves, then happily folded them up and slipped them into a zippered pocket in his pants.

"That really is just what the doctor ordered," he murmured under his breath, his mood a bit improved. He hustled back towards where the road met the river. To his surprise the two tents were already set up and, even more shocking, there was a large fire going in a shallow pit between them. He stared in amazement as the flames shot several feet into the air, the burning sticks and leaves hissing and popping loudly, the green wet wood stubbornly succumbing to the fire. He couldn't understand how they'd managed one, but was overjoyed to see it.

Paul was still on the ground. The towel wrapped around his leg was red with blood, but there was a huge grin on his round face. He may have been in pain but right then he looked decidedly happy.

"It's amazing what you can do with gasoline," he said, pointing to one of the jerry cans. "We thought we'd only grabbed cans of water. Imagine our surprise when one was filled with gas. Butch almost blew us up getting it started but I'm pretty damn happy with the final outcome."

"We'll take a break wherever we can get one," Hal chimed in. "And by that smug look on your face I'd say you found what you were looking for. Am I right?"

Ari walked up. The fire was burning so hot he couldn't get close, but the heat felt glorious on his wet skin and clothes, even in the warm air. The air was thick with the smell of gas. He drew the leaves from his pocket and held them up. They didn't look like much.

"As a matter of fact I did." He knelt down next to Paulson and by the flickering firelight gingerly unwrapped the bloody rag from his leg. The wound was already swollen and angry-looking. Fresh blood dribbled down his calf.

"So, doc, what're you going to do?" the young man asked, trying to be upbeat.

Ari carefully crushed the leaves in a tight ball before unfolding and wrapping them over and around the wound. The leaves themselves were bright green and shimmered in the firelight as if they were slightly greasy. Spread out flat each was about the size of a paperback book. Once they were in place he held them there with another strip of cloth and several rubber bands. He had four leaves left over which he stashed away in his pocket.

"Natives use these to stave off infection and to keep insects away. They're also an effective coagulant," he said. "It's no substitute for a good dose of antibiotic but it'll help for now. Just make sure you keep all this in place. And we need to keep your leg elevated, too, at least for tonight."

All four men clustered around the fire and let the heat begin drying their clothes. They were exhausted – it showed in their lowered heads and downcast eyes. Hal rolled a rock over and placed it under Paulson's leg. The young man grimaced once but then settled back and rested on his elbows. Ari looked at their small pile of remaining supplies.

"So what did we manage to salvage from the Toyota?" he finally asked.

The agent didn't look away from the fire. "Half a box of nutrition bars, three jerry cans of water, the two tents, of course, and some ammunition, most of which is for the rifles, which doesn't help because we lost them with the Toyota. Oh, we also got that bag of trinkets Raul gave you. A few other odds and ends. Nothing else."

Shit, Ari thought. "That's it? What's in Raul's bag? And please tell me someone has bug spray."

Butch materialized a can from his zippered pants pocket. He held the green can up and rattled it. "I've got about half a can left. That's it. I've also got one of the big hunting knives."

"I've still got my machete," Hal said, displaying the black blade. He stabbed it into the ground where it stuck in the soft soil. "And a flashlight."

Butch rummaged through the trinket bag. It was too dark to see inside it so he dumped the contents out onto the ground near the fire. Ari spotted a dozen or so small knives, a handful of lighters, some cheap costume jewelry, as well as several larger black boxes about four inches square. Butch held up one of the boxes.

"What the hell...?"

He opened it and a black plastic ball four inches in diameter rolled into his hand. On its side was a black number eight surrounded by a white circle. It had a flat spot on the opposite side of the number. It looked exactly like an oversized pool ball. He held it out to them.

"A Magic Eight Ball? Why the hell did your guy give us a freaking Magic Eight Ball?"

Paul was still lying on the damp ground with his injured leg elevated. He no longer seemed to be in overt pain, which was an improvement. He had levered himself onto one elbow and was staring at Butch and the black ball.

"Okay, I'll bite: what in the world is a Magic Eight Ball?"

Despite their circumstances, Ari almost permitted himself a grin. Trust Raul to come with something unique like this, he thought, even in the middle of South America. He motioned Butch to hand it to Paul. "You've never seen one of these before?"

Paulson shook his head. He rolled the ball in his hand, finally finding the flat spot that was actually a clear window. He squinted in the flickering firelight as he read the words that appeared there. The newly-named Lucky the dog sat attentively at his side.

"It says 'Outlook is good'. What the hell?"

"That's promising," Hal commented. "Considering the circumstances, I mean. Ask it a question then turn it over and back again."

Paul obliged. "Ask it a question? Anything?"

"Sure. Anything."

"Okay, I'll bite again. Um, will I get to talk to my son Taylor again soon?"

Ari had almost forgotten Paul's young son. The youngest member of their group hadn't mentioned his boy the entire trip, but he was obviously missing and thinking about him. Paulson flipped the ball over and back again, then peered at the message window as the reply materialized.

"It says 'It Is Decidedly So'." He held it toward Ari. "Well, I like that answer. What is this thing?"

"It's a novelty toy that's been around forever. Used to be very popular back in the 60s and 70s. I don't know how Raul got his hands on any or why he included them in with the other stuff, but it could make a good gift to a tribe, if it comes to that. It's different, that's for sure."

Ari took the ball and handed it back to Brubaker who slid it roughly into the box. He shoveled all the trinkets into the bag and set it aside. The four of them stared at the fire in silence for a minute with the sounds of the night all around them, a faint residual smell of gasoline still in the air. Quietly they took turns using Butch's bug spray and applying it sparingly over their bare skin. Ari helped Paul coat the uncovered area below his wound, and he was thankful to see that the insects seemed to be staying clear of it anyway. The leaves from the Flashing Flower were working better than he'd hoped. Finally Butch sat up, his back straight, and he crossed his

259

arms over his chest and inhaled deeply. He was moving his jaw back and forth as if words were fighting to escape his locked jaw.

"Okay, if no one else is going to say it, then I will," he finally began. His tone was thick, his temper just barely in check. He wasn't as angry as he'd been at Ari's front door that day so long ago, but he was close. "As far as I can see it we're pretty fucked right now. Our man here," he said, stabbing a finger towards Ari, "screwed up everything when he went and lost our transportation and most of our supplies."

Hal had been sitting there with his fingers steepled under his chin, silent and deep within his own mind. He looked up. "Stop it, Butch."

"No, I'm not going to stop," he snapped back, breathing heavily. "He's supposed to be some big-shot jungle guide that knows what he's doing, and besides fixing up the kid's leg I don't see that we're any better off than we'd be without him. Look at us! We're in the middle of BFE with almost no food, no wheels, and a banged-up kid. What the hell are we supposed to do now? You guys want to find this SOP and Ice stuff and I want to find my wife. Right now I don't see any of that happening! Hell, we'll be lucky to get out of here alive. Hey, kid, why don't you ask that little eight ball of yours how this is all going to turn out?"

Hal started to protest again, to come to Ari's aid, but Van Owen stopped him with an upraised hand. Had he seen himself in a mirror he would've been shocked at how tired he appeared; his shoulders were bowed with the weight of the expedition, Paul's injury, not to mention the loss of the Toyota. New, pinched lines had formed in the corners of his eyes and mouth, and the back of his neck ached with the strain. He stared at each man in turn, one by one. Hal and Butch each met his gaze with very different expressions, but Paulson looked away and into the fire, his thoughts hidden behind eyes that were dark and shadowed.

"No, he's right," Ari admitted finally, though it galled him to give Butch any credit. "This hasn't gone as planned, certainly not losing the Toyota. But these trips never do. Yes, I've made some mistakes along the way, and for that I apologize. Especially to you, Paul, for your leg. I violated one of my own rules back there: I rushed us by trying to cross the riverbed when I should've been much more careful. I should've made us wait and checked it out better." He sighed and rubbed his face with both hands as if he could wipe away a patina of guilt. When he inspected his open hands he looked surprised to find them empty. He didn't want to admit to them, especially to Brubaker, that he'd hurried because he was worried about Frankie, that under normal circumstances he never would've plowed ahead like that so recklessly. But the more time they took, the less likely they'd be able to find her. It was that easy.

"But that doesn't change anything," he continued, his voice resolute. "We have to keep going."

"Oh really? And how do you propose we do that?" Butch demanded to know. "We've barely got enough supplies to last a few days. Hell, we could be out here for weeks for all we know. Are we supposed to just start walking and hope for the best? Is that your plan now?"

Ari resisted the urge to scream at him that yes, that was exactly what they would do. *Frankie was still out there somewhere!* Nothing else mattered except finding her. He felt the admission boiling to the surface and trying to claw its way out, but was saved by Hal when the agent loudly cleared his throat to get their attention.

"Ari's right. We have to keep going. This is too important for us to give up already. And besides, where else should we go, back where we came from? Back to the gas station where we left those men stranded? I bet they'd love to see us again."

That poignant revelation shut them all up. Butch had a retort ready but he closed his mouth so hard his teeth clacked together. He squinted his wide eyes and swallowed his reply, but the way he sat with his arms locked around his knees and his fists clenching and unclenching spoke volumes.

"We still have a mission to complete," he continued. "There's no choice – we keep going. Case closed."

The four of them sat in uncomfortable silence as the nighttime noises began their evening ritual. Unidentifiable sounds surrounded them as huge insects dive-bombed their camp. Titi monkeys chattered at them from up in the trees, and a disturbing cry as of a baby in pain rang out somewhere in the dense brush behind them. There was nothing else to do, so eventually Ari got up and rummaged around nearby for more wood to burn. He pulled Hal's machete from the dirt and used it to hack up the larger pieces that he found. When he'd sufficiently stoked the fire he still had enough left over to make a small pile for later. The wet wood hissed and popped and added to the cacophony of sounds. He pointed the flashlight toward the river and spotted another capybara digging in the red mud near the bank. When he sat back down he noticed that Hal had already retired into his tent for the night. Paul was sitting up and inspecting his leg. Butch was nibbling on a nutrition bar.

"We should probably all call it a night," he said, making a general announcement. "Tomorrow's going to be a long day."

He offered the stick to Paulson who used it as a cane to help him stand. The young man flexed his leg several times. Lucky stood and shook residual water from its fur and stared up at him. Paul smiled and patted its head. He looked toward Butch.

"I want to thank you for helping me save Lucky back there," he told him. Butch didn't stop staring at the ground but did wave a dismissive hand in his direction. "Seriously. I owe you one. Thanks."

"Don't worry about it, kid. Glad it all worked out."

Paulson nodded at him and both he and Lucky crawled awkwardly into the tent. That left Butch and Ari alone beside the crackling fire. The two of them sat quietly for a few minutes as if they were two kids playing a game, a game where the first one who flinched lost. Ari wasn't up to any more theatrics with Butch so he quickly relented and headed into his own tent. They didn't have any way to cover up since all their bedding had floated away with the Toyota, but the night was warm enough that it wasn't necessary. The inside of the tent reeked of wet dog and mud. The one single bright spot was that their personal stench had been power-washed away in the river. Paul snorted once in his sleep and mumbled something as he moved around.

Ari closed his eyes, certain that sleep would evade him. The fact that they had lost their transportation and most of their supplies was still only secondary to the fact that they didn't appear to be any closer to finding Frankie. He drifted off seeing her face and, most of all, her green eyes that stared deep into his soul.

Chapter 15

Ari's eyes popped open and he jerked awake, banging his head on the hard ground. His heart was pounding in his chest harder than a jackhammer at a construction site. For a moment he had no idea where he was, but then the jungle noises penetrated his mind as easily as they penetrated the thin fabric of the tent, and it all came back to him. He needlessly checked his watch and saw that it was straight up five o'clock in the morning. Of course it was, he thought. What other time would it be? At Paul's feet Lucky lifted its head in curiosity then calmly eased back down, its white fur a muted grey in the dim light, the black fur completely invisible.

Van Owen waited there on his back and tried to doze again, but soon realized that additional sleep was going to elude him for now. He carefully eased out of the tent and saw that their fire was little more than red embers that puffed and shifted softly. His back to the river, he positioned more scraps of wood in a teepee shape and blew on the coals until a small flame burst back into life. Soon the fire was going again, a comforting yellow and orange glow that forced back some of the darkness surrounding them. Larger insects were still buzzing about and dive-bombing their campsite, but at least the mosquitos had relented for now. He stood and thoughtfully looked back at the river, and that was when he saw the lights.

Curious, he carefully made his way down to the river's edge. As the toes of his boots sunk in the mud he heard a rustling noise and shined the flashlight beam into the brush. A pair of eyes glowed back at him. His first panicked thought was that a caiman had survived and was coming for him, but he quickly realized it was more likely one of the capybaras he'd seen a little while ago. This second assumption was proved correct when the eyes gently blinked at him and backed away. Ari sighed and focused on the river.

The lights were there, possibly hundreds of them meandering down the now calm waterway. They were *Las Damas de Alba*, the

Ladies of the Dawn. He watched as the tiny flames flickered in the still air of the night, some clustered together as if for protection, others seeming to strive forward eagerly, like they were racing toward a destination only they knew or understood. He stared at them in mute fascination as they floated peacefully down the obsidian ribbon of the river, like stars against the backdrop of night. This was proof that they weren't alone here, that not too far upriver there were natives living their very own personal, unique lives, and that the four of them were not only strangers, but intruders in a land they could never completely understand.

Ari focused his attention on one of the flames that drifted close to shore. He flicked on the flashlight and saw that it was nothing more than a cupped leaf about the size of his hand and filled with some sort of thick oil, with a burning wick stuck through the bottom. It was simply a primitive candle when viewed that way. But when he clicked off the light it once again became something haunting and beautiful. The pull of the water tugged it away from shore, and he watched as it spun and twirled away, meeting up with other lights as they meandered down the silken surface of the river.

Ari held the flashlight to his face and clicked the beam on and off, on and off. He knew that the lights on the water were in reality nothing more than primitive lamps. But he couldn't help thinking that they somehow spoke to him and to anyone else who witnessed their random beauty. Perhaps there was a way to decipher their deeper meaning? Maybe there was some key to glean their hidden message? He was transfixed there in that spot, his boots silently sinking into the thick mud of the riverbank.

He furrowed his brow, the quizzical expression invisible in the near darkness. He held the flashlight up to his face again and clicked the beam on and off, on and off. He played the bright light on the nearest of the Ladies of the Dawn, instantly taking it from something mysterious and dark to a simple leaf filled with oil and a wick. With just a flip of the switch he could morph an object that was both haunting and mysterious to something very mundane and ordinary.

Technology was like that, he knew. The traditional way of doing something could be inefficient and clumsy, but that wasn't always the case. In fact, at times the old ways could be even more effective in the long run. Look how much more efficient a simple phone conversation could be over a day's worth of emails or texts, he considered. Just because something was new didn't mean it was inherently better. He and Frankie had their secretive posts to each other on Facebook, but for conveying meaning and feeling it paled in comparison to the times they could actually talk. Their Facebook messages and the way they worked was still rather new, but the art of imbedding hidden meanings in messages was not. People had done it for thousands of years. You just had to know what to look for, had to know what the keys were. For example, any time he wanted Frankie to check something out or get her attention he worked her initials into his post, just like his last status update: *Great catching up with old friends on FB. Who needs a cell phone nowadays??* It was easier since her initials were the same two letters at the common acronym for Facebook. There was always a key, he knew.

There was always a key…

That last realization jerked him upright, his eyes suddenly wide and knowing. Wait. Facebook? Hidden messages? *Shit, that was it!*

With absolute clarity he knew what Fawcett had been doing. He knew there were hidden messages to the Colonel's wife in those recently discovered letters from the Royal Geographic Society that he could now decipher - which meant he could figure out what Fawcett's actual location had been. Damn, why hadn't he seen it before? What was the matter with him?

He turned and ran back towards the campfire, unable to help himself from loudly calling Hal's name, his guilt at losing the

Toyota momentarily banished. The jungle sounds retreated, shocked to silence at the unexpected outburst.

It only took Ari a few seconds to run from the river to the campfire, but Hal was already out of his tent with his Glock in his hand, pivoting around and trying to spot the source of the commotion and possible trouble. He saw Las Damas de Alba down on the river but made no move to investigate.

"No, Hal, it's okay," Van Owen assured him, a little out of breath from his sprint. "There's no problem."

The agent turned back toward Ari and lowered his gun to his side. Brubaker and Paulson each stuck a wary head out of their tents and looked at the pair. Lucky appeared next to Paul, its brown eyes blinking sleepily.

"What's all the brew-ha-ha out here," Paul asked, stifling a yawn. "What time is it?"

"Just after five," Ari answered, not needing to consult his watch. He turned to Hal. "I figured it out."

Hollenbeck cocked his head at him. "Figured what out?"

"Fawcett's messages to his wife. I figured out how he was communicating his location to her all along. I know how he did it."

Brubaker groaned and his head vanished back into the tent faster than a turtle into its shell. "Crap, I thought it was something really important. Not this Fawcett nonsense again. I'm going back to sleep."

Ari shot him a withering scowl before continuing with Hal. "A few weeks before we left I received those new Fawcett writings from Sir Alex Hanes at the RGS. They've never been published, at least not yet. I read them through and through and they were much of the same stuff I've seen from him in the past: he talked about places they'd gone, plays they'd seen, parties they'd attended. All normal writings from that era."

"Yes. So?"

"So he was secretive to a fault, remember? He couldn't take a chance that anyone else could know his actual location. He was terrified some other group would use the information to find the Lost City of Z before him. And messages back then weren't like sending one today via email or text – there were no encryption programs, no way to make sure the info would stay secret, just a sealed envelope or wax seal that could be easily broken. The messages passed through too many hands and could be seen by practically anyone between here and London. So he had his own encryption program."

Hal was clearly interested now. He holstered his gun and motioned Ari to take a seat by the fire. Van Owen was too nervous and excited to sit. Instead he pushed past Paul and plunged into the tent, quickly finding and dragging out his backpack. He rummaged through it and drew out a clear plastic tube about the size of rolling pin. He popped open the top and gently slid Fawcett's papers out, careful to lay them on his lap where they wouldn't get soiled.

"I read over these a few times before we left." He leafed through several until he found the one he was looking for. "Here's the first time he mentions his wife. He talked about a time they went to see some play called The Playboy of the Western World. He says *'My dearest Nina, I shall forever cherish our evening together December last at the Camden Theatre. A pity the play paled in comparison to the magnificence of the theatre itself.'"*

Hal scratched his head in obvious confusion. It was clear he didn't understand the significance of the sentence, but Ari didn't expect him to. "So they went to a play. So what? I don't get it."

Van Owen took a deep breath. His hands were shaking. "Don't you see? The Camden Theatre was an outdoor facility. Many of the theaters of the time were."

"Yes. So?"

"So Fawcett wouldn't have taken his wife to an outdoor play in December in London. The weather would've been horrible, and women weren't used to being outside in foul weather. She was much more refined than that, a lady."

Hollenbeck began to comprehend, if not the specifics then at least the general concept. "What are you getting at? You're going to have to walk me through this epiphany, Ari."

The words tumbled from him with barely a pause or a space for punctuation. "I remember noticing this before but not making the connection. In these letters to his wife he uses the phrase 'My dearest Nina' often, a total of six times. This is the first time. If I'm looking for a key in each sentence with that salutation I should find a clue."

"Six?" Paul asked, now captivated as well. "Why six times?"

"Great question. I think it's because latitude and longitude used to be recorded in hours, minutes, and seconds, two times each. A total of six numbers. That's got to be it."

Paulson clumsily climbed out of the tent and sat by the fire. He adjusted the makeshift bandage on his leg. There was no blood to speak of on the bandage. "So what's the clue in that first sentence? The one about the theater."

Ari rustled through the letters, finally finding the phrase and stabbing it with his finger. "December. That's gotta be it. It's the twelfth month. And twelve," he said, his eyes locked on the paper, "is also the first number in the coordinates for Mato Grosso. Right where we are now." He slapped the ground with his open palm.

Paulson's mouth opened in a perfectly round "O" of shock. "No shit?"

Ari exhaled, barely able to keep his excitement in check. The papers in his hands quivered, fluttering as if he were holding a wounded bird. "No shit."

"So you can figure the rest out now?"

Van Owen stared at the letters in his hands and felt his heart drop, his earlier rush of excitement draining away. "Damn, no, I don't think so. I mean, yes, but not here. I'll need a computer and the Internet to do that. But it's a start."

Hal stood and patted Ari on the shoulder. He brushed dirt and leaves from his pants. "Good work. It also really bolsters our cover if we need to fall back on that in the future. Well done and congratulations. You've earned it." He crawled back into his tent and zipped the flap shut. Paul and Lucky did the same.

Alone now, Ari continued staring at the papers in his hands. He felt as if they were almost glowing in the firelight, glowing like some supernatural and ancient tome, one steeped in mystery and wisdom. He was both terrifically excited and crushed at the same time. To know how to decipher them and not be able to do it! He was a kid and they were Christmas presents he could hold, fondle, and shake - but not open. He knew he wouldn't be able to sleep now, not with this pending knowledge so close at hand. Thousands had died searching for Fawcett over the last century, and here he was holding the answer in his hands, the answer so many had coveted – and he couldn't do a thing with it. To be so damn close! He felt like screaming his frustration into the dark jungle night. He stayed that way until dawn when the mosquitos roused and began to break their fast on him, and even the strong DEET in the bug spray couldn't keep them at bay. He tenderly rolled up the papers and slid them into the plastic tube, then retired to the tent where he lay wide-eyed, sleepless, and impatient until the others woke for the day.

Soon after dawn they were up and about and struck camp. Thankfully the tents were made of the latest materials and didn't weigh much. However the same couldn't be said for the jerry cans of water and the single one of gasoline. Using Hal's machete they downed a small tree and fashioned it into a six-foot length with a deep notch near each end. They wrapped their one towel around the middle and slid a jerry can on each end until it settled in the notched slot. Ari, perhaps out of guilt for what happened to the Toyota, or perhaps because he was still so pumped about the Fawcett papers, volunteered to carry the load first. They lifted it onto his shoulders and he shrugged it into place. With the cargo distributed like that it was awkward but not unmanageable, the bulk of the weight pressing across his back. The rest of their meager belongings were passed around and distributed to the other three. Paul carried the least since he had to use the stick as a cane, so was relegated to the battered backpack slung over his shoulder. With a final look around the campsite to make sure nothing had been left behind they moved out, Lucky trotting beside them. Butch, who had kept to himself all morning, assumed point and led the way.

The bulk of the water in the flooded river had already receded and was shallow enough that they could cross it without undo trouble. Hal and Butch made a crisscross cradle with their hands and hoisted Paulson across, keeping his injured leg high and dry, Lucky cradled securely in his arms. Van Owen had to step carefully and inched his way across, cognizant that an errant step could easily topple him and his heavy cargo into water that was still several feet deep and moving right along. When everything and everybody was across, Ari stopped and looked back at the large rocks where they had lost Betty. He gave a sigh of regret, then they all began their hike up the slight incline and away from the river, happy to put it behind them. They moved out in silence, their slightly labored breathing easily drowned out by the raucous sounds of the jungle around them. In minutes they were back in the heavy canopy of trees with the nameless river out of sight behind them.

The going that first day was challenging, especially with Paul's injury. The gash was on the same leg as his war wound which, Ari thought, was probably better than having both legs at less than one hundred percent. At least this way he could lean on the cane for support as he went. They stopped frequently to hydrate themselves, as Ari was of the opinion that it was better to stay strong now and find more water later than to become dehydrated and weak while trying to conserve it. After noon Butch grunted and took his turn carrying the jerry cans, and the others split up the rest of the supplies. Brubaker and Van Owen didn't speak to each other or even make eye contact, which was fine with Ari and probably fine with Butch, too. When they finally stopped for the day they all crashed to the ground in exhaustion, pulling off their boots and airing out their sore, wrinkled feet.

"Okay, I admit it," Paulson said, rubbing his damp feet, "the expensive boots were worth it. Walking's not so bad, but they still don't feel like they'll ever dry out."

"I don't know much about surviving in the jungle," Hal said, tugging off his own boots and massaging his toes. "But I do know that constantly wet feet are ripe for problems, like trench foot. Soldiers in World War I had a terrible time with it, to the point where they weren't fit for duty any longer."

"Gee, sounds like a great time. This just keeps getting better and better."

They set up their tents and each man gobbled down a nutrition bar and drank deeply from the jerry can. No one commented or complained when Paul gave one of the non-chocolate bars to Lucky to eat as well. The dog didn't quite know what to make of it at first but was so ravenous that in the end it didn't care. In three bites it was gone, and the dog licked its chops and sniffed around for another. They had a fire going again thanks to their dwindling supply of gasoline, and while none of them were in the least bit cold the small blaze was a welcome addition.

Brubaker was on his back staring up at the dark canopy overhead. He had an arm thrown over his face and Ari thought he was asleep already until he swatted at some mosquitos that were buzzing around him.

"If I see another one of those peccary things I'm going to kill it and skin it," he mumbled. "I'm sure we can eat the damn thing. Those bars aren't going to last us very long."

Ari took a drink. The water was warm but still tasted delicious. If they found water they'd have to come up with a way to boil it in one of the jerry cans soon. He had a stick and was idly scratching in the dirt with it. Before he knew what he was doing he'd doodled a rough Karma wheel in the moist ground. When he saw what he'd done he quickly rubbed it out with his hand, shooting a quick, sideways look at Butch.

"Peccaries are good to eat," he said, finally. "The locals also eat monkeys and pretty much anything else they can trap and kill."

Butch didn't answer him. He scratched at the sores on his arms and neck then moved slowly into his tent without another word. Paul slapped at something biting his own arm and his hand came away with a thin trail of blood. He wiped it on his pants absently. He looked at Van Owen.

"Monkeys? They eat monkeys?"

"Sure. I've had roasted monkey, and before you ask, no, it doesn't taste like chicken. It takes more like venison, but stringier."

Paulson scrunched up his face. "That's not helping, really."

"But the locals also eat all kinds of fruits that grow around here, too. They're excellent for you, much better than most of the ones we get in the states. Acai berries, aguaje palm fruit, yumanasa berries – they're everywhere. I've been watching out for some. Just haven't seen any yet. I don't think we'll starve."

"That's fine, but I don't think Lucky here can eat any of that. I'm with Butch – the next peccary that comes our way will be invited to dinner."

All of them retired to their tents. None of them complained any further about the lack of food, but their audibly growling stomachs summed up their situation very well. They were already cinching their pants up at the waist a little more each morning.

The second day after losing Betty was much the same as the first. They continued walking along the narrow, rutted road, Paul limping but making decent time with the makeshift cane. They never came to a village or saw anyone else along the way, although they did spy worn down and flattened spots on the side of the road where others before them had camped. The last time they ran across one of those Ari took the opportunity to hike around through the increasingly dense brush, looking for something to supplement their meager food supplies. After ten minutes of searching he yelled for Hal. The agent was there right away, and found Ari standing beneath a thick, squat palm tree, its grey trunk as big around as his thigh. Van Owen pointed up at a cluster of brown, shiny, circular nuts, each the size of his fist. There had to be dozens or hundreds of them there, clustered like huge bunches of oversized grapes. He was smiling.

"So what are those?" Hal asked, just a little out of breath. He held the Glock like an extension of his hand, seemingly always at the ready.

"Just what I was telling Paul about yesterday. They're aguaje pine nuts. Very edible and very good for you. I figured natives stayed at these sites for a reason. I figured right."

Hal nodded at him in admiration. "Good thinking. Let's grab as much as we can carry and get going."

"Well," Ari said, scratching at his head, "that's not as easy as it sounds."

"Why not?"

Ari didn't answer him directly, but instead walked closer to the palm tree. After a few steps he had to jump to one side because one of the aguaje nuts came hurling down at him from up high. It thudded harmlessly at his feet, followed by an angry chittering sound up in the palm.

"Because they don't want to share, that's why."

Hal creased his forehead in confusion and peered into the tree. Thirty feet up and concealed in the palm fronds three or more monkeys were staring back at them. They were about the same size as Lucky but with thick, bushy brown fur and tiny bald heads. Their hairless faces were pink and expressive, like a baby's face. They stared down at the two men with open curiosity, their brown eyes huge.

"Did one of those monkeys just try to bean you with a nut?"

"Yes it did. In fact the first one nailed me on the head. They have very good aim."

Hollenbeck continued to stare into the tree. "What do you want me to do?"

"I figure if you shoot your gun into the air it'll scare them off. Then we can take what we want and be on our way."

Hal shrugged and pulled out his pistol. As he aimed it into the sky a tremendous explosion rent the air behind them. Ari nearly jumped out of his shoes and Hollenbeck stared at his gun accusingly, thinking that it had discharged itself unbidden. One of the monkeys from high in the tree crashed through the palms and landed with a muffled thud on the ground at their feet, a bloody hole in the soft brown fur of its unmoving chest. Its companions screamed and took off through the trees, their cries quickly fading away. Birds of all kinds and color spun into the sky in a feathered frenzy, all blues and yellows, like parade confetti in reverse. Ari spun around and saw Butch standing behind them, his own pistol in his hand, the barrel smoking.

"Why the hell'd you do that?" he shouted. "We only needed to scare them away!"

Brubaker calmly holstered his weapon and walked over to the animal. He toed it several times with his boot to make sure it was dead. It moved bonelessly as he nudged it.

"You said it before. The natives eat monkeys, so we can, too. And besides," he went on, "we can't have the kid's dog eating our supplies. It needs meat, and this is meat. I'll skin it and cook it up. Paul's already got a fire going."

He reached down and grabbed the animal by its flaccid leg and dragged it back toward the road, through the thick brush. As it bumped along it left a smeared trail of blood on the grasses and leaves. Still shocked, Ari couldn't think of a thing to say, especially since everything Butch had stated was true. Hal watched him go then started methodically plucking handfuls of the brown, slick nuts, filling his pockets. After a few seconds Ari did the same.

"Damn pragmatic of him," Hollenbeck admitted after a minute had passed and his pockets and hands were full. He tentatively peeled the shiny brown husk away, revealing an orange, pulpy interior. He looked at Ari and raised an eyebrow.

"Sure, go ahead and bite into it," Ari finally replied, still staring at the flattened, blood-soaked grasses where Butch had gone. He stooped and began slowly gathering up nuts of his own and stuffing his pockets. "You can eat them raw. They're good. I should warn you, however, that eating too many can give you the runs. Just take it easy."

The agent took a tentative nibble as if he were sampling hot pizza, then rolled the taste around in his mouth. After a moment he took a more aggressive bite and nodded in appreciation, accompanied by a small monosyllabic grunt of approval.

"That's not bad at all. Tastes like a carrot, but with a different consistency. I could get used to these."

Ari peeled one himself and began sucking on the orange pulp. It was delicious and brought back memories of his prior trips, memories of being in the other parts of the Amazon but in locales that looked just like this. He'd had some awful experiences on those journeys, but he'd enjoyed some good times as well, adventures that would never be forgotten. Good memories tended to stick around and had a better half-life than bad ones, he knew. It reminded him of past high school reunions and joking with people he hadn't always gotten along with back then – he remembered the parties and Friday night football games better than the dust-ups he'd had with some of them in the parking lot after school. He sucked the last of the meat from the nut and threw the husk over his shoulder.

"Hal, I've got to know. Why did you really bring Butch along?"

Hollenbeck continued munching on the nut, concentrating his ministrations on the orange interior. When he was finished he pitched it aside and began methodically peeling another.

"I've told you why, Ari. And look how helpful he's been already. Lucky wouldn't have been quite so lucky without him, and there'd be more caimans in the world and maybe fewer of us."

"Yeah, I know," he admitted. "Paul's very attached to that dog and I'm glad it's still alive. Regardless, I know what you told me, but there had to be more suitable people available for this. Like another agent, perhaps?"

Hal was looking down at the nut he was peeling, focusing on the thin brown skin that almost looked like the scales on a fish. "Listen. Like I said, Butch knows Frankie much more intimately than anyone, you included. You never know when that might come in handy. And he's proven very handy with a gun, which is something to consider down here. He's also quite the hunter, as we've just seen. I think he was a fine choice."

Van Owen couldn't tell if the agent was being completely sincere and honest with him or not. He also knew that if Hal had an ulterior motive that he didn't want to share, then there was no way he could pry it out of him. He spit out a piece of the brown husk that he had missed.

"Fine. Whatever. He still makes me uncomfortable to have around."

"Well, sure, that's to be expected. I'm not asking you two to be best friends, but the four of us have a mission to accomplish, and I plan on doing just that. Okay? You need to get along with him. This is important."

It was Ari's turn not to answer. He gathered up several more of the brown nuts and in silence the two men followed the blood-smeared trail back.

When they arrived Butch was squatting on the ground and working diligently on the monkey carcass with his hunting knife. His hands and arms were bloody up to the elbows. He was grunting as he tugged and ripped at the stubborn pelt. Paulson was standing some ways away and was staring at him, either in disgust or amazement, Ari couldn't tell. Lucky was sitting at Paul's feet and was staring at the grim tableau with keen interest. As they watched, Brubaker finished his gruesome task and manhandled a long stick through the center of the carcass. He had already hammered several other thick sticks into the ground on either side of the fire pit and set the bloody hunk of meat over the blaze to cook. It immediately began to hiss and sizzle as the fat caught and burned. After a few minutes he turned the spit as the meat began to blacken. Ari shook himself and tossed a few aguaje nuts to Paul.

"Here. Peel these and eat up. I think you'll like them."

Paul looked at them warily, but finally gave the nut a tentative nibble. "Hey, not bad," he admitted.

Hal deposited a few of the aguajes at Brubaker's feet and instructed him to do the same. As Butch continued turning the spit the agent picked up the bloody pelt and other unwanted body parts and walked into the woods beyond their campsite where he tossed them into the brush. Brubaker hadn't touched the nuts yet, and instead carved a hunk of charred meat off and tossed it toward the dog. Lucky sniffed it for just a second before gobbling the piece down. Licking its chops it peered at the sizzling meal with renewed interest. As time passed the entire campsite smelled like they were downwind of a Burger King fast food restaurant. Despite himself Ari's stomach rumbled.

"Well don't just stand there," Butch ordered, not unkindly. "Line up and let's eat."

It took some time but eventually, like a Greek chef manning a gyro stand, he began slicing off thin strips as they cooked. After their first bites of the rather stringy, semi-cooked meat the aguaje nuts were left on the ground forgotten. Butch's hands were caked in blood and he kept cursing as he repeatedly burned his fingers, but soon there was little left but bone and remnants no one wanted. They piled these scraps in front of Lucky who carried them one by one to the edge of the firelight and hungrily made short work of them. The four men finally sat back and nibbled on the brown nuts for desert and sipped some water. Eventually they set up the tents, stoked the fire, and crawled in for the night. The evening hoots, cries, and strange jungle noises were back again, but with their hunger temporarily assuaged, exhaustion quickly claimed them and no one noticed.

The next morning they awoke to Butch screaming. It wasn't a surprised yell, or even one meant to get somebody's attention. It was a shriek, piercing and horrified. People on fire must scream like that, Ari thought. To a man the others scrambled from their tents to find him standing there with his shirt up, staring in abject horror at his chest.

"Jesus Christ there's something in me!"

Hal hurried forward and quickly shoved his glasses on so he could see. Butch's chest was heaving in panicked gasps and the skin on his face was stretched and contorted like a reflection in an ancient, warped mirror. Sweat dampened his hair and ran unnoticed into his wild eyes.

"Look! What the fuck? There's something moving!" he shouted. His voice peaked several octaves higher than normal and was laced with panic. He sounded nothing at all like the composed hunter from the day before.

Hollenbeck reached out a tentative finger and traced it around Butch's heaving chest. Ari hurried over and stood next to him, peering close. In three or four places they could see tiny bumps on his skin in close proximity to the bites he had first complained about back in the hotel lobby. Under or near each aggravated sore a lump moved, slowly undulating back and forth. Ari rubbed his face and exhaled through puffed cheeks.

"Ah, shit. You've, ah, been infected with botflies."

"Botflies? What the fuck's a botfly?"

"Whatever bit you back in the hotel deposited some eggs under your skin. They're growing and are now in the larval stage of development."

Brubaker creased his forehead in disgust. His face went pale and he looked ready to throw up. In fact he gagged once but held everything down. "Larval stage? What the hell is in there?"

"Worms. You've got worms growing under your skin. If we don't do anything eventually they'll grow and crawl out. They'll be like big flies then, almost as big as a bee."

"Well get the damn things out of me!"

Ari stood straight and rubbed his face again. He crossed his arms. "We can't. Not here at least, and not without some medicine or other stuff."

Hal stopped staring at the bumps on Brubaker's chest. He rubbed his hands together then wiped them on his pants as if he were trying to wash them. "What do we need to do?"

"We need Vaseline, or pine tar, or even Super Glue, none of which we have. We can't just pull them out because the larvae have barbs on them to hold them in place. We might get a piece of it out but what's left can cause a nasty infection. If we let them run their course they'll crawl out on their own in a week or so."

Butch recoiled like he'd been sucker punched in the face. "A week or so? You've got to be shitting me! I can't leave these things in me for that long!"

"I'm sorry, Butch, but we don't have any choice. If we leave them alone they'll come out on their own and won't do any damage. As it stands there's nothing we can do but wait. I'm sorry."

Brubaker stood there with his mouth open and his shirt held high. Eventually he let it drop and sat down hard on the ground next to the dying fire. His face was pale and mottled, the color and texture of old parchment paper. He couldn't figure out what to do with his hands, although his fingers were curled into claws and flexing as if he were doing everything in his power not to rip open his own flesh. Finally they fell to his sides and he lowered his head.

"What kind of fucking place is this, anyway," he muttered harshly at the ground. "What a fucked up place."

Ari and the others stared at him for a moment, lost in their helplessness. Then they began striking the tents and packing up their meager belongings, preparing for another day of hiking towards their goal. When they were done Paul touched Butch's shoulder and softly told him it was time to go. Without a word he stood, shouldered his own share of the load, and together they marched on. Lucky trotted behind them, a ragged, bloody bone clamped tightly in its mouth.

The rest of the day passed without incident, as did the third. On the fourth day since losing Betty they ate the last of their nutrition bars. Paulson shared his final one with Lucky even though it was readily apparent that the young man was famished. He had already tightened his belt one notch and was about to cinch it to the next one. They found several more trees harboring aguaje nuts, but the last time they did so the inner meat was sour and bordering on rancid. They ate a few but began to suffer gut cramps so fierce they all quit and threw them away. They hadn't gotten close enough to anything Butch or Hal could kill for food. That same afternoon they drank the last sips of their water. It wasn't much, just a mouthful each, and only served to remind them how deathly thirsty they were.

Paul was no longer able to walk fast enough to keep up, even with his cane. They slowed down to his hobbled pace which was not much better than a crawl. He kept apologizing until Butch finally snapped at him to stop it. No one did much talking and even Hal was quiet and withdrawn. To the best of Ari's reckoning they were still headed in the right direction but that did little to buoy their spirits. Hungry and tired was one thing, he knew, but to have no water was something they'd have to rectify within a few days if they hoped to keep going at all. Their lips were white with dry skin.

Late that afternoon Paul stumbled and fell. Too tired and weak to even help they all shuffled to a stop and waited for him to get up, but he just rolled onto his back and threw an arm over his face. Without a word they followed his lead and slumped to the ground in boneless, exhausted heaps. With slow, deliberate motions Hal took off his glasses and tried to wipe them clean on his shirt. Even his clothes were so dirty and foul he only made matters worse. Eventually he looked at Van Owen. He tried to lick his cracked lips but there was no moisture on his tongue. When he spoke his voice was raspy, little more than sandpaper rubbing on concrete.

"We need water, Ari. Food would help, but we need water first. We can't go on much longer without any."

Van Owen nodded. "I know. We're sweating it out and not putting anything back in." He crawled over to Paulson and inspected his wounded leg. The scrap of towel wrapped around it was caked in old blood and flies covered it in an undulating mass. He shooed them away then removed the makeshift bandage and old leaves and inspected the gash; it was bright red and visibly swollen, puffy and angry-looking. The ragged edges of the cut were turning a nasty shade of purple. Hollenbeck didn't move but didn't have to in order to see how infected it was. They could all tell how bad it had become in such a short time. Paul didn't look up.

"You got any more of those leaves on you?"

Ari shook his head. "No. I used the last of them the other day. I've been watching for more of the flowers but haven't seen any." He gently wrapped the filthy scrap of cloth around the leg and secured it with rubber bands, knowing that it would at least keep the flies and insects away. One rubber band snapped. He dug into his pockets and found he still had several more. Paulson never moved or flinched during his ministrations. Van Owen motioned to Hal and the two of them ponderously stood and walked several yards away.

Ari looked back at Paul. "He's got a fever, too. He's burning up. His skin is hotter than hell."

"Damn. We've got to do something. I don't know how much longer he'll make it. Not without water and antibiotics."

Van Owen didn't need reminding. He stared down at the young man, the man he had talked into coming on this trip. Regardless of what he had done, Ari was ultimately responsible for him being here. He looked around at the thick jungle surrounding them and came to a decision.

"I'm going to go look around, off the trail. Just like when we found the aguaje nuts and the flashing flowers, they weren't on the road. I'm going to head into the jungle and look for something. I have to." The determined edge to his voice left no room for argument. In the past Hal might have attempted to stop him, to at least make an effort to keep him with the group. But that was the past and they both knew how dire their situation had become. This time pragmatism won out over safety.

"At least take a gun with you," the agent implored, holding out his Glock. "If something happens, I don't know if we'll be able to help. Please take it."

Ari began to argue the point but thought better of it, knowing Hal was right. He accepted the heavy pistol and stuffed it into the waistband of his pants rather awkwardly. He still didn't like the feel of the steel pressing against the flesh of his stomach. Hal also handed him the machete.

"You'll need this, too. Be safe out there. I'll keep an eye on the others. Just don't go too far away."

Van Owen nodded once then pushed through a small opening in the heavy foliage and disappeared from the road.

Two steps off the trail the jungle closed in on him, wrapping its leafy arms around him in a thick green embrace. What he remembered most about the untamed jungle were thorns, thorns of all shapes and sizes, some that oozed poison and others as sharp as razors. They were everywhere, seemingly on each branch and tree trunk, from tiny, nearly microscopic splinters to huge spikes four inches long. They all eagerly snagged at his skin and clothing and quite effectively demonstrated how inhospitable and dangerous this place was. Then the thick canopy overhead dimmed the sunlight until it was no brighter than an overcast dawn. The sounds changed, too, becoming heavy and muffled, the same sensation as sitting inside a car with the windows up. He remembered all this from before but it still took him a few seconds to adjust. He raised the machete and began hacking at the branches and vines blocking his way. Even the ringing of the metal blade was muted and dulled, the sound not carrying more than a few dozen feet beyond him.

He kept close attention to the ground at his feet, watching to see if it ever dipped down. Down was good. Water always flowed downhill. Past experience and common lore said if you were lost in the woods or the jungle you should always head downhill. So he kept hacking his way through the dense brush, keeping his eyes peeled for any indication that the terrain was changing in his favor. Dehydration and hunger had left him weak and his arm was beginning to tire already from swinging a blade that suddenly felt heavier than an I-beam. He switched hands and kept going, his breath coming in choppy, exhausted gasps.

He continued on, not certain how far he'd travelled. Twenty yards? Fifty? Jungle this thick was like a Fun House or some convoluted corn maze; he couldn't be sure how much ground he'd covered, not when he had to detour around huge grey trees with spreading roots and clusters of thorn bushes too thick to hack through. He used to know the names of the grey trees but he was too tired and his mind didn't seem to be firing on all cylinders at the moment. He looked up and saw the blue, cloudless sky above him through a small opening in the canopy. It had rained so much in the prior weeks, there had been so many storms, so why couldn't it rain again now? He came to an aguaje nut palm tree but it was barren. Husks of rotten nuts littered the ground. He kicked at a few then moved on.

He came to a large clearing covered in leaves, broken branches, and other jungle detritus. Happy that he could make some progress without the machete he took another step and felt his foot sink up to his calf in something sticky and cloying. His mind suddenly woke from its stupor and he jumped backwards, his heart racing like he'd touched a hot wire. With more effort than it should have taken, he pulled his boot free of the dark red muck. The entire clearing was quicksand, he realized, which explained why there were no trees or bushes growing there. Ari himself had no fear of quicksand; he knew it was almost impossible to drown if you had any sense and didn't panic, but even so it was a nasty, sticky mess that could leave you temporarily trapped and helpless. On the plus side, since quicksand here in the jungle was almost always formed by underground springs, it meant there was a high probability of water nearby. He wanted to smile but was afraid his lips would crack open and bleed. He carefully skirted the boggy area and kept going, heartened that he might be close to a natural spring or water hole.

Just past the boggy clearing he spied a game trail about a foot wide, which was more good news. The reddish dirt was flattened down and free of brush. It veered off to his left and followed a serpentine course around some saplings and bushes, quickly disappearing from view. He followed the path cautiously, his machete at the ready and cognizant of the heavy gun tucked into his waistband. He was concentrating so hard on the trail and what might be in front of him that he almost didn't notice a slight, unnatural movement farther ahead of him. He stopped and stared into the thick underbrush at whatever his peripheral vision had noticed, but there was nothing to see. It could have been anything, really, he mused; a bird, a monkey, or just a branch moving. Ari stood still for nearly a minute listening to his heart thumping in his chest, waiting, watching, peering intently into the jungle, his senses keenly alive and on edge. The machete was gripped so tightly in his hands that his fingers ached and his knuckles had gone white, a vivid contrast against the black handle. When nothing materialized, he exhaled and moved on. While he'd been in the jungle before by himself, he remembered being much fonder of it under better circumstances.

Twenty feet farther up the game trail he came to a fork. As he was deciding which direction to take he heard a twig snap somewhere to the right of him and he quickly raised the black blade of the machete, using it as both a shield and a weapon. Ari nervously pivoted from side to side and waited, loose red dirt grinding under his boot as he moved. He wanted to pull out the Glock but couldn't bring himself to pry either sweaty hand from his death grip on the machete. He waited for what felt like an hour, a week, a year, an eternity. Insects didn't share his apprehension and continued mercilessly attacking his face and neck. After waiting a minute and hearing nothing else out of the ordinary, he lowered the machete and decided to take the left fork, away from any more strange noises. Despite his dehydrated state a single drop of sweat dribbled down his forehead and stung his left eye, momentarily clouding his vision. He blinked it away and walked, slightly hunched over in a crouch. His right boot was heavy with the sticky red mud from the bog.

Another thirty slow paces passed without incident. There were hundreds or thousands of diverse plants around him, and in front of him he recognized a huge bush of white and green variegated leaves that was taller than him blocking his way. It was an *Epipremnum* bush, or what his Spanish-speaking friends for some reason called a *telefono* plant. Why he recalled the name was a mystery to him, but it put up no fight when he hacked through the wide, flat leaves, dark green lined with yellow as pale as dawn. As he cleared a path and stepped through, he stuttered to a stop.

"Oh, hot damn."

He'd arrived at a short rocky cliff draped in vines and covered in green and black moss. The cliff wasn't at all impressive as a geological formation, being little more than a rocky outcropping five or six feet tall that melded and became one with the dense green brush in both directions. Had he wanted to he could've scaled it without any trouble, even in his current debilitated state. But he had no intention of going any farther, not when he saw a thin trickle of water dribbling down a narrow, mossy channel and accumulating in a shallow puddle below it. This time he did smile. His bottom lip cracked and a thick drop of blood oozed out and hung there, defying gravity. He licked it away with a tongue that felt wrapped in wool batting, and tasted the warm wetness of it. People always said blood tasted like copper, but how did they know that? Had they licked copper before? Regardless, he knew he had to retrace his path and get Hal and at least one jerry can right away. He was pissed at himself for not bringing one along in the first place. He wasn't thinking clearly.

He turned and started back, hurrying now. He was moving faster not just because of their need, but because Ari had just recalled some additional jungle lore that warned about watering holes: they were popular with all manner of creatures, small and large, good and bad - and sometimes the bad were extremely bad. More than ever he was keenly aware of being alone and far from the others and far from top physical form. He increased his pace another notch.

He'd retraced his way and was about to step off the game trail and back onto his own hacked path he heard some commotion behind him. Something big was heading toward him from the direction of the watering hole, and it was coming fast. He stopped to listen and heard it again, some animal crashing through the jungle, something that was moving with lots of haste and zero caution. Then there was a loud grunt and a dirty brown peccary larger than Lucky burst through some knee-high scrub brush and came charging toward him, its little piggy eyes wide in abject terror. The beast either didn't see him or didn't care as it dodged through his legs, bounced gracelessly off a tree, and vanished into the thorns with a raw squeal. Two seconds later a yellow and black spotted jaguar that had been hot on the beast's heels flew toward him at a full sprint. It saw Ari and braked with all four paws spread wide, its ass and tail low to the ground as it came to an abrupt halt. Dirt and leaves flew up as it backpedalled to a stop.

Several thoughts fought for dominance in Van Owen's mind, the first being that the jaguar was small, probably a female since it weighed less than a hundred pounds. That was all relative since standing it would likely still look him square in the eye. It was winded and breathing heavily, its sides heaving in and out. Its open mouth showed huge yellow teeth each nearly as big as his thumb. He knew those teeth and its powerful jaw could crush his skull and kill him with one crunching bite as easily as he might bite into an apple.

The second and much more predominate thought was that the big cat was only about fifteen feet away from him, and he was smack dab between it and its dinner. Or, he considered with a sinking sensation, was he now dinner, the measly peccary long forgotten?

The machete was still gripped in both hands but the gun was wedged into his waistband. He doubted he'd have a chance to get the Glock out, cock it, and shoot before the beast could attack. He was oddly calm as he stared into the cat's dark, oddly liquid golden eyes. He spotted a two-inch puckered scar on its left cheek, likely a wound from some previous battle. He took a slow, measured step backwards. The spotted cat stared back at him, still breathing heavily and perhaps as shocked as Ari was at seeing something so out of the ordinary here in its domain. He managed three more steps backwards as the jaguar stood there panting, staring, its pink tongue hanging down, a single drop of milky-white saliva dangling off the end. Its short, spotted tail flipped and twisted behind faster than an agitated python. He caught a brief whiff of a musky, thick, animal smell.

Ari continued to slowly step backwards until he bumped into something hard, a tree probably, maybe even the fallow aguaje nut palm he'd run across earlier. He didn't dare break eye contact and look around, scared that to do so might flip some primitive breaker switch within the jaguar and set the cat into lethal motion. The more he considered it he had to admit that he honestly didn't know what might or might not do that, but he wasn't keen on changing a status quo that seemed to be working. He shuffled to his left and carefully put his boot down, slowly putting his weight first on his toes, then on his heel. He couldn't have known there was a dry branch underfoot. The branch snapped, the sound more jarring than a book dropped in a library, and that was all it took. The jaguar took two measured, graceful paces forward then began to move. Ari didn't wait. In a single motion he spun and sprinted back the way he had come, toward Hal and the others. He dropped the machete and felt his feet fly over the ground, moving faster than he ever believed possible, all fatigue banished by the surge of adrenaline blasted into his veins. Leaves and branches tore at his face and thorns ripped at his clothes, but nothing could hold him back. He heard the big cat crashing right behind him, closing on him with every fleeting step.

He came to the quicksand clearing and didn't pause. He reached the edge of the bog and jumped as far as he could, diving out like a swimmer from starting blocks. He sailed a dozen feet out, and when he smacked against the tranquil, leaf-covered surface he quickly discovered that it was a lot firmer than he thought it would be, so firm and hard it nearly knocked the wind out of him. The jarring thud rattled his bones and felt like he'd landed on wet sand, that type of sand right at the ocean's edge where waves kept it shifting and soaked. Spread-eagled, he skidded across the dry leaves and sticks before coming to a sudden stop, mud and twigs in his hair and clogging his mouth and nose. Winded and gasping he twisted onto his back to see the jungle cat still behind him. It had stopped at the edge of the clearing and was angrily pacing back and forth, its tail still twitching. It scampered around to the side of the boggy area and tried to get at this new prey from a different angle, advancing and putting a huge paw larger than a man's outstretched hand into the thick muck before pulling it back and shaking it with a frustrated, feral growl. It didn't like coming this close to dinner and being stymied, but it liked the quicksand even less.

Ari felt his legs sinking in the mud and did his best to stay calm, spreading out his extremities to slow his descent into the warm muck, trying to achieve some sort of neutral buoyancy. The cat bared its impressive teeth and growled again, louder this time, the ancient, primal sound causing the hair on his arms and neck to stand at rapt attention while turning his bowels to jelly. In seconds his feet were completely covered and the reddish mud was oozing over his thighs and encroaching on his groin. He tipped downward, beginning to sink as gracefully as a holed ship. As his body angled down and he sank deeper he felt something in his waistband, and remembered the Glock. With trembling hands he fumbled it out and cocked it.

"Sorry, cat. Get your meal elsewhere."

With hands covered in red muck he aimed the pistol at the patch of blue sky above him and pulled the trigger. The recoil almost ripped the gun from his slippery grasp as the blast reverberated through the trees, ricocheting around the tight clearing louder than trapped thunder. The jaguar acted just like a startled housecat and jumped two feet straight up before it landed, spun, and vanished into the jungle with an angry snarl. Just to be sure he'd scared it all the way to Bolivia he pulled the trigger and let loose another round.

Several blue and yellow macaws, their long colorful tails trailing behind them, burst from the trees, squawking at him in anger. In the near distance some tiny squirrel monkeys screamed in shock and bolted off, leaping deftly from branch to branch. Two tiny titi monkeys sat high up and stared at him, their tails entwined. Van Owen for some reason remembered just then that once titi monkeys were mated they stayed together for life.

Ari sighed and lowered the gun. The red-hot rush of adrenaline brought on by the jaguar began to dissipate, his boiling blood now cooling. He was exhausted and weak and felt an overpowering urge to simply lie back in the mud and let its warm embrace cover and protect him, like his mom had held him when he was a kid and he'd been spooked by some unknown nighttime terror in his bedroom. After everything he'd been through it was so very, very comforting. The quicksand was above his chest and he was still sinking.

Then in the distance he heard a shout, someone calling his name. Ari couldn't tell which of his party it was or how far away they were. He tried to yell but his cry was thin and hoarse and didn't carry far outside the clearing. He lifted the pistol again and let off another round. The retort made his ears ring. He hated using up their limited ammunition but there wasn't much choice, not if he wanted to be found. He tilted backwards as far as he could to slow his descent, but even so the muck was almost to his chest and had already reached the back of his neck. Deeper down the mud was thicker and heavier. It took more effort than he thought possible, but he cautiously poked around with his feet until he realized there was still no solid ground below him, at least none that he could find. The comforting feeling he'd relished just moments ago evaporated faster than fog under a tropical sun, replaced by a burst of panic more poignant than his confrontation with the jaguar.

Then to his left the brush parted and Butch pushed his way into view. Van Owen had to twist himself uncomfortably sideways to see him. The man was breathing heavily and he had red scratches on his face. He bent over and put his hands on his knees, trying to catch his breath. The two made eye contact and Ari felt a wave of relief so immediate and strong he felt momentarily lightheaded.

"Little help here?" he said. His voice was still weak but he was surprised how calm he actually sounded considering his situation.

Brubaker stared at him for a moment. He was still huffing and puffing like he'd been the one chased by the jaguar. His wide face showed no emotion, except perhaps his eyes. They squinted as if in thought, but still effectively masked what was going on hidden in the recesses behind them. He looked over his shoulder then turned and vanished back the way he had come, into the jungle, leaving Ari alone in the mud once more. Van Owen found his voice then and yelled at the spot where the man had been.

"Butch, dammit! Get back here! What the hell are you doing?"

The modicum of self-control he'd enjoyed moments before vanished and he felt himself suddenly consumed with white, blinding fear, the fear of drowning, of thick, cloying mud filling his lungs as he fought against the primal urge to breath. He thrashed in the quicksand, felt it resisting his every movement, each spasm sending him ever deeper. He screamed at the still empty spot where he'd seen Butch for several minutes before finally stopping, his own breathing heavy and labored now in his ears, his throat ripped raw from the effort. Somehow his body was still able to sweat and he felt it running into his eyes and coursing down his cheeks like tears.

He looked up at the patch of bright blue sky overhead and saw the pale white contrails of a large airliner. He considered the injustice that he could see that bit of civilization right there, directly above him and seemingly so close that he could reach out and touch it, but that the people in that other world were comfortable and completely ignorant of his plight. They'd probably just been informed that it was okay to use their portable electronic equipment, and were impatiently waiting for the drink cart.

He was sinking again and could do nothing to stop it. *It's not supposed to work this way!* He should be able to achieve neutral buoyancy and float, at least a little – but that wasn't happening. He was still going down. Mud and dead leaves reached the bottom of his chin.

Then there was another rustling in the brush, more subtle this time, stealthier, but in the direction of his feet. He craned his neck up, muscles straining, again hopeful that either Butch had returned or someone else from his party was there to help. At first he thought it was Paul since he saw a blond head peeking above another *telefono* bush at the edge of the clearing. But the dirty face was thin, not round like Paulson's, and the skin was much darker, almost as dark brown as any Amazon native. The eyes peering curiously at him were as blue as the dome of sky above his head. They blinked once before the face dropped down and noiselessly vanished behind the bush. In hindsight Ari realized that was what he'd seen before; that blond head had been the unnatural movement that had spooked him before his run-in with the jaguar, he just knew it. But it didn't make any sense. What the hell?

Chapter 16

Before she'd passed away Van Owen's maternal grandmother had been fond of a certain saying, one she'd used sparingly and only in special circumstances. But when she said it she meant it. At those times when she was really angry with someone or something she'd grit her teeth and snap, "I'm so mad I could just spit." That was how furious Ari was right now at Butch Brubaker.

He'd always known, of course, that the son of a bitch didn't like him. The feeling was mutual. It revolved mainly around their shared relationships with Frankie, but it really went beyond even that. They were from different worlds, enjoyed different activities, were of completely different mindsets, and never would've been friends under any circumstances. At a party they would have positioned themselves on opposite sides of the room, fated never to speak or mingle.

But for Butch to see him stranded in the quicksand and do nothing, to just walk away and leave him there without a word, was beyond anything Ari had imagined of the man. For any reasonable, civilized human being to do that was beyond the pale. Like his grandmother in those special moments, he was so angry he could just spit.

But there was also that last glimpse he'd had of the blond native. That tempered his anger, distracted him enough that he was no longer grinding his teeth and flailing at the muddy slop that had him trapped as effectively as hardening concrete. A blond native? How in the world had that happened? Was it a mutation? A genetic fluke? In all his time in the jungle he'd never run across a blond haired, blue-eyed native before, and it was baffling him to no end. What he wouldn't give to find that young man and talk to him, discover his personal history and how he had come to exist at all.

But not now. Now he had to do whatever he could to escape this mess. He thought back to what he knew about quicksand and how to get out. Moving slowly he flipped over onto his stomach, still keeping his arms and legs stretched out and extended as if he were making a snow angel, or in this case a mud angel. He took a deep breath and began a gentle swimming motion with his arms, trying to make his way to the side. He gauged his progress against static landmarks on either side of him, keeping his disappointment tamped down when he realized how little success he was having. He felt like screaming his frustration at the top of his lungs but knew that wouldn't help. Besides, pragmatism insisted he shouldn't waste his energy, and his throat already hurt like hell.

Unfortunately for some reason his body hadn't yet reached a level of neutral buoyancy and he was still sinking, albeit very slowly. Panic was becoming a physical thing he had to force down and out of the way before it grabbed hold and took over. He had sunk far enough that when he was on his stomach his face was almost entirely in the mud, and he had to take a deep breath before he could continue. When he was unable to hold his breath any longer he flipped to his back and rested, hoping he wouldn't continue to sink. He thought he had made some headway but couldn't be certain. He remembered the Glock he'd stuffed back in his waistband and pulled it out for another shot into the sky, then with a flash of frustration saw that the chamber and clip were empty. There would be no more help from that avenue. *Shit!*

His face was barely above the level of the mud and he had sunk so far that his ears were covered and leaves tickled his temples. Ari's nerve was nearly shot when he heard a sound and twisted his head. He couldn't believe it but Butch was back. In his hand he held what looked like a long, roughly coiled up vine. The vine was about an inch thick and covered in tiny green leaves.

"Here, catch," Butch ordered, the highs of his words clipped off and muffled by the mud in Ari's ears. He tossed one end out towards Van Owen where it nearly hit him on the head. "Careful. It's covered in little thorns. But it's the best I could do."

Ari snatched onto the vine like the lifeline it was. His mud-covered hands were slick and he had a hard time getting a solid grip on it. And Brubaker was right – he felt the thorns piercing his skin but at this point that was the least of his concerns. At first the quicksand didn't want to relinquish its cloying grasp on him, so Butch had to set his feet and put his back into it before Ari felt himself moving. With Brubaker's sustained effort he finally felt himself pulled free of the deeper muck and onto the surface. Butch dug his heels in and walked backwards, his feet slipping on the leafy ground, and finally Ari felt himself reach semi-solid, then solid dirt once more. Brubaker plopped down hard onto his butt, breathing heavily, and tossed the vine to the side. Ari simply stayed put and luxuriated in the feel of real ground underneath him. He was covered head to toe in the thick, sticky mud, and his hands stung from the thorns, but he didn't care. He rolled onto his back and breathed deeply of the heavy jungle air, fatigue threatening to claim him.

"You're welcome," Butch said after a time, sitting up and inspecting his bloody hands. He'd been holding onto the thicker part of the vine where the thorns were larger. He plucked several out of his palms. Each time he extracted one he winced, a tiny movement of his right cheek, like a nervous tic.

Ari finally rolled over and sat up. He inspected his own hands and gingerly picked a few of the larger thorns out. Others were too deep and he'd have to work on them later, although some would require the attention of antiseptic and a sharp needle, none of which they had. As with any injury in the rainforest that involved broken skin they'd both have to be wary of infection. On the plus side some of the thick mud covering him was already drying in the heat and was flaking off in big, damp chunks, as if he were a pottery project that had gone bad. He rubbed himself and more plopped off, leaving his skin stained a deep terra cotta red.

"Thanks. For a minute there when you left I was beginning to get worried."

Butch didn't look up from working on his hands. "I didn't have any way to get you out. I had to find something."

He rubbed more mud chunks off of him. He was getting quite a collection scattered around him in a rough circle. "That vine was perfect. Good work."

Brubaker picked up the fat end of the vine and held it up. "Don't thank me. I couldn't find anything and practically tripped over this thing. It was lying on the path right in front of me. Here. Check this out."

Ari inspected the end that was offered to him. It was cut cleanly as with a sharp knife. A thick, clear liquid oozed from the severed end. Van Owen looked over to where the blond native had been staring at him. There was nothing to be seen now, but the stranger had been there, he was certain of it. And before, on the trail, too.

"Hmm. Come on. Let's get back to the others. I found water...and something else."

Butch stared at him but Ari didn't feel like elaborating, not yet and not to him. He knew he should at least do a better job of thanking the man for saving his life, but Brubaker was probably just as content not talking about it either. They retrieved the machete then the two men followed their hacked path back to the others, dried clay still falling in clumps from Ari. Anyone watching would've thought he was shedding a second skin.

When they got back Hal was nowhere to be seen, but Paul was still on the ground and doing his best to mind their limited supplies. He looked Ari up and down with wide eyes.

"What the hell happened to you?"

Van Owen brushed more mud off his arms and legs. Most of it was gone now but he was still stained reddish-brown all over. "Just a little excitement, that's all. I'll explain later. Where's Hal?"

Paul motioned into the jungle. "He's out there looking for you guys."

"Damn. We need him back here right now."

Brubaker drew his pistol out and cocked it in one easy motion. He aimed it into the air. "I'll get his attention."

"No, wait – hold on," Paulson ordered. "Save your ammo. I can do this." He put the first two fingers on each hand into his mouth, then took a deep breath and blew hard. An ear-piercing whistle shattered the jungle's sonic equilibrium. It was so loud it hurt, louder than any referee's whistle Ari had ever heard, and easily loud enough to penetrate even the sound-dampening qualities of the jungle. Their hands instinctively flew to their ears.

Butch holstered his weapon. "Jesus, kid, warn us next time, okay?"

"Oh, sorry about that. Didn't even think about it."

"Where'd you learn to do that, anyway?" Brubaker asked, not unkindly.

"When I was a kid I was in charge of calling everyone home for lunch, or dinner, or whatever." He shrugged. "I've always been able to do it."

Just then Hal came up the ragged road from the other direction. He sighed deeply in relief when he saw all of them gathered together. There were scratches on his face and neck, and some fresh blood was smeared on both hands. His footfalls were heavy and slow and it was clear how exhausted he was, his tank running on fumes.

"You okay?" Paul asked when the agent finally made it to them.

He sat down heavily next to Paulson. "Yes, I'm fine. Just had some run-ins with thorns looking for you guys. Not having a machete made it a little difficult." He looked Ari up and down, finally settling on his face. "And while you look like hell, I can tell by your expression you've got some news for us. What'd you find? Good news, I hope."

"Good news, yes. Plus some news I'm not sure how to classify." He told them about the water, which immediately buoyed their spirits. Butch grabbed a jerry can and started to head for their hacked trail. "But hold on – there's more."

Hal cocked an eyebrow at him. "More?"

"Yes, more." Van Owen recounted the jaguar incident and spotting the blond native, and how Butch had saved him with the vine that had certainly been planted on the trail by the stranger. There was no other explanation. Hal and Paulson were obviously intrigued, but not nearly as much as Ari had hoped.

"Don't you get it?" he continued, looking at each of them in turn. "There are no blond natives out here. It just doesn't happen."

"I'd say the bigger question is, why did he help Butch save you?" Hal asked. "Why would he bother? He can't know you or any of us. Is there some sort of Law of the Jungle that would direct him to lend a hand?"

"A Good Samaritan sort of thing?" Paul asked the group. "He helped out of the goodness of his heart? Something like that?"

Ari raised his hands, palms out. "No, no, there's nothing like that out here, trust me. Tribes are closed and not at all altruistic. They're all aware of the limited resources available and would never go out of their way to help someone from outside their tribe, except maybe a woman, and that's for different reasons altogether. In fact there's an anthropological process called 'fissioning' that takes place when a singular tribe becomes too large, or the resources in their area are becoming too depleted. The tribe splits and one half leaves, they go their separate way to a new part of the jungle, one that can better sustain them. They're a new, individual tribe then, and rarely if ever have contact with the other group again. That's the way of the jungle."

"Well that's fine and very interesting," Hal admitted, "but I don't see how any of this pertains to our situation right now. I say we get the water and be on our way before something else happens. Jaguars first and then quicksand – what's next?"

Ari wanted to protest, to insist that the blond native had to be investigated, but he was keenly aware of their immediate need and didn't push his point. He grabbed one of the empty jerry cans and motioned to Hal.

"Come on. Let's go get some water and get going."

The agent held out a hand and Ari helped him to his feet with a long, steady pull that took more out of him than it should have. Together they followed the trail back to the quicksand bog. Its surface was whole and complete again, the disturbed leaves and muddy tracks the only sign that Van Owen had been trapped there at all. He stopped and pointed to the other side.

"That's where I saw him, over that bush right there. He was blond with blue eyes, a thin face, tanned, and he was staring at me."

"Did he say anything?"

"Nope. Not a thing. He was there, and then he wasn't."

Hal stuck a toe into the edge of the quicksand; it came away damp with red mud. He wiped it off on the ground as if it were a little offensive. They moved cautiously around the boggy area and Ari found the game trail where he had first encountered the jaguar and the peccary. He pointed the area out to Hollenbeck who said nothing but may have grasped his Glock just a little tighter. The two men followed the serpentine game trail up to and around the *telefono* bush, ending up at the low rocky wall. Ari breathed a silent sigh of relief when he saw that the trickle of water was still there; he had half believed, irrationally, that it would somehow have dried up, or worse, never been there at all.

"I know I can't," Hal whispered, staring, "but I want to put my mouth down there and drink it right now."

"Well you could, but you wouldn't like the outcome in less than twenty-four hours. I've tried that before and it never ends well.

Headache, fever, diarrhea, vomiting. It's not pretty. Come on – let's fill this and get back."

It took nearly fifteen minutes to fill the jerry can, and it would've taken longer if they hadn't finally used a leaf from the *telefono* plant as a sort of funnel. Hal took a minute and washed some of the dried blood from his hands, but Ari wouldn't let him clean any of his open scratches with the unpurified water. It was too dangerous. When it was finally topped off and they picked up the metal can it sloshed deliciously, tantalizingly as they walked. In no time at all they were back, the way now familiar.

During their absence Butch had taken the initiative and had a fire going with the last of their gasoline. Since they had no other way to suspend the jerry can over the fire they threaded Paul's walking stick through the handle and two of them had to hold it while they waited for the water to heat. A watched pot had never, ever boiled so slowly. Finally Ari took off his hat and placed it over the mouth of their second, empty jerry can.

"Okay, Hal, slowly pour it through my hat and into this one to filter out any particulate matter – bugs, dirt, stuff like that. After that let's line up and toast the end of a rather eventful day."

Just a few minutes later they were all drinking deeply of the still very hot water. Although it was bland and way too warm for comfort, and still possessed a faint, mossy flavor, none of them had ever tasted anything so sweet and delicious. Despite Ari's warning of drinking too much too fast, they downed as much as they could as quickly as they could. They drank until they were full, and almost immediately felt some welcome relief, even if they suffered some intermittent cramping as their systems fought to handle the influx. They didn't care.

Hal used a few handfuls of water to clean his face and hands, and Ari did the same to Paul's leg. The young man winced a few times when Van Owen even lightly touched the wound. He then used the last of it to rinse out the bloody rag before wrapping it up again, securing it with rubber bands. Finally he and Hollenbeck made an uneventful trip back to the watering hole for a final fill up, and when they got back they managed to boil another jerry can full of water before the fire burned too low to be effective. They strained it through Ari's hat one more time, then capped the can for later. The four of them then sat back down around the smoking embers.

"We need to keep going, if we can," Ari said, still staring at the fire. He kicked at some of the coals and a tiny flame licked up. He had located some dried palm fronds and tossed them in where they smoldered for a few seconds before catching with a small crackling sound. "We can't stay here. There's no food. That's our next objective."

No one said anything, but neither did they move. The brief joy that the water had provided was quickly dissipating as the enormity of their situation once again began to beat them down. Ari looked at Paul. The young man was pale and listless, his breathing shallow and thin. Across his forehead a fresh sheen of oily sweat glistened. He was not well. All of them could tell that he wouldn't be able to go far, not in this condition.

"I'm not sure that's a viable option," Hal said after a minute had passed. He didn't need to elaborate on why. They all knew.

Ari thought back to the conversation he and the agent had had back in Kentucky, the one where they had discussed that people in the jungle died being "just hardy". He'd had his doubts about Hollenbeck then. He'd also had doubts about Paul and his battle injury and whether he'd be able to make it. He hated to think that he'd been right all along.

But Paulson surprised him and sat up, then used his walking stick to help him to his feet. He was weaving dangerously back and forth, much like Father Ed had after half a bottle of bourbon, but he stayed upright, leaning on the stick for support. If anything he was even paler than before, his skin the same washed out color as his fair hair, but the resolute expression on his round face clearly evinced his determination.

"Come on, you guys," he said in a thin voice. "Ari says it's time to go. So let's go." He began hobbling away from them, down the road. Wordlessly Butch got up and followed. Hal raised both eyebrows at Van Owen in surprise and stood, brushing dirt and leaves from his pants. By the time Ari got to his feet the others were already a dozen yards away. He picked up the water can and started after them, shocked and more than a little proud of the young man's determination and fortitude.

They were moving like zombies and had only trudged a few hundred yards when Ari called out for them to stop. With a few seconds of delayed reaction the other three did and slowly turned around. Ari was staring at the ground at his feet. There, piled neatly one on top of the other with a small stone to hold them in place, were a handful of leaves from *Trapaeolum majus*, the medicinal plant he had found earlier.

"Where did these come from?" he asked to no one. "Who put these here?"

Hal had shuffled back to him and was staring at the leaves. "What are you talking about?"

"These leaves. They're the same ones I used earlier on Paul's leg. Did you find them?"

The agent shook his head. "No, of course not. None of us did. We don't even know what the plant looks like."

Ari picked up the small pile of broad green shiny leaves. They were most definitely *Trapaeolum majus*, there was no doubt about it. And the top one had some clear, gooey substance smeared on it that he didn't recognize, something with the same consistency of Vaseline. He touched the gooey stuff then brought his finger to his nose and smelled it: it had a faint, tangy aroma, almost like eucalyptus. He rubbed it between his fingers and the smell intensified and he swore it warmed under his touch. Ari walked over to Paul and told him to sit down.

"What's that stuff?"

Van Owen crumpled up some of the leaves and unwrapped the damp dressing. He smeared some of the clear goo around and into the wound then bound it all back up with the leaves and the rag. Almost immediately Paul's strained expression eased, the tightness around his eyes and mouth softening. His tense shoulders drooped ever so slightly.

"Damn, that feels good. What is it?"

"It's a leap of faith, that's what it is."

"What? What do you mean?"

Ari slid the rubber bands back up to hold it all in place. "It means that we may indeed have a Good Samaritan watching over us, that's what."

Just then they saw Butch's head whip around and his pistol aimed into the jungle at their right. Hal spun around and followed the barrel, his own Glock in his hand and raised, poised to shoot.

"No, wait!" Ari shouted. "Nobody move!"

Through a gap in the brush Ari saw the blond native. He was fifteen feet into the jungle and simply standing there, his long blond hair down to his shoulders, his blue eyes steady and blinking slowly. Van Owen hadn't noticed before but the native was young, not more than eighteen or nineteen years old. He had black lines painted around the lower half of his face, individual lines that nearly mimicked dark facial hair. He stared at the group for another moment then turned and walked slowly away, deeper into the jungle and away from them.

"What's going on?" Butch said in shock, not lowering his gun.

"Come on," Ari ordered. "We need to go after him."

"Go after him? What are you, high or something?" Butch asked.

Van Owen shook his head. "No, I'm not. We need to follow him. I think he's helping us."

Hollenbeck stepped up next to Ari. "Are you sure? You want us to go off into the jungle and blindly follow some native? I don't think that's a good idea at all."

Ari was still staring into the brush. He looked down again and noticed another game trail leading toward where the native had been. It would be easy to follow him. He took a step between the bushes. He pushed aside a thorny plant and motioned for the others to come along.

"Look," he said. "He's already helped save me, and he knew exactly what we needed for Paul. And looking back I think he was directing me to the water, too. He's helping us and we need to go after him."

Butch stepped up next to them. "I'm not going after some native into that jungle. No fucking way. Don't let him, Hal."

Hollenbeck looked down the road, at Paul, then where the young native had gone. In response to Butch he holstered his gun and held his hands out toward Ari, then pointed toward the game trail.

"You're the expert, Ari. This is your call and we've trusted you so far. If you say let's go, then we go."

Ari knew it was Brubaker's turn to be so mad he could just spit, but eventually he growled something foul under his breath and shook his head in frustration. He didn't mirror Hal and put his pistol away, but merely looked to the heavens as if for support. Meanwhile Ari pushed ahead into the brush, followed by Hal and, slowly, by Paul and the dog. After a few seconds Butch shook his head again in disgust and plunged in after them.

305

The native was elusive and much more at home here than they were. He was able to slide deftly through the brush, rarely seen and never heard. The four of them glimpsed his blond head only sporadically, tantalizingly, always fifteen or twenty yards distant. They were on a well-defined game trail again where the ground had been packed hard and cleared of brush by years of animals of all sizes and types tramping by. At one point not far along the ground rose and Ari figured they were walking over the shallow cliff that housed the spring he'd found earlier. He hiked on with the others behind him, Hal tentatively and Paul noisily, Lucky sticking close to his side. Butch brought up the rear and was doing an admirable job of being quiet, the hunter in him showing through once again. Several hundred yards along Ari was still able to catch an occasional glimpse of the native as he artfully kept just enough distance between them. His blond head continued to pop up here and there in front of them, his light hair in sharp contrast to the dark greens and blacks of the jungle. Each time they thought he was gone he'd appear again, still leading them on.

Thankfully, the influx of water had done wonders for their overall condition, and while they were still weak and far from one hundred percent, this impromptu detour was proving to be easier than any of them had hoped, at least in the short run. The reasonably well-defined trail helped, as did their intrigue concerning their guide. Ari himself was more than just intrigued. He still couldn't wrap his head around someone like that existing here, much less one altruistic enough to help them. None of it had made sense to him at first, but Ari was beginning to formulate a theory. No, not really a theory, but maybe a desire? Either way, he had to find a way to communicate with this native first, and to do that he had no choice but to follow him. So follow him they did.

They kept on for nearly half an hour before the game trail suddenly stopped in a clear dead-end. Ari knelt down low and looked around more closely. Hal dropped down on one knee and did the same. The young native was nowhere in sight.

"What are we looking at?" he asked.

Ari pointed to the ground at their feet. "The old trail stops here. I can see it used to continue on, but there's newer growth here, and the branches and ground cover are reclaiming the area. And look here." He pointed to his right where it was very evident that a new trail was being formed.

"I can see that. This new path is headed in a different direction. I wonder why?"

"Let's find out." Van Owen brandished the machete and began clearing the way forward. Branches and leaves fell under the blade, the tender new growth easily falling away under the sharp edge of the black steel. Several steps in he swung downward again, but this time instead of slicing through underbrush the blade stopped with a metallic clang. He swung a second time and again the blade stopped with clang of metal on metal that jarred his shoulder and arm. He pushed branches aside to see what he had struck.

"It's a fence," he called back to the others. "It's a damn chain link fence."

Paulson hobbled forward and reached out with his walking stick. He tapped it on this unlikely barrier, the same type of chain link found in backyards all across America. "Uh, forgive me for being ignorant of the jungle and all, but this really isn't supposed to be here, is it?"

Ari cleared away more brush and ripped vines away from it. He gave it a push and found it was taut, strung tightly between metal poles spaced ten feet apart. It was about seven feet tall, easily high enough to stop any of the local fauna from crossing, except the smallest ones and perhaps curious monkeys. Nothing else would be able to get over it. Except a man, of course. A person could climb over it, although it wouldn't be easy.

"No, it's not supposed to be here. Not at all."

Hal helped tear away more vines and leaves. He peered through the chain link. Without pulling his eyes away, he said, "Ari, take a look through here and tell me what you see."

Van Owen did. On the other side of the fence was a thirty-foot wide road. It was crude, just packed down reddish-brown earth, but it was clearly a thoroughfare of some kind. They could see parallel tracks running through the dust and dirt, along with a few trench-like potholes big enough to swallow an unwary compact car. A few of the largest potholes had been filled with crushed rock and gravel.

"I don't remember seeing this on any maps. Is there supposed to be something like this here?"

"No, it's not." Ari shrugged off his backpack and pulled out his trusty laminated map. He unrolled it on the ground and traced his finger here and there. "Look, here's the old road we were on. To the best of my reckoning we were somewhere around here." He pointed to a spot in the middle of a dark green area, one devoid of any markings at all. "There's not supposed to be a road here. This road is new. Very new. And I printed this off right before we left. I don't get it."

Just then Paul looked up, his head tilted. "Do you guys hear that?"

Hal pursed his lips. "Hear what?"

The young man held up his hand for silence. His young ears were more acute than theirs. "That rumbling noise. Don't you hear that?"

They all held their collective breath and listened. Finally Butch nodded. "Yeah, now I do. What is that?"

"It's a truck. It sounds like a truck's coming. It's getting closer."

Ari and Hal exchanged a quick glance as comprehension and a decision hit them simultaneously. Ari shoved the map back into his bag and put a foot up in the air. "Hal, boost me over. Quick!"

The agent didn't stop to think. They both realized that a truck meant civilization, and civilization could mean the difference between surviving or not. It meant possible medical attention for Paul and Butch, it meant food and water, and most of all – to Ari at least – it meant possible access to the Internet. They needed that truck. Hal grabbed Ari's outstretched foot with both hands and nearly tossed him cleanly over the fence. He landed awkwardly on the other side and rolled to his feet, then ran into the road, looking madly in both directions, trying to ascertain where the truck was. He tripped on one of the ruts but kept his balance.

The truck, when it rounded a bend in the distance from his right, turned out to be a huge semi loaded with long black pipes and metal girders. Ari had never seen anything like it before. He was used to the ubiquitous eighteen-wheelers from the States, of course, but this was much larger and more imposing than that. It was at least two, perhaps three times as long, with a massive black cab complete with blacked out windows. He stood in the middle of the dirt road and waved his arms back and forth madly - and belatedly hoped that they not only saw him, but that they could or would stop before running him down. With far less clearance than was comfortable, the gigantic rig's brakes hissed and it shuddered to a halt, its pitted steel bumper not ten feet from where he stood, dust billowing all around it in thick, reddish clouds. The massive machine idled there for a moment as if considering the situation, black smoke puffing from its dual exhaust pipes, before the passenger door swung open and a clean-shaven black man wearing a white Coors ball cap leaned out. He pointed a rifle directly at Ari's chest.

"Who the hell are you?" he asked in unaccented English. "And what the hell are you doing on my road?"

His name, or the only name he ever gave them, was Big Al. They found that the appellation "big" was always used before his name to describe his personality, not his physical stature. Even so, in reality the man was a tank, nearly as wide as he was tall, which in his case equated to just a whisker over five feet, four inches. His shoulders started just below his ears. He had a broad, solid face that looked capable of absorbing a sucker-punch or crowbar with nary a mark. Ari figured that anyone half a brain would realize the error of their ways, and issue sincere apologies, long before a situation could disintegrate into fisticuffs.

Big Al jumped out of the truck and Van Owen swore he could feel the ground shudder as his black boots landed solidly on the dirt road. The man's arms were so thickly muscled that the short sleeves of his T-shirt were stretched almost beyond their limit. He expertly snapped the barrel of the rifle up so it was again centered on Ari's chest.

"I said, who the hell are you and what the hell are you doing on my road?"

Ari didn't move, except to instinctively raise his hands. "My name is Ari Van Owen and I'm on an expedition to find out what happened to the legendary explorer Percy Fawcett. The other members of my team are just beyond the fence, over there." He tilted his head toward the jungle. "We ran into trouble a few days ago and we desperately need food, water, and medicine. Will you help us?"

The barrel of the gun didn't waver or budge but Big Al's eyes tracked to his left. At the fence stood Hal and Paul, clearly visible, but Butch and the dog were somewhere behind them and out of sight.

"How many in your party?"

"Four, including me. Plus a dog."

"You armed?"

"Me? No, I'm not, but we have some pistols, yes."

Big Al grunted. "Tell them to toss all their weapons over the fence. Now."

He said it with such force that Ari almost couldn't imagine saying no, like the man was employing a Jedi Mind Trick. Regardless, he did push back. "Wait. We're not here to hurt you or anything like that. We just stumbled across your fence and road. We just need help, that's all. Will you help us?"

"Tell them to toss all their weapons over the fence. Now," he repeated. His dark eyes never wavered.

Ari stared back at him. Without help he didn't think Paulson would make it, not with his infected leg. He and the others might, but not Paul – and he was responsible for bringing the young man on this journey. And besides, the blond native had led them here for a reason. He took a leap of faith, not because he wanted to but because he had to.

"Hal, Paul, Butch!" he yelled toward them. "Throw your guns over the fence. It's okay. He's going to help us."

Ari waited for several seconds. His arms were getting tired as he held them up, his shoulders beginning to ache. He couldn't be sure but he thought he heard a rather heated, albeit brief, argument on the other side of the fence. Finally he heard Butch bark out, "Fine!" and the three Glocks arced up and over the fence and landed with distinct thuds on the hard-packed ground.

"Is that it?" Big Al asked. "You do not want to hold out on me. I will not be happy if you're holding out on me."

Ari nodded once. "That's it. We lost our rifles with our transportation. Along with most of our supplies."

Big Al grunted and lowered his rifle a few inches. "Tell them to climb over and stand against the fence. Smooth and easy."

"One in our party is injured. Is it okay if I help him over?"

He didn't hesitate. "Go ahead."

Ari hustled over and waited as Hal and Butch gave Paulson a hand from their side. He caught Paul as he nearly tumbled over the

311

top and eased him to the ground. The young man was pale and shivering even in the heat, but he didn't make a sound or complain. Next came Hal, who did a pretty good job of climbing up and over, only stumbling a half step when he came down. Then Butch stretched and handed Lucky over before he himself was over the top quickly and smoothly, looking like he did this sort of thing for fun on weekends. They lined up against the metal fence.

Big Al walked from the front of the truck and surveyed the group. He shook his head from side to side and clicked his tongue. He calmly picked up the three pistols and one by one stuffed them into his waistband. He stood there for well over a minute and stared at them, and it was impossible to know what was going on behind his dark sunglasses.

"This is no place for any American citizens to be. Much less a dog." Lucky eased toward him and sniffed his pant leg once, then trotted back to Paul's side. Big Al slung the rifle up and onto his shoulder. "But I'm not about to leave any fellow Americans to die out here in this hell hole. Climb in."

With that he turned and got back into the truck, just assuming that they would follow him. The four of them exchanged glances and got in, pushing past Big Al into the large back seat. Lucky jumped in soundlessly. Behind them an American flag was tacked onto the back of the cab. The driver was a heavy-set man with long hair partially obscured by a blue bandana, a holstered pistol at his side. Big Al wordlessly pointed ahead and the massive truck moved out, bouncing along the rutted road as it surged forward.

Just a mile or so up the road they rounded a bend and came to a large, open area, a clear-cut space large enough to house several football fields. There were a dozen or so house trailers set up to the left and a large, complex metal construct being erected well off to the right. The construct itself was all silver and black pipes and girders with rigging strung up everywhere. Three huge cranes were busy lifting and stacking masses of steel pipes and I-beams as easily as a man would pick up a length of PVC tubing. There were dozens of people in hardhats milling about, several with clipboards or talking into handsets. Ari was sure the complex would make sense to someone, but not to him. All he knew was that nothing like this should have been here at all, not in the middle of the jungle. He couldn't imagine why it didn't show up on his map or anywhere else.

The truck pulled up to the first house trailer and jerked to a halt. Big Al swung open the door and motioned for them to follow. He lithely jumped out of the cab and strode into the trailer. The four men did the same, Paul with a little more difficulty but still holding his own. Ari smelled hot dirt and the burnt tang of welded steel, along with other chemical odors he couldn't place. The smooth chugging of several engines, probably generators, came from somewhere out of sight beyond the industrial complex. They entered the trailer and the cool air of a strong AC unit chilled their damp, sweaty skin. Lucky hesitated at the threshold but in the end skittered in after Paul and quickly sat down in a corner. A man at a desk covered with blueprints and other paperwork looked up.

"Doc, look these boys over and give them what they need. I'll be back to check on them later." Again he didn't wait to see if his orders would be followed or even questioned, but turned and walked back outside, shutting the door behind them. The sounds of construction were suddenly muffled to a soft murmur.

Doc was a short, swarthy balding man, very tan in a white shirt and khakis. Where Big Al was tough and hard, Doc was the opposite, soft, overweight, and had the appearance of a man accustomed to eating what he liked, when he liked, and as much as he liked. A large sandwich stuffed with lunchmeat and slathered with mayo sat on a plate, half eaten, with a big one-pound bag of Fritos next to it. A can of Diet Coke was sweating next to the plate, a small puddle of condensation pooling at its base. Doc took a deep, weary sigh, evidently miffed that his normal routine, whatever it was, had been interrupted. He looked the four of them up and down.

"I'm not even going to ask why you guys are out here or how you know Big Al, but if he says check you out then I'm going to check you out."

Ari stepped forward. "Him first," he said, putting his arm around Paul and inching him toward Doc. "He's got a badly infected leg wound and a fever, not to mention dehydration. And we haven't had much to eat in several days."

Doc handed the remainder of his sandwich to Paul. "There's plenty more where that came from. Eat up and follow me. You guys take a seat. There's food and water in the fridge." He jerked a thumb behind him and the two of them headed through a narrow hallway toward the back of the trailer.

Hal watched their retreating backs. "Excuse me, but are you really a doctor?"

Doc didn't even look back. "Nope. But I'm the closest thing you've got."

Just seconds after Doc disappeared into the back, Butch declared he was going to take him up on the offer. "If he says there's food and water in the fridge and to help ourselves, I'm gonna do just that."

There was a small, utilitarian kitchen tucked around the corner, complete with a full-sized refrigerator stocked with more lunchmeat, condiments, bread, shelves of water bottles, and much more. This sudden oasis of civilization was so unexpected and welcome that none of them could properly describe the overwhelming emotions battering them. They loaded up plates, then sat on leather couches and chewed and swallowed frantically at first, then more methodically, eating long after they were full, eventually to the point where food lost its allure and they were bloated and stuffed. And then they ate and drank more. All along Butch kept tossing scraps to

314

Lucky. They found him a bowl in a cupboard and filled it with water from bottles. The dog eagerly lapped up every drop.

Just past the kitchen there was a cramped bathroom, the very definition of a water-closet, with a toilet and both hot and cold running water. Each of them took a turn cleaning up, Hal going last. When he exited his glasses were sparkling clean for the first time in days, and while he would never bring it up Ari could tell that completing that small, personal task properly meant a lot to him, likely more than even he imagined.

Bellies finally full and cleaned up to the best of their ability, they slumped down on couches and relaxed. All three men closed their eyes. Ari could feel his body melting into the cushions and his eyelids were weighted down with weeks of fatigue and worry.

"So, Ari," Hal said, and surprisingly he didn't sound tired at all. If Van Owen could've described it, he would've said Hollenbeck was using his "agent's" voice, calculating and all business. "You've had a chance to think about it now. What's going on here? What is this place?"

Ari slowly sat up. He looked around but Doc and Paulson were still at the other end of the trailer and no one else was there. He knew Hal would've done the same before broaching the subject, but for some reason he was still nervous talking about it openly.

His voice low, Ari answered, "My guess? Illegal oil exploration and drilling, I'd say."

Hal nodded. "My guess, too. I have to question how something like this could go on here, and how you could hide it. This is no bush-league operation."

"You're right. I doubt you follow happenings down here like I do, but the Brazilian government makes a big show out of defending the Amazon. But even they know how much oil there is here, how badly the world needs it and how much it's worth. I'm sure palms could be greased and eyes paid to look the other way. When you combine two entities like the Brazilian government with one or more of the oil companies, pretty much anything can happen."

"Even hiding a huge, very visible road from satellite imaging systems?"

"I would've said no before this, but I think now how naïve that would be." He looked a hard challenge at Hollenbeck. "And are you telling me the US government couldn't do something like this if they put their minds to it?"

Hal considered that for a moment. "Point taken. What about the fence? Why the fence along the road? Are they trying to keep something in, or out?"

Ari had to think about that one. He remembered reading about other times in the past when roads like this one had been constructed through the jungle. The original intention had simply been to provide improved access across these vast tracts, but there had been unintended consequences – namely, that the indigenous, local tribes had moved all up and down the new road and erected squatter villages, further taxing limited resources and bringing much greater visibility to the entire area. That may be something this group, whoever they were, was determined to quash. He passed this along to Hal and Butch.

"Makes sense," the agent admitted, and his thoughts were so clear and obvious to Ari that he could almost reach out and touch them. They were the same as his. "I think, gentlemen, that we need to watch ourselves and tread very carefully here. Something strange is going on here."

Just then the door at the other end of the trailer opened, and Paul and Doc walked out. The young man was limping a little, but Ari had to admit that he didn't seem to be favoring it much more than before the leg wound. He stood to greet them.

"How is he?"

Doc grabbed his bag of Fritos and tossed a few into his mouth. Crunching as he talked he said, "It wasn't as nasty as it looked, but it was infected for sure. He said you used some of the local plants to help out? Good thinking, although I wouldn't touch them myself. Don't trust 'em."

Ari didn't have an answer to that, so he said nothing.

"I cleaned it and stitched him up good and tight. Mamma never taught me to sew so I can't vouch for my skill with a needle and thread, so he'll likely have a helluva scar. Gave him a Tetanus shot and a huge dose of antibiotics in the ass and started him on course of oral antibiotics just to be sure." He shook a pill container and tossed it to Van Owen. "One pill in the morning, one at night, for ten days, and he should be good to go. Get him some more food and water and he'll be a new man in no time at all."

"That's great. How do you feel, Paul?"

Paulson was eyeing the contents of the refrigerator as ravenously as the jaguar had stared at Ari. Doc gestured at the racks of food and drink with a Vanna White flourish, telling his patient to get busy, eat up, there was lots more where that came from. The young man didn't need to be told twice, and quickly tucked himself in for a grand feast. That alone answered Ari's question about how he was feeling.

"Actually," Paul finally said around a mouthful of turkey sandwich with Swiss cheese ten minutes later, crumbs littering his chest and lap and a glob of mayo in the corner of his mouth, "I started feeling a whole lot better after you smeared that clear goop on my leg. What was that, anyway?"

Ari shot him a covert look, which Doc didn't notice, busy as he was filling his mouth with more Fritos. When Van Owen spoke his voice was light and conversational, easy-going. "Just a little something I concocted. Glad it helped. Spend enough time out here and you're bound to learn a thing or two." Hal had taken note of the look and correctly interpreted what was going on.

"Yeah, Ari, that was impressive. What did you call that flower with the leaves? *Trapaeolum* something? What was it again?"

"*Trapaeolum majus*. I've used it before and I know most tribes have, too."

"Glad you spotted more of it."

Doc listened to them discuss jungle remedies for a minute before he grew bored and headed to the back room, presumably to clean up from his ministrations with Paul. His wide, pear-shaped bulk nearly filled the narrow hallway, and his heavy footfalls could be felt vibrating the whole trailer. Paul watched him go then quickly turned to the Ari.

"Okay, I'm not always the sharpest tool in the shed, but I'm guessing you don't want to talk about our Good Samaritan buddy? Why's that?"

"Because we don't know what the hell's going on here, that's why. Until we do we give away as little information as possible, I think. That means we also stick totally to the Percy Fawcett story. Your thoughts, Hal?"

"I agree one-hundred percent. The less we talk the better. And yes, it's more imperative than ever that we stick to the story."

Ari turned and addressed the group. "So, about Big Al – what do you think?"

"I'd say ex-military for sure," Paul said. "Staff Sergeant or higher is my guess, but no way he was an officer. From my time with the Corp that's what I'd say."

Both Butch and Hal agreed. The agent looked to make sure Doc wasn't coming back yet. "I agree with Paul. He's a guy who came up through the ranks, not OCS and definitely not a weekend warrior."

"I was never in the service but that's the impression I got, too." Ari looked out the window at the massive construction project taking place all around them. A crane was busy unloading all the steel piping and girders from the black semi-truck that had brought them here, and was stacking everything in neat piles off to the side. He tried to count how many people there were around the complex and came up with at least fifty before he gave up, convinced he'd missed as many as he'd counted. The place was an ant's nest of organized chaos. He finally turned to Butch.

"You should take this chance to get your botfly infections looked at, don't you think? I doubt they'll be able to extract them but they can sure start by killing them."

Brubaker didn't need any additional urging. He called back to Doc and quickly moved to the rear of the trailer, almost running to get there. Ari could hear their murmured discussion, and taking a peek down the hall saw Butch removing his shirt and pointing at a number of spots on his chest and back. Doc peered at several of them and stepped out of view, presumably to find some medicine. Ari nodded his head toward the back room.

"You think he'll stick to the story?" he asked, directly his question mainly at Hal.

"I don't see why not. I don't think he'd be able to discuss it at length or in any detail, but otherwise we should be okay."

Ari nodded. "Okay, you're a better judge of him than I am, I think you've proven that several times. My next goal is to get Internet access so I can look up more of the hidden clues in the Fawcett notes. That should also serve to bolster our story."

"Agreed." Hal shot a glance out the window. "And I think you're going to get your chance soon. Here comes Big Al."

Van Owen spun and looked out the small window. He said, "Good," and met the man at the door. Similarly to whenever he talked to Theodore Rust, Ari had to resist the impulse to salute. Even though he towered over the stocky black man by nearly a foot, he could sense the man's inherent power and felt more than a little daunted by it. He had to stop himself from taking a step backwards.

"How's your boy?" Big Al asked without preamble, motioning toward Paul. He crossed his muscled arms, putting further strain on the sleeves of his shirt. He wasn't exactly menacing, but neither did he come over as caring. Nobody would have classified him as warm and fuzzy.

"Pretty good, I think," Ari answered. "We can't thank you enough for helping us out. I don't know what would've happened otherwise."

"My guess is your boy would've died, followed in a week or two by the rest of you." He said it matter-of-factly, with little or no inflection or emotion. It was a statement of fact as he saw it, like telling them it was hot outside. "Now, with more detail this time, tell me why you're here."

So Ari did, at length and in as much detail as he felt was necessary. Big Al listened dispassionately and didn't interrupt or ask questions. Van Owen assumed he was giving the man what he wanted, so he kept on talking. After nearly ten minutes he had brought Big Al up to speed. He exhaled deeply, not realizing until just then that he'd talked so much he'd barely breathed. The only acknowledgement that their benefactor made at all was to remove his Coors ball cap and grab a bottle of water from the refrigerator. He took a sip before he said anything.

"We'll get you fixed up and then send you on your way. You can't stay here any length of time."

Hal sat up. "Can I ask why not?"

Big Al stared at him for a moment before answering. "No. You shouldn't be here at all. If you weren't Americans I never would've helped in the first place. As it is…" he trailed off. "Never mind. We'll get you cleaned and fed, then we'll haul you back where I found you. Questions?"

"Uh, yes. Can I have access to the Internet? I really need to do some additional research on what I figured out. You know, the hidden messages I told you about. I figure I can nail down his final destination pretty close if I can have some computer time."

Big Al stared at him, unblinking, as if he were reading him down to his DNA. "Yes, you can – if I have your word that you won't be emailing or otherwise contacting anyone outside of your group."

"Absolutely. You've got it."

It took him no time to decide. "Then you can. Follow me."

After telling Doc that they were going to the trailer next door, the three of them plus Lucky followed the stocky man outside. Butch stayed behind with Doc as he worked on the botflies. They stepped back out into the blistering heat, heat made all the more apparent since they were no longer under the canopy of trees but in such a huge open area. Hal fell into step next to Big Al.

"This is quite an operation you've got going here," he said, motioning around with the stem of his glasses. He blew a piece of lint off the lenses. "So what is this place?"

Big Al shot him a single glance and didn't say anything for a number of steps. "You sure ask a lot of questions. You a cop?"

Hal smiled, more of a smirk, actually. "Me, a cop? No, and don't worry – we're eternally in your debt for saving our skins. You have nothing to worry about from us."

"That's good. I consider myself a damn good judge of character. Don't prove me wrong. That wouldn't be a good idea."

They arrived at the next trailer and Big Al strode inside. This trailer was furnished much like the other, with the front rooms setup as offices with a central hallway leading to more in back. There wasn't anyone around, but there was a powerful PC on each desk, with the ubiquitous Windows logo bouncing around the otherwise darkened screens. Big Al typed something into the first one to unlock it then pulled up a browser window for Ari.

"Here you go."

Van Owen sat at the desk. From his backpack he took the clear plastic tube containing the Fawcett letters and spread them next to him on the desk. Big Al watched all this in attentive silence, his arms still crossed as he leaned against the wall.

Paulson eased himself down onto a leather couch by the door and Hal sat at the next desk. The young man closed his eyes and may have fallen asleep. Hollenbeck, on the other hand, was alert and very interested in the proceedings. He leaned forward and motioned toward Van Owen at the computer. "So I noticed when Ari here was telling you what had happened," he started, "and he was talking about our encounter when we got gas, you seemed a little interested when he mentioned this El Quemado guy, the Burned One. Why was that, if you don't mind my asking?"

Big Al didn't move, but his eyes tracked over to Hal. He considered him for a second before he said, "You do ask a lot of questions, don't you?"

Hal smiled innocently. "It's in my nature, I guess. Plus we seem to be headed in his general direction, and we'd like to know as much about him as we can. That makes sense, doesn't it? Can't blame us for that."

Their stout benefactor didn't say anything for what felt like much longer than the few moments it was. He looked back at Ari when he finally answered.

"We know the name, yes, but we don't know much about him. Not really, except everyone around here is terrified of him. He's got something going on about fifteen or twenty miles northwest of here. We don't mess with him and he doesn't mess with us. I'd stay away from him."

"That name, though, the Burned One. What's that all about?"

"We don't know. We heard him called that, too, by some natives to the south of here. Something about an accident he had that scarred him up pretty bad. But that's all rumor. We've never met anyone that's seen him face to face, which says quite a bit if you think about it."

"Is it drugs? Is that what he's doing?"

"I just said that we don't know anything about him. He doesn't bother us and we don't bother him. We have heard that he's got a lot of men, well-armed men, but so do we. If he tries anything here he'll regret it."

Hal took note of the steely edge in Big Al's voice. "Sounds like you're almost hoping he does. Try something, that is."

Again, he didn't look away from Ari, but his voice kept its hard edge. "I don't like drugs, and I don't like what they're doing to my country. If I had an opportunity to do something about it I wouldn't hesitate." He stood up to his full height such as it was and headed toward the door, their discussion over. "If you need anything just flag down anyone outside and ask for me. They'll find me. Otherwise stay in here and I'll come get you later. There's a refrigerator in the back room. Help yourself."

As he was walking out Ari looked up from the keyboard and asked, "Oh, by the way, you didn't see a young priest come through here in the last year, did you? A man named Father Sean, or something like that?"

"A priest? No, no priests or anyone else. You're the only ones, but keep in mind we've only been here for about six months."

Ari thanked him and the stocky black man left, shutting the door solidly behind him. They watched him walk purposefully toward the big cranes as he yelled something to one of the operators, pointing to somewhere outside their field of vision. He shouted at a few more workers, and in no time he was out of sight.

"Curiouser and curiouser," Hal said to himself. "Who's this Father Sean you were talking about?"

"Someone that Father Ed talked about back at the village. I was just wondering, that's all."

Van Owen bent back over the computer. He had already deciphered one more of Fawcett's riddles and was able to add the number to his short list of coordinates. It was beginning to take shape right before his eyes. His fingers trembled on the keyboard as he worked.

Meanwhile Paulson was sound asleep. He would jerk and snort periodically, his head back and his mouth slightly open and his leg twitching. Lucky was at his feet curled into a tight little ball, keeping one eye cocked open and watching the proceedings with care. Hal sat quietly at the desk and watched Ari at work, obviously captivated but not wanting to interrupt his intense train of thought. He sat very still, doing nothing, not even cleaning his glasses.

A little while later Butch tossed the door open and came in, standing at the threshold as his eyes adjusted to the lower light levels inside the trailer. He saw the three of them and sat heavily on one of the desk chairs at Hal's gesture.

"Did Doc fix you up?" the agent asked.

Brubaker lifted his shirt and they could see a dozen shiny patches on his chest, each about the size of a quarter. He held up a small tube of Superglue. "Yeah, there wasn't much he could do right now, but he checked me out then smeared this over each one of the little bastards. Said it'll suffocate them and they'll die pretty quick. Then we can enlarge the hole and get them out, or something like that. He gave me a spare tube in case there's more."

"Nasty business."

"No shit. The sooner the little suckers are dead and gone the better." He dropped his shirt and looked around. "So what's going on here?"

Hal nodded towards Ari. "Our man here is deciphering Fawcett's letters, thanks to Big Al and the Internet, and Paul is catching forty winks. I'd recommend you do the same."

"Still this Fawcett crap?"

"Yes, and this Fawcett 'crap', as you call it, just proved itself worthy and covered our story with our new friend. Thanks to Ari's passion and detail he was able to convince him our Fawcett quest was legitimate and the only reason we're out here."

"Fine. Whatever."

"Whatever? So tell me, Butch, think of this: how do we know Big Al doesn't have some sort of arrangement with this El Quemado person? How do we know he doesn't have a deal to turn over suspicious intruders or, for that matter, a deal to turn over men who are looking for their kidnapped wives? It could be just like the little village gas station back there, the one with our buddy with the bad eye and freshly broken knee. They could all be colluding to help protect each other. We just don't know, and we can't take the chance."

Butch waved a dismissive hand. "Yeah, yeah. Don't worry – I'll be a good boy and I'll keep up the Fawcett quest thing."

"Good. Please see that you do."

"And in just a bit I'll also take you up on that nap, but I'd rather check something out first." He walked to the back of the trailer where he could be heard rummaging around in the fridge, moving dishes and containers around, clanking bottles together. With a triumphant laugh he walked back and proudly displayed a can of Pabst Blue Ribbon beer as if he had won it in a contest. "Now this is what the doctor should have ordered."

"Careful," Hal warned mildly, "you're still dehydrated, and alcohol won't help you at all. You'll be thirstier than ever."

"Screw that. This is the first beer I've had in weeks. I'm not going to pass it up."

Their conversation continued but Ari didn't hear them, their voices having grown detached and distant. He was so entrenched in his search that he had no clue what was going on around him. Via the Internet and his own intuition answers were coming to him fast and furious. He wrote furiously on the notepad next to the keyboard, his handwriting sloppy and wild as the clumsy mechanics of putting thought to paper couldn't keep up with the avalanche of revelations.

Sometime later Butch and Hal wandered to the rear of the trailer and settled on the couches, kicking back and napping, but Ari kept going, his energy level soaring and his mind running a million miles an hour. He couldn't believe how useful Google and the other search engines could be for research and investigative work. After several hours of this he wrote down a final number and sat back in the chair, his eternally messed up brown hair sticking out at crazy angles. He was surprised to notice that besides Paul snoozing away he was alone at the desks, and that it had grown dark outside. The sounds of construction had ebbed and the only noise was the muffled hum of generators rumbling through the thin manufactured walls. He rubbed his eyes and looked at the dozens of pieces of paper next to the keyboard, focusing on the topmost one. On it was written six numbers in large print: 12 77 19 and 56 55 39, which he was certain translated to 12.7719' south by 56.5539' west, coordinates for sure. He plotted that compared to where he figured they were now and made two dots on the map with a pen, one their approximate current position and the other this new one. To the best of his reckoning they were only ten or twenty miles apart. More specifically and certainly more importantly, he considered thoughtfully, tapping the pen on his teeth, it looked like Fawcett's final location was very close to this El Quemado person *and* in the general vicinity of the bullet ants Hal was so interested in. In fact, all three areas were almost on top of one another. That couldn't be a coincidence.

Despite all this he finally knew what had likely been Percy Fawcett's last known location. He was so pumped and excited that for a moment, just a moment, he even forgot about Frankie Brubaker.

Chapter 18

Big Al returned for them a little while later, not at all surprised that the other three men were asleep. He reached down and scratched a wary Lucky once between the ears.

"Did you find what you were looking for?"

Ari held out the final coordinates. "I did, yes, thank you. It wasn't that difficult once I had a computer to help. You have no idea how long I've been trying to figure this out."

"This Fawcett person, why was he so secretive and how come nobody else has ever tracked him down?"

Van Owen explained in more detail about the British explorer and his belief in the Lost City of Z, and why it was so important to him. He also told him how Fawcett had encrypted his answers within the letters to his wife. Big Al didn't respond but did raise an eyebrow or two as he absorbed what Ari was saying. He looked at the two dots on the map.

"You say this one here is the location of Fawcett, and this one is us?"

"To the best of my knowledge, yes."

Big Al grunted once and took the pen. With careful consideration he made a single mark slightly to the left of Ari's. As he reached his arm out Van Owen noticed a portion of a deep blue tattoo on his outstretched arm. He only caught a portion of it, but what he could see looked like the blade of a knife piercing what could have been the Earth. It was difficult to see against the man's dark skin, but it was there. The tattoo was still clear-edged and sharp, the dark blue as yet untainted with green or smeared with age. The upper portion of it was hidden behind the shirtsleeve, but enough was visible in that split second. He set the pen back down.

"You were close. This is our current location."

Ari inspected the map again. If the placement of the two dots was correct then they were even closer to this El Quemado person than he'd thought. Probably ten miles, fifteen at the most, was all that separated them. Ari felt a rush of excitement.

Then Big Al stood, all business again. "Come on. Gather up your men and you can bed down for the night. You'll need to leave tomorrow. You can't stay here longer than that."

"Can we at least stay long enough for our guy with the botflies to get taken care of?"

"I talked to Doc. He can remove them tomorrow morning. After that you have to go."

"Okay, thanks. I mean it."

Ari knew by now that there was no point in talking or asking more questions. He gathered up his papers and map, then roused his three companions and together the five of them plus the dog exited and followed him to another trailer. They went inside. It was dark, with just a faint row of lights running down the center of it, like airplane emergency lighting. On either side were rows of bunk beds all up and down, terminating near the back in a small bathroom, complete with a shower. In most of the beds men were asleep and breathing heavily, exhausted from heavy labor in the Amazonian heat and humidity. Some read with tiny lights while others used tablets or small laptops. A few turned their heads in curiosity but went back to their business when they saw who was there. No one spoke.

"Get cleaned up and call it a night. There's soap, shampoo, and shaving cream and razors back there. Use what you need. The beds in the back are empty."

He turned and left. The four of them looked at each other until Butch headed to the back, entering the bathroom. He shut the door behind him and they soon heard water running. He was in the shower for less than five minutes, but it was long enough for the others to queue up and anxiously wait their turns. Ari was the last to go. The white fiberglass shower stall was so tight he could barely turn around, but the hot water felt glorious on his filthy skin. He could've stayed in there all night with the pounding water blasting away the stain of the journey, but he reluctantly finished and dried off. None of them wanted to put their crusty, muddy clothes back on so each man got into bed naked, the cotton sheets feeling like the coolest silk on their sensitive skin. Their clothes were piled in a foul heap on the floor. In minutes they were sound asleep.

Ari woke and knew it was five o'clock. Inside the trailer it was still dark, but the glow from the floor lighting seemed abnormally bright to his eyes. All around him he could hear men breathing heavily, some snoring lightly, a single person at the other end mumbling something unintelligible, something punctuated with a laugh and a snicker. He couldn't remember if he'd had a dream or what, but whatever vision or sensation had woken him this time hadn't been nearly as ominous or threatening. He took that as a good sign, although it was just guesswork on his part.

He eased himself out of bed and went to the bathroom. Once inside he closed the door and flicked on the light. Staring into the mirror he was shocked at how gaunt he looked. He'd shaved the night before in the shower, but had been so exhausted he hadn't paid much attention to his face, the act of shaving itself simply happening by muscle memory. He could tell he'd lost weight, which he'd expected. His already thin face was narrower than he remembered, his cheekbones etched clear, the skin around his cheeks and forehead pulled tight like the head of a snare drum. His brown, eternally tussled hair was so out of control no amount of product could've done much good, not that he cared. He turned away and used the toilet, then washed and padded softly back to his bed. The sheets still felt wonderful after so long sleeping on the hard ground. He was not looking forward to roughing it again in the wild, and only the thought of Frankie still out there urged him on. In a few minutes he was asleep again.

The early morning commotion of men preparing for work woke him. He sat up in bed and looked for his filthy clothing, but all their clothes were cleaned and folded in a tidy pile on the floor next to their beds. He was surprised none of them had heard anything, but he was more than just a little pleased to be putting on something that didn't smell like the bottom of a septic tank. Apparently Paul's pants had been too far gone to salvage as he had a brand new pair waiting for him. They all got dressed and blearily followed the workers outside, this time to a large tent on the other side of the compound that had been concealed from view by the trailers. The tent was open on all four sides but draped with thick white mosquito netting, meaning they could enjoy the morning breezes and cooler temps without sharing breakfast with the teeming insect population. It was a nice arrangement.

Once inside they lined up for breakfast. There was a huge spread of traditional American fare, with regulars like bacon, eggs, toast, and fruit. Even though they'd eaten their fill the night before they were all keenly aware that this could be their last complete meal in a while. Each of them in turn ladled a tremendous amount of food on their trays, to the point where it began to look ridiculous. They sat together at a table to one side, aware that most of the workers were staring at them curiously. There was a constant low hum of conversation around them, and for the most part Ari heard them speaking English, even if he couldn't make out what they were saying.

"These guys really know how to lay out a spread," Paul mumbled around a mouthful of waffles and real maple syrup. He had a second plate to one side which he'd heaped full of eggs and bacon.

Ari was already finished with his and had gone for seconds on the coffee. It was hot and delicious but stronger than he was used to. He hadn't realized how much he'd missed it until just then. He drained that cup and went for thirds.

Butch was gobbling down his second plate as if he were being timed. Just as he finished and sat back with a contented sigh, Doc came towards them, his ponderous bulk weaving dangerously between tables. He couldn't help but bump a few men, none of whom seemed to care or notice.

"Let's go get those out of you." He pointed a thick finger at Brubaker's chest. No one needed to ask what he was referring to.

Butch may have blanched a little at the thought of what was to come, but he gamely followed the big man out. Paul took that opportunity to slide his second plate under the netting to a waiting Lucky, who sniffed once at the hot food before digging in with gusto. In the background they could hear heavy equipment fire up as the men filed out and got to work. Within minutes the three of them were alone in the mess tent except for a few guys cleaning up dishes or sweeping the plywood floor. Hal got a cup of coffee and thoughtfully added a cream and two sugars. After a tentative sip he set the cup down.

"This place has a definite military air about it," he observed.

Ari nodded, looking around at the operation. It was neat, tidy and well-run. What he had first observed as organized chaos was actually simply organized, with each man doing his part without undue supervision or wasted motion. The entire camp was laid out with an almost geometric precision, with trailers lined up one next to another, the mess tent located equidistant from all of them, and the generators tucked out of the way yet still accessible. It was an impressive display.

"I agree. Nobody is saluting, but I wouldn't be surprised if they did."

"I know what you mean," the agent said, his eyes roving around and drinking in everything, as if he were committing the entire layout to memory. "So what did you figure out last night? Did you uncover all your Fawcett clues?"

An unabashed, happy smile broke out across his thin face, a side of Ari that was new to most of them. It was the smile of a man who'd just won the Powerball Lotto or been told his terminal medical condition had cleared up. There was no way the others could understand what a major breakthrough this was and what it meant to him. He was borderline giddy and could barely believe it himself.

"I did. Once I figured out what to look for it was just a matter of time and perseverance. And having some background knowledge didn't hurt, either."

"And?"

Van Owen eagerly took some papers and the marked-up map from his backpack. He unrolled it out on the table between them, using some salt and peppershakers to hold down the corners. "Once I got going it didn't take too long. The encryption Fawcett used was both simple and ingenious. I doubt anyone without a computer, Internet access, and solid knowledge of the times could've figured it out at all. There were too many disparate and random data sources, and no one but his wife would've been privy to all this. It was basically common knowledge to the two of them, but to nobody else. Very neat and smart."

Paul took a break from idly nibbling on a final piece of toast. "How so?"

"Well, some of it was very subtle, such as the clue he used for the number 19, right here." He pointed to the grouping of coordinates on the papers. "Remember, he always started the cypher with 'My dearest Nina', or something along those lines, which was my cue to start digging. In this case it was simply his house number. He'd written, 'My dearest Nina, I simply cannot wait to be home with you again'. The only thing he referenced was his home, which at that time was 19 Caxton Street. Thankfully he kept all the clues in order and never thought to use any secondary encryption or I might've never deciphered them."

332

"So you got all of them? You know where he was?" Hal asked, leaning forward, interested or doing a good job of acting so.

"I got them all. I plotted the coordinates and came up with a final location. He was right here." Ari pointed to his black dot on the map. "And according to our benefactor, Big Al, that's right about where this El Quemado is." He pointed to the other mark.

"Shit, we're almost right on top of it," Paul exclaimed.

Ari nodded and sketched a dotted line around an area about the size of a quarter, one that neatly encompassed the two dots. He pointed to it with his pen. "And here is where that specific species of bullet ant is that Dr. Fox found from the toxin in Garrafon's blood." He looked at Hal. "They're all three right here, together. I don't think we can call this a coincidence."

The agent stared at the map. "You know I don't believe in coincidences, and you shouldn't either. We've felt all along that this was somehow all tied together, and this proves it."

"I think so too. I think we're also going to get a chance to find out sooner than later. Big Al is pretty adamant that we can't stay any longer than today. Whatever they're up to here is secret enough that he doesn't want us around – either for our own good, or for his, I'm not sure which."

Paulson sat back and rubbed his stomach, pushing his plate away. "Well done, Sherlock. But I've got a more immediate concern: one more bite and I'm going to burst. That could get messy."

Outside the deep rumble of diesel-powered heavy equipment echoed around them. Ari turned away from his map and watched in curiosity at the construct that was slowly taking shape. At this point it was little more than steel girders making up a forty-foot tall rectangle the size of several ranch homes stacked on top of one another. Lengths of the steel tubing were running through it like an arterial system, crisscrossing in a complex pattern. Men in hard hats and welding equipment were perched at a dozen places all up and down the structure, the intense white light of arc welding so bright it hurt to look at it, even from a distance. More I-beams and metal tubes over a foot in diameter and twenty feet long were stacked neatly to the side. Hal was back to peering intently at everything, as if by staring at it hard enough its purpose might spring to mind. He finally shook his head and sat back.

"I wish I could figure out what they're doing here."

"I honestly don't know," Ari replied. "Oil exploration maybe? Do you think that's what it is?"

The agent wiped his off glasses on his now very clean shirt, obviously pleased at the result. "Maybe. But it doesn't look like any type of oil rig I've ever seen, and these men don't strike me as typical roughnecks. They're more military than that. And I'm assuming an oil rig of any kind would be a bad thing out here?"

Ari held the cup in his hands and enjoyed the warmth of it. "Yes, that'd be a huge legal and ethical breach, if that's what it is. This section of the Amazon is off-limits to anything like that. No oil drilling, no mineral exploration, no logging. There are poachers and small groups of farmers and ranchers that violate that law, and quite honestly they typically get away with it through intimidation, payoffs, and murder, but this is something different. If word of any condoned operation got out a lot of Brazil and most of the Western world would scream foul. This rainforest is special in many ways, most of which we don't understand yet."

"I agree," Hal finally said, still staring. "But that structure doesn't fit the mold for anything I've ever seen."

Ari was as baffled as the agent. "I can't tell either. And that road they put in is wide enough to cart in pretty much whatever they want shy of a space shuttle."

While they waited for Butch to return, Paul lifted the edge of the mosquito netting and surreptitiously let Lucky in. The dog quickly scooted under the white mesh and proceeded to lie down at his feet, its tail twitching. He petted it idly with one foot while his injured leg was propped up on the bench. He scratched at it vigorously, Hal watching him in approval.

"Your leg itches? That's a good sign, I'd say."

"Yeah, it's driving me nuts. I'm telling you, Ari, whatever that clear goop was that you put on it did the trick better than anything Doc did. I could feel it working right away. That stuff was awesome."

"I'm glad it's feeling better. Can you walk on it now okay, do you think?"

"It feels great, better than ever. The stitches hurt and are a little stiff, but it's nothing like it was before. I'm ready to go whenever you are."

Van Owen was both relieved and thrilled that their young companion was on the mend. The fact that so many weeks ago he'd been involved in Frankie's disappearance was no longer a factor in their relationship. Paul Paulson was a friend now, a friend he cared about. He vowed that he would do whatever he could to make sure he made it through this in one piece, and that he made it back home to his son. Ari swore a personal oath right then that he would help save Frankie, then get them all home, even Butch - no matter the cost.

Brubaker came back a few minutes later. He was indeed a shade or two paler than before, but the satisfied grin on his face told them all they needed to know.

"So you get your little tenants evicted?" Paul asked.

"I did. You don't want to know you how they did it, but the little hitchhikers are gone, and good riddance." He lifted his shirt and showed off a dozen bandages taped to his chest, each one complete with a small dot of blood that had soaked through. "My back's the same way, but at least they're gone."

As they all stared at Doc's ministrations, Big Al walked up to them, still in jeans and a black short sleeve shirt and white Coors hat, looking as solid as a boat anchor. Seeing the man jogged Ari's

335

memory, and he leaned over to Paul. "If you can, check out the tattoo on his arm. It's hard to see, but try."

Paulson was about to ask a question, but before he could the man stopped outside the mess tent and stared inside. "You've been fed and looked after and you should've had your fill to drink. Now it's time to go. Gather up any gear you've got and follow me." He turned and walked through the trailers, confident as always that the four of them would be right behind him.

They arrived back at Doc's trailer. Lined up outside on the ground were four black backpacks, free of markings or brand names of any kind. On top of three of them were the Glocks he'd taken from them the day before. There were also four new machetes, each one catching the early morning sun along their sharpened edges. The backpacks had a sleeve on the side that held a black metal water bottle complete with an odd spout on top. He went over and hefted a backpack as if it were weightless.

"Inside each one of these is two weeks' worth of MREs, plus water purification tablets. Two of them have first aid kits. There is a box of ammunition for each weapon, and the weapons themselves have full clips plus one in the chamber. You've each got a tactical flashlight in the side pocket that's basically unbreakable. The water bottles themselves do a good job of purifying water on the spot, although we've found that the filters clog easy. Do you know what a Camelbak is?" All four of them nodded. "Good. The back of each of these packs is filled with water now, accessed by this tube. It should be enough for a day or two, but no more. You'll have to find more as you go. Don't get dehydrated." He handed a pack to each man.

Ari stared at him. "I don't know what to say."

"Then don't. I'll bring a truck around and drop you back off where I found you. I'll get you through the fence then you're on your own."

Ari considered, not for the first time, what a man of few words Big Al was. He almost seemed to treat each utterance as special and precious, as if once spoken his words were no longer his.

"Yeah, okay. Thanks."

He grunted and left, returning just a few minutes later behind the wheel of a huge Ford pickup truck. Hal, Butch, and Paulson had already strapped on their sidearms, and all four of them had their backpacks on, the straps adjusted for comfort. They were heavy, Van Owen quickly discovered, but the thick, padded straps and narrow profile made them surprisingly comfortable. They piled into the truck and were on their way in no time, the trailers, mess tent, and strange steel structure gone from view in an instant, their only scenery now the wide dirt road and the green wall of jungle on either side of them. Colorful birds of all kinds flitted through the trees and across their path, for the most part indifferent to their passage.

The trip in the pickup truck went much faster than in the huge semi, and before long Big Al had pulled over and the killed the engine. This section of road looked pretty much like any other to Ari, but somehow their benefactor knew this was the spot. Just as he was about to say something they heard a deep rumbling noise and another one of the huge black semi-trucks trundled toward them on its way to the site. On the long trailer were two massive, stainless steel vats, each twenty feet in diameter and just as tall, solid except for a few openings on the sides and top. They reminded Van Owen of some brass beer vats he'd seen at a brew-pub back in Louisville, only these were much larger. All of them watched the truck drive by, its thirty-six wheels kicking up clouds of thick red dust that settled slowly in the still air. Big Al's expression was impossible to read but for some reason Van Owen felt he wasn't pleased they'd seen this particular cargo. He finally turned and stared hard at Ari.

"This is where I found you. I'm going to get you through the fence, then I want you to forget you were ever here."

Ari was still at a loss for words, only managing to say, "Again, I don't know how to thank you."

Big Al got out of the truck and pulled a large pair of bolt cutters from the bed, along with a small roll of heavy gauge wire. With expert motions he snipped out a flap in the chain-link fence large enough for them to squeeze through, which they quickly did. With equally precise skill he wired it shut behind them, crimping the ends so tightly no one would get through that opening again without pliers and determination. Butch, Paul, and Hollenbeck were already out of sight in the brush, but Ari hung back for a moment. He looked at Big Al.

"Just answer me this one question, please. Why? You didn't have to do any of this. Why'd you help us?"

Big Al just stared at him for a few moments, and Van Owen thought he might not deign to reply. When he finally did his voice was firm and strong and the statement was delivered with such feeling he could've been reciting an oath.

"Because you're Americans. That's why. And this El Quemado we talked about? I'd stay far away from him if I were you."

With those final few words he slung the bolt cutters over his thick, muscled shoulder and walked back to the truck. He fired up the Ford and moved out. Ari watched it go, then pushed through the underbrush to catch up with the others.

His companions were waiting for him on the game trail. Together they hiked back to the road, the trip back going much easier than it had that last, frantic time following the blond native. Lucky scampered ahead, searching and sniffing about, running back every few minutes to make sure its de facto owner hadn't strayed from the pack, its herding instincts clear.

Paulson himself was limping, but no worse than he had before gashing his leg on the Toyota. The speed at which he was healing was remarkable, Van Owen marveled, thoroughly impressed with the clear goop he'd applied and the job it was doing. With their supplies and renewed physical condition he was feeling more optimistic about this journey than he had in a long, long time, since before they'd lost their transportation. Plus Frankie was clear and sharp in his mind now, to the point where the closer they got the clearer her face and features became. That couldn't be the case, he knew, but it felt that way regardless. It quickened his pace enough that he had to be careful not to run into the back of Hal.

They arrived at the dirt road and found their supplies right where they'd left them, not that they expected otherwise in a place so devoid of people. All four of them began gathering their things together, preparing to head out.

"Hey, Ari," Paul said as he snugged tight the straps around a rolled up tent, "I got a quick look at Big Al's tattoo, just like you said."

Van Owen had nearly forgotten that. "You did? Good. What was it?"

"We were right. Big Al was a jarhead, for sure. That tattoo is a typical Marine marking. Our man was definitely in the Corp."

Ari nodded. "I thought that might be the case. I wonder about the rest of the men there, the workers. Think they were, too?"

"I don't know, but I wouldn't be surprised. Did you see how they went about their business? They were efficient as hell and never questioned him, not even Doc – although I don't think he was ever in the service, not in the kind of shape he's in."

"Maybe, maybe not," Hal observed, slinging their canvas bag of trinkets over his shoulder. He surreptitiously dipped his head toward Brubaker. "People change in time and aren't always what you thought they were. Right, Ari?"

Van Owen understood that statement was directed at him and Butch, and like it or not he was right. He didn't like dwelling on how much help Frankie's husband had been, and how he'd likely saved his skin several times. He'd spent years harboring a deep resentment for the man, and that was proving a difficult rock to budge. Instead of responding he just grunted and continued gathering their things together, not looking up. He hefted their jerry can of water and pointed down the narrow dirt road, motioning ahead. Hal allowed himself the smallest of smiles and left his statement hanging in the thick, humid air.

"Let's move out," Ari said, keeping his head down and ignoring the agent. "We've still got a long way to go."

In silence they finished rounding up their gear and began walking, Paul's limp evident but not slowing him down. In fact there was a slight spring in his step that none of them had seen since the beginning of the journey. He didn't even need his walking stick any longer.

They'd only gone a few hundred yards when Ari, in the lead, motioned excitedly for them to stop. Standing in the narrow road in front of them was the blond native, the same one from the day before, Ari was certain of it. However this time he made no attempt at hiding but stood in the middle of the road with his arms at his side and his head held high. Van Owen could see that not only was he blond, but he was tall for a native, too. His body shape was not typical for this part of the world, either, as he was proportioned more like an American teenager during that gangly, awkward phase of life, not the stocky, squared-off shape Ari was accustomed to seeing. The black markings on his face were in sharp contrast to his light brown skin, the lines continuing down his neck to his chest, where they radiated out and traced his ribcage. He was naked save for a leather wrap secured around his waist, almost like a short kilt, and he wore no shoes. But it was his blue eyes that stood out, blue eyes that stared at them and blinked slowly, thoughtfully. Behind him he heard either Butch or Hal draw their weapon.

"You three stay here, and keep the dog with you, Paul," he commanded. He slid off the backpack and set it noiselessly on the ground at his feet next to the jerry can. The youth in front of them stayed still, but may have swayed a little. Looking him over more closely Ari could see how thin he was, the black markings across his chest and stomach not hiding the ribs showing through.

"What's your plan, Ari?" Hal whispered.

Ari kept his hands to his sides and slowly walked toward him. "I'm going to try and communicate with him. Stay put."

"It could be a trap or something," Butch hissed. "There could be more of them."

Van Owen couldn't say why, but he didn't think so. He began walking toward the youth, slowly covering the twenty yards that separated them. Behind him the others were talking in low tones, punctuated by louder protests from Brubaker. When he was only five feet away, he stopped. He was considering how to proceed when the young native looked him up and down. Then he shifted his gaze over Ari's shoulder and walked right past him, stepping up to Paul. When he stood before him the native bowed low once, deeply, then stood. Paulson didn't move but shifted his gaze side to side in confusion.

"Are you from the Father?" he asked in slow, precise English, English clearly laced with a British accent. "Are you here to save us?"

Chapter 19

During Ari's gap year he'd spent time traveling around Europe, including a very pleasant month in and around London. It was late spring and he knew that to fully appreciate his stay in Great Britain he had to attend a soccer game, or football match as it was called there. Like baseball in North America, there were many levels of professional football in England, the most prestigious of which was the Premier League. A Premier League match, being some of the best football in Europe, was what he really wanted to see.

Van Owen had been staying in a hostel in southwest London with a dozen other travelers. Nearly all the locals in that part of the city were fans of Fulham Football Club. Ari had mentioned over breakfast one Saturday his desire to see a Premier League match, and that was all it took. Before he knew it his friends had somehow procured tickets to a Fulham match, and he was dressed in a borrowed black and white jersey, or "kit". Soon they were marching down a wide sidewalk along the shore of the Thames and singing songs, some raunchy and bawdy and most as old as the club itself, as the crowd neared a quaint stadium known as Craven Cottage.

He and his companions were early and took their seats behind one of the goals on the home side, the white-lined playing field before them more perfect and pristine than an English garden. Some of the players were already out on the pitch warming up and taking shots on goal, blistering, thunderous blasts that looked strong enough to tear right through the back of the net. Ari turned to comment on this when an errant shot went wide into the stands, catching him on the side of the head. He dimly remembered seeing a bright white flash before waking up in the first aid station quite a while later, the match nearly over, with a head still ringing and a neck so sore he hoped someone had noted the license plate of the truck that had clobbered him.

342

That was how stunned he was at that moment in the jungle, so stunned that another soccer ball to the head would've nearly gone unnoticed. *This young native had just spoken English, and with a British accent!* How in the hell was that even possible?

Hal's expression mirrored Ari's. "Did he just speak English?"

Van Owen nodded. "Yes, he did. And with a British accent. Did you catch that?"

"I did. And pardon me for sounding ignorant, but where in the world would a person in his circumstances learn to speak English, British accent or not? It wouldn't be like Ernesto back at the gas station, would it? A priest or something like that?"

"But with a British accent? And out here, this far away from anything? I just don't think it's possible. I don't know."

Ari had so many questions careening through his head he felt it might burst, and in fact almost couldn't decide what to ask first. He tentatively eased up to Paulson. His young companion's white eyebrows were arched high, almost comically so, and his blue eyes were wide in sustained surprise and amazement. Paul chanced a quick look at Ari, just a shift of his gaze without moving his head, as if any movement might spook the native and ruin everything.

"Um, a little help here, Ari?" he mumbled out the corner of his mouth. "What's going on?"

"Are you from the Father?" the young native repeated as he stared intently at Paul and ignoring the others. Each word, each syllable, actually, was spoken precisely and slowly, as if practiced or memorized. There was also an edge of something in those five words that the accent couldn't hide, Ari noted. Maybe desperation?

"Who are you? What's your name?" Van Owen finally brought himself to ask.

"Name?" the young man repeated after a moment, turning his blue-eyes on Ari. He was clearly running the word through his head. He blinked once. "My name…is Josiah."

"Josiah, where did you learn to speak English? Who taught you?"

Josiah's static expression never wavered and it took him a few seconds to answer, as if he were laboring to form a coherent sentence. Those mannerisms and pauses reminded Ari of himself in high school, completely unprepared and struggling to answer his teacher all the way back in freshman French.

"We...we all learn English," he finally replied. "The Father...says we must."

Ari realized then that he had to keep this simple. Short sentences, easy words, all spoken slowly. "The Father. Who is the Father?"

Josiah kept looking back at Paul, as if transfixed. He edged slightly closer and looked ready to touch him. "The Father is...the Father," he finally answered, a single line of confusion creasing his tanned brow. "He is the Father."

Ari chanced a look at Hal, who nodded encouragement at him. "Can you take us to him?"

Again Josiah thought before replying. "No. The Father is...no more. He is dead."

"The Father is dead. Um, can you take us to your tribe?"

The young native clearly didn't understand. He stared at Ari but didn't or couldn't answer. Van Owen tried again. "Your people. Where are your people? Your family?"

"My family...is dead. They are no more. My people are..." He concentrated then rattled off a string of something in a local, sharp-edged dialect that Ari didn't know, the native openly frustrated at his inability to communicate better. If pressed Ari would've guessed the young man had just roundly cursed. Finally Josiah marshaled his thoughts and tried again, his British accent still clear. "I do not have...the words. Sorry."

"Can you take us to your people? Can you do that?"

344

Josiah pointed away from them, not quite down the road, but into the deep brush. "My people are there. At home. But it is…not safe. Death. Much danger."

"Why is it not safe? Why is there much danger?"

"Because of him…because of El Quemado. He is death. He is killing us."

At the name El Quemado, the Burned One, all of them – Hal, Butch, and Paul – all physically jerked and stared hard at each other. Paul's eyes, if possible, opened even wider. The warning from both Big Al and Ernesto from the gas station was still etched clear in their minds, the warning to stay away from this person. Hal took off his glasses and wiped them clean, Josiah watching the unfamiliar action with muted curiosity, intrigued at his glasses.

"There's no such thing as a coincidence in all this, of course. We've talked about that before several times," he said, his voice intentionally low.

No, Ari had to agree, there was no such thing, not any longer. "I don't know if we can figure out from Josiah what's going on, but this El Quemado person is at the heart of all this. He has to be."

"SOP, Ice, Frankie's abduction, the attempted kidnapping of you in your garage, and now Josiah. It all revolves around him."

"It does, yes. So what do we do? What's our next step?"

Hal replaced his glasses and wiggled them back and forth to settle them properly. He smoothed his still clean shirt and looked in the direction the young native had indicated, his vision distant. "We originally set out to find the source of SOP and Ice, and to find Butch's wife. I don't think we have any choice but to keep going, do you?"

Ari didn't. He did notice that his hands were shaking a little and didn't know if he was anxious, excited, or simply afraid. He crossed his arms to hide the trembling he was certain the others could see. Eventually he nodded once.

Just then Brubaker stepped up and grabbed Josiah's arm. "My wife? Does this El Quemado guy have my wife? Is my wife there?"

Josiah took a step back and tried to process the question, but failed. Ari could tell that he simply didn't have the vocabulary or the ability to comprehend.

"Easy, Butch," he said a little impatiently, "let me try. He only knows the basics. Josiah, do you know what a woman is? Or a girl?"

After a moment he nodded. "Woman? Yes, I know this."

"Good. Is there a woman with El Quemado, one who speaks English, like us?"

"Oh, yes, there is a woman. Frankie is there. She…helps us. She is…nice." He pronounced her name oddly, the R in Frankie coming across as a rolled D sound. But it was definitely her name, there was no mistaking that.

All four men stared at each other again, although suddenly Butch became agitated and looked ready to bolt into the jungle toward El Quemado, warnings and caution be damned. Hal placed a calming, restraining hand on his shoulder and kept it there even though Brubaker stared daggers at him and tried to shrug it off.

"Frankie is there," Van Owen confirmed with Josiah, who nodded again, outwardly pleased he had made this visible connection. "Is she okay? Is Frankie okay?"

"Oh, yes, she is…okay. She is sad. She helps us."

The fact that she was sad, as Josiah said, tore at Ari's heart. He couldn't help but think back to the dreams of Frankie all by herself around the fire, scared and alone, as the hands roughly grabbed her and dragged her away. He could see her there, her green eyes staring into and through him, terrified, alone. He couldn't stand to think of her like that, so he quickly turned back to the others.

"This El Quemado guy has Frankie and is certainly tied up in SOP and Ice. That's clear now." Hal and Paul nodded while Butch stared beyond him, into the jungle. "Hal, I think it's time you took over. This is more in your wheelhouse than mine, that's for sure. I can get us through the jungle, but that's about it. What's our next step?"

The agent didn't hesitate. "We came here to find the source of SOP and Ice, and it's very evident that this Burned One is at the epicenter of it all. We go find him and figure out what's going on if we can, then we get out and report back. That's it."

Butch jumped in. "And rescue my wife! That's why I'm here, dammit!"

"Of course we will, we'll do our best," Hollenbeck assured him, although Ari had to wonder at his sincerity. "But our first priority has always been to locate the source of all this, then report to my superiors and let them handle it. We can't hope to take him on directly– we don't have the men or the firepower. You know that. Big Al said as much, and he's a professional."

Butch growled low in his throat but didn't say anything else. As badly as Ari wanted to rescue Frankie, he was afraid Brubaker might do something rash and screw everything up. And while this was no shock to Van Owen, it may have been eye-opening for the others: Hal's statement very clearly reiterated what the agent's priorities were and what he was prepared to do. Hollenbeck continued to prove that he was level-headed and sensible to a fault, and his mission would come first, always.

"So how do you plan on doing that?" Paul asked. "I hope you're not just going to waltz in there and introduce yourself."

"No, not exactly. Remember - we've got a secret weapon now. We've got Josiah." The young native hadn't been able to follow their rapid-fire conversation, but knew his name when he heard it. He tore his gaze from Paul's face and gave a tentative smile, his even white teeth bright against the dark lines on the lower part of his face. "We've got someone who knows this area intimately and seems willing to help us out. I'd say our odds of success just improved dramatically."

"I hope you know what you're doing," Van Owen finally said to him and the group. They began to gather up their meager belongings, shrugging on their backpacks. "I've got a feeling this could get ugly."

Within minutes they were ready to go. Ari was going to try and explain as much as he could to the native, to ask him to carefully lead them to his people and El Quemado, but the young man stumbled and almost fell over where he stood. Ari realized then that the poor kid must be starving. Who knew how long he'd been out here on his own and the last time he had eaten anything? He swung off his backpack and removed one of the MREs and tore open the foil pouch. The main entrée in this one was tuna, which Josiah sniffed a few times before taking a tentative bite. When he figured out it was fish he dove in and had it consumed in seconds, licking the remnants and juice from his fingers. They let him drink his fill from one of the filtered canisters, and after he'd gotten the hang of it he finished it off in one long chug. When it was gone he stared at it and shook it once, as if mystified that it was empty.

"So are you thinking what I'm thinking?" Hal asked Ari while Josiah ate.

"Probably, but I'm never really sure. What are you thinking?"

The agent nodded toward Josiah, who was still picking through the scraps of his MRE. Paul took a moment and handed him another one, which the young native opened on his own this time. This particular food packet was cheese ravioli, which he began eating but didn't seem as thrilled with as the tuna. Paulson knelt down next to him and helped open the smaller inner packets. In one was a Snickers bar, which Josiah ate in one bite, his eyes lighting up with joy at the unfamiliar flavors.

"I'm thinking of course that the Father he's talking about was your Colonel Fawcett, that he ended up with Josiah's tribe and started his own, shall we say, bloodline. How else would you get a tall, blond native that speaks some English with a British accent? There's no other explanation."

Ari of course had been thinking the same thing, but he just couldn't believe it. With all the research he'd done on the Colonel over the years this was one possibility that had kept coming up again and again, that Fawcett had gone native and had never returned home. He remembered the quote he'd read so long ago, one from Fawcett himself: *"Civilization has a relatively precarious hold upon us and there is an undoubted attraction in a life of absolute freedom once it has been tasted. The 'call o' the wild' is in the blood of many of us and finds its safety valve in adventure."* Could he have abandoned his wife, his country, his very culture and settled down here in the middle of nowhere? Ari hadn't thought so before, but here was proof right in front of them, a young man with blond hair and blue eyes who was busy licking chocolate from his fingers.

"I don't know, I really don't, but I can't think of anything else." He mirrored Paul and crouched down next to Josiah. The young man looked up at him expectantly.

"Josiah, you asked us if we were from the Father, if we were here to save you."

It took a moment for the blond native to consider his words. "Yes."

"Who is the Father? Was he a man named Percy Fawcett?"

"The Father…is the Father," he simply said, unable to express his thoughts any clearer than that. "He is the Father."

"Why do you think this man," he said, resting a hand on Paulson's shoulder, "Why do you think he is from the Father?"

Again it took him a few moments to translate the question in his head. "Because you speak…English, although strangely, and this one…" he pointed to Paul, "this one has white…" He stuttered to a halt but touched Paul's blond hair. He considered a bit longer, but couldn't come up with anything else, and instead broke into his native tongue and spoke quickly and in frustration, angry at himself for not being able to get his point across. Finally he sat back and could only say, "Sorry, but I do not have the words."

Ari nodded and stood, moving back to Hal, shaking his head in disbelief. "That's got to be it, although I never would've thought it possible. Fawcett went native and started a family here in the middle of the Amazon jungle. I'll be damned."

"And young Josiah thinks Paul's either a reincarnation of Fawcett or was sent by him to save his people."

"That's it. That's got to be it."

"Does he look like Fawcett?"

Van Owen envisioned the Colonel, the thin face and sandy brown hair that was going grey. "In the face, no, not really. But he was tall and lanky, that much I know for sure. There are plenty of pics of him, but most of them grainy and dark."

"Regardless, let's find out what else he knows that can help. Agreed?"

Ari did, although after another ten minutes of halting discussion it was evident that either Josiah didn't know much more, or didn't have the means to explain himself. The only additional information they could glean from him was that El Quemado wasn't originally from here, that he had many men with him, and that they were armed. Josiah didn't know the word for "gun", but he was quick to point to their sidearms. With a visible shudder and a great deal of respect he mimicked pointing a gun and making a loud bang sound. Many of his people had died because of the Burned One and his weapons, he managed to get across, a point not lost on any of them, especially Hollenbeck.

Paul had been listening in as well. "The more I hear about this El Quemado guy the less I like him. And remember what Ernesto back at the gas stations said? That our buddy with the red eye works for him? And so does the giant that took Butch's wife and tried to take you."

"I know," Ari said, still staring at Josiah. "If what he said is true he's already slaughtered many of his people for some reason. We've got to be extremely careful."

"Agreed," Hal stated flatly. "We get close enough to find out what's going on, determine the exact location of his operation, and see if we can get Frankie Brubaker out. That's it."

When it was clear their young native had eaten enough they cleaned up the remnants of the MREs and headed out. Ari had given Josiah instructions that they wanted to go to his tribe, to see his village, but not so close they might be seen. He thought and hoped that the native had understood. Josiah was eager and ready, clearly hopeful that this group was here to help. He was still convinced that they were sent here from the Father, and in a way, Ari admitted to himself, they were.

Chapter 20

They kept to what was left of their now familiar road for a mile or so, then Josiah turned right on a nearly invisible trail and they left it behind forever. They pushed through dense brush and thorns, and the terrain quickly became hilly with scattered small, rocky cliffs, similar to the outcropping where Ari had discovered water earlier. They soon found themselves hiking up and down gradually growing hills, sometimes forced to climb the low cliffs, and more often than not having to detour around swampy areas filled with black, stagnant water. Here the flying insects were so thick they were an undulating, living fog, moving in eerie unison. The bugs didn't seem to bother the native much, but they zeroed in on the Americans with gusto. They all sparingly applied more bug spray but that only seemed to make the larger marauders angry and more determined. The three of them took turns walking single-file so whoever was behind could swat them off the back of the man directly in front. It was a good system expect for the last man in line, who found himself squirming and twitching under their onslaught. Ahead of them Josiah walked quietly and moved with an easy, fluid grace through the brush, almost more animal than human, and more than once glanced back in irritation at the continued commotion from his charges. At one point he stopped short with an exasperated huff and grabbed a thick green stem from a plant just off the trail. Then he looked around for a few moments and found a bush laden with dark red berries that Ari didn't recognize. Each berry was roughly the size of a peanut M&M. He crushed them in his palms and thin juice the color of pink lemonade filled his hands. He squeezed a few drops from the stem and combined it with juice from the berries. He wiped this all over his own body, through his hair, and on the outside of his kilt-like garment, then handed another clump and a stem to Ari and motioned for him to do the same. Van Owen did so without hesitation, and almost immediately the flying pests ignored him.

"You've seen these before?" Hal asked him.

"No, but I won't forget them in the future, that's for sure."

Paul mimicked the others and rubbed the juice everywhere, including his hair, as soon as Josiah gave him some of the berries and a stem. The air around them was suddenly filled with a spicy, heavy aroma, like burnt cinnamon toast mixed with oranges. It was a pleasant, comforting smell.

"Ari, you told us before that the jungle holds a lot of surprises, and now I know what you mean. First that clear gel stuff he got for my leg, and now this? Seriously, what's next?"

Even Butch was impressed, although he never said as much. At first he took the berries and tentatively squeezed one, raising an eyebrow at the amount of pink juice that spurted on his palm. He combined the two and carefully spread some on his arm, perhaps doubting anything positive would happen, or perhaps worried something negative would.

"Come on, Butch," Paul chided easily, "go for it. This stuff is great."

When nothing bad happened he followed suit and covered the rest of his body, wrinkling his nose at the unexpected smell. His expression still conveyed nothing but doubt and wariness, and he kept looking at his exposed flesh as if he expected boils to flare up or his skin to melt any second.

The five started hiking again, this time free of at least one major distraction. They still had to contend with the thorns and spikes that seemed to be on every branch, every leaf, and even on vines that dangled across their path. The machetes with their honed blades did a fine job of clearing the way, but they couldn't help but get snagged once in a while, generally with bloodied results. They all suffered except for Josiah, who seemed to swim through the underbrush without ever coming into contact with anything but air. His ability to pass through unscathed was amazing.

They traveled on that way for several long, grueling hours, and finally Van Owen called for a halt. Immediately Josiah dropped down to a squat, where he seemed perfectly content and comfortable. The others dropped their gear with a heavy thud and plopped down with much less grace than their native guide had. They all drank from their backpacks or water bottles, Paul sharing his supply with Lucky and Ari handing his to Josiah. The MREs he'd eaten earlier had done wonders for his stamina, as he hardly looked fatigued or winded.

By mutual consent they pitched their tents for the night, Josiah looking on in curiosity at the two-man pup tents. They each ate an MRE and sprawled out on the ground, pleased beyond belief that for once they didn't have to worry about being eaten alive by the flying denizens of the jungle. They wanted to start a fire but thought better of it, being as close to El Quemado as they were, so they sat around and talked in low tones until the darkness was nearly complete. Ari was wondering where they were all going to bed down, thinking that perhaps three of them could fit into one tent if necessary, when the young native stood and climbed a nearby kapok tree. He was up into the thick, gray branches faster than a man could climb a ladder, his back against the trunk and his legs dangling on either side of stout smooth branch. The rest of them crawled wearily into their tents and were asleep in seconds, Lucky snuggled down near Paul's feet. The night sounds were loud and raucous, filling the darkness with the calls of titi monkeys and a thousand different species of birds, but no one heard a thing.

Ari's eyes popped open at five o'clock, as he'd known they would. There was no panicked sensation this time, no shortness of breath, no night sweats. He wondered why he was so calm for once, and figured it must be because of his proximity to Frankie. Lying there, he recalled that for fun during his sophomore year at college he'd taken a psychology course that had dealt with the Id, the Ego, and the Super-ego, the three parts of the psychic apparatus defined in Sigmund Freud's structural model of the psyche. These Frankie dreams were likely being driven by the Ego portion of his psyche, he considered, and for once the Super Ego had stepped in to cut him some slack. If that was the case, he was eternally grateful to himself.

After a few moments he roused himself to go answer a call of nature and eased out of the tent. Once outside he realized he could see the night sky through an opening in the canopy overhead. Above him he could see a million stars like holes in the sky, bright and unpolluted by any other light source. The Milky Way galaxy was a thick ribbon of glittering diamond dust spread in a wide swath above him, clearer and more beautiful than he'd ever seen before. In that moment he felt small and insignificant, his troubles and problems paling against the majesty of God and nature. He stared at the wonder that was the universe before taking care of his mundane, crude personal business. The sensation of being totally insignificant remained with him well after he'd crawled back into the tent and dozed again.

At first light they were up and moving. Josiah was pleased when he'd found more ingredients to make their bug repellant and they all reapplied the juice to their skin and clothing. Hal noticed that he'd developed a light red rash, and after further inspection the others found patches of it on their skin as well. Josiah, on the other hand, showed no effects at all.

"Something with the berries?" Hollenbeck asked the others. "But if that's the case then why doesn't our young friend show anything?"

Ari found a dozen places where he was breaking out, too, but only where he'd applied berry juice directly to his flesh. His arms and neck were the worst. The rash stopped abruptly where his clothing started. It didn't itch or burn, and in fact didn't bother them at all, it just looked like hell. They tried to ask Josiah about it but he just shrugged, and they couldn't be sure if he didn't understand or didn't care.

Paul was inspecting his red arms. "Maybe he's used to it? He's probably been using it his whole life."

"Maybe so," Ari agreed. "But rash or not it still beats the hell out of getting eaten alive. I vote we keep using it for now and just watch for any other side effects."

Butch continued to look dubious, but even he had to admit it was better than the alternative, especially after what he'd been through with the bot-flies. With a grunt he applied the juice all over him, concentrating more on his chest than anywhere else. When he was done they started down the trail again.

Several hours into the morning their guide stopped and crouched low. He silently turned and motioned for the others to do the same, which they did almost noiselessly except for a knee pop from Hal. Lucky, who'd been padding along silently next to Paul, stopped and sniffed the air. The dog didn't make a sound but the fur along its back bristled in either fear or anger. Ari strained but couldn't hear anything out of the ordinary, but he took a deep breath through his nose. Wait, what was that smell? Was it...? It was tobacco, burning tobacco. Someone not too far away was smoking, he was certain of it. He tapped the shoulders of his companions and signaled for them to head back the way they'd come.

A few hundred yards back they all crouched again, their heads close together and nearly touching. Ari pointed up the trail to where they'd been.

"Did you smell that?"

"I did," Hal whispered, his Glock in his hand. "Was someone smoking? I thought I smelled a cigarette."

The others had caught the same scent. Ari turned to Josiah. "Are your people here? Are they nearby?"

It took the native a few moments to translate the question. "Yes, close."

Van Owen sniffed and pointed to his nose. "I smelled something. Bad man?"

He nodded slowly. "Yes. Bad man. Danger."

Suddenly Ari's palms were sweaty. He wiped them on his pants, trying to dry them, but with no success. He was forcefully reminded that this sort of dangerous field work was outside his limited training, not to mention his comfort zone. He was a researcher, not a soldier. Only his desire to save Frankie was keeping him going now. When he spoke again he was certain his voice would sound shaky and nervous, and was relieved and surprised when it didn't.

"Hal, what's our next move? What do we do now?"

Hollenbeck checked to make sure his Glock was loaded and cocked, the metallic *click-click* sound loud and foreign in this environment. He slid off his backpack and set it at his feet. With a deep breath he said, "Josiah and I are going to check this out. You all stay here and wait for us. If we're not back in thirty minutes it means something's gone wrong. If that happens you head out, fast, and make your way back to Big Al."

Butch's eyes flashed in anger. "I'm not going without my wife!"

"We're not leaving without you," Ari hissed. "No way."

The agent kept his voice low. "Listen. If I'm not back in thirty minutes then you take off, got it? There's nothing you can do here. Get back to Big Al and convince him to help you get out of here. Ari, you know these coordinates. Get back to civilization and contact my office and tell them what happened. Butch, I don't intend to get close enough, but if I get a shot I'll do my best to get your wife. I promise."

Brubaker didn't look convinced and Ari was afraid Hal would have to do something extreme to keep him in check. But Hollenbeck

357

placed a hand on his arm and looked earnestly into the man's dark eyes.

"I promise, Butch, I'll do what I can. I'm trained for this sort of thing, and you're not. You getting killed isn't going to help Frankie. Let me do my job." Hollenbeck stood and pointed toward the smell of the smoke. "Josiah, let's go."

Confusion passed across the native's young face. "He is from the Father. He is here to save us," he said, pointing at Paul.

"It's okay, Josiah. Go with him now," Paulson said calmly. "Help him."

After a moment he nodded and stood, but still didn't appear convinced. Paul assured him again that they were all here to help, Hollenbeck included. The two of them finally moved toward the smoke smell. Just before the jungle enveloped them Hal glanced back.

"Remember. Give me thirty minutes, that's all."

Then they were gone, moving quickly and silently into the brush, and that was the last time Ari ever saw Hal Hollenbeck.

Chapter 21

Thirty minutes had never gone so slowly before, even though Ari was reminded of several instances in his past that rivaled it: flipping through old magazines in a doctor's waiting room, or stuck on hold for tech support. But those examples didn't have the same weight or anxiety. This was his friend, someone he'd known and admired for years, and that made all the difference. Add to that the realization that Hollenbeck was one of his only friends, and that made it even more poignant. He was worried sick, to the point where he actually had an upset stomach. Pacing helped burn off some nervous energy, but only a little.

"I'm sure he'll be fine," Paul assured him sympathetically. "He's a pro. He knows what he's doing."

And of course that was true, Van Owen had to admit, but that didn't make it any easier. "I know," he finally said, not slowing his pacing. Every so often he'd stop and cup an ear toward the jungle, straining to hear a shout or some noise to indicate what was happening, but there was nothing besides the normal chittering of wildlife and the endless droning of flying insects. A quick look at Butch showed that despite his characteristic low-key nature even he appeared nervous; he couldn't seem to figure out what to do with his hands, and he took turns fiddling with his gun or drumming his fingers on his thighs. He kept his eyes focused on the ground at his feet.

When thirty minutes were up no one said anything, they just continued passing time in their own tense ways. Then forty-five minutes ticked by and the three of them began to get restive. When an hour came and went they looked at each other.

"I'm not going back to Big Al," Ari stated. "I don't care what Hal said."

Paul and Butch each stood, each brushing dirt and leaves from their pants. Brubaker nodded, his dark eyes set. "Me neither. I'm not leaving without Frankie. That's final."

Paulson looked from one to the other, measuring Hollenbeck's last order against the will of the two men standing with him. "I kind of figured that'd be the case," he said, pulling back the barrel of the Glock and chambering a round with a loud *click-click*. "So what's our next step? Just charge in after them?"

"I don't think so. Butch, you're the hunter and you know how to move through the woods, so I'd like you to take point. But let's circle around and come at them from a different angle. I'd hate to go the same way Hal and Josiah did if they're waiting for us. Your thoughts?"

"Yeah. Let's leave everything here so we can move easy. No additional weight. Nothing but pistols and machetes. Nothing to slow us down."

"But what about Lucky?" Paul asked, concern for his dog written across his young face. "He can't come with us. Not now."

They bantered this around for much longer than Ari liked, and not for the first time he was annoyed at Paulson for bringing the dog along in the first place. In the end they quickly set up a tent and left water and food inside. The thin material wouldn't do much to stop a predator from getting at Paul's pet, but it was better than just tying it to a tree like a wounded goat. They opened several MREs and left water as well. With a ruffle on its head the young man placed the dog inside and zipped it up. It wasn't a great solution, they all knew, but it was better than nothing.

That task completed they piled their belongings together next to the rest of their supplies. Paul and Ari looked to Butch who dipped his head and together they moved out, single-file, painfully aware of every branch and leaf that crunched underfoot and each thorn that ripped at their skin. Even their hacks with the machete were slow and measured, each swing making no more noise than the monkeys now leaping from branch to branch far overhead. Their progress was slow, sometimes only a few feet per minute. Van Owen was torn by his desire to get there faster for Hal and Frankie, and his anxiety about what dangers might lay ahead. He was not proud of the fear he felt and tried to shove it down and away from him, deep enough that he couldn't feel it. Instead the fear just twisted his gut into a hot, dark mass until he was afraid he might puke. Some hero I am, he thought.

Half an hour into their search Brubaker held up a hand and pointed to his nose. Ari recognized the smell of tobacco again, although much fainter this time, just a whiff that was there and gone in an instant. Their pace slowed even more and they got lower to the ground, until they were on hands and knees below much of the brush. Suddenly they heard voices, people talking. It had the sound of general conversation, nothing heated or anxious, more like two or three people passing the time of day or discussing the weather.

Butch silently eased himself down to his stomach and slowly army-crawled through the dense brush, Ari and Paul following. To Van Owen's ears they were making far too much noise, but in reality they were creeping along very quietly. Brubaker stopped and motioned them to come level with him. As they pulled up to either side he pointed to his eyes then motioned ahead, his message clear: *check this out.* Ari pushed through the underbrush, his head down low and his eyes opened wide.

At first it looked like any other jungle village he'd ever seen, and he'd seen plenty. They couldn't see the entire village from their location, but they could pick out a dozen or more small thatched huts in a rough circle around a central, larger structure, open at the sides and positioned in the middle of a central dirt plaza. Many times, he knew, this larger hut would be a communal gathering place where the men would come together in the evenings to eat, talk, and boast of the day's hunt. He could just make out its thickly thatched roof and a stout, central post holding up the structure that made him think of a circus tent. The biggest difference here was that, unlike some of the less remote villages he'd visited in his travels, there were no generators, no black satellite dishes, none of the modern conveniences he'd come to expect in those that were geographically closer to western civilization. Then Butch nudged him and pointed to the left, beyond the village itself. He followed the man's finger.

Partially obscured by overhanging trees was a large metal and wood structure standing about twenty feet high and consisting of a complex series of pipes and black hoses. The most striking feature, however, were two large brass vats, each standing next to each other and almost completely hidden within the bowels of the jungle itself. The vats were each about six feet tall and three feet wide and were blackened at the bottoms, as if they'd been exposed to a constant heat source. The brass above the blackened area was tainted a shimmering, bluish green. From overhead the entire construct would've been invisible, tucked away as it was. Paul slithered around and came up beside him. He put his mouth up to Ari's ear, so close his lips almost touched.

"Tell me that doesn't look familiar," he whispered.

It took Van Owen just a second to comprehend what the young Marine meant, and when it clicked he had to smother a gasp. The vats and the surrounding structure were a scaled-down version of what was under construction at Big Al's camp. Maybe a twentieth of the size, to be sure, but the design was too similar to be a coincidence – and as Hal always said, there was no such thing as coincidence.

He was so busy staring at it that he nearly neglected to see the two men walking the perimeter of the clearing and coming closer. They were no more than fifteen feet away when they stopped. The one he could clearly see was short and sturdily built, with a wide-brimmed straw hat and a dark chocolate complexion, his skin tone a combination of genetics and years of near-equatorial sunshine. He had a cigarette dangling from his mouth, his lips hidden by a full, thick moustache. He loosely held some sort of automatic rifle in the crook of his arm, and he was talking to... *Oh, shit.*

Ari's blood chilled. He was talking to the giant, the man who had tried to abduct Ari from his own garage, the man who had tossed Frankie into the back of the SUV. There was no mistaking him, there was no way anyone could mistake him. He'd been hidden from view by some leaves, but when he stepped clear Van Owen could see how he towered over the first man, his black eyes hooded underneath his Neanderthal brow, the long dark hair parted in the middle and hanging in his face to partially conceal his scarred features. He was talking in low tones and gesturing about, pointing, clearly issuing orders. With this prolonged look Ari could see that he held his left arm oddly, as if it had been broken at some point and hadn't healed correctly. They stopped as the giant motioned to several other spots around the outside of the village, the smaller man nodding repeatedly and vigorously, eager to please. The big man looked around him once, almost seeming to stare directly at their hiding spot, before he lumbered away, toward the center of the village. He did indeed lumber ponderously, but Van Owen wasn't fooled; he had witnessed how fast the giant could move when conditions warranted. The nervous shaking in his hands redoubled and sweat ran into his eyes, burning like acid and forcing him to blink ferociously. He'd been holding his breath without realizing it, and he made himself let it out in a slow, controlled exhale. Seeing the giant made him flashback to his garage and what had happened there, including the bloody mass that had once been a living person. That vision was clear and bright in his mind, all black, white, and red. Mostly red.

Butch touched both their shoulders and motioned them backwards. Taking extreme caution to move quietly, they finally crept back far enough away that whispering was okay. Paul was the first to speak.

"So you saw that contraption back there, right? It looks like a mini-me version of what Big Al's group was building. What the hell is it?"

"My guess is it's what he uses to make Ice," Ari offered, looking back toward the village. "And if that's the case, then here's another question: why's Big Al making one? And for whom?"

"An Ice Maker? Nice." A slight smirk crossed Paul's face before he turned serious again. "But for who? What do you mean, for who?"

"I just got the impression that Big Al didn't like what they were doing there, that's all. He clearly wasn't enthusiastic about it. You heard what he said about drugs: he doesn't like them and what they're doing to our country. He was pretty emphatic about that."

"Yeah, I do. But if he's under orders, just doing what he's told, you know, like a good soldier..." His voice trailed off.

Ari grasped his meaning immediately. "If he's following orders like a good soldier, then maybe what's going on back there is bigger than we thought. Big enough that someone involved has reason enough to keep this hidden from everyone. Big enough and powerful enough to make sure it won't show up on satellite images."

"Could the US Government do that?"

"I don't know, but if anyone could it'd be them, I'd think."

The enormity of that realization was beginning to hit home when Butch stirred impatiently. "I don't know and I don't care," he nearly hissed, effectively dismissing their conversation. "I just want to get Frankie and get the hell out of here. She's gotta be in one of those huts."

"But Hal's probably there now too," Ari said. "And Josiah. I agree. Right now I don't care much about Ice or SOP or any of that either. Right now we've got to figure out a way to get them out. Ideas?"

The three of them fell silent, their heads turned toward the village as they considered their limited options, manpower, and firepower. In the end it was decided that they should split up and each take up positions around the perimeter of the village where they could see what was going on, see how many men there were, and figure out what to do next. They would meet back at this spot at dusk and compare notes. Ari was amazed at how poised and calm Paul was, his earlier youthfulness and carefree attitude gone and replaced by something harder and cold. The Marine in him was shining through. Van Owen himself was a nervous wreck.

Each man headed out in a different direction. Butch planned on returning to the spot they had just vacated, Ari would go left and Paulson would head right. The young man's eyes were chilling in their intensity and his jaw was set as he moved out. Butch's expression, on the other hand, was unreadable to Ari, but he was used to that by now.

Feeling very vulnerable without any protection, Van Owen fought through the brush for almost thirty minutes, swinging wide and creeping up to the edge of the village on his hands and knees. Certain he was making more noise than a peccary chased through the brush, he made slow progress as he gently pushed aside thorns and spikes longer than his finger. All three of them would be torn up and bloody when this was over, he knew. As he came close enough to peer at the huts through the dense foliage he realized with a start that he'd gone much farther than he thought, almost within a stone's throw of the structure housing the two vats. He peeked through the leaves and thought he saw something else there, something eerily familiar. His breath caught in his chest and he had to force himself to exhale for the second time that day. Not far from the vats he could see a rudimentary fire pit, no more than a few stones circling blackened coals. Just beyond the dead coals was a bench that was no more than a rough plank sitting atop two tree stumps, exactly as he'd seen in his dreams. He had no idea how this was happening, how in the world he was seeing this now, but it both unnerved and excited him more than he could describe. His heart was racing since this was even more proof, as illogical and unlikely as it was, that Frankie was here.

As he watched the village he saw a handful of woman and children walking quietly about, singly or in pairs. They were subdued and moved from one hut to another, their eyes down, never talking or lifting their heads. Most were short and thick through the middle, with long black hair. Their thick legs and bare feet shuffled through the dust. But he was less surprised than he thought he'd be when he spotted several others that were tall with fair skin and lighter colored hair, much more European in their body shape, much more like Josiah. Almost all were bare-chested and wearing nothing but a wispy skirt made of decorated animal skins. All were adorned with black body paint in various, swooping, curling designs and a few had bright yellow and red feathers woven into their long hair.

More importantly he spotted over a dozen armed men stationed outside huts and sitting inside the communal building. These men were clearly not natives, since all were dressed in conventional Western clothing and hats. Several walked around with rifles over their shoulders and were scanning the jungle, guards patrolling the perimeter. If they already had Hal, Ari thought, they must know or at least guessed that there might be others out here. That realization didn't help calm him one bit.

As he continued watching, he noticed that several of the armed men were hanging around a specific hut just beyond the communal building. This one was partially shielded from view by other huts, but it was larger than most, probably double or triple the circumference of the others. While he was staring he saw a tall, dark-haired man walk behind it. Moments later the sound of an engine drifted across the open space to him. It had to be a generator. A native girl in her early teens that was walking across the open area barely took notice of the foreign, mechanical sound.

When the shadows were lengthening across the village and the face of the huts were masked in deep shadow he pulled back and started making his way to the rendezvous spot. He got turned around more often than he thought possible before, scratched and frustrated, he finally arrived. Paul was already there, calmly munching on an MRE and drinking water from his backpack. Ari's stomach rumbled but he didn't think he could eat anything. Just a few minutes later Butch materialized and all three of them sat down.

"I spotted at least fourteen men, all armed," Paul began around a mouthful of cold beef stew. "I circled the entire camp. I also saw several generators with cables going everywhere. There's a larger hut near the back that's newer and constructed differently. It's sturdier and made of wood, not just that thatch stuff, and they pay a lot of attention to it. Lots of men hanging around."

Ari was impressed; he hadn't thought to move from his initial hiding spot at all. Butch nodded and opened a food packet and began shoveling the contents into his mouth.

"Also," he continued, "I didn't see a single adult native male in the entire place. Lots of women and children, but no guys at all. It's creepy, you know? And I tried to get close to the Ice Maker machine to check it out but couldn't. They've got several more guards hovering around it. It wasn't worth getting caught to see it."

Van Owen was a little ashamed that he hadn't seen anyone around the contraption, confirming once again that he wasn't very good at this and would've made a lousy field agent or soldier. He'd stared at it for hours and hadn't noticed a thing.

Butch jerked a thumb behind them toward the village. "I counted the same number of men. Fourteen at least, and maybe more inside the buildings. Good catch on the larger hut."

"If I had to guess," Paulson continued, "I'd say they were keeping any prisoners inside that one. Stands to reason."

"Agreed," Butch said. "Anyone could force their way out of one of those thatched huts if they wanted to."

"So what's next?" the young man asked. "How do we get them out? The best time to try this would be just before dawn. That's when their guard should be lowest."

"Agreed again. I say we head back to the tent and lay low, then come back and try it just before dusk. We'll circle around and come at the bigger hut from behind. We'll firm up plans when we get closer and we get a feel for the lay of the land."

"That sounds great in principle," Paulson said. "But none of us have an alarm or will know when to go. And we need to catch some shuteye or we won't be worth a shit. Once I'm out I'm toast for the whole night. I probably won't wake up till first light."

That caught Ari's attention. "What time should we move out? Would five o'clock in the morning be about right?"

Paul and Butch both nodded. "Sure," Paulson said. "That sounds about right. Why?"

"I think I can take care of that. Trust me."

Chapter 22

They got back to the tent and let Lucky out to stretch its legs and answer nature's call. The black and white dog was overjoyed to see Paul and wouldn't let him out of its sight, its tail wagging so hard its butt swung back and forth. All three of them agreed they should strike camp and set it up elsewhere in preparation for night, just in case their position had been compromised. Half an hour later their new camp was set up on a small spit of land deep in a swampy, boot-sucking area half a mile or more from El Quemado. Ari forced himself to eat something even though he wasn't hungry. Whatever was in the MRE tasted more like paste from a jar, cold and cloying in his mouth, and from there it sat like a stone in his gut. When the sun had dipped below the trees and the shadows once again claimed the daylight, he and Paul crawled into the tent with Lucky at their feet. True to form and to Van Owen's amazement the young man was out in seconds. Ari didn't believe he could follow suit, but after thirty minutes even he fell into a fitful, restless doze. He didn't have any dreams that he could recall, not really, but like clockwork just before five he jerked awake, his body covered in sweat. After taking a few breaths to steady himself he nudged Paul.

"Wake up. It's time to go."

"How'd you do that, anyway?" the young man asked, instantly awake.

"Long story," was all he said.

They hadn't undressed so were out of the tent and ready to go in seconds. Butch had heard them moving around and was outside waiting for them already. Lucky didn't look at all thrilled to be zipped back up in the tent, but they knew there wasn't any choice. The little dog scratched at the zipper but made no other sounds, not a whimper, not a whine.

Each man had his flashlight, courtesy of Big Al. They turned them to their lowest light level, which produced a soft orange glow

369

that barely illuminated the ground at their feet. Even with the flashlights to help all three soon discovered that moving through the jungle in the dark was much more problematic than they'd imagined, and as often as not they found themselves tangled in vines or tripping over roots. Fortunately even at this early hour the rainforest was alive with noises that helped cover their clumsy progress.

Nearly thirty minutes passed before they could locate their previous camp, but once there the going was easier. Ari was almost surprised when Butch, in the lead, carefully pushed through some thick brush and stepped into the village itself, not far from the firepot. Lights off now, they crouched at the edge of the village, keeping low, ready to dive into the brush if necessary. They spent what felt like several lifetimes surveying the black, open space, looking for movement, listening for sounds, straining to sense if there were guards around. No one could detect anything. Brubaker tapped them on the shoulders and they continued circling, always moving toward the larger hut they had spotted at the back. Ari was so jittery he nearly dropped his flashlight a score of times and he had a sudden, overwhelming urge to pee.

They made good time over the flattened, open dirt, mercifully unencumbered by the jungle. If they made any noise at all it was simply the scuff of a shoe on dirt or the rustle of their clothing as they moved. Van Owen felt naked without a weapon, but he knew he'd feel even more awkward with one. He almost envied the other two their Glocks.

Before he knew it they were behind the hut. Ari could only see Butch's faint outline against the darkness, but he tapped them on their shoulders and gently pushed them down. *Stay here* was his message. He got down on all fours and slowly crawled toward the sturdy hut. Ari could barely make out his darker silhouette against the lighter ground, and he realized that the stars overhead were as bright as far away Christmas lights in the velvet sky, their constellations unfamiliar below the equator. There was no moon, at least not now. Crouching there, shaking with nervous energy, he realized that, even though he would never like him or could ever call him a friend, Butch had shown blind determination and nerve throughout this entire ordeal. Grudgingly he had to admire that. The man's love for Frankie was complete, and he discovered that he was feeling remorse for how he continued to carry a torch for her. As Yvonne had bluntly stated so long ago back at his house, it wasn't fair to anyone, Frankie included.

Brubaker was back in no time. He tapped their shoulders again and motioned them away from the hut. When they were thirty or more feet away he whispered, his voice so low it could have been a breeze fluttering leaves around them.

"I didn't see anything or anyone. I don't get it."

"Nothing?" Paul whispered. "That doesn't make sense. Where is everyone?"

"I don't know. There's a door on the far side and I could see a little light through it, but nothing else. I'm going to check it out."

"I'm coming, too," Paulson insisted.

Butch didn't say anything but headed out again, the young man right behind him. Ari brought up the rear. They quickly arrived at the door and saw there was a tiny sliver of light along one edge, just a faint glow, like a candle or small fire flickering on the other side. Brubaker gently eased the door open a crack, his Glock held up and at the ready. As he moved to peer inside the night around them exploded into incandescent brilliance. All three spun about in shock, Butch and Paul with arms outstretched and guns ready, their eyes blinking madly in the sudden, blinding brightness.

"Drop your weapons," came a familiar voice from beyond the light, light that came from a dozen spotlights mounted under the eaves of the huts, high in branches, and on tripods scattered around them. They heard the metallic *click-click* of dozens of weapons being loaded. "Drop your weapons or you will be shot dead where you stand."

Ari squinted into the darkness beyond the spotlights. Ten or more people were there in the shadows. Three of them began to walk toward them. First their shoes became visible, then their legs and torsos. Van Owen's heart sank as the three of them stepped fully into the light and fully revealed themselves.

Before them stood the giant, and next to him was the translator from his garage. A step in front of the pair was the man in the fedora. He was slender and well-built, his face in shadow and hidden by an arc of darkness under the rim of the hat, his mouth the only feature visible. Even white teeth smiled at them. He spoke softly in what was probably Spanish, and the translator, the voice they had heard moments before, worked his magic in that instantaneous translation.

"Butch, how nice of you to finally join us. I had instructed you to do whatever it took to get these people here, but I didn't expect you to sneak in like this." He shrugged. "No matter. You are here now and that is what I wanted. Welcome! Come join me. Come stand by my side."

Ari felt his knees beginning to go weak. Butch? Working with El Quemado? He heard a shuffling noise to his left and saw the butt of a rifle coming toward his face. He raised his hands in self-defense, but was too slow. The heavy blunt end crashed into the side of his head and his mind flared white before a stygian black enveloped him completely.

Van Owen woke slowly, the banging in his head on par with the morning after his tequila bender with Yvonne. Before he could even open his eyes he heard a female voice humming softly, soothingly, and he felt a damp cloth on his forehead. He levered himself up onto an elbow and tried to look around. Frankie stared back at him, her lovely green eyes soft and filled with concern. When she saw him sit up she moved closer.

"Arjen Van Owen, what in the world are you doing here?"

Nobody else could use his full first name without it raising his ire. But somehow when she said *Arjen* it sounded perfect to him, and always brought a smile to his face. She invoked it infrequently, as if saying his full name too often would attenuate and dull the magic. But to hear it now was a gift, a present he had pined for but never truly thought he would receive. She misinterpreted his silence, the corners of her green eyes pulling down in alarm.

"Ari, are you okay? I was starting to get worried about you."

He refrained from saying something corny like, "I am now," even though it was the first thing that came to mind and was exactly how he felt. No, what he actually felt, he realized, was an overwhelming urge to grab her and hold her tight, put his face in her hair and breathe of it deeply. *Frankie was here with him!* But he was afraid that if he did that he'd never let her go, and that wasn't why he was here. He couldn't believe they were actually this close to one another and he couldn't do anything about it.

He found he was on a hard cot of some sort, so he slowly swung his feet down and sat up all the way. The damp rag on his forehead fell into his lap. He reached up and touched a large, tender goose egg located just above his temple. It was sore and swollen and was positioned right above where an eyeglass stem would go. Frankie saw him wince and gently placed the cloth back on the bump, applying gentle pressure, the caregiver in her showing through. The touch of her fingers on his bare skin sent a tingle of electricity through him to the point where he had to pull away. She peered at him oddly but didn't say anything. If she had felt the sensation as well she didn't give any indication of it.

He took a moment and looked at her deeply, drinking in her presence, marveling how closely she resembled what he'd seen in his dream. Her blondish-brown hair was pulled back in a loose

373

ponytail and fell well past her shoulders, subtle streaks of sun-induced highlights just visible in the low light. Her face was half in shadow but was indeed thinner than he remembered, but her petite nose and full mouth were the same. The white T-shirt was there, stained and dirty, and couldn't do much to hide the outline of her small breasts. Her fingernails were cracked and short, which, Ari thought, probably bothered her more than anything. Yet her green eyes still pierced his soul, especially when she tilted her head to the side the way she did. He had almost forgotten that look, and didn't realize until then how desperately he'd missed it. She was as beautiful as he remembered, maybe more so due to the passage of time and his relief at finding her.

"Well, the short answer is we're here to save you," he finally managed, his voice little more than a smoker's croak. "Um, what happened?" He felt shaky, and the throbbing in his head was so loud he wondered if she could hear it.

Frankie kept up the slight pressure with the damp cloth. "They hit you and knocked you unconscious. You've been out cold for over an hour."

It was all starting to dribble back to him then. Sneaking up to the hut, the bright lights, the confrontation with El Quemado. The bitter realization that they'd been caught. The butt of the rifle angling toward his head and putting a quick end to their short-lived rescue. Darkness.

"Then they dragged you in here. Your friend Paul is here, too."

Ari looked up quickly and immediately regretted the sudden movement as his head swam and pulsed anew. Paulson came up and knelt beside him, looking none the worse for wear. "How you doing, Ari?" the young man asked, concern thick in his voice.

"Where are we?"

Paul looked around him. "In the hut, the one we were trying to look in. Just like we thought, it's made to look like the others but it's made of wood and pretty damn solid. They've got guards all around." He paused. "We're not going anywhere."

"Where's Butch?"

Paulson looked at Frankie, passing the question to her. The expression on her face was unreadable, a subtle softening around her eyes combined with a tightening around her mouth, as if she couldn't make up her mind what to think. "He's with him."

"With him? With El Quemado?"

"El Quemado? Oh, yes, him. But we don't call him that here. His name's Roberto, at least that's what he likes to be called."

"But…why?"

"Because they're working together, that's why," she spit out, not able to meet his gaze and staring pointedly down at the ground. "Turns out they've been working together the whole time. They're partners of some sort, I guess."

So it *was* true. What El Quemado had said when they'd been captured was the truth. Butch had betrayed them. He tried to catch Frankie's eye but she wouldn't look up. Finally he glanced at Paul who stiffly nodded his head.

"Roberto makes his drugs here, the stuff Paul said is called Ice back home," she continued, "and he uses Butch to help bring it into the States. With all his shipping connections in UPS and contact with pilots and crew it's easy for him to smuggle it in."

"But hold on," Paul chimed in, apparently hearing this for the first time. "How can that be? They've got all kinds of security set up to stop that from happening. You can't just bring drugs into the country all willy-nilly like that. Dogs, checkpoints, TSA. They're not stupid."

"Sure, for conventional drugs they've got security in place, but not for Ice. It isn't like anything they've ever seen before. That contraption out there, the one with the big vats, makes it and condenses it down to a kind of brown paste that's easy to ship. It doesn't set off any alarms and it gets past dogs and whatever because it's totally new and different. It's not an opiate, it's not marijuana, it's not like any of those. They can't detect what they don't know and understand. And when it's back in the States it's easy to reconstitute and sell."

It was all beginning to make terrifying sense now. Ari had a sudden flashback to the first time Butch had come to his house: his fingers had been tainted brown, like a smoker's fingers – but Butch didn't smoke. He had to have been handling the condensed form of Ice. Butch had been playing them the entire time…

He sat up all the way and tried to gather his wits, finally sure he wasn't going to vomit. He looked around the hut and saw several other people there, barely visible in the low light from the single gas lamp sitting on the dirt floor. One tall man in particular was pacing back and forth at the other end, in the near dark. He'd take five steps, turn, and do five steps back. The pacing was the same each time, precisely five steps each way, even though the hut was large and he had more room than that. He was muttering something too low to hear, and he held something in his hand, a rectangular object, perhaps a book. Ari looked back to Frankie, who was staring at him.

"Okay, I get it. Your husband was helping smuggle condensed Ice into the country. Why were people suddenly getting paralyzed and dying? Like those two pilots that crashed in Louisville?"

"That passenger plane? That was horrible." She shivered.

"Yeah, that one. A flight attendant who survived saw the pilots in the cockpit right before the crash. She described them as paralyzed and unable to move. All red in the face and shaking, like they were sick and feverish. She was the only survivor."

Frankie blanched, her naturally tan skin going pale. She had trouble meeting his gaze again. "I saw that, just a week before I was…taken. The pilot was Eric Handler and was a friend of Butch's. They used to golf together all the time. I think he was helping him bring the condensed Ice drug into the country. He had some money problems and he was being paid good money to do it. Gambling or something, I don't know. Roberto's told me some of this, but not everything. The only thing I can figure is that he came into contact with the condensed drug and somehow overdosed. If he had even the smallest cut on his hand, or touched his eye, or something like that, that's all it takes for some people. I've seen it happen before…" Her voice trailed off then, and if she said something else he didn't hear it. Her shoulders sagged and a shaky hand drifted up to cover her face. She sobbed once, deep and shuddering, and he was so touched that he couldn't help but reach out and lay a hand on her arm. She didn't pull away but her sobs continued. Paul and Ari could do nothing but watch and wait.

She finally regained a measure of composure and wiped her face. The tears left dirty smudges across her cheeks, smudges that could have been deep bruises around her eyes. She breathed deeply and tried to calm herself. Ari reluctantly pulled his hand back.

"I've seen that happen before, too many damn times. Roberto…he tests his drugs on the men of the village, trying to get the right mixture and concentration. It's not so bad now because he's got it pretty well figured out, but so many of these poor men have died being guinea pigs for him."

"Just the men?" he asked.

She wiped away a rim of moisture gathering on her lower eyelid. "Yes, and really he can only test it on the mixed-race villagers, the ones without pure Amazonian heritage. I don't know how much you've seen, but the people here are either 'pure' natives like you're used to, or they're mixed with European genes. Those are the taller ones, usually with brown or blond hair. The pure natives aren't affected by the drug for some reason, so he can't test it on them. Something about prolonged exposure to the base ingredients for so many generations, I think. He can only test it on the mixed-race villagers."

"Like Josiah?" Paul asked, his eyes wide. "He's a mixed-race one, right?"

Frankie spun to look at him. "Yes, like Josiah. How in the world do you know him? Did you see him? Is he safe?"

"These mixed-race natives," Van Owen said, pressing her. "Where did they come from? How can they even be here? Tell me," he asked, steadying himself, prepared for disappointment once again, "are they descendants of Percy Fawcett?"

For the first time that morning she blessed him with a small smile. It wasn't much, really, just a fleeting lifting of her lips that never made it to her teeth. It still struck him as wonderful.

"I don't know for sure since everyone here just calls him The Father," she admitted, "but it would make sense, wouldn't it? It would seem, Ari, that you may have found your mystery man at last."

After the initial surprise of Frankie's statement had worn off, Van Owen turned to Paulson. His voice was soft, and he spoke as if still in mild shock. So much new information. So much had happened. Back in the jungle they had guessed this might be the case, but these new facts may have clinched it. "What happened after they knocked me out?"

The young man's face hardened. "I tried to help but a couple of them jumped on me and held me back. El Quemado, or Roberto, or whatever he's called, told Butch to follow him and they all went away somewhere, to one of the other huts, I think. The big guy and the translator went with him. Then they tossed me in here with you and we've been waiting for you to wake up. That's pretty much it." He smacked his fist into his open palm in sudden anger. "I can't believe Butch is working for that guy! I trusted him!"

Frankie stood and brushed dirt off her knees. "Don't worry. He fooled all of us, including me, and I'm married to him." She stared at Ari for a moment then sat down on the other end of the cot. He could tell she was fighting to hold back more tears. He hadn't had time to consider how she must be feeling throughout all this: her sense of betrayal by the man she called her husband had to be tearing her up inside.

But he'd been so damn convincing, he thought. Butch's intensity and desire to save his wife had seemed so genuine. There was no way he'd been acting. Or had Ari simply been blinded by his own desire to help her? By his own admission he'd been unable to read the guy well. He shook his head, now angry with himself for being duped. If only he'd seen through him earlier, then maybe they wouldn't be in this mess now.

"He fooled us all," he finally admitted, although it pained him to acknowledge he'd been taken in, too. "Now we've got to figure out how to get out of here. Is there any sign of Hal?"

"No, I haven't seen him."

Frankie looked up. "You mean the man they caught yesterday? He's here, in one of the other huts. They were questioning him."

"So he's still alive? Is he okay? What about Josiah? Is he here, too?"

She shook her head. "No, I don't think so. At least I haven't seen him. And from what I heard they weren't too pleased with your friend, either. I don't think he was being very cooperative."

"That sounds like Hal," Paul said with pride. "I doubt he'll say very much."

Ari shakily stood and took in his surroundings and the people sharing the hut with them. He pointed to the tall man pacing back and forth like an automaton. He motioned to him. "Who's that?"

Frankie's eyes softened again and she stood and moved toward the tall man. Always the caregiver, she placed a calming hand on his arm and he stopped walking. His low muttering didn't stop. "I don't know his real name. I think he used to be a priest. Roberto experimented on him before I got here and something went wrong. Something happened and his mind is...gone. Fried, I guess you'd say."

Ari walked over and stood in front of him, their eyes level. The man's hair was long and in clumps, knotted and filthy, like unkempt dreadlocks. His four-inch long beard was untrimmed, and Van Owen could just make out a red tint to it in the dim light. In his one filthy hand he clutched an old, tattered bible. In the other, the one he held to his mouth, he clasped rosary beads, which he kept sliding through his fingers as he mouthed nearly silent words. Frankie's caring, gentle touch continued on his arm and her tone, when she spoke again, was filled with compassion and sadness.

"Now Roberto just keeps him around, for fun or something. He's harmless and lost in his own world. Sometimes he talks or shouts out loud or quotes scripture, but for the most part he simply wanders around like this. I feel so bad for him. We all help take care of him but we don't know what else to do."

Van Owen looked into the priest's wild eyes. They locked stares for just a moment, and for a split-second the man seemed almost lucid, as if a thick veil in his mind had been lifted. Then the veil slammed shut and the low muttering began again, and Ari could see he was counting beads on the rosary.

"Father Sean? Are you Father Sean?"

The name did little more than make the man twitch, and maybe his head canted to one side for no more than a heartbeat. The rosary beads, worn and shiny from use, moved deftly through his fingers, although maybe with more urgency now. The beads clicked together with a sound of a mouse scurrying across a tile floor.

"How do you know this guy?" Paulson asked, clearly shocked and impressed.

Ari realized Paul had either been absent or asleep each time he'd talked about him before. "Father Ed mentioned him, and I asked Big Al about him, too. He passed through Ed's village last year and hasn't been heard of since. It has to be him." He gently took the man's shoulders in his hands. There was little flesh and muscle there. Ari felt angular bone through the man's filthy black T-shirt.

"Father Sean, others are worried about you. Father Ed is worried about you."

"He is no longer here," came a thin voice from the shadows at the other end of the hut. Again Ari was shocked to hear English with a British accent, but at this point he guessed he shouldn't be. "The body remains but his soul has left us. He is off his chump. He is little more than a *pulhaja*, a…husk. If that is spoken correct."

The man in the shadows stood and wobbled into the light. He was short and spare, his legs and arms thin with age and so frail they could barely hold him upright. His broad face was painted in black lines like Josiah's, but whereas the young native's had been sharp and clean this man's had faded and blurred with time. When he walked slowly towards them Ari couldn't believe how ancient he was. He guessed his age at eighty or ninety, but out here in the harshness of the jungle there was no way to know for sure.

Frankie smiled at him and rested a gentle hand on his arm. "Ari, this is Moises. He's the leader of his people here."

"He speaks English, too, just like Josiah," Ari said.

Moises' face scrunched up, the many wrinkles twisting his features in mock pain until they resembled an apple left to dry in the sun. "Like Josiah? Crikey, no. He is full of footle and is a poor student who never paids attention to his lessons, and never learned the English as he shoulds. He was always too busy huntings and concerning himself with girls. Daft boy."

Ari looked from Frankie to Paul, then back at Moises. "You speak English very well."

"Yeah, no kidding," Paul agreed. "But what kind of English is that?"

Ari couldn't look away. The odd words like *crikey* and *footle* were the key. "I think it's what they were taught. It's British English, for sure, but from the early 1900s."

The old man tottered toward them then eased himself down on Ari's cot, and even that short walk was almost more than his fading body could handle. He sighed deeply and seemed to shrink into himself as he exhaled. "Yes, we were tolds to learn English by The Father. He said that one day other Whites would come and we would needs to know, we would needs to know to protect us. So we learns exactly as he instructed, trying to keeps the language pure, and we teach each other, and we practices. And now the Whites have come, and we talks to them, and they do little more than kills us."

Van Owen got down on one knee in front of the old man. "You all talk about The Father. Who was The Father? Tell me, Moises, was he a man named Percy Fawcett?"

The chief stared at him with very clear, dark brown eyes. Ari could see that the man's body was failing him but his mind was still sharp and whole, that there was an intelligence there that belied his outward appearance. Stuck out here in the jungle the man had obviously never had a chance to learn much more than needed in order to survive, but ignorance and intelligence were not always mutually exclusive, he reminded himself.

"I do not knows this bloke you call 'Percy Fawcett'," Moises replied, saying the Colonel's name badly, the unfamiliar name hard for him to pronounce. "We follows the commands and the teachings of The Father. He ordered us to learns, so we learns."

"What happened to him? Why was he here?"

Moises scratched at his ear and sighed. His ears had piercings of tiny white bones running up and down the backs, just in front of the cartilage. "Many years ago he cames to us, wounded and with the grippe, all alone. His leg was badly injured. We cared for him and in exchange he showed us many things and taught us to better survive in our own world. With his help our people became stronger and we grew in numbers. We were happy and strong. Years passed, then The Father died, back when I was just a child, but not before he sired many children with many different women. For years we were left alone and we had no more visitors and saw no one." He paused and drew a deep breath and he stared over their shoulders, his mind far away yet peering deep within himself. "And then these others cames, and my people have died. We are almost…no more." His eyes closed and he sat there, small and tiny, his hands twitching in his lap.

Ari stood quickly, excitement overruling his anxiety at their predicament. "It had to be him. Fawcett survived and ended up here," he said to all of them and to none of them. "He had children, probably lots of children from what I've seen so far. He grew old and died here. I'll be damned."

Moises wore a shawl of white beads around his neck and over his shoulders. When he shrugged the beads rattled softly, clicking together as they moved with a sibilant rustling noise. It was the sound of an ancient people, a people living within the confines of the jungle and having no need or desire to exert dominance over it, a people who had come to terms with their place in life. Ari thought back and remembered a controversial topic in some random philosophy class in college. The subject was *environmental determinism*, a theory used for centuries to understand why some cultures or civilizations were more advanced than others. Largely disproven in modern times, he was forced then to rethink how this predatory and vicious environment had certainly kept tribes like this from advancing into a more modern society. There had to be some validity to it, he thought. It would explain so much.

But now there were more immediate demands and no time for random musings. He turned away from the small chief and addressed Frankie. "So a lot of this is starting to make sense," he said, "but I don't get why you were kidnapped. That doesn't fit in with any of this."

She sat down next to the chief and rested a hand on his boney knee. "I don't know, I mean they never told me. The big man –

Gonzalez, his name is Gonzalez, by the way – grabbed me in the hospital parking lot. We drove to some tiny airport outside of Louisville and flew for hours. We stopped twice to refuel, I think, and finally landed at another small airstrip. Roberto has a helicopter and they brought me here, to the village. I've been here ever since. I'm not even sure where we are."

"You're in western Brazil, in the state of Mato Grosso, if that helps."

"Well, no, not really. But thanks. Geography was never my thing."

Father Sean suddenly stopped and held the tattered bible in the air. In a loud, deep voice that vibrated the walls, he proclaimed, "And it came to pass on the morrow, that the evil spirit from God came upon Saul, and he prophesied in the midst of the house: and David played with his hand, as at other times, and there was a javelin in Saul's hand." He held the bible aloft for a few moments before letting it fall, as if its weight were now too much to bear. He held it tightly against his chest and began pacing again, the rosary beads clicking ever so softly.

The four of them watched this display, mostly with curiosity but also with compassion, especially Frankie. "That's pretty much all he does. He gets the scripture right most of the time, although I've never been able to figure out if he's trying to tell us something or if he's just tossing out random verses."

"Beats me," Paul said, "I went to catechism in junior high but didn't learn much. Mainly I just went to meet girls."

From his place on the cot Moises shook his head sadly. "You may resembles The Father, but you acts like Josiah, a right josser. I do not know what this *catch-a-chism* is, but if it is a place of study then you should have beens studying and not dwellings on young hoydens."

Paulson's faced flushed and he sat down next to the ancient native. They began talking about school and church and Paul was

384

trying his best to explain what catechism was all about, while trying to understand just what a "hoyden" was. For just a moment no one was paying any attention to Ari or Frankie. She stood and stepped close to him, so close he could feel her warm breath on his face and neck. But when she spoke her voice was stern.

"You shouldn't be here. What are you doing? And you came here with Butch? How did that even happen?"

He had to think before he answered, picking his words carefully. "I couldn't stand you being in danger. I know we...can't be together, but I had to find you. I had to be sure you were safe. You understand that, right? I couldn't just leave you out here."

Frankie looked up at him and he stared into those deep green eyes, and in that moment all that they'd once meant to each other, all their past feelings and shared history, passed effortlessly through that link. Her face relaxed, the muscles down her jawline easing, and she finally allowed herself a real smile, one filled with all their yesterdays. In that moment Ari felt as if he was completely alone with her at last, and despite himself, despite telling himself again that she could never be with him, his heart swelled. He again resisted the urge to hold her tight.

"Thanks," she finally said. "And...I'm glad you're here."

Chapter 23

Later that day, when the hut was heating up and the still air inside was so hot and stifling it was difficult to breathe, the door opened and a female native wordlessly deposited food and drink inside. The meal was simple, fruits and some sort of coarse flatbread, along with several clay bowls of water. There wasn't much, not nearly enough to fill anyone's stomach, but the water seemed pure and clean. Ari was happy to see that they weren't planning to starve them at least.

They divided up the meal, and against his insistence Frankie made sure Moises took a share, too. As there was nothing else to do they sat and talked, mainly Ari bringing her up to date on what had happened. He told her about his attempted abduction and the explosion that had damaged the Firebird and killed one of the intruders. Telling that part was still difficult for him, time not blurring the memory nearly enough. Paul filled in some of the gaps of their journey here, momentarily becoming very upset when he realized that Lucky was still in the tent.

"He's still there! Shit, he's trapped in that tent. I gotta get him out."

No amount of consoling could settle him down, and he began pacing the length of the hut right along with Father Sean. The two of them nearly collided several times. Paul's face had turned hard and cold, and once more Ari could see the determination there that marked him as a Marine, a seasoned warrior, a man desperate for justice and right. He wouldn't want to be the one to stand in his way if it ever came to that. Moises watched him with interest, studying him. Eventually the young man sat down hard on the dirt floor, deep within his own thoughts.

An hour later the door to the hut opened and Gonzalez stood there silhouetted in the bright light, the low, narrow doorway overflowing with his bulk. He had to crouch to come inside, and Van Owen and Frankie both involuntarily shied away from him. Paulson stopped pacing and stared daggers in his direction, undaunted by the man's immense size and presence. With the light behind him they could only catch bits and pieces of his features, and with his long hair hanging in his face his eyes were no more than two black spaces devoid of life or emotion. When he stood his head brushed the ceiling. He pointed to Van Owen and Frankie with a finger larger than a bratwurst. In his other massive hand he gripped a black cigar that in comparison looked smaller than a cigarette butt. The end glowed a deep red and the smell of tobacco quickly filled the hut.

"Come with me," he said, his voice impossibly low, as if a diesel engine were rumbling in his chest. He spoke heavily accented English but it was clear enough to understand. The two of them looked at each other and stood to follow.

Paul had been sitting on the ground and as the two moved toward the door he stood up and crossed his arms, staring hard at Gonzalez, appraising him. The giant caught the movement and casually looked the blond Marine up and down, sensing a challenge. There was a tense stillness in the thick air, made all the more poignant by the cloying cigar smoke now hanging in layers all around them. Ari's mind grasped the situation and he was about to command Paulson to stand down when the huge man chuckled once and turned away, dismissing the threat as too minor to warrant further attention. However, Paul's point had been made: *I'm not afraid of you.* Van Owen was proud of his young friend's David versus Goliath bravado, but thought Paulson must be crazy. He himself was terrified of the giant.

They exited the hut into bright afternoon sunshine. The temperature had to be in the upper eighties but the slight breeze on his skin felt wonderful and cooling, quickly drying some of the thick sweat that covered him. Well-armed men fell into step on either side of them and they followed Gonzalez through a warren of smaller huts to one near the middle of the village. Here there was a smaller structure. It had a thatched roof and was open at three sides, with a fan spinning slowly overhead and powered by some unseen electrical source. Sitting underneath the overhang was an antique wooden table, dark walnut or some other exotic wood, the edges beautifully carved in complex shapes and with thick, curving legs. It was completely out of place in this primitive jungle setting. Behind the table sat El Quemado, still wearing the brown fedora. He was casually eating from platters and dishes of fine china, and there was red wine in a tall-stemmed glass near his right hand. Oddly, even in this stifling heat, he was wearing an obviously expensive long sleeve white shirt secured with gold cufflinks. The smell of steak and cooked vegetables hit Ari's nose, and despite himself his mouth watered and his stomach gurgled, the unwelcome Pavlovian reaction catching him off guard. It was all he could do not to lick his dry lips.

Flanking El Quemado on his left was the translator, his long black hair still in a braided ponytail and the sides of his head shaved short, as before. He didn't move but his bulging eyes tracked the two as they approached. He was leaning back in an equally ornate chair and appeared eminently relaxed, almost boneless. On the other end of the table was Butch. When he saw Frankie he jumped up and started toward her, but El Quemado quickly raised a hand and Brubaker stopped short, his frozen position awkward and unbalanced. He grimaced once and a shadow crossed his wide face, then he slowly sat back down, the chair squeaking softly as his weight settled. Ari and Frankie stood there in the hot sun while their host continued his meal. Two, then three minutes passed and all they could hear was the distant buzzing of cicadas and the clinking of silverware on china as he cut his meat and chewed methodically. Still they waited.

Finally he pushed the plate away and dabbed at the corners of his mouth with a white napkin, and it was then that Ari noticed his hands. As Paulson had described back in Louisville they were visibly scarred almost down to his fingers. The patchwork flesh was different colors and looked mismatched, a ghoulish tapestry of skin. If the scarring went any further up his arms it was hidden by the long shirtsleeves. He casually swirled the wine within the glass and took a small sip, sucking in air afterwards. He spoke in Spanish and the translator said, nearly in real-time, "I believe it was Ralph Waldo Emerson who said, 'Give me wine to wash me clean of the weather-stains of care.' He was a wise man, no? Wine is one of the many pleasures of life, one that I would never care to do without again."

It was Frankie who spoke next. She took a step forward and Ari nearly put out a hand to stop her. "Roberto, what do you want? Why are we being held like this? I don't understand. I've always had my freedom here in the village."

"Excellent question, my dear. I find that circumstances have suddenly changed. Simply put, these men that have intruded into my village are here to do me great harm. They are from the US Government and in particular the FBI. I can't have that, surely you can understand. I can't be interfered with."

"No, I'm just here to save my wife," Butch blurted out. "You know that!"

Roberto pointed a sharp knife at him, the blade glittering. There was an undercurrent of menace in his otherwise easy voice, like a drop of arsenic in champagne. "You're a different story, my friend. I know why you're here."

Ari finally found his voice. "What do you mean?"

Roberto settled back in his chair. "It's quite simple. For the past year my friend Butch Brubaker has been helping me smuggle the condensed version of the drug you call Ice into your country. His connections in the shipping and transport business have been invaluable to me. But like all small men he became greedy and demanded more for his services. Tell us all, Butch, what happened next?"

Brubaker glowered at him for several moments before he caught himself and stared at the ground instead. El Quemado eventually shrugged. "Ah, being your normal, stubborn self? Fine. I shall tell them." He set the knife down and lined it up with his other utensils.

"What happened is what always happens when small men smell money," he stated through the translator. "They get a whiff and suddenly it fills their nostrils and they want more. I was paying Butch handsomely for his services and my shipments were beginning to make it into the United States very nicely, but then suddenly this ass, this *pendejo,* decides he wants more. So what does he do? He threatens to cut off shipping all together unless I double his pay." He leaned forward and slapped his open palm on the table. China and silverware jumped and his wineglass toppled over, a splash of the deep red burgundy spilling across the tabletop. "That was unacceptable! No one will hold my operation hostage, especially not a little shipping boy whose greed exceeded his intelligence. So Mr. Gonzalez and I took a trip to America and picked up, shall we say, an insurance policy, and now we are operating smoothly again. Right, Butch?"

Brubaker didn't react, not in any way that could be seen by Roberto or the translator. But Ari saw his hands clenching and unclenching between his knees. His knuckles were white, the color of bleached driftwood tossed up on a beach.

"But somehow you all determined where I was, or at least my general vicinity, and for that I give you credit. When the FBI agent Hal Hollenbeck contacted Butch and asked him to come down here to search for his wife, he didn't know what to do. What's the expression you use? He 'freaked out' a bit? In a panic he contacted me and I told him to join your group and to do whatever he could to make sure you made it here safe and sound. I had to capture you so I could find out everything you know, and could properly plan my next moves. I believe it was your own Benjamin Franklin who said

'An investment in knowledge always pays the best interest'. My investment in your capture will pay handsome dividends, I'll make sure of it."

Ari suppressed a groan. He had a sudden flashback to a conversation he and Hal had had when they were putting their team together back at his house in Louisville. He recalled the agent saying that he'd contacted his man, and after several days he'd agreed to come along. That man of course had been Butch, and he should have wondered back then why Frankie's husband had taken days to answer Hal, why he hadn't agreed to join right away, especially as fervently as he'd been searching for her since then. Now he knew why. Now it all made sense. He'd needed to get in touch with El Quemado to figure out what to do. Yes, the son of a bitch had betrayed them all.

"Where's Hal?" Ari asked. "Where are you keeping him?"

A flash of annoyance crossed Roberto's face at the interruption, a small twitch of the muscles around his mouth and eyes. But it quickly passed and he grinned, his even teeth white under the fedora. "He is here and he is safe, or at least safe enough." He snapped his fingers and a tall, bronzed native woman appeared and scurried to his side where she began bussing his dishes and mopping up the spilled wine. Her brown hair was interwoven with beads and she had dark tattooed or painted markings down her bare chest. The markings were not straight-line and symmetrical like Moises' or Josiah's, but curved and swirled around in a random pattern across her mid-section. If he stretched his imagination Ari could possibly see a blooming flower there. She was clearly one of the mixed-race villagers. Roberto paid her little attention but waited patiently until she finished and retreated.

"But enough talk of past transgressions. Now we shall have some entertainment," he said, his voice light again. He motioned again and two of his guards strode out of a nearby hut with Josiah sandwiched between them, each man holding him tightly by a bicep, their fingers digging deep into his flesh. The young man appeared unhurt but terrified, his blue eyes wide and darting. He saw Ari and Frankie and stumbled a little, the two men forced to hold him upright.

Roberto reached behind him on the ground and picked up a small canvas bag that Ari hadn't noticed. He set it on the table in front of him where it clunked softly. "And by the way, we also found your camp in the swamp. I took it upon myself to bring all your supplies and possessions here. I was quite taken and intrigued by one specific item that we found." He reached into the bag and brought out one of their Magic Eight Balls. He held it up and admired its shiny surface, moving it this way and that. Even in the shade of his enclosure the black orb gleamed brightly in his scarred hand.

"This thing is fascinating, and I must admit I've known many people in my life who would've been better off using its decision-making abilities instead of their own. So let's give it a test, shall we? A simple question first. Magic Eight Ball, is it going to rain today?" He inverted the ball and shook it, then turned it upside down to read the reply in the message window. *Signs Point To Yes.* Well, looking at the blue sky above us I can't say that it's always right, but what can you do?"

Frankie watched the display in confusion, then looked away toward Josiah. The young man appeared stunned and lost, his eyes still wild and afraid. The two men had a grip so tight on his arms that it must have hurt, but he didn't seem to notice. She turned back to Roberto.

"Why are you holding him? He's harmless, you know that. He's just a boy."

"Harmless? I think not," he replied through the translator. "He violated standing orders and left the village. He found these men and brought them here. There's no telling what other damage he's done that could jeopardize my operation. No, he's far from harmless. We shall have to make sure he doesn't disobey again."

At that he crooked a finger at someone out of sight and a man came forward pulling an old couple with him. They were natives of the pure indigenous type, short and very dark, with wide, stout bodies and thick legs. Their straight black hair gleamed in the hot sun as brightly as the Eight Ball. Both were clearly terrified as they were herded forward. Josiah saw them and if possible his eyes opened even wider. He said something unintelligible to them and the man said something back. Frankie made a move in their direction but one of their guards roughly grabbed her arm to restrain her. Butch twitched in his seat.

"The family hierarchy here is confusing at best," Roberto explained calmly, barely paying the couple any attention, his eyes still on the Eight Ball. "It's not traditional in the least, not by our Western standards. It's a much more open set of relationships based on a less defined structure. For example, 'marriage' as we know it isn't practiced here and something they find quite humorous, a very Christian and puritanical arrangement they never adopted. No, if they want to have sex with one another it's a complicated series of requests and barter more reminiscent of your 'free love' period in the 60s. Honestly, I don't claim to understand it and it's a little barbaric for my tastes. But, it seems to work for them on some level, and I'm not one to judge."

"Roberto, what are you doing? These two people haven't done you any harm!" Frankie shouted, still vainly trying to pull away from her captor.

"Of course they haven't, and how could they? I have all the power here. No, my continued ability to control this village comes down to obedience. Thoreau once said 'Disobedience is the true foundation of liberty. The obedient must be slaves'. These people cannot for a moment believe that they are free. I may have need of young Josiah's bloodlines in the future, so one of these people must be punished for him. His mother and father are long dead and he has no other immediate family. These two," he waved at the couple casually, "are his aunt and uncle, or second cousins, or something like that. It's difficult to figure out for sure. So one of them will suffer for his sins."

"Please, Roberto, no!" Her struggles were becoming manic.

He ignored her pleas. "But I'm not a cruel person at heart. I won't make that decision myself – I'll let this new tool choose for us. We shall do as it instructs." He shook the black orb and asked, "Magic Eight Ball, should I punish the man?" He turned it over and read out loud, "*My Sources Say No*. See? True to my word I will not punish the man. Now let's ask again. Should I punish the woman?" He shook the black ball and read from the message window. "*Without A Doubt*. There, you see? We have our answer." He spoke in Spanish to the guard holding the couple, something the translator didn't repeat. The guard calmly pushed the man away then pulled out his pistol and shot the woman in the side of the head.

The gun's report was deafening this close, loud and sharp enough to make Ari and Frankie jump. He watched in horror as a geyser of blood as thick as his thumb sprayed from her head. Her thick legs melted under her and she fell in a heap, her limbs and body sprawled in that awkward jumble that only the dead can achieve. The old man screamed something and ran to her, holding her slack cheeks in his shaking hands, hands that were now coated with her blood. Frankie stopped struggling and hid her face in her own hands, her shoulders shaking. Both Ari and Butch stared at the grisly scene and fought to grasp what had just happened, and Van Owen had to swallow bile that abruptly bubbled into his mouth. Roberto calmly set the Magic Eight Ball down and absently scratched under his jaw with a manicured finger.

"Now young Josiah sees the result of his disobedience. Now he knows what happens if I am not obeyed." He opened his arms wide, taking in everything around him. "This village and its people are mine. Never forget that. Now take her away."

He wiped his hands on the white napkin as if cleansing himself of the deed. Then he stood and left, the translator a step or two behind him. After a few seconds Butch followed slowly, his feet dragging in the dust. Their audience, such as it was, was over.

When they were back in their hut with Paulson and the others, Frankie collapsed heavily onto the cot. Tears streamed down her swollen, puffy cheeks, and the green of her eyes were overpowered by red.

"What happened?" Paul asked, looking from one to the other and back again. "We heard a gunshot and some screaming. I was afraid something had happened to you guys."

Ari touched his shoulder and they moved away from Frankie. He explained their audience with El Quemado, the Magic Eight Ball, and the murder of the old woman. Paul listened intently and quietly, but his jaw clenched and his fingers curled into fists. When Ari had finished the young man turned and strode to the door. Van Owen grabbed at him but it was like trying to stop a train.

"Paul, stop!" Ari commanded. "There's nothing you can do!"

Paulson threw open the door but was balked by two guards with rifles pointed directly at his gut. He stood there with his chest heaving, the injustice of the world pounding in his skull and urging him forward. Ari had never seen him like this, not with this berserker rage pulsing from him in palpable, murderous waves. He knew if he didn't do something fast his young friend would be slaughtered on the spot. But before he could act another figure quickly interposed himself between Paul and the guards. It was Father Sean, his right arm outstretched and his other clasping the ragged bible to his chest. His wild eyes were lifted to the skies.

"Thou shalt not avenge, nor bear any grudge against the children of thy people, but thou shalt love they neighbor as thyself."

Paul stuttered to a halt, his face a twisted mixture of hate and confusion. He made a move to go around the emaciated priest but Father Sean spread his arms wide and refused to let him pass. After a few seconds of this some of the fire left the young man and he spun around, stalking towards the back of the hut, his shoulders still hunched in anger and frustration. Ari let out a slow breath and calmly eased the door shut again, the inside of the hut suddenly dark and quiet. Seeing Paul like this he could understand anew why the young man would make a fine law enforcement officer, and why the bribe had caused him so much guilt; his unfailing belief in justice and his desire to help were overriding and overwhelming personality traits. He may eventually find that life was not fair and a measure of cynicism could creep in, but he wasn't there yet. Father Sean began pacing again, the rosary beads clicking softly in his hand. Van Owen went back to Paul.

"Don't do that again," he ordered softly over the young man's shoulder. "There may come a time for action, but it's not now. Anything you do now will just get you killed. Remember: Think, plan, then act. Okay?"

Paul took some time to react to his own motto before slowly nodding, his white-blond hair clearly visible even in the shadowy darkness of the hut. Head still down, he slumped to the dirt floor and stared at his hands, hands that quivered with the unused adrenaline surging through his veins. Ari patted him on the shoulder then made his way back to Frankie. Her tears had stopped but her face was blank and empty. He sat next to her, but not so close that they were touching.

"How could this be happening?" she asked, clearly knowing there was no answer forthcoming. "How did Butch get involved in all this? We were happy, Butch and I. We had our problems like anyone else, sure, and most of them revolved around money, but that happens to everyone." She wiped her face and stared at her broken nails. "Butch never went to college, you know? He always felt like he should be able to make more money, always wanted to do better." She turned her head and looked briefly at Ari. "I don't know, maybe he always thought he couldn't do as well as you. He never talked about you, about us, but I think it always ate at him. You made him feel...inadequate."

Ari didn't have an answer for that. He felt a momentary spasm of guilt for his own involvement in this: his continued conversations with Frankie, the way he couldn't let her go, the way he still felt about her. He had been far from innocent, he knew. His post-tequila conversation with Yvonne thrust itself into his mind. She'd urged him to let her go once and for all, that Frankie would always be miserable knowing he was still there, that they might someday be together somehow. It would never, she had insisted, get better until he was out of the picture.

Damn it to hell, he thought. Perhaps Butch was right to think the way he did.

Sometime later more simple food and water was brought to the hut. The four of them ate in silence. At one point Moises asked about the woman who had been killed, and Frankie described her to him. He nodded. "Ah, Loyis. She was a good woman. She was quick to scolds but had a full heart. She thought herself a fine cook, but she could burns water more often than not. She told fine jokes."

Ari couldn't help but notice that the villagers all seemed to have biblical names of sorts. Not exactly like the originals, but quite close. The natives may have kept the English language reasonably pure, but over years the names had been slightly warped and distorted. And some of Moise's vocabulary and expressions were nearly a hundred years out of date, too, but that was to be expected with no outside influence. They were lucky to be able to communicate at all.

Later that evening the door opened again. Gonzalez stood there, his bulk overpowering the doorway. In his hand he held a small sack. The meager light from inside illuminated his face just enough that they could see his pocked skin and the purple scar that ran down his cheek. His long hair couldn't hide the thick, Neanderthal ridge over his black eyes. The menace he generally exuded wasn't completely absent, not really, but nor was there compassion in his gaze. He tossed the sack at Ari's feet.

"This is for you," he said in thick English. "You will eat with him soon."

The door shut behind his massive form. Ari gathered up the sack and rolled out the Magic Eight Ball, holding the smooth orb in his hand. He stared at the toy as if it could strike him down where he sat. He quickly threw it away from him on the dusty ground where it rolled towards Moises. The old man cautiously gathered it up and slowly spun it around in his ancient, gnarled hands.

"What is this thing?"

Ari didn't answer, still horrified that the device had been instrumental in Loyis' death. Paul stared at it before moving to the old man's side. He took the ball from the chief. "It's a child's toy. You can ask it a question and it's supposed to answer you. Let me show you." He shook the ball and said, "Magic Eight Ball, will I see my son Taylor again soon?" He turned the sphere over and read from the message window: "*Outlook Good.* Hmph. Fat chance of that."

Moises reverently took the ball back. He slowly spun it around, tracing his crooked finger over its unnaturally smooth surface. He sniffed it, his eyes widening fractionally at its complete lack of smell. He tapped at the message window and scratched a fingernail over the painted number eight. It was clear he had never seen anything like it.

"This is a...toy?"

Paul nodded, his face softening. "For kids, yes. It doesn't really mean anything. Don't read too much into it."

Moises gently shook the ball up and down, once, twice, in a clumsy attempt at mimicking Paul. "Magic Eight Ball, will this evils be purged from my village?" He slowly turned it over and mouthed the words he saw there. Ari was impressed that not only could he speak English, but could read it as well. His impression of the man's intelligence took another upward leap. "*Cannot Predict Now.* How is this thing possible? This is serious *tejerha-na*. This is magics."

"No, not magic. It's a toy," Paulson insisted. "It doesn't mean anything. Really."

No matter what they said the chief continued to be amazed by the black orb, shaking it and peering at its answers over and over. They could hear him talking to it in both English and his native tongue. The chief was surprised when the message window always delivered its answer in the same blue English print. Ari didn't remember how many possible responses there were but after a while he was sure they started repeating themselves. Moises wasn't fazed and his enthusiasm never dimmed, his yellowed eyes alight.

Shortly after that, the door opened and Gonzalez was back again. He motioned for Ari, Frankie, and Paul to follow him. Paulson stared death at the huge man, which Gonzalez found humorous, Van Owen noticed, but the giant was cagy enough to keep the young Marine in front of him at all times as they walked. They bypassed the smaller structure where they had met with El Quemado before, and made their way to the large communal building. Along the way they noticed some children playing an obscure game with a stick and two leather-wrapped balls, squealing and giggling as they ran about in the big open area, carefree, the weight of current issues beyond them. Women of both the native and European types were walking in pairs or small groups and talking quietly, some carrying bundles of plants or rudimentary crockery. All the women in the village were bare-chested and sported black tattoos emblazoned from their waists up. One younger girl in her late teens and with longer blond hair stared at them openly as the group passed by. Her chest tattoo looked like a black phoenix exploding up from below, the upturned head and beak between her tiny breasts. An older lady snatched at her arm and dragged her along.

The group continued following Gonzalez. When they arrived at the communal hut a large table was set up, complete with a white tablecloth and four place settings of china, three on one side and a single one opposite. They took their seats in front of the three and waited while several armed men took up stations around them. El Quemado may enjoy strict obedience, Ari reflected, but he definitely doesn't take any chances.

Minutes later Roberto walked up, the tall translator in his wake as always. Van Owen remembered what Theodore had said back at the hospital and paid special attention to the man's shoes. He caught a brief glimpse and saw that, yes, they looked very expensive and probably Italian, as the ex-soldier had observed. Ari inspected him further and, even though he himself was more practical when it came to everyday clothing, he was familiar enough with higher quality items that he could tell their captor was no stranger to the finest stores. His slacks fit with crisp, tailored precision, the cuffs just brushing the top of his shoes, and his white shirt was gathered just so at the waist, accentuating his slimness. Theodore would have been suitably impressed, but also would've frowned in disapproval at the man's insistence at never removing his fedora. From what Ari had seen so far, their captor was very full of himself, and enjoyed showing off his material possessions.

He sat across from them and smiled grandly, his white teeth gleaming. Through the translator he said, "My apologies to all of you. I rarely have guests and I've forgotten my manners. You've been kept in that stuffy hut all day without so much as a decent bite to eat. We'll address that now." He snapped his fingers and several native women deposited large platters of food in front of them; green beans, zucchini, and other types of vegetables not grown locally and flown in, plus several bowls of fruit, more of the flatbread, and a huge slab of prime rib dripping in a dark red *au jus* sauce. For the second time that day Ari's mouth watered almost uncontrollably and he had to swallow several times. He looked to his left and right and saw Paul staring wide-eyed at the food as well, his Adam's apple bouncing up and down as he gulped repeatedly.

Roberto produced a dark bottle of red wine and deftly uncorked it. "It's a 2005 Cabernet," he said, sniffing the cork then setting the open bottle on the table. "It's a very good year and one of my favorites, actually, and is obscenely expensive. I purchased several dozen cases of it last year but I'm afraid it's nearly gone already. I will have to secure more from my contact overseas at this rate. Let's let it breathe a little then we can enjoy it."

Ari looked away from the steaming food before them. "Where's Hal Hollenbeck? I want to see him."

"It's amazing how much a fine bottle can go for these days," he continued, taking no notice of Ari's question. "A fine vintage like this would cost more than I made in a month when I was younger. Now I'm afraid I'm quite spoiled. I realize now that if I hadn't seen such riches I could live with being poor."

Frankie sat up a little straighter in her chair and addressed him, her voice cautious yet firm. "Roberto, where is their friend? What have you done with him?"

He spun the bottle to inspect the brown and gold label, then sighed and tilted his head at her. He scratched at his chin. "Your precious FBI agent hasn't been harmed, although he isn't enjoying a meal as fine as this. He is my guest as well."

"I still want to see him," Ari stated, pushing the subject.

El Quemado's face flushed but he held his temper in check. It took him a moment to master himself before he said, "No. Now we will enjoy our meal and you will see that I am a just, fair man at heart. Eat now."

He poured each of them a few fingers of the dark red wine, expertly spinning the bottle with a showy flourish so as not to spill a drop. Then he ladled food onto his plate and motioned for each of them to do the same. Frankie accepted a token amount, but Ari refused, his resolute silence communicating his sentiment better than any words could. Paul on the other hand scooped so much onto his plate that some beans slopped over onto the tablecloth. He tossed back the wine and began devouring the food, his eyes never straying from his meal. Roberto appeared annoyed at Ari but amused at the young Marine. He himself chewed slowly, savoring each bite, occasionally closing his eyes and leaning back in his chair. He was clearly relishing the meal and his time as their host.

He pointed a fork at Van Owen. "Are you sure you won't join me? It's really quite excellent, considering where we are."

Frankie nibbled at her small portion without any enthusiasm. After what Ari had witnessed earlier that afternoon, he found that no matter what his body's reaction was to the feast, his mind wouldn't allow him to break bread with this man. Roberto kept eating, finally accepting that Van Owen was going to rebuff his offer, and still amused at the vast quantities of food Paul shoveled into his mouth. When their host had finished he sat back and dabbed at his mouth with his napkin. This close they could all see how ravaged the skin on his hands was. A friend of Ari's in high school had once been burned on the arm with hot tar while doing some commercial roofing. These scars looked like that, a patchwork of multicolored and shiny skin that was, for the most part, hairless and smooth. Roberto sipped at his wine, inhaling noisily after each drink, letting air flow over his tongue to enhance the full body of the drink.

"You've got questions, I can see that. I'm not sure if it's the wine or such a fine meal, but I'm feeling generous. Ask what you will."

Paul paused in his chewing for just a moment. He poured himself more wine, tossed that back, and belched once. "Who's that big gorilla you've got hanging around? I don't like him much. He's starting to piss me off."

Roberto grinned and slapped the table in amusement. "You mean Mr. Gonzalez? I doubt anyone has called him a big gorilla to his face and gotten away with it. He is an employee, nothing more and nothing less. In my line of work you occasionally need people like him. I had initially tried to locate someone else, a crazy little man with a bit of a reputation, but he seems to have come up missing. Sadly that's not uncommon in this line of work." He leaned forward earnestly. "You may not realize it, but Mr. Gonzalez is actually quite intelligent. Much more than anyone would suspect. He also has quite a knack for surviving calamities that would claim a lesser man. But I must say, my young friend, I like your nerve. You've come a long way from our brief encounter at the hospital."

"Yeah, and you still owe me five thousand dollars, don't forget. I did my part."

It took their captor a moment to recall what he meant, then he clapped his hands together and laughed out loud. Ari himself wondered what the hell Paulson was up to: this combative attitude and baiting wasn't like him at all. "As a matter of fact I do! And you shall have your money before this is all over, I promise you." He turned to Van Owen. "And what about you? I'm sure you have questions for me."

"Yes, I do. This drug you're smuggling into the States, Ice. What is it? What does it do?"

"Excellent questions. But let's back up a little bit as it will make more sense that way. First and foremost, I consider myself a businessman, an entrepreneur, if you will. Several years ago I found myself, shall we say, less than welcome in my own country of Bolivia, due to some business endeavors I was involved in. So I left and subsequently set up a base of operations several miles from here, away from prying eyes, fickle police, and two-faced politicians. We were beginning to dabble with different types of drugs, different combinations, trying to come up with something new, something no one had ever seen before, or at least a variant of

403

an existing product that would stand out." He leaned forward and his eyes were dancing now, warming to his subject. He was also delighted at hearing the sound of his own voice, Ari was quickly learning. "The problem with today's market is that the run-of-the-mill drugs like marijuana, cocaine, LSD, and heroin – they've all become commoditized."

"Commoditized?" Paulson asked around a mouthful of food.

"Yes, they've become little more than commodities, like milk or bread. They can be bought cheaply from nearly anyone, anywhere, any time, on any big city corner in America. There's no exclusivity and the market is a glutted mess. And don't even get me started on methamphetamines or the fact that some states in your USA have legalized marijuana and are selling it in storefronts, like cigarettes or beer. No, for the most part anyone with half a brain can make and distribute these commodities, to the point where the price has plummeted and dealers are more concerned with killing each other than breaking new ground. They're idiots, but they're vicious idiots. It's a jungle out there." He chuckled at his own joke.

"But to make real money, to be truly successful, then you need something new, something fresh, a drug no one else has and that doesn't routinely kill your customer base. That's what I wanted." He paused and took a measured sip of his wine. The translator never moved, just relaxed in his chair and waited for him to talk again. The instant Spanish to English translation still amazed Ari, and despite himself he was intrigued at the man's story.

"As I said, with my hasty exit from Bolivia I came here, to the jungle. I'd heard whispers and tales of tribes that had some truly amazing concoctions derived from indigenous plants and insects, and I was hoping to find something that would fit my needs."

Ari thought back to the bug repellant and the clear gel-like substance Josiah had produced and that they'd used on Paulson's leg. Both were nothing short of miraculous. He nodded.

"I'd been experimenting not far from here with some of my people when there was an...accident. An explosion. To be completely honest, I was near death when one of the people from this village found me and nursed me back to health. And it was then that I uncovered some of the amazing medical wonders this particular tribe had discovered over the centuries. The most intriguing substance, the one that truly caught my eye, was a concoction they used sparingly and infrequently, part of a male purification ceremony. They tried to describe it to me and I even tried their version once myself. It was perfect. Exactly what I was looking for. You can imagine my excitement! After time and much work my men managed to synthesize it in greater quantities than ever before, and even improved upon it. It was this drug that you call Ice."

"But what does it do? Besides kill some people, like that baseball player in Ohio, that one named Garrafon?"

The joy and amusement in Roberto's face quickly leeched away at the mention of that name. His expression turned dour and it took him several breaths before he could continue, but deep down Ari had a funny feeling the man was acting, that he wasn't all that torn up. "Ah, young Carlos. He was my nephew, my sister's son. He found out I was working on Ice and begged me to let him try it. I was reluctant but he was very insistent. Honestly, he was desperate. His career was not going well and he felt he needed help to regain his prior form." He leaned forward, his elbows on the table, sadness drawing down the corners of his dark eyes. His voice grew soft. "I'm sorry to say that I hadn't quite perfected the mixture yet. He saw amazing results right away. His career took off again with that other team."

"With Cincinnati. The Reds," Paul pointed out.

"Yes, with them. But eventually, as you have likely guessed, he used too much. I'm afraid in the end it killed him."

"I bet that makes family gatherings a little awkward," Paulson said around a mouthful of prime rib. Ari thought Roberto might not take Paul's quip well, that he might not appreciate the snarky comment, especially as quick to anger as he'd shown to be. But their captor sniffed and patted at the corners of his eyes with the napkin. When he finally spoke again his voice held the slightest quiver. As phenomenal as his abilities were, however, the translator didn't or couldn't replicate the trembling.

"I haven't seen my sister since, and I don't know when I will again. It's very sad."

No one knew quite what to say at that point, although Ari didn't feel any great sorrow at his loss, not with what they'd seen from Roberto since. That, and Ari still had a feeling that the man wasn't as torn up as he wanted them to believe. In fact, a sneaking suspicion tugged at the back of his mind that perhaps, just perhaps, El Quemado had planted the idea with his nephew to try his new drug so he could see how well it worked in a high-pressure professional sports setting. How else would Garrafon have heard about Ice and what it could do? The ensuing silence was punctuated by the distant buzzing of cicadas, the complaining of several monkeys in a nearby tree, and the sharp clanking of silverware on fine china as Paul continued to eat unabated. When enough time had elapsed Ari cleared his throat.

"You still haven't told me what Ice actually does."

"What does it do? Well, it's difficult to describe since I've only tried it the one time, and that was the less potent tribal version. From what I've seen and been told it produces a sense of...clarity, I guess is the best word. The external world seems to almost slow down, or perhaps it's better described as if the mind speeds up."

"So it's an amphetamine?" Ari asked. "That's it? There's a million of those out there already. Those are nothing new."

"No, no, it's not that simple. Amphetamines are used for many purposes, recreationally of course, and also in the treatment of

ADHD and narcolepsy. One of its effects on humans is the perception of what it does instead of what it actually does. Yes, athletes use it to increase performance, students use it as a study aid, and plenty of people take it for recreational purposes. But Ice is different."

"How so?"

"Because someone on Ice actually sees and experiences the outside world in a completely different way. Time is not frozen, but almost seems to slow down, to give the user more of an opportunity to think and react. Before he died this is what Carlos told me: if a baseball player on Ice is at bat and the pitcher throws a 95 mile per hour fastball, instead of the ball reaching him in a split second it seems to be traveling much slower, so slow the batter has more time to see it. He can decide whether or not to swing, and to adjust his swing accordingly. He can even tell what spin is on the ball by the way the seams are moving. Or in the field, when a ball is hit toward him he has so much more time to decide how to play the ball, to judge how it's coming toward him, where it will bounce, plus what the other players around him are doing. It's nothing short of fantastic."

"That's why Garrafon was doing so much better, in the end," Ari said.

"Exactly. The month before he died he was on Ice for every game. His play during that period was spectacular. I saw many of his games in person. If you watched him you could see it. His batting average more than doubled and his fielding was unparalleled."

Paulson lifted his eyes from his plate. "Until it killed him."

"Yes, until it killed him. But consider it: what athlete out there wouldn't use Ice to improve his performance? Performance is money, and fame, and prestige, and so many of them are always striving for more of them all. It could easily be used in football, soccer, hockey, boxing. And there's no reason to stop there. Think about any endeavor where reaction time is a factor: driving, flying, or any activity where the ability to see outside events at a much slower pace is enhanced. And these athletes command huge paychecks. So tell me – which of them wouldn't be happy to pay handsomely to maintain or increase their levels of performance? Answer? Almost all would."

Paul finally finished his meal. He'd been quiet for the most part, listening without appearing to. He pushed his plate away and idly picked at a tooth with his index finger. Finally he said, "A soldier would kill for that ability."

Roberto considered this for several seconds. When he spoke it was as if he were thinking aloud. "In a heated battle, on the ground against an enemy? Yes, he would. He wouldn't be invincible, of course. He couldn't dodge a bullet, but he could see the entire field of battle in a vastly superior way. His chances of survival and winning would be increased tenfold at least." Roberto tilted his head back and looked to the heavens, now deep in thought. He tapped his finger on the table in a steady cadence and Ari could see the dollar signs multiplying in his mind. "I may have underestimated you, my young man. That is an entirely new market I hadn't considered before. Imagine government militaries vying for my business. Imagine the bidding…" He turned to Paulson, admiration clear in his voice. "Well done. I may owe you more than five thousand dollars for that. Someone once said that 'vision is seeing before believing.' My vision of what Ice will be continues to expand."

Ari wished that Paul hadn't said anything. They didn't need to give this lunatic any more ideas, and helping him was the last thing he wanted to do. Had he been able to kick Paul underneath the table he would have done so. He shot him a quick, withering look that the young man ignored.

Roberto reached into his pocket and deposited a small black bag on the table. He reached into the bag and withdrew several identical objects, each about the size and shape of large marble. But they were made of thin, malleable plastic instead of glass, and each one had a stubby needle protruding from one side and a hoop attached on the other. To Ari they looked like evil Ring Pops.

"What are those?" he asked.

Roberto held it out, admiring it. "To work effectively the drug needs to be injected into the bloodstream. Once the brown paste is reconstituted and made into doses of Ice, I knew I needed a way for an individual to quickly and easily administer the drug, especially if there wasn't time to use more traditional syringes. My people came up with this. Inside each pouch is an exact dose of Ice. You slide this ring on," he said, carefully sliding it onto his middle finger so that the pouch containing the drug was in his palm, needle out, and could be neatly hidden from view. "When you're ready you simply slap the needle against your arm or leg and press down, injecting the drug. It's quick and easy and can be done unobtrusively. And unlike syringes that tend to be used over and over, sometimes with very grave consequences, these ampules are single use only. I'll be selling Ice this way around the world." He smiled wide, pleased with himself. "As I said, I don't believe in killing my customers, unlike most idiotic drug dealers." He held the device out like a jeweler admiring an expensive bauble, then put them all back in the bag and pocketed them again.

Roberto pushed himself away from the table, his enthusiasm blossoming. "But enough talk. Let's take a walk and I will show you my operation firsthand. I think you'll be impressed. Come with me."

Everyone at the table stood and followed as he strode away, their captor rightly assuming they'd be right behind him. They made their way through the village and across the open expanse of dirt, the translator and two armed guards quietly shadowing them. They walked towards the contraption with the two vats, the machine Paul had dubbed the Ice Maker. This close they could see three large propane tanks tucked off to the side, big white tanks each about the size of a refrigerator. They could hear a steady hissing noise as blue flames licked the bottom of each vat. The vats themselves gurgled and pinged softly as the contents were kept at a steady boil. They went around the Ice Maker and followed another narrow path through the thick underbrush. They'd gone several hundred yards when they came upon a second clearing, this one much newer than the one housing the village, evidenced by stumps cut low to the ground and the ragged ends of bushes and branches all around them. In the center of this football field-sized opening was a white helicopter with dark markings. Ari didn't know anything about aircraft, but to him it looked like traffic copters he'd seen flying low over cities, or ones the news stations used to report breaking stories. Roberto affectionately brushed his hand along its smooth flank then continued on, following another path. It was hot outside, and when the sun hit them it felt like an actual weight had settled on their heads.

They walked for another ten minutes before El Quemado motioned them to a halt. Through the ubiquitous translator he said, "Up ahead you will have to stay on the path. At times we'll be walking on an elevated walkway. For your own safety, don't stray."

Ari's natural curiosity begged to ask why, but before he could say anything their captor moved on. They followed again and soon found themselves on a narrow walkway made of rough lumber, not more than two feet wide, moving up into the jungle. At this low height there were no handrails, but at this point they were only a foot or so up, just high enough to stay above the jungle floor. Soon, however, the elevation increased to where they were nearly ten feet off the ground and looking down on foliage that appeared untouched, a green expanse marked here and there with yellow and red flowers, striated leaves, and huge trees that opened up into the canopy overhead. Van Owen began to see bright yellow bags suspended on thick sticks just above the plane of the underbrush. At first there were just a few dotting the vast area below them, but the concentration of the bags increased the farther they walked until

410

there was one every few feet. The bags were not much bigger than a saline bag in a hospital, but they were open at the top. He couldn't imagine what they were for.

Now there was a railing on one side, which was a blessing since they were at least fifteen feet up and crossing a wide, slow-moving creek. The sluggish body of water was less than twenty feet from shore to shore at this point, but very deep, the bottom hidden well below its murky depths. Something large and dark moved down there and caused a sudden ripple in the black water. Ari looked up and saw that the blue sky from earlier had given way to clouds, thick heavy ones that marched across the narrow break in the canopy. Still they walked on, the wooden pathway creaking and swaying under their combined weight. Paulson seemed quite at home at this elevation and never bothered reaching for the railing, but Frankie held on tightly as she walked, sometimes with two hands. With a start Ari realized he hadn't known she was afraid of heights. After crossing over the creek he could see wooden ladders that gave access to the jungle floor positioned every so often. Just as he was about to ask what was going on Roberto stopped. He motioned down to the jungle's surface and pointed out a dozen or so of the yellow bags placed randomly below them. Van Owen saw some movement down there. He peered more closely and picked out one of the villagers tending to a yellow bag. The man was one of the non-European natives, a pure Amazonian tribesman, built stout and short, his torso thick, his black hair as smooth and shiny as an oil-slicked rock. He was naked except for a swatch of cloth around his middle. He reached into one of the yellow bags with a long set of tweezers. He plucked something out, inspected it, and inserted it into a pouch clipped onto a rope around his waist. They were too far away to see exactly what he was doing, but Ari thought he knew.

"Those are bullet ants he's gathering up, aren't they?"

"Very good, Arjen Van Owen," Roberto said, and Ari felt the familiar wave of annoyance at the use of his full first name. Did the man know it would piss him off? But on the plus side he could tell that El Quemado was both a little surprised and miffed that someone had stolen his thunder, which gave him a small measure of satisfaction. "There are many other workers down here that you can't see, and they're all collecting bullet ants. Or, since you seem to know so much, you may also know them as *Paraponera clavata*. In the yellow sacks is a thick liquid, a gel. It's infused with the essence of a bullet ant queen to attract the ants. They can't help themselves when they capture her scent. They climb up the post and fall into the bag and are stuck in the gel. My workers go from sack to sack and collect the ants, putting them in those pouches you see at their waists. When their pouch is full they bring them back to the processing machine, then head back out for more."

It was clear this was all new to Frankie. As much as she knew, there was still much she didn't. She was watching the native carefully, concern clear in her voice. "But what if they get bitten? The bites from those ants are supposed to be excruciating, almost debilitating."

Roberto held up a finger and smiled. "That's why this village and these people are so vital to the operation. Over the centuries and generations the men here have developed an incredible immunity to the bites. What would take down you or me feels like nothing more than a mosquito bite to them. It's quite fascinating, really. And what is truly amazing is that because of this immunity I can't even test my drug on them. It works, but to such a lesser degree that as test subjects they're almost worthless. But that's where the other men, the mixed-breed types, come in. With their European genes they make perfect test subjects."

It was all clear to Ari now. "You've got the pure-bred tribesmen to do the work, and the European ones to use as guinea pigs."

"Exactly. Thanks to significant trial and error on these villagers I've finally got the dosage and concentration down to a science. The concentrated compound, the brown paste that's so easy to transport

412

and move into your country and that can cause what you call sudden onset paralysis, is nearly ready to be reconstituted and sold in individual doses in the ampules. The first few batches that made it into your country were not quite ready, I must admit, but now I'm ready to go to market. I'm the sole possessor of Ice and I will be able to sell it to the highest bidders, and I will finally be rich beyond my dreams. My vision will become reality."

Paulson had been listening intently. He hadn't said anything in a while, but when he spoke his voice was measured and hard, a steel rod wrapped in cotton. "You realize that hundreds of people have died because of you, right? And perhaps thousands have had their lives disrupted or damaged because of all this?"

"Who do you mean? These savages? Tell me truthfully, my young friend – who will miss them if they vanish forever? No one even knows they exist. The plane going down was unfortunate, of course. The idiot pilots must have somehow come in contact with the condensed paste. Any break in the skin or any other way the concentrated paste could make it into the bloodstream can mean an overdose and death for some, but not all. Most people, like your husband, Mrs. Brubaker, can touch it without recourse, as he has with preliminary batches several times in the past. These foolish pilots should have never touched it. The fault and the deaths of those people are on their shoulders, not mine."

Ari couldn't believe his ears, couldn't fathom what El Quemado had just said. The fact that the man accepted no responsibility for his actions nearly floored him. How could someone be that incredibly delusional?

"And besides," he went on, quite sincerely, "tell me how this differs from a gun manufacturer? He simply makes the weapon, he doesn't open fire on a theater full of people. There's no difference here. I'm simply providing the product. How it is used from that point is outside my control."

413

Van Owen was watching both Frankie and Paulson. He knew there would be no arguing with this man, and he was hoping the other two realized that as well. When he was a boy his mother used to say that you couldn't argue with crazy, and El Quemado was one hundred percent crazy. Paul was holding any emotion in check, but it looked like Frankie was about to burst. Her sense of fairness and humanity was clear. Before either of them could do anything rash he asked, "So what then? What happens after they collect the bullet ants?"

"They take them back to the processing machine, the one we passed near the large clearing, and we begin the process. It takes literally several thousand ants before I can begin each batch. Each ant contains such a tiny amount of the poneratoxin. The insects themselves are ground up and a rather complex process of fermentation and filtering begins. We use several varieties of local plants as well as a substantial amount of water and heat in the procedure, which takes more than two weeks to complete. When that's done we have a small quantity of the brown paste, an amount about the size of a golf ball. From that ball I can reconstitute the drug into several hundred doses of Ice."

"Sounds like you've got all this figured out," Paulson said.

"Of course I do. This has been planned for months. I've got my initial contacts in the US waiting for this batch, and we'll begin sales in earnest soon. The crash of the airliner in Kentucky set me back a month or so, but I'll be back on track in just a few weeks. And even though the first few batches of Ice that hit the States over the last few months were not exactly perfect, they were still received quite well. I've got many, many orders to fill. My network is coming along nicely, starting on the east coast and moving west. Word on the street is getting out, virally, just as I had planned. Excitement is ramping up."

Below them they could see more of the natives picking their way carefully through the jungle. One man several dozen yards away shouted in surprise and held up a yellow bag. Inside they could see a black mass squirming. While none of them could make out details from this distance Ari just knew the bag was full to the brim with the prized ants. The native quickly and with surgical precision plucked out twenty or thirty of the nearly half-inch long insects and deftly shoved them in his pouch. He looked up at El Quemado and smiled.

"That man and his family shall be eating well tonight. I know how to show proper appreciation for good work."

As they watched, fat raindrops began pelting them, a smattering at first that quickly grew into a steady shower. El Quemado looked to the heavens and shrugged. He spoke softly, almost to himself, and the translator repeated, "Well look at that. The Eight Ball was right after all. It's raining." He glared at the translator who simply stared back at him dispassionately, his huge, bulging eyes indifferent. Apparently he wasn't supposed to translate that last sentence. Their captor growled something at him then turned and squeezed past them all, the lesson completed. They stood there in the rain until the armed guards nudged them and they followed him back the way they had come.

Chapter 24

On their walk back, their captor said that from this point on they would have free reign of the village, and didn't see any reason to restrict them to the hut. Compliance, they all knew, was guaranteed after what had happened to the old woman. Regardless, everyone felt the small hut was home base and headed back there, especially since it was now pouring outside and there was nowhere else to go. When they got back Butch was waiting inside for them. His flat face and wide-set eyes were haunted and deep, despair written in the lines etched across his forehead. When he saw Frankie he jumped up from the cot and embraced her. For nearly a minute they all stood still and watched them. Frankie didn't return the hug at first, but in time her arms drifted up around his neck. Ari felt a strange combination of emotions in his gut that he fought to keep from his face. Finally Butch broke the embrace but wouldn't let her go completely, holding her at arm's length.

"I'm so, so sorry," he said to her, his voice low and trembling. They all felt like intruders on their conversation, but in the small hut it couldn't be helped. "It was never supposed to be like this. I...I screwed everything up."

Frankie didn't immediately reply. Off to the side they could hear Father Sean mumbling into his hand and the clicking of his rosary beads as he paced. Paul went and sat on the ground next to Moises, perfectly comfortable with the elderly native. Ari didn't know what to do so he stood by the door in silence, emotions battling with logic within his heart and mind. Seeing the two of them together was almost more than he could handle and he nearly walked out, pouring rain or not. All this time it had been relatively easy to tell himself he was only doing this to find Frankie, that saving her was his one true goal. But now that he was here with her and seeing how she reacted to Butch, seeing them together...it nearly crushed him and he felt a part of his soul cry out.

"Yes, you did. What were you thinking?"

"I was just trying to give you everything you ever wanted. I wanted to make you happy. That's all."

She touched his cheek tenderly, just two fingertips that traced his jawline before drifting up to his lips. It was a motion she'd done to Ari back when they were together but one that was theirs now. "But don't you understand? I was happy. I've always been happy with you. We had everything we ever wanted or needed."

He dipped his head and Ari knew the man was close to tears. This was a side of Butch he'd never seen before, and it impacted him more than he thought possible. "I...I know, I guess. But I wanted to do more, and this was a way to get that. I love you and I just wanted the best for you. That's all I ever wanted."

Frankie guided him to the cot and the two of them sat down, Butch a little clumsily. "I love you, too, my dearest," she said softly, her head now resting on his shoulder. Her ponytail had fallen in front of her and was draped across his chest. "I didn't need or want anything else. I had you, and that's all I need."

From where he sat Paulson spoke up. "Super. I'm glad to see you two lovebirds are together again. But, really, Judas, thanks for tossing all of us under the bus." He swept out a hand to encompass the group. "Now what? How are we going to get out of here? You know he's never going to let us go, right?"

Brubaker glanced up, his eyes momentarily distant and unfocused. "What do you mean?"

"I mean, our happy host's got you now. He'll hold onto your wife forever just to make sure you don't screw up again. He's never going to let the rest of us go. Me, Hal, and Ari here, he'll either keep us prisoners or kill us and keep your wife forever. Either way, we're all pretty screwed. Thanks a lot."

Butch stared at him. Ari could tell that he'd been so intent on finding his wife that he hadn't thought beyond that event. He'd been so driven to save Frankie that he'd never considered the

417

ramifications or potential final outcome. Realization that Paulson was right finally began to move across his face, and he almost seemed to crumple in on himself, to shrink in size and stature. His head fell into his hands and he moaned as if in pain.

"Paul's right," Ari said, trying not to feel pity for the man. "We're probably dead men walking. He's having fun now showing off his plans and operation, strutting around, being full of himself. Deep down I think he's pretty insecure and paranoid, and as soon as he's got what information he wants from Hal I think we'll end up like that poor old lady did, with bullets in our heads."

Ari could see Butch adding all this up in his head, and he impatiently waited for the man to come to that inevitable conclusion. He resisted the urge to yell at him to get there faster. Butch's dark eyes shifted left and right as he thought everything through, and when he'd factored in all the future variables he sat up.

"You're right," he admitted to all of them. "We're screwed. I've fucked it all up for sure. He'll never let you go. He'll keep Frankie here forever. We'll never be free of him. What have I done?"

"So what was your end-game here, Butch?" Paulson asked. "Were you in on this the whole time? Were you just trying to get us here for our happy host?"

Brubaker shook his head, his eyes wide and pleading. "No, I mean, not really. When Hal asked me to come I nearly freaked out. I mean, I had just found out that she'd been kidnapped and who had her. I had to call *him* and see what he wanted me to do." He was talking fast and had to stop to take a deep breath. "He said to help you get down here, especially Hal, so he could find out everything the FBI knew. I agreed to help, I had to, but I really wanted to get here, steal Frankie out under his nose, and just get back to the States. I just wanted her to be safe, and now..."

Paulson stared at him for a few moments, then nodded. No one could tell if he was forgiving Butch his actions, or if he was simply acknowledging them. When no one said anything else Ari pushed off the door. Everyone looked his way.

"That's all well and good, but we're all stuck here. So the question becomes, how do we get out of here? Or how do we stop him?"

He looked from person to person, hopefully, but to that question no one had an immediate answer.

Over the next few days they had unencumbered freedom around the immediate village. They were stopped from taking the path to the helicopter, which also kept them from the wooden walkway leading to the harvesting area with the yellow bags. Josiah was free as well, and he and Paul spent quite a bit of time together doing little more than talking and walking around. They had to suffer through several more meals with their captor, but as the days passed he seemed to grow bored with that and they saw him less and less. There was never a time when the man wasn't protected by at least two or three guards and the translator, and many times the giant, Gonzalez, was with him, too. None of them had any hopes of killing their host in order to put an end to this, much to their dismay. Worst of all, to Ari at least, was that he wasn't allowed access to Hal.

"He's in the hut at the far end, I just know it," Paul said. "There are always guards at the door and any time I get near it someone shoves a gun up my nose."

Van Owen had to agree. He'd brought the agent's name up several times and was summarily shot down by their captor. Now that he imagined that his death was not far off, he found he was much bolder than before. During one meal with El Quemado he'd pushed so far for an audience with Hal that for a second he was certain their host was going to shoot him dead over his plate of chicken and rice. But at the last second their captor had taken a deep breath and poured another glass of wine, finally grinning. Even so, Ari could sense how close he'd come to death.

419

Several days later, when Paul was idly walking around the village, Gonzalez rounded a hut and they nearly collided. Both men stopped and faced one another, neither man willing to step aside, testosterone practically dripping onto the ground around them. Paulson had to crane his neck to meet the giant's black eyes.

"What are you looking at, you big ape?" he said loudly, so loud that others around the village turned to see what was happening. "Get out of my way."

Ari saw what was certain to be a bloody, nasty outcome and hustled over, interposing his body between the two men and forcibly pushing the young man back. He leaned into the Marine, his face close. He could see Paulson's nostrils flaring and the rush of red in his cheeks.

"What the hell are you doing?" he hissed. "Are you trying to get yourself killed? That guy'll tear you apart!"

"I don't care. I don't like him and he's getting on my nerves!"

In prior encounters Gonzalez had appeared amused with Paul and his bravado, but this time was different. The giant was clearly annoyed and Ari was afraid the brute was going to lash out with one of those cantaloupe-sized fists. He couldn't imagine the damage the behemoth could do when angered. He forced Paulson back and away from a confrontation the young man couldn't hope to win. In the distance he spotted El Quemado watching safely from between two armed men. Their captor stared for a moment before moving on.

"What the hell was that all about?" he asked him, but Paul wouldn't say anything. He shook off Ari's hands and stalked away, his back stiff. He watched as Josiah fell into step next to him and together they rounded another hut and were gone. He couldn't understand what Paulson was doing.

Back at their home base he found Frankie and Butch together on the cot, a spot they frequented often. Moises was quietly holding court with the Eight Ball, and Father Sean was doing little besides wearing a deeper path in the dirt floor as he paced. His mumbling had receded into the background, no more obtrusive than a neighbor's lawnmower on a lazy summer day.

"Have any of you talked to Paul lately? I'm worried about him."

No one had. Moises looked up from the black orb. "He confers with Josiah oftens. About what I don't knows. Josiah looks up to him."

Van Owen nodded. The two of them had been spending a lot of time together. He'd noticed that, too. He just wished that Paul would open up to him and tell him what he was thinking. He was afraid the young man was reaching a breaking point and would do something rash, something that might get him killed. Their situation was slowly grinding them all down. The waiting and their inability to act was the worst.

Paul and Gonzalez got into it the next day, and this time Ari wasn't there to intercede. Before anyone knew about it the confrontation was over, and a very dazed and bewildered Paul was helped into the hut by Josiah. The young Marine could barely stand and was gasping for breath. Frankie and Ari rushed to help Josiah and together they settled him onto the cot.

"What happened?" Van Owen demanded urgently.

"He fought with the big man," Josiah said, his English already greatly improved. The time spent with Paulson had done wonders. "He did not win the fight."

Frankie pushed them all aside and knelt next to him. "What exactly happened? Did he get hit in the head? Did he lose consciousness? I need details!"

She had spoken so fast there wasn't a prayer Josiah could follow her. Ari saw Moises watching and told him to translate, which he did. The young native listened then answered him quickly.

"He was not hit hards, and not in the head," the chief said. "The large bloke hit him in the chest and this one fell and hit his head on the ground."

Paul pushed their hands away and sat up, his breathing easing up. He rubbed the back of his head and winced at the bump there. "I'm okay, really. I'm fine."

"Dammit, Paul, why do you keep picking fights with that monster? He's going to kill you!" Ari barked at him, both concern and anger lacing his tone.

"True dat," Josiah said, clear as a bell.

Van Owen did a double-take. *True dat?* Apparently Paulson was teaching him colloquial English along the way. It was impressive how much he'd picked up in such a short amount of time. Despite their current situation he took a moment to consider how far the young native had come, and how intelligent he must truly be. English was a terribly difficult language to pick up, what with all its idioms and exceptions to rules and odd conjugations. There were many speakers born to the language that still managed to mangle it on a daily basis.

Paul stood and brushed them away. "I'm fine, guys. Don't worry about it."

"Fine? That monster could stomp you like a grape if he wanted to!"

But the young man wouldn't say any else. He went and sat on the ground by Moises and closed his eyes, his arms wrapped around drawn-up knees. Ari and the rest were left to wonder what was going on with him, and to worry what stupid stunt he might pull next. Despite how much he'd helped during the trip, Van Owen was left to wish he'd never brought him along in the first place. The idiot was bound and determined to get himself killed.

Gonzalez came to their hut the next morning. "Come with me," he rumbled, his accent as heavy and thick as ever. The two armed

422

guards with him motioned with their rifles and everyone but Father Sean fell into step behind them. They followed the trio to the open area beyond the communal hut where they spotted El Quemado. The ornate table from their first formal meeting had been set up and he was seated behind it, lording over the growing crowd, a king holding court. All his guards were standing around in a wide circle, one probably fifty feet in diameter. Ari counted fifteen of them, which he was pretty sure was the entire contingent. The translator of course was seated next to him, still appearing as relaxed and at ease as ever. His bulging eyes tracked them dispassionately as they approached. When they all stood before the table their captor spoke.

"I believe it's time for some entertainment," he began. "With my latest batch of the condensed drug nearly ready we will soon be too busy to spare a minute."

"What are you talking about?" Ari demanded, stepping forward.

"I'm talking about having some fun, of course. We've all seen the bad blood between your young man, Mr. Paulson, and my own Mr. Gonzalez. I think it's time they were able to settle things once and for all. They will fight."

"No! That's insane! Paul can't fight that giant. He'll be killed!"

"Roberto, please no," Frankie pleaded, her hands out, beseeching him. She ran up to his table. "Please don't do this!"

El Quemado ignored them and stood, brushing her aside. He clapped his hands several times and yelled out for everyone to gather around. He barked orders to several of the guards who hustled off and rounded up any of the women and children who were in the village and not currently burdened with chores. He stood behind the ornate table in his crisply pressed slacks and white shirt, his dark fedora shielding his face, and waited patiently, dark eyes tracking people as they approached. When it looked like everyone was present Ari figured there had to be fifty or more people in a ragged circle, most of them natives, and all of them murmuring quietly with each other. Finally Roberto said something in Spanish to Gonzalez, who was standing nearby. The huge man listened then compressed his lips and shook his head no, crossing his arms in defiance. Roberto snapped at him again and still the huge man refused to budge. Their captor's face flushed bright red and he rattled off something fast and angry at several of his men. They raised their guns and aimed them at the giant, the black muzzles pointed unwavering at his massive, shaggy head. Gonzalez stared hot death at El Quemado but finally nodded and stepped into the open area in front of the table. Paul took a deep breath and started toward him. Ari grabbed him.

"No! You can't do this!"

Roberto snapped off a command and another guard raised his rifle and pointed it at Frankie. "Yes, I can, and I will," the translator said. "You forget who is in charge of this village and everyone here. If you interfere I will have her shot in the stomach. She will suffer horribly and it will be on your head. The choice is yours."

Paul turned and stared directly into Ari's eyes. In a low, measured voice, he said very clearly, "Don't worry. This is what I want and it's why I'm here. To fix what I did wrong back in Louisville."

"It's time," El Quemado declared from behind the table, impatience turning the normal tone of his voice harsh. "As Faulker once said, 'Men have been pacifists for every reason under the sun except to avoid danger and fighting.' Neither of you are pacifists. I've seen it in your eyes. Now!"

Van Owen leaned in close. "But, Paul. He'll kill you."

And then Paulson did something Ari never saw coming. The young man smiled at him and winked. "I don't think so. Remember – think, plan, then attack." He reached down and unzipped a pocket on his pant leg. From it he withdrew one of the Ice ampules that their captor had showed them several days before. *Where had he gotten that?* In one smooth motion he slapped it against his arm and pressed hard, keeping it there for several seconds. His eyes closed and Ari could see a shiver run up and down his body. His light skin flushed with a reddish hue. He breathed deeply and stepped away. He looked up at Gonzalez.

"Welcome to Thunderdome, bitch," he growled.

And then something amazing happened. The two men squared off and the fight began, and in no time it was clear that Paul was winning.

Chapter 25

As far as accommodations went, Hal Hollenbeck considered, he'd seen and experienced a lot worse in his day. A *lot* worse. The time in Afghanistan was foremost in his mind and picked up the Trip Advisor five-star rating for the biggest hell-hole of his entire career. The Taliban had snatched him from a remote outpost and tossed him in a pit no larger than the trunk of a Buick, located somewhere deep in the mountains. No light, water, or toilet facilities for days, and worst of all he'd had to share the squalid quarters with a dead Afghan soldier. No, he thought, that wasn't the worst part of it – the fact that nobody had known he was there ranked right up there, too. He'd gone to the outpost undercover so no one in the military or FBI would even acknowledge his existence. He'd been terrified he'd die there and nobody would ever miss him. With no wife, kids, or close relatives he was sure he'd simply vanish and end up as a memorial star on the walls of FBI headquarters, just one more agent killed in the line of duty who would be mourned and slowly, inexorably forgotten.

He sat back against the sturdy center post in the hut and cleaned his glasses absently. This casual, calming act had begun years earlier as an affectation, a forced pause designed to give him time to think during interrogations, operations, or any other time he needed an extra moment. People tended to give a person cleaning their glasses those few additional seconds, no matter now impatient they really were. But he'd been doing it for so long now that it had become an ingrained habit, an act he did without realizing it. He held the glasses up to the meager light shining around the closed door and, satisfied they were as clean as possible, slid them back on. Honestly, he could see rather well without them, but their presence was soothing and he appreciated having them.

The hut was like any of the others in the village: small, made of thin but stout tree trunks, and covered with thatch that had to be augmented or replaced frequently due to mold, rain, or wind. Pushing through a wall wouldn't have been too difficult, but the armed guards always stationed outside would have been alerted to his actions immediately, not to mention he was secured to a large wooden stake in the ground by a thick metal chain shackled to his ankle. He'd tugged and yanked at that stake and chain so long his hands were blistered and raw, but the fire-hardened spike was driven so far into the ground he was surprised it hadn't struck oil. He was not going to break free of that, he was certain, not without tools or additional muscle.

He leaned back against the central post and relaxed. The remains of a simple meal were on a metal plate next to him. There was a hunk of crust left from earlier and he picked it up and munched on it absently. Hal was thirsty but his small water ration was long gone. He was worried, but he didn't allow that worry to translate to fear. He had known going into this what could happen, and had accepted the consequences. What would paralyze most other people, people like his friend Ari, didn't have the same effect on him: it was training, yes, but it was also a state of mind that separated him from others. It was an acceptance of his current situation, but an acceptance that he wouldn't permit to equate to defeat, not without a fight.

Thinking of Ari did cause him concern, however. His friend had suspected that the agent was holding back information, and of course he was right. Hal had known much more than he'd been able to share with any of his travel companions. He felt a twinge of guilt at this, but only a twinge. It fell under the auspices of the age-old adage that some of this was on a need to know basis, and they hadn't needed to know everything.

For example, he was well aware that Butch was involved in this from before they'd left Kentucky. The Bureau hadn't known exactly what had brought the airliner down, but they'd been able to work backwards to the time when the handoff to the pilot, Eric Handler, had been made in Brasilia. What had been passed to Handler they'd had no idea, but drugs had always been suspected. They had informants on the payroll everywhere – in the airports, in the city, and even a few around the outskirts of Brasilia itself - and while they weren't always reliable, the FBI had learned after 9/11 that having locals on the ground with their eyes and ears open was still better than the mass collection of data that was going on at the NSA and CIA. They'd also concluded that Butch was somehow involved soon after the crash, and had quickly determined that he was probably a conduit of some sort. That was why he needed him on the trip, to keep an eye on him and to help lead them to the source. Hal considered him a glorified delivery boy, same as their captor. But in the end it was the head honcho they'd wanted, this man he now knew as El Quemado, or Roberto.

He'd also known Ari's whereabouts for several months prior to visiting him that first day. He'd had a feeling they might need the man again, so he'd spent considerable time and resources finding and keeping tabs on him. His friend was smart, granted, but few people could evade the FBI for long, especially anyone living in the US.

Another reason he hadn't shared more with Ari and the rest was because of his current predicament. The less they knew the less they could tell, as simple as that. And besides, anything he'd told Butch could've ended up in El Quemado's lap directly. That was unacceptable and couldn't be tolerated.

He kicked at the metal plate and tried to get comfortable. A few hours had passed since the behemoth, the one they called Gonzalez, had been back to see him. Oddly the big enforcer never actually touched or harmed Hal, much to the agent's surprise. He'd had him pegged as being the muscle of the bunch, all brawn and no brains. Instead, he typically stood there with the translator, who asked questions and demanded information on the giant's behalf. Now that man, the one he had started calling Frog Eyes, fascinated him. The guy was talented beyond belief and Hal would've loved to get him back to the States and put him on the FBI's payroll. There was always a place for someone like him. Rain dollars on a person like that and they could become an ally, or at least an ally of convenience. Anyway, the two of them would stand there and demand information while the guards went about their business with him. When it came to torture and extracting information these people were rookies, he mused: their tactics were stuck in the past, back when simple beatings, slaps, screams, and humiliation were all the rage. The circumstances following the downing of the Twin Towers and all that had transpired at Gitmo had reiterated to the intelligence community that these methods were about 99% unreliable, nearly useless. People in extreme pain tended to tell you what you wanted to hear, to implicate innocents, to sell out even their wife and kids, to say whatever they had to say to make the agony end. Sure, some of his peers would admit, 99% of the time you got crap - but there was always a chance of garnering that useful one percent. That single nugget of intel could save an American's life or thwart an attack, they'd insist. It could, maybe, but was the cost worth it? Not to Hal Hollenbeck. It wasn't worth selling his soul on that one, tiny chance, not for all the long-term harm it did.

The agent painfully stood and stretched. His jaw was sore and he felt several teeth move under his tongue from an earlier beating. He had suffered no broken bones that he could tell, but under his clothes he was a patchwork of blues, blacks, and greens, all the somber colors at the dark end of the spectrum. He hadn't cracked, at least not yet. He hadn't told them anything they didn't already know. The bulk of his knowledge was still locked away in his disciplined mind, and that was where it would remain. If he didn't make it out of here he wanted to be sure his captor felt as safe and secure as possible. Safe and secure people grew lax in their defenses, and he needed to make sure El Quemado didn't do anything drastic – like move his operation or change his delivery methods. That could be disastrous and set them back to square one. Again, that wasn't acceptable.

Hal gave a desultory tug on the chain keeping him in place. The chain itself was only about five feet long and secured to his ankle and the stake by shackles and heavy locks. He jerked on the chain again but could've been shackled to a tank for all the give he felt.

Assuming he could ever break free he had his plans locked down. First order of business was to kill El Quemado, to strike off the head of the serpent. That maniac was the sole leader and enjoyed a certain cult of personality among his men. Once that was accomplished he would destroy the machine that produced the condensed Ice drug. After that, assuming he was still alive, he would take it one step at a time, hopefully killing as many guards as possible before he was taken out himself. He truly wanted to do what he could to save Ari, Frankie, and Paul, but he doubted he'd get that far. Sorry, Ari, he thought. I had hoped it wouldn't turn out this way. I truly did.

Outside the hut he began to hear some commotion. It was just muffled voices at first, a murmur that increased in volume like a crowded concert hall when the lights dimmed, signaling the band was coming on stage. His hut was far away from the large open area so he couldn't make out any specifics voices, not that he could understand the native language. He wondered what the hell was going on.

To be honest, more than anything he was still pissed at himself for getting caught. He and Josiah had been extremely careful. Even looking back he couldn't think of anything they'd done wrong, really. They'd been patient and silent, not talking or making any noise. What he hadn't counted on was the obvious fact that because of Butch their captor had known they were coming and had been waiting. They'd walked right into an ambush and hadn't had a chance. He was still fuming about that one. He'd been too full of himself and his abilities and it had cost them all.

Just then the door crashed open and a glare filled the narrow doorway. After so much time in near darkness the light nearly blinded him and Hal tilted his head away and shielded his eyes. He still couldn't see anything but he heard a clanking noise as someone moved into the hut with him. The door swung shut and the light retreated. Hal looked up and his heart froze, all his plans suddenly put on hold.

"Amigo, como estas?" came a young voice. Hal also understood Spanish fairly well, another fact he'd withheld from his group as something they hadn't needed to know. In his head he translated: *How are you, my friend?*

The young man in the John Deere hat, the one they called Red-eye, moved closer to him on metal crutches, clanking each time the crutches came down on the hard-packed ground. His knee was bandaged and visibly swollen and his hat was pulled low, but his grin was bright white and crazy even in the gloom. At his hip was a holstered gun, and grasped in his other hand, along with the handle of the crutch, was the large hunting knife. He eased forward and cocked his head at the tethered agent.

"Vamos a jugar, eh?"

Let's play, eh? Hal thought. Fine, let's. The agent took a step back to give the chain some slack and to give him additional room to maneuver, then waited for Red-eye to come closer, hopefully into his limited range.

Red-eye's grin grew wider and he stepped toward him, weapons at the ready.

Ari had seen black and white film clips of Muhammad Ali fights, back when the lean boxer still called himself Cassius Clay. The man had been so incredibly fast and gifted he'd been able to make the most experienced opponent look positively inept in the ring. Ali would dart in close, land several lightning-fast punches, and retreat before his adversary had known that Ali was even in the

431

same zip code. Van Owen wasn't a huge fan of the brutality of boxing, but to witness the lightning speed and unique talent of The Great One had been nothing short of enthralling. When he fought it was more akin to an elegant dance than a bone-crunching boxing match between two opponents.

To his complete amazement that was how Paul looked now. It wasn't that his young friend was much faster or more skilled than before, but fueled by Ice he seemed able to anticipate each move by Gonzalez almost before the giant made one. If the hulking brute swung a huge roundhouse in his direction Paul would dance backwards so fast the massive fist connected with nothing but air. If he lunged forward to grab at him Paulson would suddenly be behind the man landing rabbit punches at his kidneys. By the time Gonzalez, as fast as he was, turned around with a snarl, Paul would launch several punches up at his grotesque face. Even Ali would've been impressed, Van Owen thought, maybe enough to rattle off one of his famous, quick-witted poems about it.

As the battle raged past the first few minutes, Ari could see that Gonzalez was getting both pissed and frustrated, but he was suffering, too. Paul saw it and skittered back a few steps and waited for the giant to make a move. With one meaty hand the big man wiped blood from his face and flicked it on the ground angrily where it splatted in the dust. He tried a few fast jabs but Paul's head snapped back and out of the way or side to side almost before the punches were thrown. Perhaps emulating Hal's move back at the gas station he twisted to one side and kicked out at the giant's knee. Gonzalez attempted to step back but was too slow and Paul's boot smashed into the side of his leg, causing him to stumble and trip. Paul struck again at the man's face, one, two, three blows that connected in quick succession around his nose and hooded eyes, stunning him. The giant roared in anger and disbelief but couldn't stop from reeling backwards, blood filling his eyes from multiple cuts and open gashes that were bleeding freely. His eyes were swelling and were now just tiny slits nestled between puffy flesh. Blood flowed from his nose and down his face, drenching his white shirt.

Ari chanced a quick look to see what El Quemado was making of all this, thinking he'd order his men to stop the fight now that it was clear his hired muscle wasn't holding his own. But to his surprise the man wasn't making a move at all. Instead he was staring in amused amazement as the battle raged in front of him. No, Van Owen thought, he wasn't amazed, he was *proud.* He was filled with pride at the result of his drug, his creation, and what it could do.

The crowd was getting into it, too. The natives gathered around were smiling and laughing, their faces reflecting mock pain each time Gonzalez took another hit. Paulson connected with a powerful roundhouse to the giant's head, a blow that clearly staggered him. They were urging Paul on, yelling and encouraging him. Even the guards were smiling, their weapons down at their sides or cradled loosely in their arms. The atmosphere was oddly joyous and happy, akin to the first weekend at a county fair in any small, Midwestern town. After so much oppression even this diversion was welcome.

Paulson took a step back, his chest heaving in and out, sweat beaded on his forehead and running down the sides of his red-tinged face. He was untouched. His head moved back and forth in quick, economical jerks. The precise movements took everything in, like a bird of prey surrounded by slow-moving game. He allowed himself the smallest of smiles then danced toward Gonzalez and landed a series of rapid-fire punches. The huge man's head whiplashed backwards on his neck as if on a hinge and he fell to one knee, stunned, his entire massive body swaying and barely staying upright. His bloodied eyes were unfocused and he managed a slow, cumbersome swing at Paul, not even coming close to connecting with this annoying, elusive foe. Then Paulson began walking around the woozy giant, slowly at first, then jogging, taunting the big man with slaps to his head that the swaying Gonzalez never saw coming and could do nothing to prevent. He sped up then, almost running, smiling, everyone around him laughing at the spectacle. And then Paulson did something that no one expected, not Ari, not the guards, and certainly not their captor.

Paul ran. He ran directly at El Quemado.

He snatched a rifle from an unwary guard's grasp and sprinted toward Roberto. Before anyone could react he hurdled the table where their captor sat, knocking him off his chair and onto the dusty ground. The fedora went flying as Roberto shouted in surprise and rage, kicking his legs and waving his arms in the air like a turtle on its back. At that moment Ari could finally see why they called him El Quemado, the Burned One. Without the fedora they could all see how horribly ravaged his head and scalp were, how badly burned he had been by the explosion in the jungle. He was almost completely hairless from his forehead to just above the back of his neck, nothing but purple, stretched and raw skin that was shocking to see. They had all noticed the scarring on his hands, but the ravaged skin of his head was so much worse. And to a vain man like El Quemado, Ari quickly understood, to a man who reveled in the finest things in life, to have everyone see firsthand how mangled and horrific he looked would have been abhorrent to him, and more than he could stand.

For a moment everyone stood still in shock, staring at him, unsure what to do. El Quemado himself was less interested in Paulson than in snatching up his hat and slamming it back on his wasted head, hiding his shame. When he finally had it jammed back on, crooked and dusty, he pointed towards Paul's rapidly retreating back with a quivering finger.

"Que estas esperando? Deje de el!" he screamed, his voice two octaves higher than normal and thick with fury. His face was bright red, but unlike Paulson it had nothing to do with an Ice injection.

Ari didn't need the frog-eyed translator in order to understand him. The guards all jumped and took off running, although Paul had a lead of at least a hundred feet and was easily outpacing them, even

434

with his gimpy leg. The gathered natives were talking and gesturing amongst themselves but not moving, staring at the odd tableau around them, most in shock or sniggering to each other behind cupped hands.

Paul was still pulling away, his arms pumping madly. The guards didn't know if they should shoot him or simply chase him down, but when they saw where he was headed they all ran faster, screaming commands at him in Spanish. He was sprinting directly at the Ice Maker. Fifty feet away from the machine Paulson pulled up short, got down on one knee, and pointed his pilfered rifle just to the left of the two vats. Ari instantly figured out what his friend was doing: Paul, he knew, was a quick learner and a good listener. He lunged for Frankie.

"Get down!" he screamed, tackling her around the waist and taking her to the ground. Butch was standing next to her and Van Owen could see his face twist in jealous anger at Ari's actions with his wife, that he was even touching her. But a half second later his head snapped up and his eyes went wide as he put two and two together: he'd listened to Ari's stories and suddenly realized what was coming, too. All three hit the ground just as they heard a loud *crack!* coming from Paul's direction as he squeezed off a single round. Ari chanced a quick look and saw Paulson throw himself to the red dirt just as a massive fireball erupted next to the Ice Maker, followed by two more deafening explosions.

Paul had shot the huge propane tanks.

Even from this distance Van Owen felt a wash of hot air roll over him as the propane tanks exploded. Three angry black, red, and orange balls of flame boiled upwards into the blue sky. They twisted and turned on themselves, expanding, the three separate explosions combining to form a single, massive fireball. Nearby trees were singed and blackened and birds burst from their hiding places and soared off into the sky, their terrified cries trailing behind them.

But none of that worried Ari. He'd experienced this before, back in the garage, and knew they weren't close enough for the fire to harm them: it was the shrapnel that was the problem. He stayed low and both heard and felt shards of the propane tanks flying and skittering past him, whizzing right over his head. A jagged, charred hunk the size of a pizza box landed just a few feet away from him and slammed in the dusty earth with a thud that he felt through the ground. Butch saw all this too and kept his head down, his eyes wide in shock. Two natives close by screamed and slapped at their arms as several smaller shards tore open their skin. A guard close to Paul flew backwards and collapsed when a piece of pipe the size of a baseball bat impaled him in the chest. He cried out and thrashed for a few seconds in the dust then went still, blood pooling around his suddenly still form, the pipe draining his life away like a gruesome spigot.

The massive fireball boiled up into the sky, slowly dissipating, then gracefully thinned out and was gone. Thick, acrid smoke continued streaming upwards as trees and equipment around the explosion caught fire and burned. A few taller trees nearby were fully engulfed, their wet wood popping and crackling loudly. Ari knew the rough wooden bench had been destroyed: it had been almost on top of the tanks. He felt an odd sense of loss thinking that the vision from his dreams was gone.

He hadn't known what Paul was up to at the time, but the young man's plan had worked to perfection. It was clear to Ari now what had been going on, that Paulson had been egging on Gonzalez these past few days on purpose. He had known about El Quemado's penchant for entertainment, and had been making a show of his dislike for the huge Mexican, hoping that eventually their host would pit them against each other. He'd needed all the guards there, too, so he could have an opportunity to take out the Ice Maker without interference. And the Ice Maker, Ari saw, oh, the Ice Maker, it had not fared well at all, and there would be hell to pay for that.

One of the vats was toppled over and the other had suffered a mortal gash several feet long. Like the blood around the impaled guard, the fluids in both vats were spilling out on the thirsty ground and soaking into the dusty, blackened soil. Pipes and hoses were twisted and mangled as if an angry child had crushed his toy in a burst of frustration. However close that batch of condensed Ice had been to completion, Ari knew, it no longer mattered. Paul had effectively destroyed it, setting their captor back weeks or months in his plans. Good job, Paul, he thought in appreciation. Well done.

That thought of Paulson made him sit up in alarm. He'd been so much closer to the explosion than the rest of them. He hoped and prayed the young Marine was unhurt. Ari stood and looked and saw Paul's supine form on the ground, unmoving. He began running toward him. Fear grabbed at his heart.

"Paul! Paul, are you okay?"

Paulson rolled over and slowly got to his knees, then to his feet. He picked up the rifle and began jogging away from Ari and everyone else.

"Paul!"

But Paulson either didn't hear him or was ignoring him. He picked up speed and broke for the jungle, his limp still evident but not slowing him too much. He crashed into the brush and was gone, leaving Ari to stutter to a halt far behind him. Van Owen meant to go after him but heard a shout from behind. He stopped and turned. There was El Quemado standing over Butch and Frankie, a pistol in his hand, the muzzle aimed at the pair. The man rattled something off in Spanish, something Ari didn't understand, but he didn't need to speak the language to comprehend his meaning. He glanced back where Paul had disappeared, then slowly began walking back towards the group, knowing that if he disobeyed at this point either Butch or Frankie would be killed.

"Just keep running, Paul," he ordered under his breath. "Just keep running, and don't look back."

Chapter 26

Ari was sure El Quemado was going to kill all three of them on the spot. He'd never seen anyone so furious before. The man's rage was so engulfing, so complete, it made Butch's rant on his front doorstep seem no more vicious than a temper tantrum.

Luckily both Butch and Frankie were unhurt by the explosion. El Quemado had avoided injury as well, although the translator appeared shaken up and either wouldn't or couldn't talk just then. His bulging eyes were wide and he was shocked and shaken, as if these recent events were just a bit more than he had bargained for. Roberto was screaming orders in Spanish at anyone and everyone, and pointing into the jungle where Paul had vanished. He leveled his pistol at the spot and squeezed off three quick rounds in frustration, causing some of the natives to dive to the ground in fear. Besides the one guard who had been killed several others were lightly injured, blood staining their clothes and faces. Two others took off after Paul and crashed into the brush, trying to run him down. El Quemado turned to the three of them. His face was stretched and taut and his dark eyes wild and crazed, twin doors that briefly let them glimpse the madness within him. But there was more than madness, there. There was murder.

"Go to the hut," he commanded in slow, heavily accented English.

Frankie pointed to some of the injured natives. If she noticed the palpable aura of death he radiated she ignored it. "People are hurt. Let me help them. Please."

"Go to the hut," he repeated.

Ari and Brubaker gathered themselves up and began to walk away, following his command, Butch's hand on his wife's arm to drag her along if necessary. Ari was still fearful that they'd be shot where they stood. Each step farther away slightly decreased his conviction that they were dead on their feet. But before they'd gone more than a few paces a guard rushed up and said something fast and urgent to their captor, motioning back toward the huts.

"Que?" Roberto screamed.

The guard flinched and repeated his news. He pointed again to the huts and they could see another guard helping the young man they'd come to know as Red-eye hobble toward them. Ari was momentarily shocked since he hadn't known the cruel youth was even in the village. Regardless, the guard had his arm around Red-eye's waist and was helping him along. El Quemado didn't move toward them but simply waited. Ari could see their captor's chest heaving in and out. He didn't look away from the oncoming pair but barked an order toward the translator. Frog-eyes looked like he'd rather roll around on a bullet ant nest instead of obeying, but eventually he stepped forward. His huge eyes were darting and wary. Roberto turned to them.

"It seems that in all the commotion your FBI friend overpowered my idiot nephew here and somehow escaped," he said tersely. "Like your Mr. Paulson he took off into the jungle. What he hopes to accomplish there is beyond me, but he is gone. It seems he has deserted you."

None of them had known Red-eye was his nephew, not that it changed anything. The young man approached and stood there, weaving side to side. His face was bloodied and bruised and it was clear that his injured leg was in worse shape than before. The swelling was now so great the fabric of his jeans was stretched to the limit and was ready to pop. He wouldn't look up at his uncle. Tears ran down his face and traced dirty paths in the dirt and blood caked there. His lips twitched in fear. The guard who had helped him took a few cautious steps away, as if the young man might explode.

El Quemado turned to his nephew and the two of them had a brief conversation, just the two of them. Red-eye mumbled a few words, and it was clear in his voice that he was pleading with his uncle, explaining and asking for forgiveness at the same time. El

Quemado listened and his face softened, the hard lines easing. Red-eye saw this and he sighed in relief. His uncle nodded once and smiled, a small smile, one of understanding and maybe a little compassion. Then he aimed the pistol down and shot his nephew in his good leg.

This blast of the gun was deafening, more so since it was so unexpected. Red-eye screamed and fell to the ground, grabbing at his bloodied knee and writhing in the dust. Roberto knelt down and patted him once on the shoulder, then barked an order at the guard. The man quickly hoisted the wounded nephew up and dragged him away.

"Roberto, what are you doing?" Frankie finally asked, staring aghast at the trail of blood the nephew left in the dirt. "Why did you shoot him?"

Through the translator he replied, "He failed me again. He violated orders and delayed you at the village, and he foolishly sought revenge just now and allowed the FBI agent to escape. He's lucky I let him live."

"But to shoot him in cold blood like that?"

"He'll live. If he weren't my nephew he'd be dead right now."

"Well I'm going to go help him." She turned and started after the pair, the blood trail easy to follow. Ari didn't much care what happened to the young man, but he had to admire her dedication and desire to help. That was the Frankie he knew and he would've expected nothing less of her. It was one of the things he loved about her.

El Quemado started to object, but she was already moving away. Her force of will overruled any opinion he had, and it seemed he had something of a soft spot for her. Ari was interested to note she could get her way and act with measured impunity where no one else could. Their captor ordered a guard to stay with her, then stared after her before turning back to Ari and Butch. As if to prove his dominance over them, he brusquely reiterated his order through the translator.

"Back to the hut, both of you. I will deal with you later. Now I have to assess the situation and what your Mr. Paulson has done." He waved the gun at them and pointed in the direction of their hut. Neither man felt they could do anything else at that time, so they obeyed and started walking side by side, another guard behind them, his rifle out and aimed at their backs.

As they walked Ari realized he'd rarely been with Butch alone before, not since he'd help pull him from the quicksand. It still felt odd, and likely always would. Brubaker looked to where his wife had gone and was clearly eager and tempted to follow her. Ari took hold of his elbow and instead guided him towards the hut. He resisted at first then allowed himself to be directed. The guard behind them followed five or ten feet to their rear.

"Paulson has got some serious balls," Butch finally said. "I don't think I could've done what he just did."

Ari was terrified for his young friend. But he was tremendously proud of him, too. "Me neither. He's come a long way since Louisville."

"So what do we do now? Paul's gone. Hal's gone. But what can they do? What can we do?"

"I don't know. As long as he's got any of us he'll be able to do whatever the hell he wants. We can look for a chance to run, but I bet he'll be more paranoid than ever of losing us. Especially Frankie. He can control you through her. Forever."

Butch finally nodded. His lips vanished into a thin line as he considered their options. "We've got to get out of here. All of us. It's the only way."

Ari agreed. But he didn't see how they could. At least not yet.

When they were ushered back into the hut Van Owen saw that Father Sean and the old chief, Moises, were there. The young priest was still pacing back and forth with the rosary beads up to his mouth, incoherent mumbling leaking through his fingers, the old bible clenched tightly in his other hand. Moises was seated on the cot with the Eight Ball grasped firmly in his ancient hands. The polished black surface of the toy was greasy with his fingerprints.

"I heards the explosion," the old man said. "The thing that makes the *grilich-ta*, what we use in the ceremony, what you calls Ice. It is…dead?"

Ari nodded yes. "It's dead. Paul shot it and blew it up."

"Good. El Quemado should not be making *grilich-ta*. It is sacred, and only for my people. Bollocks, we shoulds have never showed him this secret."

Van Owen agreed wholeheartedly. He sat down next to the chief and exhaled loudly, staring at his hands folded in his lap. Butch couldn't stay still and paced around the hut alongside the young priest, too nervous and anxious to contain himself, worry for his wife driving his actions. The only sounds were the shuffling of their feet and Father Sean's muttering.

Ari considered their options. What he'd said to Butch was true. As long as El Quemado held Frankie there was nothing either one of them could do. Shy of killing the man and his guards he couldn't see a way out, at least not yet. He wished Paul had told him what he'd had up his sleeve; they might have been able to work his plan into something grander and more final, but that point was now moot. On the other hand both Paul and Hal were loose in the jungle, at least for the time being, and the Ice Maker was out of commission. They might be able to do some incremental damage to the guards searching for them, but with no food or water he wasn't sure how long the two of them could hope to survive out there. Neither one had any jungle survival training to speak of, and with night coming in a few hours it would get very dicey out there fast. Maybe, he thought hopefully, just maybe they'll be able to find each other. Two people had a better chance of making it than just one. But neither one knew the other was free, so what were the odds of that happening?

As he considered and rejected their options, Frankie came back with an armed guard in her wake, which appeared to be the new normal. When her husband saw her he ran and embraced her, an embrace she quickly returned. He was reluctant to let her go but after a minute she gently pushed away.

"They haven't found either Paul or your FBI agent yet," she said. "They forced some of the natives to help but from what I heard and saw they weren't doing much good. The villagers just wandered around and insisted they couldn't find a trail. I think they were intentionally being helpless."

"Good for them," Ari said, looking away. Watching the two of them hug was something he couldn't get used to.

"And I'm not sure that young boy's leg can be saved. The bullet passed right through but there was a lot of damage. I wish there was more I could do."

Ari and Butch shared a rare, knowing and friendly glance at each other, neither of them disturbed in the least at Red-eye's plight. Brubaker looked at Frankie and shook his head, feigning sadness and doing a poor job of it. His wife looked from man to man and couldn't understand this new level of camaraderie between them. Ari wasn't sure if she was baffled at their reaction, or that they had a shared joke. Before she could delve into this further, Father Sean stopped and flipped open his bible to a random page. In a loud voice he proclaimed, "Saul tried to pin him to the wall with his spear, but David eluded him as Saul drove the spear into the wall. That night David made good his escape." Then the rosary beads went up to his mouth again and he started his pacing anew. Ari stared at him in mild fascination, glad for the distraction.

"So how much do you figure he really understands? Those quotes sometimes hit the mark and seem pretty damn relevant."

444

Frankie walked to the priest and placed a tender, motherly arm on his shoulder. Whether she cared more for him as a man or a man of the cloth was impossible to tell. "I don't know. Sometimes he makes more sense than others. All I know is what Moises and the others have told me, that he was one of the first true non-natives to have Ice tested on him. The dosage was way off and he overdosed and went into a coma. When he woke up he was like this. It's like his brain was partially fried. It's so sad. He was only here to evangelize, to spread the Word of God. It was his calling."

The priest stared at her with eyes that held no more recognition or understanding than a newborn infant. He pulled away from her and started pacing again, mumbling and walking back and forth with the beads gently clicking in his hand. They all watched him in silence. There was nothing left to say, and each of them were left to dwell within their own thoughts. Eventually night came and the light from around the door faded and was gone.

The next morning a small, spare meal was delivered by one of the bare-chested female villagers. Moises spoke to her in their native tongue before the armed guard hustled her out.

"Your friends have not been founds. Many men looked through the night but could not finds them. El Quemado is not pleased."

"Thank god for that," Ari said, relieved. "They may not have much of a chance surviving the jungle, but it's a better than being caught."

"Maybe they'll make it to civilization," Frankie said hopefully.

"Yeah, maybe," Van Owen answered, but his answer lacked conviction.

They quietly ate their meager breakfast of bread and fruit. Moises declined but Frankie insisted he eat something, and he finally settled on a few bits of bread and a sip of water. Father Sean mechanically ate whatever was placed in front of him, but didn't show any need or desire for more. Ari's stomach still rumbled when all the food was gone, and he drank some water to try and trick his body into thinking he was fuller than he was. His pants were getting loose and he hitched his belt a notch tighter. They would all have to eat more than this in order to keep their strength up, he knew. Even if they could escape they might be too weak to go far. Perhaps that was part of El Quemado's plan for them.

Later in the morning the door opened and their captor stood there. He was fully under control and composed again, his expression calm yet firm, but empty of his earlier charm and bravado. The destruction of the Ice Maker was not sitting well with him. He was dressed as usual in crisp dark slacks and a neatly pressed white shirt. His Italian shoes fairly glittered. The fedora was firmly in place on his head. The translator, as always, was at his side and spoke for him.

"It would seem that during the commotion yesterday someone else managed to escape. The young native, the one you call Josiah, is gone, too. His disappearance is less worrisome than the others, but he disobeyed my orders for a second time and that cannot be permitted. When they are all back in my control there will be retribution." He pointed at Ari. "I need Butch Brubaker to assist in shipping Ice, and I need his wife here as an inducement for him to continue his duties. However, I don't have any need of you."

Frankie jumped up and ran to face him. "Roberto, no! He's done nothing!"

Their captor pushed her back and shut the door roughly, the discussion over. Ari stared at the spot where he'd been and pursed his lips. The others in the hut stared at him in shock or simply looked away, unable to come to grips with his death sentence. Dread hung over the group.

Oddly enough, El Quemado's words had just the opposite effect on Ari. For the first time in as long as he could remember, at the very least since he and Frankie had been together, he felt a sense of release, a lightening of the morass that had settled on his soul. He looked at Frankie and her husband and knew the two of them were meant to be together, that he'd been holding on to a memory of him and Frankie that wasn't meant to be. Yvonne was right, he realized. He needed to move on and let her get on with her life. He needed to be out of this picture so she could draw her own future, a future that didn't include him. Karma was a bitch, he thought, but in the end it always came out on top. He turned to them, and when he spoke his voice was light, almost cheerful. He couldn't believe how good he felt. Conversely, he couldn't believe how lousy he'd felt for so long.

"Well that's that, isn't it? Not the kind of thing you want to hear right after breakfast, is it?"

Frankie stared at him. "No, that's not it. We've got to figure out a way to stop him. He can't just kill you! I won't let him."

Van Owen smiled warmly at her and brushed her cheek with a fingertip. It was a gentle touch, but one that held no deeper significance. Butch tilted his head, somehow sensing the change that had come over his onetime rival, and for once wasn't jealous at the physical contact with his wife. His wide-set eyes blinked once, slowly, in recognition of the new Arjen Van Owen. He nodded as if in thanks.

"Moises, what's your Magic Eight Ball say my chances are of making it through all this in one piece?"

The old chief raised an eyebrow at his strange behavior and question, but mumbled under his breath and shook the black toy. He spun it upside-down and read what he saw in the window.

"It says '*Reply hazy, try again later.*' Bollocks. Shall I tries again?"

"No, don't bother. That's not too reassuring." He clapped his hands together and smiled, a real smile, one that he hadn't felt in a very long time. He could almost feel the atrophied muscles in his face rebel at the strange, unfamiliar configuration. He walked over and patted the old man on the boney shoulder warmly. "Thanks,

447

Moises, you've just confirmed what I haven't been able to admit to myself, and what a very pretty girl in Louisville tried to tell me."

"What is that?"

Ari grinned down at him, staring down at the man's ancient and wise face. The faded tattooed lines on his face were indistinct in the dim light of the hut. "That it's time to move on, that's what."

Frankie spoke up then, an edge of concern audible in her voice. "What do you mean?"

He smiled again, an honest and sincere one, the second one in as many minutes. It felt awesome. "What's Paul always say? Think, plan, then act? But sometimes you just have to act."

Ari strode purposefully to the door and opened it. There were two guards stationed there that jumped up and spun around at the sudden movement. Their guns snapped to attention and were aimed at his chest before he could even blink. He said something to one of them, something his companions couldn't hear. After a few moments the guard nodded and motioned for him to start walking. The door shut.

Less than thirty minutes later he returned. No matter what anyone did or said he wouldn't explain where he'd been or what he'd been doing. He sat on the cot next to Moises and the two chatted amiably on and off for the next few hours until dinner came. They ate their spare meal in silence, the group - and especially Frankie, Ari could see - marveling and concerned at the amazing change that had come over him, how at peace he'd become.

As the evening dragged on Van Owen got down off the cot and taught the old chief how to play tic-tac-toe in the dust of the hut floor. Neither Frankie nor Butch could bring themselves to join in, distraught as they were, but Moises enjoyed himself to no end, quickly becoming so adept he was virtually unbeatable. Eventually, however, even that diversion foundered, and Ari saw everyone dozing off. The Magic Eight Ball was grasped tightly in Moises' hands as he crawled back up onto the cot and slept. He smiled and settled himself on the ground near the door and cleared his mind, and was asleep in under a minute.

Chapter 27

Paulson had no time to rest, even though his exhaustion was so complete his arms and legs felt thick and sluggish, as if his blood had been replaced with heavy syrup. The prior night had been harrowing to say the least. After he'd outrun his captors he'd only managed to snatch a few minutes of sleep high in the boughs of a tree, and even then the bugs, snakes, and monkeys had made it quite clear he wasn't welcome. And he was thirsty, so damn thirsty that his throat felt raw and coated in hot gravel. He was still sweating, which was good, but he knew he'd have to find water soon or he'd start going downhill fast. One thing he'd learned in all this was that if you were weak or sick your chances of survival in the jungle were extremely diminished. Okay, not just diminished - nearly nonexistent. Ari'd been right, he considered; the jungle didn't care what you did, since it would always win in the end.

He pushed through some thick bushes and cursed as hidden thorns several inches long raked at his hands and arms. The damn things were everywhere! As were bugs the size of compact cars, snakes that were so massive they might have been left over from the Jurassic, and things that growled and snarled in the distance that made his sphincter pucker and his skin erupt in primal goose-bumps. He'd survived his tour of duty in Afghanistan, yes, and as horrific as that had been this was worse because everything here was after you. Everything. He slapped at a dozen mosquitos queuing up to dine on his exposed hands and face and kept slogging along. Some ways back he'd noticed the land was sloping downward at a very slight angle and he was following Ari's advice; downward meant water eventually. He hoped.

He thought about his escape from the village. He'd planned the whole thing out, and he was proud of the preparation and execution of that. But when he'd injected himself with the Ice ampule that Josiah had stolen for him, well, that not only cemented his plan but had augmented it as well. In the Marines he'd gotten high before, sure, had snorted a little coke, and had even dabbled in magic mushrooms one time. But those altered experiences couldn't begin to describe what Ice was like. El Quemado was a complete whack-job, but he hadn't emphasized how incredibly awesome and powerful the stuff was. Looking back at the fight with Gonzalez he understood now that the giant hadn't had a chance. Paul had been able to *see* in ways he'd never imagined before, to anticipate what his opponent was going to do even before he'd made a move. It wasn't exactly prescience, since he knew that was impossible, but everything had moved so... *slowly* that he'd had time to notice all the subtle cues of his opponent: a tiny twitch of an eye looking here, the minute tightening of a muscle there, the smallest shifting of feet from one direction to another that signaled an attack. He'd had so much time to see and gather all these assorted cues that when his assailant finally began his assault Paul had his own next four moves planned out and ready to execute, as if he were a chess-master going head to head with someone who'd been expecting a relaxing game of checkers. The fight was so unfair and lopsided it had been ridiculous.

And shooting the Ice Maker? He managed a grin, one that stung as it cracked his dry lips. Blowing up the Ice Maker was simply a bonus, something he'd figured out was possible almost right away. From the get-go the entire fight had been orchestrated so that Josiah could escape with plenty of time to get away. Paul had given the young native one task, just one thing to do. He could only hope and pray he'd gotten it done. If not then all this was for nothing and they'd probably die out here in the jungle, and that would suck and was most definitely not part of the plan.

No, the plan was that he would soon get home to his son Taylor. After all, he'd promised him he would. And, Paul thought warmly, he wanted to get back to see Yvonne again. He smiled at the image of her, his cracked lip be damned. They'd hit it off surprisingly well in the short time they'd known each other during the rehab sessions working on his leg. He thought about her all the time - too much, probably - and he was pretty sure she felt the same way about him. She was smart, super hot, funny, and she looked at him in a way that melted him from the inside out. He'd had fantasies about the two of them that were probably illegal in certain parts of Kentucky, and that was okay with him.

He was so deeply entrenched in daydreaming about Yvonne that he wasn't paying proper attention and stumbled over his own feet, nearly toppling over. Exhaustion was making him clumsy, and he knew that around here clumsy was dangerous. He allowed himself a break and slumped down onto a fallen log for a rest, his breath coming in quick, choppy gasps that didn't sound at all good. He decided to take a five-minute break, only five minutes, hopefully just long enough to gather his wits about him and get a second wind. As he sat there he wished for either water or, better yet, maybe another Ice dose. Even now he could feel a slight tingle in his head and everything around him was still moving a little slower than it should, almost like a television dream sequence. He didn't crave another dose, he wasn't hooked on it like heroin or meth, but he knew how helpful it would be in his current predicament. The shit was amazing.

For the most part his Ice dosage from the day before had run its course in about an hour, but that had been long enough to get him far away from the village. He'd heard the guards crashing and cursing behind him for a while, but after fifteen or twenty minutes he'd lost them for good. The night before the fight he'd confided in Moises what was going to happen and what he'd planned to do. The ancient chief had smiled and assured him that the villagers wouldn't willingly help find him if he ran off, wouldn't help track him down. They wanted El Quemado gone as badly as he did and would do what they could to muddle his trail. The chief was a great guy, Paul mused, and he hoped he could do something to help him and his people.

The five minutes ticked over to ten, then fifteen. He was nearly dozing on the old log when he heard a sound not too far off, one that chilled him to his core. It was a feral growl, deep and menacing, the sound of a big cat of some sort. He'd heard the same growl the previous night some distance away, followed by a horrific screeching of an unlucky animal in its death throes. The sounds had bored into him on such a primitive, ancient level he'd nearly peed himself. He'd never admitted it to Ari or anyone else in the group but this whole jungle thing scared the shit out of him. The bugs and heat were bad enough, but what truly freaked him out were the weird animals, especially the big ones, the ones with huge teeth that wouldn't mind a midnight Paul-snack.

As a kid of four or five years old his parents had taken him to the Cincinnati Zoo one hot summer day. He vividly remembered the foreign and not entirely pleasant smell of the place, the underlying reek of exotic animals caged up on a humid Ohio afternoon. The sounds were so weird, too, the grunts and cries of creatures not meant to live in a Midwestern city. He felt sorry for most of them, sad and penned up as they were, especially the small, cute ones.

Near the end of the visit they'd stopped by the bear pit. Inside and down below was a huge brown Kodiak with clumpy, mangy fur. It had some silly name like Trippy, or Tippy. He couldn't remember. When it stood up it was nearly ten feet tall, but to young Paul Paulson it looked twice that size, massive and imposing, even standing in the bottom of the pit as it was. The bear had stared directly up at him with its dark, deadly eyes and opened its mouth. Then it roared. It roared so loud it vibrated the bars surrounding the pit, bars that little Paul was gripping fiercely in his tiny, sweaty hands. It roared and its huge gums flapped and fluttered and saliva flew out in greasy strings. That deep, wild and primordial sound had terrified Paul so badly, had violated his psyche on such a basic level, that he had indeed peed himself where he stood. His parents had laughed and several children standing nearby had pointed and snickered, their jeers going unheard by him. He had been so terrified he couldn't move, his sneakers rooted to the concrete as urine puddled around them.

That was the same sensation he felt now, that deep-seated terror that somehow circumvented all intelligence. Without thinking he sprung to his feet and took off through the jungle, his survival instinct screaming in his mind and overruling his need for hydration or anything else. Then he heard the growl again, only closer this time and to his right, shadowing him. *Damn!* He shifted direction and headed left, moving faster and faster and ignoring the thorns and needles that assailed his exposed flesh. He was making more noise than he liked but fear was dictating his actions now and caution had been evicted from his mind.

He burst into a clearing and spied a tree on the far side, forty or fifty feet away, one of the grey ones with smooth bark and low branches. An easy climber. Whatever was behind him couldn't be outrun by a mere man, he knew, and a voice from an ancient recess of his brain told him to go up, to get above the ground and keep climbing. Up was good. Up was defensible. He angled for the tree and ran over the uneven terrain, once again thankful that Ari had insisted on good boots.

He was less than twenty feet away when a massive yellow and black spotted jaguar bounded into the clearing and blocked his path. This was no diminutive female of the species, he knew instinctively. Ari had described that one to him and had placed its weight at around a hundred pounds. This brute had to be twice that size with a big, square head the size of a mastiff's and yellowed teeth almost as long as his fingers. It paced in front of him but it's liquid golden eyes never left Paul's face. Its long tongue licked around its muzzle. Paulson was no musician, but the deep rumble from the big cat reminded him of a sustained bass guitar note played through huge speakers.

Paul kept his head steady but his eyes were busy tracking left and right, looking for an avenue of escape or a means to defend himself. The rifle he'd snatched from the guard had only contained that single bullet for some reason, the one he'd used to blow up the propane tanks, and he roundly cursed the damn Barney Fife guard for not having a full clip. He still had the heavy weapon, however, and he hefted it like a baseball bat, determined to get at least one good blow on the jaguar if it decided to make a move. He doubted he'd do much but piss it off, but he'd be damned if he wasn't going to go down swinging. He just hoped he wouldn't wet himself like back at the bear pit as a kid. It took everything he had, all the will power he could muster, to stand there with his wholly inadequate weapon and stare the big cat down.

"Alright, you big son of a bitch," he said, nearly shouting, full of false bravado. "Let's do this!" He raised his head and screamed as loud as he could, his own version of a primal challenge, hoping if nothing else to throw the cat off its game. Then he brought his fingers to his lips and blew – hard. The piercing whistle that he'd used as a kid to call his siblings home shattered the normal jungle noises, reverberating through the trees. A sudden silence fell all around him as every creature nearby suddenly hushed, startled, now aware of the battle about to take place below. The jaguar didn't care for the loud whistle at all. It stopped pacing and cocked its head to one side, staring at Paul, perhaps waiting for another blast, or maybe just thinking. It sniffed the air. Then it crouched down, its tail thicker than a man's arm whipping and lashing at the air, and prepared to attack. Paul grabbed the rifle tightly and waited for it.

But the attack never came. The big cat stopped and sniffed the air again, its head up and its wet nose twitching. Its ears, which had been laid back flat against its square head, popped up and twisted, listening for something. There was a rustling in the brush behind it, a twig snapped, and then to Paul's complete shock his missing dog ran out, looking from side to side, no doubt drawn there by his master's whistle.

"Lucky! Oh my god!"

The poor dog was in worse shape than he was. It was clearly malnourished and likely dehydrated as well. Its black and white fur was matted and filthy and there was dried blood from a long cut on its nose that had stained its white fur sometime in the recent past. But when it saw Paul it wagged its tail in excitement. Then it spotted the huge cat and its demeanor changed in a heartbeat. It dropped its head and spread out its front paws and a low growl escaped from between its bared teeth. Paul stared at it. He'd never heard his pet growl before.

The jaguar wasn't sure what to do for a moment. Paul figured it wasn't used to anything standing up to it, much less two strange creatures like this. Its thick tail flipped around as of its own accord and its golden eyes flicked back and forth between the two of them. And then Lucky did something Paul hadn't seen coming at all. His dog began to bark. Loud, piercing barks that were so sharp they hurt his ears. The big cat didn't know what to make of that at all, he was pleased to see, so he figured he'd join in.

"Take off, hoser!" he screamed. "Get the hell out of here!" He picked up a rock at his feet and launched it at the jaguar's head. It hit the ground shy of the cat but bounced up and smacked it in the ribs. The cat jerked as if it had been shocked and spun to find the cause of the strike. Lucky darted in and snapped at the cat, still barking loud and strong. The jaguar took a swipe at it, but the dog had already dodged back and out of range.

Paul tossed another handful of rocks to distract it and draw its attention away from his dog. The huge cat snarled and hissed at both of them. He continued yelling and screaming and throwing whatever he could find and Lucky kept up the barking. The frustrated cat growled deep in its throat and backed up a few paces, slowly. It looked like it was about to give up on this whole affair when Lucky darted in too close. The jaguar swiped a massive claw and caught the dog just behind the head, above its shoulder. Lucky's barks cut off and the dog spun like a Frisbee and landed in the dust five feet away, blood on its fur, suddenly still.

"No!" Paul screamed.

Without thinking he launched himself at the jaguar and began pummeling the cat with the butt of the rifle. His swings were manic and ferocious, not focusing on anything but doing as much damage as possible. Without a lingering trace of Ice in his system he would've perished in moments, but there was enough left to give him that little something extra, that needed edge. The butt of the rifle was bloody and covered in clumps of fur, and still he continued battering the shrieking cat.

This was clearly not what the jaguar had in mind or had expected. It rolled onto its back but couldn't reach him as Paulson connected with the rifle again and again. Paul was screaming obscenities and curses all the while, heedless of any personal danger as the rifle connected with the force of a sledgehammer. He felt the wooden stock splinter but he wouldn't stop. Ten, fifteen more powerful blows rained down on the big cat as it rolled and tried to escape his fury. Suddenly it bounded to its feet and scrambled a few paces away, blood caked about its eyes and mouth, its ears flat against its head, a single tooth broken clean off, its sides heaving in and out. It limped around a moment before it crouched down and prepared to pounce. Paul stood his ground with the remains of the rifle held in both hands, ready for it. It almost seemed as if his Ice dosage had had a resurgence within him, and he could *see* what the cat was about to do. His own breath was hot and heavy in his chest and sweat blanketed his face. The jaguar snarled and leapt at him and Paul began a final swing of the rifle.

At that same instant he heard a loud *crack!* Then the full force of the cat's two hundred pounds crashed into him, bowling him over. He cried out and felt hot blood wash over him, covering his face and upper body. He rolled and kept rolling and shoved the heavy cat away, then jumped to his feet. Panting, he looked down and saw that a fist-sized chunk of the jaguar's head was gone, blown away by what had to be a high caliber bullet. A mass of bone and flesh and blood was all he could see there. The cat's chest heaved once and then stopped, and its one remaining eye glazed over and stared at nothing. It twitched and then moved no more.

Paul stood over it for no more than a second, then tossed the rifle down and ran to his dog. Lucky had fared better than the cat, but not by much. There were three long gashes down its flank, from its neck to its ribs. There wasn't much blood, he saw, but that was probably because the poor thing was so dehydrated. It was panting heavily, its tongue lolling in the dust. Paul dropped down and cradled its head in his lap, petting it gently and saying soothing nothings, telling Lucky what a good dog he was, how proud he was. He felt tears on his cheek and could only think that he was wasting water when his dog needed it so badly.

Then he heard noises coming from beyond the tree, men talking in low voices, the sounds of people treading carefully through the brush. He turned back to his dog, not caring at all that he was about to be captured and taken back to the village. He had an idea what was in store for him there, but it didn't matter. He just knew they wouldn't separate him from his dog. Never. Of that he was sure.

He waited, still petting Lucky tenderly, and they came for him.

Hal wasn't faring much better. The prior night had been rough, admittedly, but while he wasn't aware of Paul's secret fear of the jungle, the agent didn't share his *hylophobia* either. As at any time in the rainforest he'd had to contend with all manner of voracious predators and nuisances, including of course the swarms of insects, snakes, and everything else that slithered, crawled, bit, or stung.

Like Paul he'd taken refuge high in a tree for the night, but whatever action he took he was still hindered by the length of chain resolutely shackled to his ankle. On the plus side, Hal considered, he had two serviceable weapons at hand; the knife and the pistol, courtesy of Red-eye.

He forged ahead through the thick brush, all the while holding onto the chain in his left hand and the knife in his right. He wished he had a machete to better hack his way through the dense foliage, but in a pinch he could use the knife to slice open a narrow path, or swing the chain to smash open up a trail if he had to. They didn't work nearly as well as the machete, and swinging the chain tired him out quickly, but he made do with what he had.

He had a destination in mind, Big Al's camp. But his directional sense wasn't the best and he could only hope he was headed in the right direction. He wasn't at all certain what Big Al's group was up to out here, but they had computers and the Internet, and he was determined to make it there in one piece. All he needed was a few minutes online and he could call for backup. Thanks to Ari he knew the exact coordinates of El Quemado's camp, and nothing could stop him from calling in and demanding a strike force. He would kill two birds with one stone; hopefully save Ari, Paul, Butch, and Frankie, and take out the camp at the same time. Beyond that he no longer cared what happened to him, was no longer concerned if he made it or not. If it meant a memorial star on the wall of FBI headquarters, well, so be it. His duty and obligations were clear to him, and his personal security and well-being were secondary.

He stopped for a few minutes and leaned against a tree. He could feel his strength fading and he knew he needed to rest, if just for a moment. He wouldn't be able to help anyone if he passed out from exhaustion or dehydration. Hal wrapped the chain around a low branch and closed his eyes, his thoughts drifting back to the village.

Red-eye had been an impulsive idiot, thankfully. He'd been overly cocky and confident because he'd been armed and the agent had been securely moored to the stake. Easy pickings, or so he thought. One of the first things a rookie FBI agent learned was to never underestimate an opponent, something Red-eye had obviously never considered. Hal had realized right away that the young thug was acting on his own or he would've used the gun first thing. No, he'd stepped in close to use the knife and Hal had delivered a rudimentary front snap-kick to his bad knee again. Amateur. The impetuous youth had hit the ground like he'd been tazed and it was a simple matter for Hollenbeck to disarm him, before delivering a crunching blow to his head with the butt of the pistol. The hardest part had been digging out the stake with the knife to free himself. That had taken some time, time he wasn't sure he'd had, even though with all the commotion and shouting going on elsewhere at the camp in the long run he hadn't needed to rush. Once again he'd had to decide whether or not to eliminate Red-eye, and once again he'd passed on the opportunity for some reason he couldn't fathom. Maybe he was getting soft, he didn't know. Regardless, once he'd dug the stake out he was able to flee the village unseen and unimpeded, right past the four generators that powered their captor's equipment. Their raucous rumbling had covered his clanking progress nicely.

He pushed away from the tree and started off again, the heavy chain looped around his hand. The gun jammed into the tightened waist of his pants provided him some measure of comfort against the coming night. He didn't want to use it unless he had no other choice as the loud report could give away his position. Plus he only had four bullets, one in the chamber and three in the clip. Enough to protect himself against jungle denizens, but not enough if more than a few guards found him.

He wondered again what the huge explosion was shortly after he'd gotten away. Whatever had caused it he sincerely hoped it was the Ice Maker. He couldn't imagine how that might have happened, but it was the only source he could think of around here that could blow up like that. Unless El Quemado's helicopter had exploded? Hopefully with their captor onboard? That was an intriguing thought, one that had buoyed his spirits and had kept him content throughout the previous night.

Hal pushed ahead. The ground beneath his feet was for the most part flat, but periodically it angled slightly downward, and like Paul he recalled Ari's words about water always being at a low point. He wasn't sure what he might do if he found any since it would likely be a potentially lethal microbial soup, but at this point he was certain he'd drink anything shy of mud and worry about the consequences later. If he made it to Big Al's they would surely have medicine to counteract anything he'd ingest. And if he didn't make it then nothing he did in the short term would matter.

Just a few hundred feet farther on he suddenly felt light-headed and woozy, the lack of food and water hitting him hard. He recognized the sick feeling. It was the same way he'd felt back in the cave in Afghanistan when he'd been malnourished from weeks with little to eat or drink. His entire body was shaking and he felt nauseous. He slumped to the ground and removed his glasses, then put his head down low, between his knees. Thankfully after a few minutes of forced deep breathing the sensation passed. As he sat there he felt a lump in his pocket and he withdrew a large coin. He held it up and almost grinned. It was a Challenge Coin, something an agent or the FBI itself gave to individuals who stepped up and assisted the agency. Hal took the significance of the coins very seriously, and had only presented three before in his entire career, the most recent one to the Army corporal who'd been instrumental in freeing him from the cave in the Mideast. He'd carried the coin with him since Louisville and had intended to give it to Paulson if the young man had been as helpful as he'd hoped. The coin was larger than a fifty-cent piece, and heavy. It was bronze, and on one side it showed the red, white, and gold crest of the Federal Bureau of Investigation, with the words *Fidelity, Bravery,* and *Integrity* on a ribbon below the crest, all on a blue background. On the flip side there was an eagle clenching arrows in its talons. There was some dried mud caked in some of the letters, and he spent a few precious minutes cleaning them out with a long thorn, happy to finally find a useful purpose for the nasty things. He breathed on the coin and buffed it against his shirt, then pocketed it again. He hoped against hope to be able to deliver it to Paul and hand it to him personally as the young man deserved it. He'd been happily surprised at how well Paulson had carried himself the entire mission.

Hal finally stood and took another moment to clean his glasses. He wasn't able to do a very thorough job, and this bothered him ever so slightly. His fellow agents back in Cincinnati always chided him for being so neat and tidy, he knew, but he didn't care. Deep down he hated being dirty. No, that wasn't quite right. It wasn't the actual dirt or germs that bothered him, but the fact that not being clean seemed, well, unorganized to him, and being unorganized made him nervous and more than a little anxious. He preferred things tidy and orderly, and anything outside that paradigm was upsetting to him. That was one of the main reasons he'd gone into law enforcement; laws and the American legal system kept society orderly, and without them he knew humanity could slide into chaos and eventual anarchy. He couldn't stand for that. Hal sighed and pressed his lips together in frustration at the smudges he couldn't seem to clean off his lenses, then started walking again.

It was getting late and he hadn't found anything to eat or drink yet. The sun was already setting below the trees and he knew he'd have to find shelter or a tree to climb soon. He was worried anew that time was potentially running out for his friends back at the village, and he was upset he hadn't stumbled across either the new road or Big Al's camp yet. Of course he could have missed it by a few hundred feet and he'd never know it, but he had to pray that hadn't happened. He shoved that possibility into one of the small, organized cubbies in his mind labeled *Unhelpful Thoughts* and continued pushing ahead.

The sun was setting faster now and locating a place to shelter for the night was becoming paramount. Some distance away he thought he heard something, something faint and muffled by the thick foliage. It could have been a distant gunshot, or it could have been something as benign as a branch falling nearby. He momentarily considered ignoring it, but his physical condition was quickly deteriorating and even something as insignificant as this could be cause for concern. Not to mention that it was out of the ordinary, which of course rubbed raw his inner sense of tidiness. That was enough for him. He adjusted his path and headed toward the noise. He slid the knife into his belt and pulled out the pistol, checking again to make sure the round was still chambered. The handle felt both cool and reassuring in his hand.

Ten minutes of muted cursing through the brush and he hadn't heard anything else. He was about to adjust his course back toward Big Al's when he noticed that the jungle around him was eerily quiet. The insects were still there, including a swarm of gnats that hovered in front of his face and defied all attempts by him to swat them away. But the normal chittering and screams of monkeys was gone, and the thousands of birds had fallen silent. Something was going on. Apprehension and adrenaline shot up and he hurried behind the trunk of a large tree, ears straining to hear something, anything, out of the ordinary. He stood that way for several minutes, frozen, almost part of the tree, his ears trying so hard to catch the slightest unusual noise that his brain ended up devising sounds on its own accord. A few more minutes passed and nothing else happened. He exhaled and turned away from the tree, ready to be on his way, when a figure stepped out of the brush to his left. The gun jumped up and his finger reflexively tightened on the trigger, the pressure building, squeezing firmly and evenly just as he'd been taught. Then at the last second he saw who it was and he exhaled through pursed lips, the pistol dropping heavily to his side.

"Well I didn't expect to see you here," he said after a moment.

Chapter 28

Ari's eyes popped open. The inside of the hut was dark, with just a small puddle of light surrounding the small lamp on the floor that never made it to the corners, as if it were afraid to venture too far into the night. He knew it was five in the morning without even checking his watch, although he held it out to the meager light just to be sure. Yes, it was 5:01, just as he'd thought. Some things never changed, and for once he was happy about it.

He quietly stood and crept toward the door. Just as he was about to open it he heard a tiny movement and turned. Frankie was standing there, right behind him. Her face was in complete shadow but somehow he could still feel her green eyes on him, staring at him, through him. She touched his arm and leaned close.

"What are you doing?" she whispered, her voice no louder than a breeze.

Despite himself the touch of her hand on his bare skin still caused a flutter to run up and down his spine. He did his best to ignore that sensation, but if backed into a corner would have to admit that he wasn't very successful. More importantly, right now the last thing he wanted was anyone else waking up. He moved his mouth close to her ear, not at all confident he could whisper as softly as she had.

"Don't worry. Go back to sleep."

He couldn't see her expression, but could tell that she shook her head. "No. Tell me what you're doing."

"Why are you even awake? Please go back to sleep."

Behind her Butch moved a little, his clothes making small rustling sounds. They waited for a few moments to be sure he was still sound asleep. Her mouth moved to his ear and she whispered again, but with more force this time.

"Do you think you're the only one that wakes up at five o'clock every morning?"

Ari drew back from her in shock. He'd never known that about Frankie, had no idea she went through that every morning just like him. Finding this out bent his resolve for a heartbeat, but didn't break it. It was time to leave Frankie and Butch to their lives forever. Karma, he reminded himself, was a bitch that couldn't be avoided.

"I'm sorry," he whispered in her ear, "but you need to stay here. I'll be fine. I have to do this."

"What are you going to do?"

"I'm going to make sure you and Butch and the others get out of here. Trust me."

"No. Not until you tell me what you're up to. I...I don't want anything to happen to you."

Ari was touched but he wouldn't let it stop him or change his mind. "Please, Frankie, just go back and lay down. Stay with Butch. I need to do this by myself." He tenderly placed his hand on her cheek and found that it was wet. She was crying, but so softly he hadn't noticed. He took her hand in his own and turned hers palm up. With his tear-stained finger he traced their Karma sign on her palm, the wagon wheel with eight spokes. Then he closed her hand, gently pressing on her fingers.

"Go, and have a happy, long life. You and Butch. Okay? Now go!" Those last two words he uttered with such strength and conviction that she took a step back in shock. He forced himself to turn away from her and, without another glance behind him, squared his shoulders and opened the door.

Before she could do anything or attempt to follow, he shut it firmly behind him and stepped into a dim pool of light outside the hut. The light came from a low wattage bulb hanging from a wire a dozen feet away. On the fringe of the lighted area sat a guard in a rickety chair, a rifle across his lap. He may have been dozing or in that relaxed state just before sleep, but either way when he saw Ari he was instantly alert, jumping up and leveling the weapon at him.

Van Owen held up his hands and walked toward him. He was amazed at how calm he felt, how at ease he was. He thought back to the moment before he pulled the trigger in his garage, when he'd blown up the propane tank, and recognized the same sense of calm in himself. He wondered if perhaps this was how Hal always felt during tense moments? If so he envied him that professional poise. He continued walking towards the guard, smiling all the while, that same game show announcer smile he'd used back at the gas station where they'd first met El Quemado's nephew, Red-eye.

"Alto!" the guard barked, not at all concerned with waking the neighbors.

Ari didn't know the word but it took no effort to understand the body language and meaning. He kept his hands in the air and took a few more steps toward the man. He hadn't paid much attention to the guards since they'd been at the village, but he paused a moment to scrutinize this one. As most of them were, the man was short and swarthy with curly black hair that stuck out from under a white straw hat. He had on a long-sleeve white shirt and dark pants, and had a blue bandana wrapped around his neck, probably to ward off mosquitos. The way the gun was shaking, he didn't look at all comfortable with this sudden and unexpected confrontation. He motioned with the gun barrel toward the door of the hut.

"Vuelve a la cabaña!" the guard snapped.

Ari stared at the gun and marveled again at how relaxed he was. The hole in the end of the barrel was a tiny black circle no larger than the thickness of a pencil. It was so insignificant, such a small thing, but he knew how quickly it could take his life. He eased forward another few steps then stopped, his smile innocent and serene.

"Hi, there, how are you tonight?" he asked softly. "So tell me, what do you guys do for fun around here?"

Under his straw hat the man's face crinkled up in confusion. "Que?"

467

"No, really. I hope you're getting paid a lot for this gig. This does not look like fun."

The guard was getting more and more frustrated with Van Owen and his nonstop gibberish. He pushed the gun barrel into Ari's chest and repeated, "Vuelve a la cabaña. Ahora!"

"Okay, let's try this. Take me to your leader."

The man growled low and turned his head to shout something out, probably to alert his companions. Just then a monstrous form materialized behind him and a huge fist bigger than a bowling ball crashed down on the man's head. The guard crumpled into a boneless heap at Ari's feet, the white straw hat a mangled mess on the ground next to his body. Gonzalez stepped into the light, his already terrifying face made all the more horrible from the bruises and gashes inflicted by Paul. He walked with a distinct limp and his left arm was held awkwardly at his side. He nudged the guard with a size eighteen boot and grunted in satisfaction at his handiwork. Calm or not, standing this close to the behemoth still gave Ari the willies. Regardless, he looked up at him, his voice stern.

"You're late. I said five o'clock. I thought he was going to sound the alarm."

In his deep, basso voice, Gonzalez replied, "Slow. My English is not good."

"Never mind. Thanks for your help."

"Yes. My help. De nada."

Ari bent over and started dragging the unconscious guard out of sight and behind the hut. Before he could get far Gonzalez grabbed the man's arm and tossed him into the shadows more easily than Ari might have hefted a bag groceries. Still in the shadows, he turned to the huge man.

"Okay. Now let's get El Quemado."

"Yes. Vamos."

Together they began slipping from shadow to shadow, avoiding the hanging lights, walking quickly but silently, Ari in the lead with

Gonzalez close behind. For such a massive individual, he noted, the guy could move like a cat. They'd only gone a few dozen yards when Van Owen stopped and pointed ahead. He was about to confirm with his newfound ally that they were going in the right direction, when all around them the world exploded.

Shots rang out from all directions, and not handguns, either. These were high caliber weapons, big, booming guns that rocked the night and silenced the jungle. There were so many rounds it sounded like a string of M80s blowing up, one after another. Ari heard confused screams and shouts coming from everywhere around the village, and saw several guards running madly between the puddles of light. He spun to Gonzalez.

"What's going on?" he shouted, trying to make himself heard over the din.

The big man cocked his head and listened. "Others. Not guards."

Others? Ari wondered. What others? What the hell was going on? This wasn't part of his plan.

One of El Quemado's men sprinted past him and he recognized him as the one who had killed the old woman. The man's eyes were wide in fear and he ran right under one of the bulbs, his form momentarily and clearly visible. As he did so Van Owen saw a flash in the distance and the running guard was launched sideways, like he'd been blindsided by an invisible car. He tumbled in the dust and lay still, blood as black as ink leaking out from a crater in his side. His legs spasmed grotesquely as life left him.

"Guard the hut," Ari commanded Gonzalez. "Do you understand? Guard the hut and my friends. I'll take care of El Quemado. Understand?"

For a moment it didn't look like the giant planned on following orders, and Ari was worried because he had no idea how to make him obey if he chose not to. He looked this way and that, taking in

469

the mayhem around them. To Van Owen's relief the behemoth finally nodded and trotted back toward the Frankie and the others, his massive form quickly and quietly vanishing in the darkness. After he'd gone Ari pressed himself up against the closest hut and tried to make sense of what was going on, peering out toward the noise.

More guards were shouting and running everywhere, the full compliment up and active now. After their initial confusion and surprise it looked like they were massing at the other end of the village, back toward the ruined Ice Maker. He counted at least ten men, all well armed. Someone somewhere flicked a switch and more lights came on, the same batch that El Quemado had used when he, Paul, and Butch had been captured. The village was now bathed in stark white light. He was desperately looking for El Quemado but hadn't spotted him yet. *Damn!*

Movement at the other end of the village caught his eye. Several figures in black outfits and dark stocking caps were moving towards him, keeping low and sprinting from one shred of cover to another, large rifles clasped diagonally in front of them. The way they advanced, first one, then another, looked so professional, so practiced. Whoever they were they had been trained very, very well. One man threw himself down and looked side to side before waving a black-clad hand, motioning the next group forward. Three others advanced and the lead man did the same. The man on the ground must have seen something because he ripped off three quick shots that were deafening, even this far away. Ari heard a muffled scream back toward the Ice Maker and knew another guard had been hit. He tried to become one with the wall of the hut as he watched the melee unfold before him.

A few moments later the black-clothed men were almost even with him. He realized he was a little too close to the action for comfort, but also knew that he hadn't seen El Quemado anywhere yet. He was about to circle behind the attacking force to try and get to the far side of the village where their captor's hut was located when he felt a light tap on his shoulder. He jumped and spun around, ready to fight but not knowing exactly how, when a strong hand grabbed his arm and another covered his mouth. He started to panic until he realized who it was.

Big Al was standing there next to him. His head was covered by a dark cap and head to toe he was garbed in a black, tight-fitting outfit. His dark skin blended right in, but his bright white eyes were clearly visible. He removed his hand from Ari's arm and put a single finger to his lips, the universal sign to be quiet. When Van Owen finally nodded he dropped his finger.

"You okay?" the short, stocky man asked, his voice so low it was nearly inaudible. "Just nod yes or no."

Ari nodded yes.

"Good. Stay low and remain here. Let us do our jobs."

"What? How? I don't understand."

Big Al pressed his lips together as Ari questioned his orders. "We're going to take him and his operation out."

Van Owen didn't need to ask who he was talking about. But his natural curiosity got the better of him and he couldn't remain quiet. "Why? Who are you guys?"

The shorter man was watching his men advance, but took a second to answer. "Paulson sent the native kid, Josiah, to find us. That was the whole reason he got into that fight, to distract everyone. He'd told the kid to find us and taught him to say one thing: *Semper Fi*. Marines don't let Marines die in the jungle or anywhere else. Paulson knew we were brothers and that we'd come. We came. Now stay low and let us do our job." He started to move away, but Ari grabbed his shirt.

"What about Paul? And Hal?"

"We've got both of them. And the dog, too. We found Paulson right after he took on a jaguar, believe it or not, the crazy bastard. Josiah stumbled across Hal just a little bit later, on our way here.

They were suffering from exposure and dehydration, but the dog was hurt. Josiah made some medicine from stuff he found in the jungle, a clear gel of some kind, and used it on the dog. Whatever it was did the trick. We had one of our men take them back to our camp. They'll be fine." He removed Ari's hand from his shirt and pushed him back up against the hut. He put his finger to his lips again and quietly moved out, leaving Van Owen behind.

Ari stayed there for a few minutes and watched Big Al's men advance. He was right – they were professionals, and he knew the disorganized and panicked guards wouldn't stand a chance against them. This would likely be over in no time at all, but it would be a hollow victory if they couldn't find and stop their leader. He waited there for what felt like an eternity and then edged out again, back behind Big Al's men, planning to circle around behind them. Their captor's hut was only a few hundred yards away, and he'd be damned if he'd let that maniac get away.

He'd only gone a short distance when intense fighting broke out toward the Ice Maker. He was sure that the desperate guards were hunkered down and defending themselves, which meant that Big Al's men might be busy for a while. And if El Quemado wasn't there it could be perfect cover for him to escape. He picked up his pace and began sprinting between the huts, hoping and praying that he wouldn't be mistaken for a guard and get shot. His breath was coming hard and fast in his chest and the humidity was so thick he could have been running through melted butter.

Finally his destination was in sight, but at that moment ten or fifteen shots rang out nearby and he was forced to hit the dirt in a clumsy dive, skinning the flesh of his hands. Someone nearby was yelling orders but he couldn't make out what they were saying. He waited a few seconds and was about to burst into the hut when he heard a strange noise several hundred yards away. It was a mechanical whine that quickly escalated into a familiar thudding, the sound of a powerful motor. It was a helicopter. El Quemado's helicopter.

Ari looked around desperately and finally spotted Big Al hunkered down near the communal hut, the man's back to a thick post. He yelled to get his attention, and when the Marine saw him Van Owen dashed to his side, keeping his head down. He grabbed at his husky shoulder.

"The helicopter! He's getting away!"

Big Al needed no additional urging. Despite the bullets that were zipping everywhere like angry bees he stood and looked toward the sound. After a few seconds they could just make out the pale shape of the chopper lifting above the trees, branches blowing wildly. In his haste El Quemado had failed to douse all the running lights, so while they could only dimly see the chopper itself they could clearly track its path as it fought for altitude.

"It's him. Take it out!" Ari shouted, needlessly pointing.

Big Al lifted his rifle and sighted down the barrel before calmly squeezing off three shots, triangulating around the lights. Ari swore he could feel the sonic blast of the bullets as they left the barrel. The helicopter bucked twice and a spit of flame shot out from the rear, near the exhaust. The smooth purr of the motor became a thumping, clanking roar and the chopper began a slow, almost graceful spin. The bird began losing altitude and thundered directly over their heads, hot air and noise blasting them, the chopper now only a few dozen feet in the air and throwing up clouds of dust and sand. A foreign, acrid stench of burnt rubber and plastic filled their nostrils. Flames were shooting from the back of the fuselage as it careened by, the engine now just barely chugging along, spitting and hissing in mechanized death throes. They could hear the rotors slicing the air and feel its massive bulk as it hurtled overhead. It vanished over the huts and they heard the snapping of trees and a tremendous boom as it crashed out of sight beyond them.

During the final moments of the chopper's life the almost steady stream of gunfire had ceased, likely with everyone's attention on the dying bird, Ari thought. But with the death of the helicopter the guards must have known their end was near. They opened up with a new, vicious salvo that caught Big Al's men off guard. Ari grabbed him and pointed back toward where the chopper had crashed.

"You take care of these guys. I'll go after him."

Big Al only hesitated a moment before nodding and refocusing his attention on the enemies clustered around the Ice Maker and taking sustained pot-shots at his men. Ari kept his head down and sprinted toward the crash site, more intent on this task than on anything he'd ever done. He had the presence of mind to stay to the shadows, ducking around the pools of light whenever he could. He ran by their hut and noted with dismay that Gonzalez was nowhere to be seen, and he hoped his friends at least had the presence of mind to stay inside and keep down. The shaky alliance he'd arranged the night before with Gonzalez apparently hadn't been worth much. He'd convinced the giant that El Quemado was dangerous and more than a little crazy, not just to Ari and his friends, but to Gonzalez as well. The fight the giant had been forced into was still very fresh in the big man's mind, and he needed very little additional convincing. They'd planned to meet at five o'clock outside Ari's hut, and to do whatever they could to take El Quemado out, once and for all. So much for planning.

Ari dismissed Gonzalez and their tenuous allegiance, and kept running, his breath loud in his head. Once outside the village proper, beyond the perimeter and among the trees and brush, he could see a few small flames dancing in the dark. That had to be the downed helicopter. He angled toward it, picking up his pace once more.

He skidded to halt right where the jungle started. He saw that the chopper had plowed a ragged path through the trees, shedding bits and pieces of itself along the way. Shards and ribbons of metal and other unrecognizable parts were strewn about, a few still smoldering. He had to pick his way carefully through the debris field, stepping over broken branches and random helicopter pieces. The chopper itself was on its side about fifty feet into the brush, its landing struts sheered off and laying like steel pretzels several feet shy of the fuselage. The huge rotors had snapped off clean and were nowhere to be seen. Flames licked at the rear of the body and lighted up the immediate area, yellow and blue flames that hinted of fuel burning. The door of the copter was completely gone, along with the windshield.

Ari continued to step carefully among the wreckage, wary of burning branches and sharp metal edges that could easily slice open a leg or arm. He frantically looked side to side, peering under and around everything, carefully shifting debris, searching for El Quemado, all while the fire from the chopper hissed and popped softly. He was starting to wonder if his quarry had been thrown far clear of the accident when he heard a moan near the copter itself. He hustled closer, aware of the flames but heedless of the danger.

El Quemado, or Roberto as he called himself, the source of all their troubles and pain, was on his back, his lower legs pinned under the helicopter's fuselage. His hat was gone and blood had soaked into his white shirt in a dozen places. His arms flapped uselessly at the air around him, moving in random, aimless circles. Ari could tell he was in a terrific amount of pain. He walked to him and knelt by his side.

Without his hat and with the flickering, uneven light of the fire to illuminate him, his scarred head was ghastly to behold, a patchwork of scars marred with scruffy tufts of hair. One sleeve of his white shirt had been shredded in the crash and Ari could see the ugly scars that tracked up and down his bare arm, hard ridges of skin that reminded him of alligator flesh. The scarring was so horrific that Ari wondered how the man had even survived that first explosion. When El Quemado heard Ari kneel down he opened his pain-filled eyes.

"Help...me..." he pleaded, his voice thin and laced with agony. His two front teeth had been knocked out in the crash and that new lisp, along with his accent, made it even harder to understand him. "Please help me..."

Ari hunkered down next to him, making no move to assist. "Help you? Really? After all you've done? Let's see - you were responsible for the death of hundreds on that plane; you've killed dozens of the villagers; your own nephew died because of you; and you kidnapped Frankie." He leaned in close, so close he could smell the stench of terror on the trapped man. "So tell me; why would I do that?"

"Please. Help me..."

Ari heard a rustling in the brush behind him and looked around, startled, then relaxed when he saw it was Moises and another native, a young girl who looked vaguely familiar to him. The chief stepped carefully over the debris in his bare feet, aided by the young girl who steadied him with a hand on his elbow. The two of them stood next to Ari before the old man sat down with a deep, contended sigh. In his hand he held the Magic Eight Ball.

"He wants help," Ari informed him. "But honestly, I don't think I can make that decision. I'm going to leave that up to you. You helped him once before and he repaid you and your people with death and misery. I know what I would do, but it's your choice now."

Moises stared at El Quemado, the light from the burning chopper making his eyes look yellow and odd, little more than cold glass marbles. Without emotion he stared at the stricken man for nearly a minute, impervious to his groans and pleas. El Quemado winced and gritted his teeth, his breath coming rough and fast like a panting dog. His arms continued to flail aimlessly, his fingers grasping for something invisible before him. Finally Moises held out the Eight Ball.

"We shall lets the Magic Eight Ball decide," he said, his voice toneless. He shook it gently once, twice, and asked, "Oh Magic Eight Ball, should we helps this man?" He slowly turned it over and strained to read its answer in the flickering light.

"What's it say?" Ari asked.

"It says, *Don't Count On It*," he stated solemnly. He turned to the girl and spoke to her in their native tongue. She nodded and scampered off into the jungle but away from the fighting. She vanished into the darkness, her footfalls audible for only moments afterwards. Moises watched her go then looked back at El Quemado.

"You haves killed my people. You haves tried to destroy our ways of life. But worst of all you haves tainted our sacred ceremonies by stealing *grilich-ta*, what you call Ice. To us that ceremony is more precious than life itself and you have soiled it forever. For this you shall pay."

"What do you plan to do?" Ari asked, amazed at how genuinely unconcerned he was for a person trapped and squirming in agony at his feet. This new lack of compassion for human life bothered him on a deep, fundamental level. No, it wasn't all human life, he corrected himself, it was *this* particular human life. As he watched Moises he noticed again the facial tattoos the men sported, it finally dawning on him that none of the male villagers could grow facial hair on their own. The tattoos must be in homage to Percy Fawcett, a man who he knew sported a beard at times, especially on his adventures. He wondered why he hadn't connected those dots before.

"Do not worry. This man shall suffers an appropriate punishment."

Just then the girl returned, out of breath but with a smile on her young face. In her hand she held one of the yellow bags of gel used to attract and ensnare the bullet ants. She handed it to the old chief, who summarily poured the contents all over El Quemado. The trapped man sputtered and spit as the thick liquid got into his mouth and eyes, feebly trying to shove the chief's hands away. Moises ceremoniously slathered it over the man's face and arms, completely covering him. It took Ari less than a second to understand what would happen next, and when he did a tiny splinter of pity pierced his heart: the ants, he'd learned, were attracted to the liquid, and they would come. They would come en masse and they would cover him, and El Quemado would suffer horribly. He would endure dozens, perhaps hundreds of the bites, each one the equivalent of being shot. It would be a terrible way to die.

Again he almost felt sorry for the man. Almost. He stared at the person who had caused so much grief and pain to so many, the man who was likely about to die a terrible death. He thought back to a history class he'd had in college and to something he'd read and always remembered, a quote that had stuck with him all these years. It seemed perfectly appropriate. He knelt down, his face close to El Quemado's.

"Since you seem to like quotes so much, here's a final one for you: 'I do not see why man should not be just as cruel as nature.' Think about that one. Goodbye."

Moises stood with the help of the young girl and the three of them picked their way through the broken branches and mangled remains of the helicopter. The fire in the aft section was burning hotter now, bright enough that it threw their dancing, monstrous shadows before them. El Quemado's cries for help increased in volume and intensity. His screams changed to curses, some in English but most in his native Spanish. The three of them were nearly out of the jungle when the first bullet ant bit him. His cries of rage jumped several octaves and became a screech of agony, a feral, animalistic squealing.

Moises turned to Ari. "That thing you said. Who was it from? Very interesting."

Ari kept walking with his eyes straight ahead. "Just some crazy German from the 1940s. It seemed fitting, that's all."

There was no way the old chief knew who Ari was referencing, but he was wise enough to understand the gist of Ari's comment. He said nothing as the two of them exited the rim of the jungle.

The sun was starting to rise now, a pearly glow that bathed the far side of the village. The darkness had already receded to the point where the lights strung around the huts were no longer necessary, and they could all see each other's faces, if only barely. A single figure detached itself from a nearby hut. It was Father Sean, the ratty old bible still clutched in one hand and the rosary beads up near his mouth in the other. He started walking towards them. Moises touched Ari's arm to get his attention.

"What will you do now?" he asked kindly.

Ari listened and took note that the shooting everywhere had stopped. The level of daylight all around was increasing by the second, and in the distance he could make out some of Big Al's men milling around and several guards face-down on the ground, the men in black standing over them with rifles aimed down at their heads or boots firmly planted on their necks. Big Al spied their group and began walking toward them, his stout frame as unyielding as an anchor. Ari could tell in the calm way he moved that the brief battle was over and that he and his men were in control, and he let out a deep breath of relief. Behind them El Quemado's screams reached a new, higher pitch, a continuous wail that was more animal than human. Ari tried to block out the sound. The rest of them seemed to be able to ignore it without a problem.

Moises' question rattled around in his head. So what was he going to do now? That was something he'd avoided thinking about for quite some time. There was nothing for him back in Louisville, not really; the Firebird was a wreck and his heart wasn't into starting over. He had no job, no close friends, and he'd unequivocally promised himself it was time to be gone from Frankie's life. When it came right down to it he could think of no reason to return to Kentucky.

And then there was Fawcett. Even his passionate quest for Percy Fawcett was over and done. The Colonel had stumbled into this village, sired who knows how many kids, and had grown old and died here. Ari could take that news back to civilization and publish his findings, but that would undoubtedly open up this village and these people to more publicity and scrutiny than ever from the outside world, and they didn't deserve that. They'd already suffered so much under El Quemado. No, he would have to be satisfied that he knew what had befallen Colonel Fawcett. That would have to be enough.

Big Al stopped next to Ari, Moises, and the young girl. He may have been shorter than each of them but he projected such a presence that no one would ever notice his diminutive height. His black outfit, complete with Camelbak and water purification bottle, was scuffed up and dirty but he looked none the worse for wear. A machete was slung from a holster at his hip. He quickly inspected each of them in turn.

"Everybody okay?"

Ari nodded. "Yeah, we're fine."

Big Al peered between them as the screeches of agony clawed their way out of the jungle. The sound was no longer remotely human. It reminded Ari of two tomcats who'd fought a turf war outside his window, back when he was a kid. With a raised eyebrow the stout man tilted his head toward the crashed helicopter.

"So you took care of this El Quemado person, I'm guessing. Should I ask what the hell is going on back there?"

Ari thought for a moment before replying. "Karma. That's what's going on back there. Karma."

As he uttered that last word there was a tremendous explosion as the chopper's gas tank caught fire. The blast of super-heated air barely made it to where they stood, washing over them as a warm breeze that briefly fluttered their hair and was gone. El Quemado's screams died abruptly. All of them twisted around and craned their necks to watch the angry fireball roil into the sky and vanish into the dawn. The fire around the blackened hulk burned briefly before fluttering out, the green wood providing no real fuel. In no time at all, Ari knew, the jungle would reclaim that area and all traces of the man and chopper would be gone.

"Bloody hell," Moises mumbled, staring at the charred wreck.

Big Al squinted at the old chief and Ari was certain the man was wondering where an Amazonian native had learned a phrase like that. He considered explaining about this village being Fawcett's final destination, but thought better of it for the same reason he wouldn't be publishing his findings. This village and these people had endured enough and it was time to let them be.

"So tell me," Van Owen said, his attention swiveling back towards Big Al. His tone was more than a little accusatory. "What exactly are you and your people doing out here in the jungle? I've got a pretty good idea, but I'd like to hear it from you."

Big Al peered at him, his expression purposefully blank, a poker-face perfected. "What do you think we're doing? I'd like to know."

Ari had already figured it out, or at least he thought he had. "I think you're making your own version of the Ice drug. Somehow the US Military found out what it can do and how it can enhance your soldiers' abilities, so you decided to make your own. Am I close?"

Big Al blinked. "Go on."

"Does there need to be more than that? After seeing Paul fight Gonzalez I can understand why you'd want this stuff, but is the price worth it? You know once the military gets its hands on Ice it will eventually make it onto the street. You'll have another type of drug out there killing people. Is that what you want?"

Big Al's jaw moved as if he'd taken a bite of something rotten, but something he couldn't spit out. "No, that's not what I want, but that doesn't matter. I've got my orders."

"Orders from who?"

"I can't tell you that. But I can tell you this much; for years people have thought that mechanically enhanced soldiers would be the next wave in battlefield combat. Science fiction is full of the stuff. Cybernetics, augmented strength, increased speed, body armor. You name it. Even low-level individual flight capabilities. Miniaturized weaponry. Billions have been pumped into R&D for all of this."

"Sounds like you're talking about a damn Iron Man movie."

"On a very rudimentary scale, yes. But everything we've done so far has been a bust. It all comes down to power, to energy. Or better yet, the lack of it. We have no way of powering this type of individualized combat equipment for more than a few minutes. Battery technology hasn't kept up with the need and is woefully inadequate for our purposes. It's not going well and doesn't look as promising as it once did."

Ari saw it then. "So you decided to go a different route. When your people heard about Ice they figured out that a biological enhancement is easier and more attainable than a mechanical one. So that's your plan? Dose each soldier right before a battle or a mission? And what happens when other countries or bad guys figure this out? They'll come up with their own version of Ice, and what then? This will escalate. You know it will. It always does."

The stocky soldier didn't respond immediately. When he did he simply fell back on, "I've got my orders."

"Back at your camp you told me that you hated what drugs had done to your country. Our country. This has the potential to be just as bad if not worse than what we've seen so far. Please – don't continue with this."

Again Big Al paused. He turned to stare at the ruined Ice Maker behind him, and hard as he tried Ari couldn't tell what was passing through his military mind. Eventually he turned back, still stoic.

"We'll see."

That would have to do, Van Owen thought. That would have to do for now.

Villagers were emerging from their huts and he knew it was just a matter of time before Frankie and Butch did, too. He didn't want to be around when that happened. He heard a muted clicking sound and saw that Father Sean was standing next to him, the rosary beads up to his mouth and the old bible in his hand. Something about the bible nagged at him. It was old, very old, much older than Father Sean himself. He had a flickering notion lighting up the back of his mind, a will o' the wisp that was just out of reach and maddeningly elusive. He placed a tender hand on the priest's arm.

"Father Sean, can you understand me? I've got a question for you."

The young priest stared at him with the rosary beads clicking away. His eyes blinked slowly, but nothing in his expression or manner gave any indication he understood. Ari kept staring at the priest but addressed Moises.

"Chief, what can you tell me about this bible. Did he have it when he showed up here?"

Moises shook his head. "Blimey no, when he came to us he hads nothing but the clothes on his back. His travels had beens difficult."

"Then where did he get it? And the rosary beads?"

"They were here, in the village. They belonged to The Father. We kept them when he died."

Ari's heart skipped a beat and his mouth was suddenly dry, so dry he had to clear his throat and swallow in order to speak. "So you're saying that these belonged to The Father? To Percy Fawcett?"

"That name again? We do not knows that name. We only knows him as The Father."

Van Owen took a half step toward Father Sean. The priest didn't move, just tracked him with his eyes. He may have clutched the bible a little closer to his chest.

"Father Sean, I need to see the bible for a minute. Just a minute, then I'll give it right back. I promise. Please." He reached for the battered leather book. For a second it appeared that the priest would refuse, but something in his face changed. Perhaps he somehow understood how important this was. Maybe in some remote section of his mind he still felt the need to spread the Word of God. Ari didn't know, but when he gently took hold of the book Father Sean let it slide from his grasp.

Ari inspected the bible. As he'd noticed before it was battered and well used, the leather almost worn through in places. The binding was broken but the yellowed pages were still intact. Van Owen reverently opened the cover and a name written at the top of the first page jumped out at him. The script was controlled and neat, not a signature but a name the owner had penciled in.

Raleigh Rimmell.

Oh my god, he thought, stunned to silence. All the sounds and people around him vanished as he tried to sort this out. The jungle noises receded, the smell of the dwindling fire disappeared, and he could have been standing there completely alone, his mind working furiously as random pieces fell into place, like a shattered bottle coming together in slow motion.

Percy Fawcett wasn't The Father at all - it was Raleigh Rimmell, it had always been him, the third member of Fawcett's party. *It all made sense!* No wonder Josiah had gravitated to Paul at their first encounter. Paul's leg had been injured. He'd been bleeding and limping, just like when Raleigh Rimmell had arrived at the village so long ago. In hindsight Paul even looked a little like Raleigh, with his youthful looks and long hair. Fawcett had never made it to this village. It was Raleigh Rimmell. He was The Father. But that meant...

That meant that his Fawcett quest wasn't over. The mystery of the Colonel was still out there. The coordinates he'd uncovered were for the last *known* location of Fawcett, but not for his *final* location.

He flipped through the bible madly. Near the back he discovered an old photograph jammed in the pages, a black and white, grainy picture taken of the intrepid trio at some point before their journey. There, on the right side, was Raleigh Rimmell. Happy, smiling, blond, naïve Raleigh Rimmell. My god, he did look like Paul...

Ari slowly shut the bible and handed it back to Father Sean. The priest accepted it wordlessly and clasped it to his chest, as protective as any father with a newborn. The others in the group were looking at him in open curiosity. Van Owen stared at each of them in turn, his final gaze settling on Big Al. The resolve in his face was unyielding.

"I've got one last favor to ask of you," he said, his voice surprisingly calm considering how hard his heart was hammering in his chest. "Your equipment. Your Camelbak and machete. Can I have them?"

Big Al tilted his head but didn't ask what was going on. He efficiently stripped off his equipment and handed everything to Ari, including the water purification bottle. He also passed over a belt that contained additional supplies, such as waterproof matches and mosquito spray. Van Owen gathered them all up and put them on, having to tighten the belt to fit his waist.

"What are you planning on doing?" he asked as Ari worked.

Van Owen didn't reply. When he was done he looked at the diminutive soldier. "Please take care of everyone. Paul, Hal, and Frankie. And remember what I said about Ice. Don't let it get out into the world, please."

"You're leaving." It was a statement.

485

"Yes, I am. There's something I have to do."

Big Al cocked his head to the side. "And what's that?"

Van Owen grinned an easy, satisfied grin, one that hadn't graced his face in years, and swept his hand across the dark expanse of jungle behind him. He was remarkably at peace with himself. It felt good.

"I have to...go find a friend." he replied, then turned and walked toward the jungle. He didn't look back. Ari followed the trail of destruction caused by the downed helicopter, detoured around the smoldering debris, and was gone. For a few seconds they could hear the ringing of the machete as he cleared a path, then even those sounds faded away.

After a few moments Moises and the girl left, followed shortly by Big Al. Father Sean stood there a while longer, and eventually lifted the bible in the air. In a strong voice he shouted out a final passage of scripture.

"Instantly there dropped from his eyes what seemed to be scales, and he could see once more..."

Then he dropped the old book to his side, turned, and slowly walked away.

Author's Note

Colonel Percy Fawcett was real.

Several years ago I was holed up in a suburban Cleveland hotel for the evening, a dozen or so pages away from completing my first novel, Straw Man. During a short break from typing, I was flipping through channels on the hotel television and stopped briefly on the Discovery Channel. I soon found myself intrigued by a biography on Percy Fawcett. As I watched I soon realized I had never heard of the man before, which floored me since he'd apparently been so instrumental in the exploration of the Amazon jungle. How had Fawcett, his son Jack, and Raleigh Rimmell all flown under my radar all these years? My only conclusion was that since they were British and hadn't been involved with opening up North America, they had somehow slipped through the sieve that was my public education. Not only that, but all my beta-readers were certain he was an imagined character, right along with Ari Van Owen, Frankie Brubaker, and the rest.

That is far from true.

Fawcett and his companions were real. Dead Horse Camp in Mato Grosso was real, as was the Colonel's fervent belief in the Lost City of Z. The trio did indeed vanish without a trace in 1925, and many hundreds of people have died while attempting to retrace his steps and determine his fate. Conflicting stories have emerged throughout the years of his possible demise, but none have been corroborated. Most people believe he was killed by natives and his end will never truly be determined, but others insist he finally succumbed to his urge to "go native", and lived out his remaining days in the jungle.

Whatever end finally befell him, I like to believe Fawcett continues to wander the rainforest, even to this day. That would, after all, be a fitting end for such a man – and of course makes for a much better tale.

In my mind the Colonel will live forever.

David Kettlehake

If you enjoyed *Fever*, please check out my first novel, *Straw Man* – available on Amazon.

And for updates on upcoming projects or for my contact information, please visit me at www.davidkettlehake.com.

Thanks so much, and read on...

Made in the USA
Lexington, KY
11 October 2016